"Danie Ware's first novel is not so much ———————————— e. This is science fiction with the safety catch off. I hope she never runs out of ammunition." ADAM NEVILL, AUTHOR OF *APARTMENT 16*

"*Ecko Rising* explodes onto the page with the manic energy of Richard Morgan's cyberpunk novels before taking a surprise turn into Thomas Convenant territory. It is strange, surprising, haunting and exceedingly well written. Not to be missed." LAVIE TIDHAR, AUTHOR OF *THE VIOLENT CENTURY*

"*Ecko Rising* messes with your head in unexpected and exciting ways." MIKE CAREY, AUTHOR OF *THE FELIX CASTOR SERIES*

"I motored through this book. It's a page turner and I'll be getting hold of the next one." NEAL ASHER, AUTHOR OF *THE AGENT CORMAC SERIES*

"The best debut novel I've read in years." ANDY REMIC, AUTHOR OF *SPIRAL*

"One of the most intriguing and original blends of fantasy and science fiction I've read in a long time." ADRIAN TCHAIKOVSKY, AUTHOR OF *EMPIRE IN BLACK AND GOLD*

"This may be Ware's first novel, but she's been intimately tied to the science fiction, fantasy and horror genres for years through her publicity work. That exposure and experience come to the fore with Ecko Rising, a novel that blends fantasy and science fiction together into an epic story about the titular anti-hero who aims to do nothing less than save the entire world from extinction." *KIRKUS REVIEWS*

"A curious genre-bender that thrusts its anti-hero from a dystopian future into a traditional, Tolkienesque fantasy world... marks Ware as one to watch." *INDEPENDENT ON SUNDAY*

ECKO ENDGAME

ECKO ENDGAME

DANIE WARE

TITAN BOOKS

Ecko Endgame
Print edition ISBN: 9781783294558
E-book ISBN: 9781783294565

Published by Titan Books
A division of Titan Publishing Group Ltd
144 Southwark Street, London SE1 0UP

First edition: November 2015
1 3 5 7 9 10 8 6 4 2

A CIP catalogue record for this title is available from the British Library.

Printed and bound in the United States.

What did you think of this book?
We love to hear from our readers. Please email us at:
readerfeedback@titanemail.com, or write to us at the above address.

To receive advance information, news, competitions, and exclusive offers
online, please sign up for the Titan newsletter on our website.

www.titanbooks.com

FOR TWO PEOPLE WHOSE
PATIENCE HAS BEEN LIMITLESS,
AND WHO HAVE MADE ECKO POSSIBLE

FOR JAN, MY MUM,
AND ISAAC, MY SON,
WITH ALL MY LOVE

CONTENTS

PART 1: MUSTER

PART 2: WAR

PART 3: FRACTAL REALISATION

PART 4: FADE TO GREY

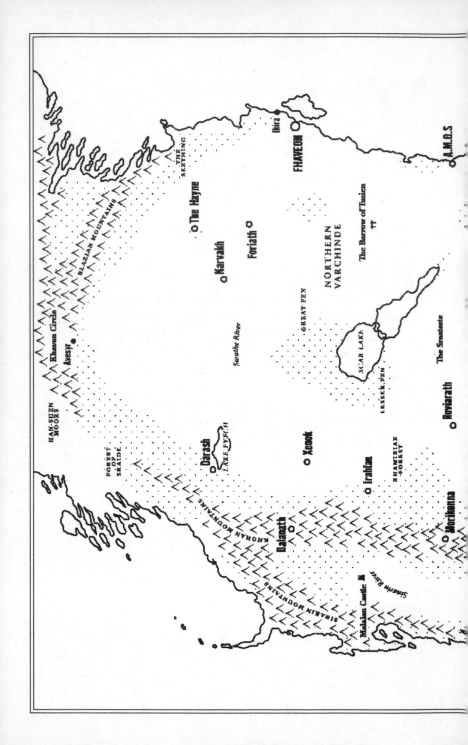

Map by Danie Ware, from an original by A D Oliver.

PROLOGUE THE KUANNE, WEST OF THE KARTIAH

Mountains.

Stark and cold, bitter as blades. They slant like a crooked spine, from southern slopes of rough grey scree to a northern winter, proud and jagged. Here, they throw out a backwards angle, a tumble of ground forgotten, as raw as the stone itself. Beneath it, the forests are pale and sharp, the rivers white with rage.

Nothing moves here, only the water.

But down there – there! – a black speck, shifting.

The motion is tiny, alone. It seems improbable, some lost mote, and yet it's as loud as a shout, the only thing living in the stillness. It scrabbles insect-like up into the foothills and then higher, but it falters often and seeks about itself for understanding, or direction. It's too small for the mountains to notice, too small for the winter, and yet it's somehow indomitable.

It refuses to stop.

As the speck scuttles onwards, the sun slowly dies on the peaks before it, stretching their shadow long across the ground and striping the high clouds with vivid shades of threat and promise. Darkness rises, as if it spreads from the broken castle, now long since left behind. It steals west until it swallows the tiny figure, swallows the land entire. The sun's last farewell is a sullen red, and then it is gone, and the cold really begins.

The figure stops.

Its arms are wrapped about itself now, its heavy shoulders hunched and its hands shoved clumsily into its sleeves, seeking warmth. Its breath plumes. It pauses to search its pockets, looks at its findings with confusion.

"Alexander," the figure says, its voice creaking with cold. "Alexander David Eastermann."

But the words fall frozen; they make no sense.

The man's belongings scatter from his shaking hands, and he kneels to pick them up. In among them, there is a tiny red light that bathes his bearded face in a sudden flash of glare. He holds it up, pointing it in the direction he's been walking.

"Yeah, yeah all right, I know. Dunno where you're takin' me, mate, but you're the only thing that makes any fuckin' sense round 'ere. You an' me, we're goin' places."

He looks through the remainder of his things, his bafflement apparent. He swigs from a small flask, puts everything back in the pockets of his battered leather jacket. Then he sighs, pulls the zip as high as it will go, pushes his hands back into his sleeves, and keeps walking.

The night deepens.

The mountains rise savage, teeth bared at black sky – no stars, no moons. The man stumbles on, crossing chasms that radiate cold nacre, lighting his way and blinding him, bright from below. One stops him completely, too wide to step across, and he sways on its edge a long time before he jumps.

He walks on. His progress becomes erratic and he falls often. Several times, he stops and coughs, harsh in the silence, doubled over with the violence of it. Then he swigs from the flask and keeps walking.

The cold becomes bitter, frosting his breath and beard.

After a time, he becomes aware of a sound, a liquid and crystal chiming, and he breaks into a shambling run. He crosses into a maze. Stone pillars, carved into fabulous shapes by wind and dust, rise tall round him, but he pays them no heed as he reaches the river. Here, he throws himself flat and drinks, ice-cold swallows that make him shudder and wrap his hands over his skull in sudden pain.

And then he curls in upon himself, hoarding heat, and sleeps.

Sunlight seeps across dead ground, touching the sleeping figure with tendrils of warmth.

He stirs, shuddering, dangerously cold.

As he turns over, groaning with stiffness and flexing numb fingers, he comes to focus on the bizarre shapes of the pillars that stand over him, tips now gleaming with the rising light. Blinking, sitting up and coughing a dark, splattering phlegm, he struggles to see them clearly.

"'Oo the 'ell are you? Some fuckin' army?" Still blinking, he gouges a thumb and forefinger into his eyes, refocuses. "What you doin' out 'ere? Turned to stone – like, I dunno, trolls or summin'."

He looks at the mountains, the water, his hands. They hurt with returning circulation. Confused, he flexes them into claws and back, then turns them over to stare at the dry palms, the old burns, the heavy calluses.

"I remember... I was a kid, and me 'ands were turnin' into dragons. Sky fulla colour. Bleedin' bonkers. Where was I? What the 'ell was I doin'?"

Then he says, in a voice like an engine starting, "Oh fuck me bloody *ragged*."

He palms himself in the forehead, groaning.

The pillars don't respond, but he tells them anyway, "I'm *trippin'*. I'm trippin' me bleedin' *nuts* off. Alex bastard Eastermann bollocks, I'm Lugan – an' I was... I was..."

A flood of images, jumbled like traffic, noisy – he pounds his forehand with the palm of his hand, jarring them. The Bike Lodge, the tavern, the Bard, Ecko gone missing, the pitch darkness of the old Underground, Thera's lights, Mom... He'd left Roderick there, and had gone seeking answers, seeking Ecko – gone all the way to the offices of Mortimer, Hiner and Thompson...

And then what?

"So, what the 'ell 'appened to me? What did they...?"

The stones say nothing.

"Bugger me. Was the 'ole bloody *thing* even real – the tavern, the tunnels, any of it? Some fucktard's fuckin' *spiked* me! *Tell* me I ain't been that bleedin' stupid?"

His voice falls on empty winter – but the realisation makes everything fit.

"*Fuck* it."

Angry now, he kicks at a pile of stones with his big black boot, making it tumble over. Then he stands up straight, winces, and looks back at the little red light.

"Right then," he says, "guess you're the only answer I got."

With a back-cracking stretch, he lumbers into motion, heading for the angled whiteness of the rising mountains.

Behind him, the pillars stand watch.

PART 1: MUSTER

1: THE COUNT OF TIME <small>AMOS</small>

The grass was dead.

Across the huge emptiness of the Varchinde plain, the bright colours of autumn had faded and blown away, and the soil and stone were scoured clean, bared to a bleak sky. The trees were stark, hard angles against a rising bank of cloud; the wind was harsh, spiralling the last stalks into tiny tornado whirls. The chill made Triqueta huddle in her saddle, her hood drawn up and her heavy cloak wrapped tight. Desert-blooded as she was, she'd never felt the season bite this deep before. She found herself shuddering as the early winter seemed to crawl under her skin, sinking cold claws into muscle and bone.

Beneath the cloak her hands itched and she held them still, refusing to scratch them. She could feel her age this morning, whatever the rhez it was; feel the curse that the daemon Tarvi had laid upon her, and the weight of the whole damned Count of Time.

...dunno why she took your time and not mine...

Ecko's words were in the wind, taunting her lean, lined face, her chapped hands. Tarvi's kiss had taken ten – fifteen? – returns from her life. It had left her aged and self-conscious, bitter with regret.

By the rhez. Enough!

Beneath her, the mare snuffled and shifted. The horse was a city creature, spraddle-legged and hang-bellied, lacking in spirit. She didn't like the empty plainland, or the cold, and her ears were flat-back, expressing her disapproval.

But Triq held the beast between her knees. They'd come out here, just as they did every morning, to look for something – hope, answers – and she wasn't done searching. She tightened her thighs and the horse started forward reluctantly, her wide hooves dragging at the muck.

The wind gusted, blew Triq's hood back and her hair across her face, white strands among the yellow. She freed a hand to hold it back, and there – there! – just for a moment, she saw it: a horizon shadow, dark against the southern sky. Her heart thundered. She was up in the stirrups, craning to see something, anything, even as her rational mind berated her for being so foolish. She'd seen the shadow before, half-man and half-creature; she'd dreamed it and danced with it over and again. It was the hallucination she'd brought from the horrors they'd faced at Aeona, the hope that ghosted constantly at the corners of her vision. Like her memory of Tarvi's curse, it wouldn't damned well leave her be...

Redlock.

She was out here looking for Redlock – on some damned fool quest for her lost lover.

Or what was left of him.

She knew how crazed it was, but she couldn't help it, couldn't leave it alone. Every night, she saw those last moments: Aeona's collapse as its alchemist master perished, the freed Kas, the daemon, as it fled north to its new host, the twisted red-maned monstrosity they'd glimpsed in the shattered tower. And every morning, she came up here to stare southeast along the coastline at the distant and unseen Gleam Wood, at the destruction they'd left behind them. They had won their fight, saved Ecko's life, perhaps the life of the world entire – but the *cost*...

Her hopes were folly and she knew it, but she came anyway, unable to let go of the hope, the fear, the shreds of denial that such a thing could have happened to him, to them. Day after day, she rode through Amos's ramshackle outskirts and out into the chill; day after day, she returned to the taverns on the wharves and drowned herself in a blur of ales and spirits, and in the heated embraces of those whose names and faces she didn't even care to remember.

She knew, she *knew*, how loco this was. Some part of her mind asked what the rhez she thought she was doing. Even if Redlock had survived Aeona's collapse, there was no way he'd be – *it* would be out here, when it had the whole dead Varchinde to run in. No way it'd know she was here and...

...and *what*?

Aeona had been a disaster. Its master had twisted Redlock into a beast, speechless and mindless and horrified, and he'd come within a moment of sacrificing Ecko and damning them all. They'd freed Ecko, but not swiftly enough – and the damage had been done. Kas Vahl Zaxaar, daemon possessor and the Varchinde's long-feared foe, had loosed himself from the alchemist's flesh to rage northward to Fhaveon, Lord city.

And now, Triq was afraid.

Afraid that their time was up, afraid the aftermath of Aeona would prove too much, afraid that the blight and the rising winter would finish them all.

Another gust caught her, and she shivered. It was cold as pure frost, sending tumbles of the dead grass across the hilltop. Though the Varchinde's "little death" was a natural thing, a normal part of the cycling of elements and seasons, somehow it still all seemed like some Gods-damned portent.

Like the grass would die for good, and there would be no spring.

The mare shook her mane, snorted steam and scorn like some saga charger. The shadow, whatever it was, had gone.

The shadow had never even been there, for the Gods' sakes, had never been more than Triqueta's own hair, scudding across her vision. She pulled the mass back, retied it.

The mare was agitated now, ears flicking.

"Come on then." She stroked the creature's neck. "We'll go home."

They turned back to the city. Out over the sea, the sky had sunk to an ominous glower. The cloud was thick and flat, almost metallic. Even as they moved, the mass was flash-lit, and the grey water ignited to an instant of glittering fire.

The rumble reached them a moment later.

Triq gave one last look southward, but there was nothing there – by the rhez, there was never going to *be* anything there. Telling herself she wouldn't come here again, she tightened her knees and urged the horse onwards – to the city, and to shelter.

And as she went, she raised her face to the wind – was surprised to find it ice-cold on her cheeks, as if it dried water she hadn't even known was there.

A dark sprawl between rising hillsides, Amos was a city changed.

With the onslaught of the blight, the Varchinde's quintessential terhnwood crop had been devastated, and its absence damned the plains' trade cycle and the lives of the cities that depended upon it. In Amos, Lord CityWarden Nivrotar had no intention of letting the resulting chaos assault the streets of her home, to gut Amos as it had done Fhaveon.

When the blight had first browned the crops and grasses that surrounded her, Nivrotar had sent teams to help the harvest and to tally and stockpile everything they could, to defend or burn where necessary, and to teach calm to the farmers and workers. Trust in your city, the Lord told her people, your city will hold her word to care for you.

And she did.

At the Lord's insistence, her bazaars and tithehalls remained open – and guarded – while her craftmasters and bookkeepers were kept recompensed and busy, vital to the continued cycle. Terhnwood still came into the city, rationed and managed. A portion of it was still stored, and its equivalent weight and value in goods was still traded back to the farmlands, and beyond. Where Fhaveon had slammed shut her trade-borders and hoarded what crop she still had, so Amos tallied the absolute minimums she'd need to maintain herself and her farmlands, and then sent bretir outwards on various carefully plotted routes with offers of what little remained.

Around Amos, the trade cycle limped into motion once more. Control was merciless, violence inevitable, justice savage and swift. Local freemen and warriors were recompensed in food and kit, and they defended the city to her last.

The system was shaky, but it held. Perhaps due to Nivrotar's power and reputation, perhaps to her ruthless Tundran intellect, Amos was still in business.

Seeking the work, more warriors came.

And more traders came.

And after them, in a steady trail of hope, came the refugees.

Amos was a city changed.

Her inherent darkness had become a beacon, a flag of stained hope. About her walls a new life had grown, a patchwork of fabric slum, swollen with life and colour. Here, gathering for shelter against the blight and the fear and the "little death", had come the people who had nowhere else to go.

When Triqueta had first ridden from the city's southernmost gate, the area had been a trade-road bazaar, loud and rough and muddy, a haven for smugglers and pirates. Now, it was a crazed tessellation of scents and shouts and smoke, tents and lean-tos, all growing one into another like lichens in the wet. There were old hangings and tacked-together cloaks, scavenged parts of stalls, salvaged pieces of wood and stone, all carbuncled against the buttresses, or collaged in corners as if they had been flung there.

The main roadway was puddled and rutted, strewn with garbage – and seething with people, some directionless and underfoot, others purposeful and frustrated. As Triq tried to shoulder the mare through the mass, beggars crowded about her, held out dirty bowls and dirtier hands; they owned only what they stood in and crying children clung to their legs. In a moment, she and the horse were surrounded by voices and pleas, by the stink of piss and urgency.

She dismounted, found herself walled in by flesh – the refugee village seemed to have swelled even since the birth of the sun. For a moment, she thought of her own crazed wealth – the hoarded metal from the Elementalist Maugrim's peculiar treasure chamber. Even if she'd had it with her, it would have been useless – some ludicrous jest of the Gods.

The rain grew heavier, cold from the sea, and the lightning flashed again. As she came closer to the dark rise of the gate itself, the roadway grew clearer and the crowd began to drift away, back towards their makeshift homes, and whatever hope they could find.

She wished she had some of her own to spare for them.

Amos was a city changed.

At the open southernmost gate, Triq found a cluster of freemen and women gathered round a firebox. Their weapons were close but not in hand, and they bore their colours with the casual attitude of soldiers who'd not worn them in training.

They eyed her as she came near but they seemed unworried, grumbling among themselves with affable discontent.

"Breakfast?" She grinned at them, and they grunted in return.

To the landward of where they stood, spreading all the way back to the city wall, there was a cleared plaza, thick with caking mud. Here, there was a square of more regular tents – a hospice, a foodhall, a tithehall – all makeshift but functioning. Smoke curled into the air, and cloaked figures scurried.

Above them, the black wall rose like the end of the world.

"Triq!"

Through the scattering rain, the sound of her name startled her – it had come from the front of one of the tents.

"*Triq!*"

There – was that someone waving?

At the far side of the square there was a wide sprawl of greenish tent, its awning bulging with water and its guy-lines strained tight. Triqueta blinked, wiped her eyes. Under the awning was a slim, pale-haired figure.

Amethea.

Friend and apothecary, with a resilience that had faced down Aeona's nightmare figments, she was tired and filthy-faced, stained with mud and fluids. Her pale skin was flecked with darkness like the missing pieces of lives.

As she saw Triqueta look, she ducked out of the doorway and ran, the mud clinging thickly to her boots. It was sheltered from the wind here, and Triq could hear her shouting, words falling over themselves.

"Triq! Oh, thank the Goddess you're here! She's – Gods! – you have to see her for yourself. I can't even think... been awake for a day and half..." She caught up, panting, and stopped to speak, stroking the walking horse's nose. The mare snorted at her smell. "Gods, this is so *crazed*—!"

"Whoah!" Triqueta put a hand on her friend's shoulder.

"Start at the beginning. I have to see who?"

Amethea blinked water. Rain ran down her face like tears; her garments were soaked through, bloodstains blossoming into sodden flowers of pink. She gestured back at the tent. "I can't... You have to come and see her for yourself."

"See *who*?" Alarmed now, Triq's heart was thumping, echoing anxious like the distant, thunderous rumble. "Thea. Make sense."

The teacher shook her head. "Look, Taegh'll take the horse." She nodded at a sodden, tow-haired lad, his own shirt spattered with the Gods-alone-knew-what. "I've... Gods, I didn't know what else... I've had to put her right at the back of the tent 'til I can work out what to do with her." Amethea was striving not to cry, but whether from panic or horror or pure exhaustion, Triq couldn't tell. "We have to get her to the Palace. To the Bard. He was her *friend*, he has to see what happened to her—"

"Amethea." Triqueta put the other hand on the other shoulder. "What the rhez are you talking about?"

"Come on. You have to see."

Amos was a city that would never be the same again.

The two women splashed through the mud, then ducked under the swollen awning.

And Triqueta stopped dead, her hands covering her face.

Dear Gods.

The tent was closeness and reek, layers of blood and rot and shit and panic, of herbs and horror and hope. Over their heads, the rain faded to a steady drumming, claustrophobic and ominous; under their boots, the mud was covered in old matting that was mouldering in the wet, stamped into mulch.

And the *people*...

Triqueta didn't deal well with illness – like her hard-jesting

Banned family, she faced incapacity with a bravado that picked despair up by the throat and shook it, daring it to do its worst.

This clustered mess of hurt, this helplessness – it scared her to the core of her soul.

By the rhez.

Closest to her, almost under her feet, was a young man, a soldier by the look of him – pale-haired and pale-skinned, his face contorted round a harm she couldn't bear to witness, but couldn't tear herself away from. As she watched him, he bunched, folding in on himself, knees to his chest, and began to shudder, spasms racking his body. Triq looked for help, for someone to come to him, but Amethea shook her head.

She turned away. Drew Triqueta with her.

Something in that movement was fatal, final   whatever was the matter with him, there was nothing she could do.

And she knew it.

For no reason, Triqueta saw the dying Feren, Redlock's kinsman slain by the centaurs. It seemed like a lifetime ago, when the Varchinde still blazed with both hope and summer, when she and Ress had ridden from the Bard's fears in The Wanderer to Maugrim's swelling power at the centre of the plains. The boy's memory was shadowed like a figment, deep in the skin of the soldier's face.

The thunder sounded again, laughing at her.

Helpless, she followed Amethea's tug, picking her way carefully to one of the tent's long, rounded ends. As they came though the crush to a makeshift curtain, Amethea paused and glanced back.

"I hope you skipped breakfast."

"Skipped...?"

The question died as the curtain came back and Triqueta saw who – what – Amethea had found.

No.

The denial was inevitable, reflexive. Triqueta found herself backing away. The thing in the tent was shrivelled and shrunken, lined and cracked; its face was a hollow, and it was curled in upon itself as if it had tried to carry the entire Count of Time upon its thin shoulders.

It – *she* – was dead.

Dead of vast age, of returns beyond number.

Unspeaking, tense with a nauseous roil of memory and horror, Triqueta stared, her hands to her mouth and her mind roaring wordless. Refusal knotted in her belly, rose in her throat, burned hot at the backs of her eyes. She couldn't pull her gaze away; the woman's face was a mapwork of life's experience, now stilled.

Skipped breakfast.

It took a moment for Triqueta to realise – she knew who this was.

Had been.

Dear Gods.

As the full understanding hit her, she was on her knees in the mulch, swallowing hard, burning her throat with bile. Shocked tears were hot on her skin. She knew exactly what she was seeing – knew it, by the rhez, knew it intimately. She wanted to shake herself, to wake up, to cry denial, to realise that this was one of Aeona's damned figments, something from the Gleam Wood, some nightmare they'd found or brought with them...

It had to be. Didn't it.

Didn't it?

But when she blinked, the aged thing was still there.

Triq swallowed again, acid and horror. Her heart was already pounding from the storm, from the hovels outside – now it shuddered like the unsettled sky. Her throat afire, she said stupidly, "No... This is some jest, some coincidence. It can't..."

"I wish to every God it was." Amethea's voice caught and she staggered, caught herself on Triqueta's shoulder. She didn't let go, and Triq put a hand over her friend's, both of them transfixed by the rotten thing that lay on the pallet.

Then Amethea rallied, stood up straight.

"Triq," she said, "I really need your help. I know this is hard for you, but I need to understand what's happened to her, what's..." Amethea gestured helplessly, seeking words. "It's like what happened to you. With Tarvi. Like her time was... just... sucked away."

"No." Triqueta was shaking. "No." When Amethea didn't respond, Triq glanced sideways at her friend. "It can't be, it *can't* be. I killed that damned daemon bitch Tarvi myself. And Vahl Zaxaar—"

"Was defeated," Amethea said. "He went raging to Fhaveon and Rhan threw him down, Nivrotar told us." Her eyes met her friend's. "But, Triq, think. If that's true, then who did this? *What* did this?" Her eyes shone with the horror of it. She blinked moisture, took a long and shaking breath. "And to Karine?"

Karine.

Capable, outspoken, no-nonsense Karine. The heart of The Wanderer, the Bard's ward and word and organisation...

Triqueta stared at the shrivelled thing.

Karine.

If the Bard himself had been The Wanderer's motivation, the tavern's soul and purpose, then Karine had been its fire, its sheer efficiency. Her vibrancy had been palpable; she'd been a constant whirl of energy, equally good-humoured, annoying and relentless. To see her like this, her returns literally sucked from her skin...

Triqueta's throat burned; figments of other memories taunted her.

Tarvi's kiss. Glorious. A moment of absolute passion, incredible. And a cost beyond words, beyond comprehension.

But Tarvi was gone: she'd killed that damned bitch-thing

herself. What else was there that could do this, could drain the very Count of Time from the flesh of a friend? Vahl Zaxaar? The – what were they called? – the "vialer"? More of Aeona's flesh-crafted creations?

For the tiniest moment, Triqueta wondered if they should suspect the Bard himself – the change in him was chilling. Since the loss of The Wanderer and his return from Ecko's world, he was a lean, savage shadow and nothing like the man he had been.

The whole damn world's gone loco. Really this time...

She swallowed again, trying to rid herself of memory, of clamouring fear, of the awful, awful burning in her throat.

Karine.

The tent side strained against the harsh wind. Water dripped from the bottom edge and seeped under their feet.

"Triqueta." Amethea gripped her shoulders, looked into her face. The girl's blue eyes were as dark as the storm-ridden sky, and then it was all there in the air between them. Not only Karine and the Bard and the lost Wanderer, but Tarvi's kiss, Maugrim's flame, the figments at Aeona, Redlock's monstrous transformation – everything they'd seen and shared, everything they'd lived through and fought for and been helpless to prevent. The summer had left them, the autumn had faded; the winter had come and the grass had died. The vast and empty plainland stood barren, scoured to the bone.

Everything that'd brought them this far had gone, or changed beyond the telling of it.

Distantly, the thunder grumbled again – some creature defeated, and waiting.

"You know what this is," Amethea said softly. She shook her friend gently. "You do, don't you? You know." Her face was grey as parchment; there were shadows under her eyes. "You've *felt* this."

"No, I haven't, this is crazed, this is *loco*." Triqueta broke her friend's grip, almost snapped it at her. "Look at her, Thea, look! How could I know? How could anyone? How could anyone understand... that? Karine..." Her voice cracked. "Dammit, Karine doesn't hold some secret, any more than... any more than Redlock did..." Then she lost it, and she was really crying, coughing as she spoke, tears mingling with the rain on her face. "Thea." She spoke through sobs, almost unintelligible. "This is all crazed. I can't do this any more, I can't do this, it's too much. I want..."

I want all this to never have happened. I want the summer, I want The Wanderer. I want the plains to be free and the figments and the horrors all gone. I want to ride, and laugh, and know that we have a future ahead of us...

I want my damned youth back!

The last thought caught and tripped her, made her look back at the shrunken thing.

Youth, by the rhez.

At least I'm still here. Still fighting.

Still able to fight.

Amethea put her bloodied arms around her friend's shoulders and they held each other for a moment. But the teacher did not bow her head, did not flinch or cry.

Her voice tinged with stone, she said, "We'll see this through to the end. For Karine. For Feren. For Redlock. For The Wanderer and all of her people, for Roderick's vision. For Ecko. For our damned *selves*."

On the other side of the curtain, a voice cried out; there were echoes of panic. The rain, slackening now, pattered on the top of the tent.

After a moment, Triqueta stood, rubbing her hands over her face. She nodded, understanding settling on her like ash.

Amethea said, "We'll take this to Nivrotar. And you'll have to tell her, Triq, tell her everything. What it felt like, if you could've stopped it..."

Don't you think I would have?

Triq's face must have changed because Amethea flushed, her cheekbones bright against her pale skin.

She said, "We need to understand. Tarvi said she was Kas, like Vahl Zaxaar, and that they needed time to live. Whatever did this, we need to know. Because I don't think this is over."

2: HEAL AND HARM FHAVEON

His voice soft with fear, the apothecary said, "My Lord, I don't know if I should wake her."

Rhan Elensiel, Seneschal of Fhaveon, stood silent, his arms crossed and his expression sombre. They were high above the city's chaos here, and the shutters were closed against the struggling below, against the two moons bright over the water.

The apothecary was shivering, though the air was not cold. Chillflesh prickled his arms and he rubbed at them almost absently, his attention compelled by the young woman who lay sweating in the midst of the great and tangled bed.

Selana Valiembor, last child of the House of Saluvarith. Lord Foundersdaughter of Fhaveon, ruler of the dying Varchinde – a tiny figure now curled below the great wooden headboard carved by her forebears. Her body twitched as if with some unseen plague, her eyes flickered beneath closed lids. Every few moments, a shudder went through her as if she fought some figment they could not see, strove to awaken herself from a nightmare beyond words.

Rhan watched over her as he always had, always would. Fhaveon was his home, his charge, his purpose. Without it...

The apothecary rubbed at his forearms, ventured, "My Lord?"

But the words rolled from the Seneschal like the chill, unheeded.

The old bed taunted Rhan with memories not his own, with crimes he'd not committed. Standing in this room, those shadows still flickered at the edge of his awareness, misdeeds unspeakable.

Misdeeds with which Phylos had taunted him: the murder of the Foundersson, this haunted child's father. The rape of his wife. *Screaming. All the way down.*

"My Lord?" the apothecary tried again.

Belatedly, Rhan realised he'd been asked a question.

"Wake her?" He looked up, stared at the apothecary for a moment. This was the man who'd found the bravery to defy Phylos's bid for power and to spare the life of Mostak, military commander. He was now here, his slender body shuddering even as his Lord's did likewise.

"Yes, my Lord. Should we wake her? From whatever figments torment her sleeping?"

The young man's confusion was as tangled as the sheets, as loud as a shout in the night's cool. He wasn't asking for guidance, he was asking for Rhan to take responsibility for the decision.

Rhan recollected himself; shook away the loitering fears. He laid one white hand on the man's shoulder, said gently, "I don't think I know your name."

"I'm Kallye, my Lord." The apothecary gave a wary, weary chuckle. "I was with Tan Commander Mostak, if you remember, when—"

"I haven't forgotten." Rhan flickered a smile, gave the man a tight momentary clasp. "You're owed a debt the city will respect and repay, given time. I trust your judgement, but wakening someone in nightmare is— Samiel's *teeth*!"

Cutting him cold, Selana had sat upright and cried out, wordless and shattering-loud. Her eyes were wide open, staring, lit to uncanny intensity by a shutter-stripe of moonslight that fell across her face. She was breathing shallow and fast, her chest and shoulders shaking under her pale shift.

Kallye fell back, hands to his mouth. Rhan moved forwards, almost expecting her to speak, to utter some profound and obscure truth, some wondrous vision... but she only stared, her eyes crazed in that strip of light.

For a moment, she sat absolutely still – then she fell back to the huge bed as if she'd been hit in the face.

Her eyes closed. She shuddered, and was still.

Shivering, Kallye muttered, "Dear Gods."

Rhan suppressed a shiver of his own. Selana's gaze seemed burned into the air; two points of light seared into both of them, horror and flesh. Under her, the bed was crouched and angered, this vast beast that had embraced Lords for generations and now glowered round the last of them, protective or aggressive or both...

By the Gods! Enough!

Rhan drew a breath, shook himself free from whimsy and sat on the bed's edge as if daring it. Carefully, he laid one hand on Selana's fine, pale throat, feeling the flutter of life within. Kallye hovered, anxious and fidgeting, while Rhan watched the shadows that moved in the girl's face, the back-and-forth flicker of her now-closed eyes.

He wondered what she could see.

And he wondered if he knew perfectly damned well.

Fool me once, my brother. But fool me twice?

Laughter sounded in his ears, his mind. Her eyes were open, staring at the bed's fabric canopy with that same crazed intensity, that same appalling sear. Vahl himself was there in her gaze, was blazing—

Her eyes were closed.

Rhan shuddered, looked again.

Her eyes were closed.

Lord Foundersdaughter Selana Valiembor slept like a little child, like she once had in her bassinet, her parents standing over her and glowing with love.

But Rhan stared at her as if those eyes held worlds unspoken, horrors checked only by vein-pale lids.

Are you in there, Vahl? Coiled? Waiting?

Rhan had won the fight for the city. Blazing white wrath, he'd torn his brother Kas Vahl Zaxaar asunder, rent Phylos's flesh and his creatures of alchemy and stone. Long, long returns of plotting and patience and power, and all of it had been over in a brief, savage burn of glory. Phylos, for all his Archipelagan arrogance and ambition, had been broken beyond redemption or help – Rhan had few fears that the scheming Merchant Master would manifest in figment and market-tale undeath.

But Vahl...

That was another matter entirely. Four hundred returns, and Rhan could not believe that his brother would give up that easily.

Or are you just lost without him, Dael Rhan Elensiel, pointless and bereft of purpose?

And the truth of *that* thought was barbed.

On the bed, Selana had lost her childlike aspect. She was shaking again, her mouth moving wordless, framing fragments of images that lived only in her mind. Four hundred returns Vahl had led them to believe he'd been hiding on Rammouthe Island – just to keep their attention from Aeona. Surely...

Surely this was not just... what... wishful thinking?

The girl swallowed, shuddered again, and Rhan moved his hand, smoothing her hair back from her forehead.

Samiel's *bollocks*, it was all shadows, dammit, he'd no idea what he was seeing – what was figment and what was real, what was in his head and what was in hers. Perhaps this was all just the price he was paying for the end of Penya's specialist herbology.

Then, on the pallet, the Lord strung taut as a bowstring, her face stretched in a scream she couldn't voice.

"Gods!" Kallye was there beside her, almost shoving Rhan and his doubts out of the way. He sat on the huge bed talking softly and stroking her pale hand for lack of any other way to help. Distress was etched into the long lines below his eyes, lines that carved his face with empathy and weariness and fear. He glanced back at Rhan, said, "Please, my Lord. Can you see... can you see what troubles her?"

"No more than I can see my own backside." Rhan's answer was subdued, his sardonic humour almost reflex. "I'm going in endless circles, Kallye – a nartuk chasing his tail."

He stood up, watched the moonlight tumble through the shutters. "Old stories tell us such dream-figments are pieces of ourselves, manifest moments of our days, our hopes and fears." From somewhere outside, voices were raised, chanting and jeering as if Fhaveon herself were sharing the nightmare of her Lord. There was a flare of flame.

Making a decision, Rhan said, "We must leave her."

"What? Why?" The apothecary looked up in objection. "You can't just leave her to—"

"I can and I will." Rhan's voice was stone, the foundation of the city herself. "You'll have her watched, Kallye – I'll watch her myself as I have the time."

The apothecary looked at him, wide-eyed. "My Lord, please... You can't leave her like this."

"You've got a good heart." Rhan gentled, freed the embroidered coverlet from the girl's feet and straightened it. "But be wary, this may be only nightmare but it may also be more than it seems. I wish I could tell the difference."

"What do you mean? More than what seems?"

"I don't know." *So many doubts and shadows. Where were the ink patterns in her skin, those writhing sigils that marked Vahl's presence?* "Gods help me, I don't know. Not yet. When she wakens, tell me."

"Yes, my Lord." Kallye's voice was layered with reluctance and doubt.

The shouts from outside came again, further away. There were sounds of hooves, then a dull, uneasy boom.

The apothecary glanced up at the shutters, though there was nothing to see. "What's happening out there?"

"Trouble," Rhan said bleakly. He gathered a sigh. "Phylos may be gone, but his figments remain. I can feel them, moving through the city." He caught Kallye's eyes, made the words matter. "The Council is disbanded, the city's in rubble, the terhnwood crop's rotted. We have no markets, no trade, and we'll run out of food before the winter is over. And even if we manage those miracles, there's... there'll still be other things to face. Other monsters." He looked back down at the sleeping girl. "I want reports from the hospice, Kallye, first thing every morning. Numbers, symptoms, deaths. Everything. We have to get control of all of this."

"Yes, my Lord." The apothecary had withdrawn his hand from Selana's sweating skin and was staring at her as if she'd manifest into some alchemical monstrosity.

Rhan gripped his shoulder, said, "It'll be all right. Trust me."

"Yes, my Lord."

Rhan gave a brief grin. "You can, you know."

"Yes, my Lord."

From outside, there came a second boom, deeper and closer. The shutters juddered. Rhan tweaked a corner, looked down at the descending madness below – at the lights and flames and shouts and chaos that had once been the Lord city, the courage of the Varchinde.

Now in turmoil.

Phylos and his damned greed – between that and the blight, Fhaveon's barely crawling. I'd pull his fool head off – if I hadn't already.

He watched for a moment, the swarming and the desperation,

then he gave a brief, bitter chuckle. If he stopped to think – to try to understand where his own responsibility for what had happened lay – it was too much. Throwing down Phylos had been Rhan's first step towards his absolution...

...but there were still many more steps to take.

Who says the Gods don't have a sense of humour?

He closed the shutter and turned back to the huge bed, to the tangle of slender girl within. In some ways, her unconsciousness was a mercy; she was at least spared the burden of trying to rebuild the shattered city. In her face, shadows shifted as if she dreamed of tragedy. Of rebuilding – with the winter climbing like frost about the walls. Rebuilding – with a populace terrified and hungry; with a military divided by flags and political rhetoric; with broken stone and little hope; and with a terrifying shortage of terhnwood and its corresponding trade. Her eyes flickered as if she followed his every thought. Rhan had sat content and unchallenged for so many returns, and now all of this was piling on his shoulders and he barely knew where to begin.

Whatever had happened to Vahl, the city had a very long way to go to reach the light.

There was a rap on the door – the short, efficient sound of the duty soldier.

Rhan checked a sigh, and stood up.

And wondered what else they could bring him.

Back at Garland House, the place still in scattered crates of confusion from Phylos's brief occupancy, the Seneschal had a guest.

In Rhan's wide main room, hands held before him in an attitude of glowering submission, stood a young man with familiar poise, his head and gaze lowered. His hair was knotted, his garments torn and his skin scattered with scratches and dirt. He looked like he'd been dragged here, and had fought every step.

When Rhan entered, he didn't look up.

The Seneschal caught his breath.

Scythe.

Samiel's teeth. They'd found *Scythe.*

There were two people on Rhan's Most Wanted list – both of them laden with Phylos's intentions for the future of the city. Scythe was one of them, Rhan's administrator who had deferred to Phylos when the Merchant Master had come to power. The other was Ythalla, Phylos's military commander, apparently fled for the city's now-lawless skirting and still courting the divided soldiery.

Ythalla would know more – but Rhan's issues with Scythe were *personal.*

Savage hope, sudden fear and a rush of opportunity all clamoured in his blood. For the moment, he stood unspeaking, staring at the head-down young man. He needed to be calm, to think about this.

Flanking Scythe was a city soldier in Palace colours. Her face was calm and cool, her eyes dark.

She gave him a curt nod. "My Lord Seneschal. You asked to be informed?"

"I did."

At the sound of Rhan's voice, Scythe lifted his chin far enough to look out from under his brows. It was a dark look of absolute loathing, a challenge laden with venom.

Do your damned worst. I dare you.

Rhan quelled the urge to grab the faithless little bastard by the neck of his shirt and shake him like an esphen. With effort, he responded only, "Thank you, tan. Please wait outside. I'll call you if I need you."

"My Lord." Cool and efficient, the woman was gone from the room.

Scythe didn't move but his gaze held Rhan's, a silent smoulder of hate. Rhan watched him in return, unspeaking.

After a moment, Scythe raised his head.

"So," he said. "Now what?" There was no fear in his tone; he oozed scorn. "Do we smoke the last of the euritu or do we host an orgy? Or do you just execute me without a hearing?" He hawked and spat. "You treasonous bastard."

"Treasonous?"

For a moment, the sensation of needing that hard, simple solution came again, stronger. Something in him wasn't ready to tackle all of this, to untangle the political rhetoric and give new faith and purpose to soldiers, merchants and populace. Something in him wanted only the pure light, the release, to answer the man's mocking challenge with the satisfaction of violence, purge the city's turmoil with a flash of laughter and the thunder of pure, exultant power.

By the Gods, it would be so easy...

But that wasn't the solution, not any more. The city below him was weak and chaotic, roiling with fear and fury. She needed to rally, to muster her resources, recover, and then to face the blight that had destroyed her terhnwood crop and now ate its way inwards, to the heart of the Varchinde.

Rhan gave Scythe a brief, brutal smile. *Screaming for his death.*

"No, Scythe. Nothing so... formal." His voice was as cold as Scythe's own. "My days of drugs and orgies are long gone. You and I are going to have a *talk*."

The talk was a long one.

Much later, as the sky paled towards the winter dawn, Rhan stood on his balcony, looking out over the hurting city below.

The air was crisp and clear and cold, absolutely still; a light frost glittered on the balcony's edge, chilling his hands. Calarinde, yellow moon, lost love, hung almost full; her pale brother smaller and higher, harder to see in the rising light.

Under their watch, scattered down the zigzag streets, the rocklights were faint; from somewhere came the smell of burning. Rhan looked for the fire, for its reflection in the crystal trees, but couldn't see it.

He was weary now; Scythe's blood stained his skin.

In the stillness, he could hear Vahl's voice.

Don't you remember how she felt, Kas Rhan Elensiel? How she tasted? Calarinde rises in glory above you every night of your immortal life, and you can never touch her again... Samiel set you up, you fool, and then he damned you for it. And still, you've failed.

The scent of the smoke had faded, thinned into nothing. The light from the Goddess made the frost into gemstones.

Look at you. Indolent, selfish, bored. The world rotted because of you... I bring change, brother, new life. Progress.

The city seemed to hold her breath, listening.

Am I the daemon, Rhan?

Or are you?

Fhaveon should be waking – that view he'd watched so many times, mornings numberless and oblivious and...

Samiel's teeth. The word was innocent.

Innocent mornings of peace, of hangovers, of damned blissful ignorance.

Down there stirring in the half-light should be that early play of yawns and feet and voices, animals and wood smoke and brewing herbal. The faint thrub of hooves and the creak of wheels as the bazaars begin their morning; the flickers of sympathetic laughter at the winter's chill in the air.

But there was nothing; the city only shifted with tension. She was restless, agitated, turning in on herself like an injured animal. Her streets were littered with the fallen – lives, leaves, debris, the cast down and the unwanted. Tan Commander Mostak, Selana's uncle and military leader, had mustered what militia would follow him. He was clearing the mess leftover from the fighting: the dead and the wreckage, the remnants of the nightmares that had ripped from the walls and torn into the lives of the people... But too many had believed Phylos's propaganda, and Rhan's rivals still thundered their drums, even as he strove to stop them.

They were still finding the horned tattooed vialer hiding in the lower areas, or trying to flee for the trade-roads – the alchemical creatures were bold and unrepentant, mocking and vicious. Rhan's request to locate their base – if they had one – had so far met with only failure, and he had few resources to spare.

Am I the daemon, Rhan?

He may have thrown Vahl down, torn Phylos a new one, but his Lord was damaged and his city ruined, devastated. Down there, opportunity came only to those who took it, merciless and uncaring – as the light rose, so grey figures scuttled from shadow to shadow, stealth and spy and ambush. Unable to trade, the people had gathered into hard communities to protect themselves, bunched into petty gangs and fiefdoms, guarding their tiny areas of land against each other and against the blight. Violence was everywhere, vicious, sporadic and harsh as coughing – as if Fhaveon was gasping for air.

Behind him, there was a sharp wet inhalation, a bloody and nasal splutter.

Sounds of struggling, movement.

Or are you?

Kas Rhan Elensiel.

Sometimes, Rhan figured, the line between himself and his brother was very thin indeed.

Sprawled out on the rug, Scythe was coming round, his face pulped with gore, several teeth cracked or missing. In the rocklight, Rhan's knuckles and elbows were dark and bloody. There were Kartian craftmasters who'd elevated information retrieval to a delicate art based on touch and hearing, but Rhan had neither the time nor the skill.

Though, in fairness, he did have certain advantages.

Coughing gouts of scarlet, Scythe pushed himself to his elbows and tried to kneel. Rhan placed a boot between his shoulders and flattened him, hard, back down to his belly. Decisive action removed Rhan's confusion, made him feel focused and stronger – not something he wanted to think about too closely.

"Scythe," Rhan said. How many times had Scythe picked him up from this very floor? Stepped over him as he lay upon it? He snorted. "You of all people know who and what I am, what I can do to you. You know that spitting blood and defiance is both charming and pointless." His voice was flat. "I must help this city. And to do so, I must know everything that Phylos intended, everything he hoarded, and where, and what he intended to do with that hoard. What plans he had to face the blight, and whether he understood its origin or solution. I need to know if he planned its cause, or its cure. And you're going to tell me."

Scythe made a noise, inarticulate, but its meaning clear. Rhan removed his boot, stepped back and crouched, looking at the broken figure of his one-time friend. He grabbed a handful of the young man's hair, pulled his chin up.

"You attended his meetings, his guests, his ritual gutting of my home." It was a statement; he didn't need an answer to that one. "I want his plans for the city. For the food-tithes of the manors; for the terhnwood crop he hoarded; for uniting the army. For what he would do after Vahl rose." Scythe sneered, spat. "He had a plan, Scythe. What was it? What was supposed to happen next?"

Scythe lifted his head high enough to meet Rhan's gaze with a look that promised a back-alley murder. Rhan chuckled.

"Are you familiar, Scythe, with one of the Gods' oldest rules?

It's very straightforward – it's why apothecaries train with weapons, why the Elementalists of old were called 'Priests of the People'. Simply? There's balance in all things – the Powerflux energy flows, soul to soul, it gives us day and night, and summer and winter. And it gives us the poled opposites of 'Heal and Harm' – none may learn one without learning the other. Am I boring you?" He crouched closer, taking a firmer grip. "Perhaps a demonstration. This, my old friend, would be 'harm'."

With a swift, vicious motion, he slammed Scythe's already bloody face into the rug, hard enough to hit the floor beneath, to crack his nose, the sound sharp and audible. Scythe swore, bubbled muffled hate and pain.

"Must do something about this rug," Rhan muttered. "Good thing it wasn't actually mine."

Still holding Scythe's hair, he leaned forward to speak almost in his ear. "Now," he said. "Just in case you've forgotten…"

He placed his other hand on the young man's broken face, felt the warmth of his blood and pain, his mortal life. In a moment Rhan could call a whole world of power, that massive elemental force, to his fingertips, could close himself away from the three unfamiliar elements and attune himself to the one that mattered – to the OrSil, the sunken Soul of Light. As he'd thrown down Phylos, defeated Vahl, and healed Mael, so now he could access just the faintest glimmer of that strength and insight.

And he could touch it to the pulse of elements that ran through the mortal body.

Change them.

Under his fingers, Scythe's face healed, bone and bruise and break. In its place, an odd red lightning mark jagged through his skin. After a moment of fearful, stock-still rigidity as he felt the flow of light and power, Scythe began to shake with a real terror.

"What… what are you doing? What are you—?"

"Healing you," Rhan said, still conversational but sharp as

an edge of bone. "It's not mercy, it's to make you think through its *implications*." As an element, light could be cruel and garish and raw; it could reach into the darkest places of a man's soul, confront him with his own figments. "Not only can I heal you so that I can torture you all over again, but also..." He moved his hand, sat back on his heels. "Scythe, think about what I am. When I ask you a question, you'll answer it. You'll answer every question I have, or by the hairy balls of Samiel himself, I'll beat you to a bloody death, pour life back into your poor broken body, and then I'll do it again. Any fool can torture you to death. I can do so *repeatedly*. Now. Tell me about Phylos."

For a moment, Scythe looked at him, blinking almost as if he was measuring his chances – wondering if Rhan was calling his bluff. Then he sagged and lowered his head, rested it for a moment on the bloody rug.

He muttered, "This isn't finished. You bloody bastard. Somehow, *somehow*, I'll get you back for all of this, for everything you've done. To me, to the city you've damned."

"I don't know what Phylos told you," Rhan said. "But he offered more shit than the paddocks on market day. I'm trying to save Fhaveon, save the Varchinde entire. I swear on the love of Calarinde herself, I'm not... not..." His words faltered, ran aground.

Vahl was laughing at him.

Am I the daemon, Rhan?

Scythe lifted his head, stared at Rhan for a moment. The red mark on his skin burned like a scar. When he started to speak, the words fell from his mouth and flooded through the room as if to drown them both in some grey sea of horror, as if the world's very ending would take place as they huddled here, listening to the rage.

And slowly, Rhan began to understand the sheer vastness of what Vahl had planned.

3: NIVROTAR'S GAMBLE AMOS

Nivrotar's audience hall was empty.

Weary of her performers, philosophers and sycophants, the Lord of Amos had set them a new task – to discover the source of the blight. Amos was an ancient city steeped in lore; if anywhere held understanding, it was here.

Without them, the hall was a suggestion of shadow, the silence as bleak as the winter chill.

Behind the great seat, her stone aperios spread black wings, its beak turned as if it watched the door from one sharp eye. But the steps below it now led down to a bare, cold floor, shining inlays clear of both feet and despair.

Only one pair of boots rested on that floor. Soft-soled, laced tight, blacker than the aperios itself, they rose into narrow, many-pocketed trews, and a long, lean figure, face mostly hidden. A figure as taut as a throne-room assassin.

The Bard, Roderick of Avesyr, stood unspeaking, his stance cold and his gaze flat, showing nothing of his thoughts. When the sharp boom of a knock came upon the great doors, he did not react, and as they parted and a chink of rocklight spread to an arc across the gleaming floor, he neither spoke nor moved.

The Lord of Amos herself watched the doors open, her head to one side like a girl's. She sat on the bottom step of the huge seat as if she were somehow unworthy, the child of its rightful occupant. Her face was pale and unadorned, her hair a tight blue-black braid. Chin in one flawless hand, she watched the long shadows in that arc of light, shadows that stretched from silhouettes, hesitant and small in the doorway.

On the other side of Nivrotar's seat was another pair of feet, now jumping back to avoid the spreading illumination. They were small feet, agile and swift, covered in locally crafted soft shoes that fit poorly.

The arc grew wider as the doors swung wide, letting in the cold of the archway outside.

"Jeez, shut the fuckin' doors willya?" Quelling an urge to scuff his toes against the elaborate shining inlay, Ecko stood in the open, sore thumb visible in his stupid new clothes, his shirt and trews both too big for him and clumsily fitted. The fabric was coarse and itchy, loose at his back and ankles; it was gonna drive him batshit before too much longer.

Yeah, so this is what I've sunk to. Rodders goes to London an' gets cool-dude-street-assassin; I stay the fuck here an' get a wool sack an' pants made outta hair...

Not that long ago Ecko would've been the assassin, maybe up there on the shadowed balcony or spider clung to the wall. Now he was stuck out here like some lost kid because he'd left his stealth-cloak in Aeona; because he had a long pink scar down his chest; because he was wearing a fucking *shirt*; because he couldn't trust himself to remain hidden, for fucksake, against a background of black stone...

Yeah, I know what you're doin'. Psyche 101. Still peelin' back the layers of defences, makin' me face the truth or find my core self or whatever the hell it is...

Hell, he might've capitulated in the face of Triqueta's rescue and Roderick's return – he might've agreed to play along the

game-path of this reality, to be good and save the world and go
to bed early and all that hero shit, but he was fucking damned
if he was giving up his attitude. Changing his choice was one
thing, but changing himself? She knew what she could do with
that shit...

You still hearin' me, Eliza? Runnin' my program? Tickin'
your li'l boxes? Checkin' to see I'm bein' a good li'l minion
now? Jus' cos I'm playin' ball, don't think I'm gonna roll over...

Chances of successful scenario at...

If the peeling layers was a thing, she hadn't even gotten
close. Ecko still had shit he wasn't gonna give up – the stuff
Mom'd given him, the stuff he'd sold his soul and sanity for.
His enhanced adrenaline spiked, making his skin shiver; his
ocular telescopics spun almost without him thinking... and he
was watching the figures as they came into the hall.

Triqueta, muddied and wide-eyed; Amethea, pale and tired
and spattered with gore.

Between them, they bore some sort of stretcher, some sort
of...

His reflexive sarcasm screeched to an unruly halt, leaving
tire-scars.

What the fuck?

Beside him, Nivrotar came slowly to her feet, her girlish
aspect gone. She said nothing, only pointed to bring the
stretcher to the floor before her.

Amethea and Triqueta exchanged a glance. Ecko watched
them as they both looked at the Bard.

His adrenaline dumped so hard he nearly chucked his lunch.

Oh this so *can't be good...*

The outside guard closed the door, and a draught of
nervousness skittered across the empty stone. Nivrotar took a
final step down to the floor, her feet bare and white. Even as she
moved, Ecko's mind was reeling. He had a sense of impending
doom the size of your average Balrog.

Hell, whaddaya know, I jus' learned premonition.
Plus five. Helluva download.

Triqueta and Amethea laid the stretcher down, then they both backed right up as if the Lord would blow them into the middle of next week.

Trembling with tension, nauseous with the unused adrenaline, Ecko crouched tight by the side of the steps – though, in the kit he had on, that was gonna do him fuck all good. He spun his telos again, his brain making silent wagers...

It's a clue, it's a key. It's the McGuffin who's gonna gasp three words about where the bad guys're at, then croak right here on the floor...

But when one of Nivrotar's long white hands pulled back the covering, he saw who it was.

And he stopped.

Holy shit.

In that split-second of recognition, of pure, cold shock, his heart rate hammered protest. He was blinking fire, swallowing sand. Hers had been the very first voice he'd heard; she'd been there, the heart of The Wanderer, right from the start...

His oculars flatlined, refused to work – he couldn't process what he was seeing. His eyes were blinking, blinking.

Shit!

But another's reaction was far, far stronger.

And Ecko realised with some loopy, detached clarity that it hadn't been Nivrotar that the two women had backed away from.

"No."

The Bard's voice was soft, like the first tremble of the coming tsunami.

As he moved, even the city's Lord gave him ground.

"No..."

Again, that reflexive denial – always, *always* the first reaction to death, like it would make some fucking difference. The potence of it shivered in the still air of the great hall, made shudders of the dust. Ecko had the creepiest feeling that if Roderick wanted, he could shatter the windows like an opera singer, bring the whole stone ceiling down in body-splatting chunks...

Jesus Harry Christ. I know you got some London tech, dude, but what the hell...?

For his life, though, he could not have moved.

"No..."

Louder this time, more a strike than a shiver. Roderick dropped to his knees by the stretcher, his long hands pulling the coverings away so he could see what had happened. He touched his fingers to her shrunken face, her thin shoulders, gently – as if he were afraid to hurt her, to wake her, afraid for her to be real.

Hellfire and fucking damnation. What's this, rise of the living dead, now? Zombie apocalypse time?

But even Ecko's savage humour was subdued; he said nothing aloud. He watched, his own denial still shouting at him, raw. Karine had been too vital, too real – too recent. This was all batshit, it had to be...

"No."

The fourth time. It was a statement, the Bard's voice still soft but gathering strength. He looked for a moment like he was going to pick the girl up, hold her to him and howl, but she was wasted and tiny, too fragile. Instead, he sat back on his heels – on his black London Converse – and looked at his shaking hands, touched them to his own face, the scarf across his jaw, as if to reassure himself it was still there.

Okay. Here we go...

But there was no roof-reaving bawl of doom. Instead, the Bard stayed like that for a moment – like he was some fucking bomb about to take out the building and all of them with it – and then he came to his feet in a single, marionette motion.

His back was straight, his face now uncovered, revealing the seething, sensual, mechanical mess of his throat, and the blacklight veins that ran up and into his ears like maggots.

For just a moment, the entire room watched him as if he would bring death to them all.

"So." His voice was a low rumble like a distant train. The hall thrummed with tension and acoustic. "This is our message, is it?"

What?

"That's *it*?" Ecko's words were out before he could stop them – their harsh rasp was a slap. All heads snapped to look at him. Uncomfortable under that many eyes, he sprang up the side of the steps and curled his lip, exposed black teeth. Grief manifested as anger, and he threw it back. His skin shifted with the shadows of the great hall. "Chrissakes, what the hell happened to you? Karine was like, I dunno, your fucking kid, your daughter. Jeez, thought *I* was fucked up—"

"Quiet." Roderick's look should have flayed skin from bone. He looked back down at the pitifully aged woman. "The time for riddles is past. Tell me, where did this come from?"

"*She*, where did *she* come from." Ecko's adrenaline was still singing along his nerves. He found himself halfway over the seat itself, staring down at the Bard, incredulous. "Chrissakes, I'm the sane one now? What the hell did Mom do to you?"

While you were screaming.

Down there in the dark.

Heat pulsed through the Bard's throat like tension. He didn't answer.

But Ecko had found his voice now, his release. The words were a torrent of force, catharsis and fury, and he couldn't hold them back. He crouched in the Lord's seat, an old embroidered cushion under his shoes, and aimed himself at the Bard's black hood.

"What the hell's goin' on here, anyhow? You come back from Mom's lair and – bam! – you're the supernasty? You got the black hat? You're the one with all the *tech*, now?" The word was an accusation – he was being childish and he knew it, but he didn't fucking *care*. "One day-trip ticket to the London Underground, two rounds with Mom's operating table, and hey whaddaya know, you're a new man!"

The strike was casual, a backhand slap. But it was so quick that, even adrenalised as he was, even with his targetters tracking, the Bard's fingers caught him. The impact didn't hurt, but the sound rang, inside and out, smarting. And the fact that it'd made contact at all…

Ecko spat outrage. "You fucking *dare*—!"

"I said, quiet."

"Fuck *you*."

"*Enough!*" Nivrotar's voice rang from the dark vaults of the roof. Like children they subsided, glaring.

Cold as winter wind, she said, "There is no combat in my presence without my word. I see grief, I see envy – I understand. But these things will not be aired in here." She added no threat, no warning of punishment or consequence – she had no need to. Instead she came to stand by Karine, the light making hollows of her perfect white cheeks. She turned to look back up at them. "We must understand this. Control yourselves, all of you, and tell me how this… atrocity… came to occur in my city."

"Outta my ass." Ecko's snipe was not aimed at anyone in particular.

"This is no jest." The Lord's voice was calm; she looked from one face to another. "Only the Kas – or those crafted from them – drain time." She cocked an eyebrow at Roderick. "Vahl may be gone, but the Varchinde is in pieces, the cities in turmoil. Blight eats our crops and we know not its source. Fhaveon lies gutless and ruined, the Council is broken. And if there are creatures of this ability within my city walls, should I just part my thighs and let them ravage me?" The sentence was delivered without a flicker of humour or vulnerability. "How comes this discovery? If Vahl lives again, if his craftings walk the streets of Amos, then I *will* know."

Amethea shook her head, her denial deeper than just disbelief. She was grey-pale, like ash, her body temperature too low; sheer bloody-mindedness was keeping her on her feet.

She said, "Karine was with me yesterday, yesterday morning. She went to secure supplies, herbs, food – she was helping. No one haggles like Karine." Her smile was brief, sad. "Couple of guards brought her back. I tried…" her voice cracked and she looked up at the Lord of Amos, blinking "…I tried to understand, I really tried. But how – where – no one knew. The bazaar was heaving, no one saw a thing."

"No one ever does." Triqueta's comment was bleak.

"Vahl's *gone*," Amethea rounded on her friend, plaintive, angry, defiant. "Rhan won, Fhaveon's free – the bretir came with the message. You told us!" She looked back at the city's Lord, gave a short laugh like the edge of hysteria. "That bit's supposed to be *over*—"

Ecko snorted, loud and confrontational, echoing in the empty hall. When they all stared at him, eyes upon eyes, he bared his teeth.

"Yeah an' the bad guys never come back after you kill 'em." He grinned, malicious. "Answer me this – this Kiss, Kas, this Vahl must-be-a-bad-guy-'cause-his-name's-got-a-'z'-in-it – what's he want?"

"Fhaveon," Nivrotar said. "To defeat his brother and cast down the city of Saluvarith—"

"Fuck legend." Ecko was agitated. He was onto something and he wasn't sure what – it was like throwing a hot piece of metal from hand to hand. "When he got the city, what was he gonna do with it? Open schools? Build social housing projects, what? Hold an open-house party for all his daemon buddies?" His own jibe brought him up short – something had just occurred to him. "Like *Tarvi*?"

Triqueta flinched, said nothing.

Nivrotar watched Ecko. "What do you mean?"

"I mean..." The new thought was gathering pace; as he spoke, he understood what it was that he was trying to say. "Shit! Like – how many of these fuckers are there? Were there? Really? You talk about Vahl and the Kas, and we've seen – what – two? One big an' one little? Where are the *rest* of them? The army of Kiss Vahl Thingies, the army of Tarvis just waitin' to *snog* everything to death. I *mean*—"

"You mean, where are his friends?" Amethea's voice was soft as the smothering pillow.

"Something else you've *forgotten*?" Ecko's voice was jagged, and it tore.

Nivrotar rocked backwards, said nothing. She turned to look at the Bard, and they exchanged a long glance laden with fuck alone knew what. For a moment, their mutual Tundran resemblance was strong.

And the Lord of Amos looked old, older by far than Roderick, older even than the carved beastie behind her throne...

She looked *exhausted*.

Then Ecko blinked, and the look was gone – she was pale and perfect, elegant as ever.

"There was always suspicion," Roderick said, his voice like the plainland's empty wind. "All my life, Ecko, scrabbling for pieces. Fragments of forgotten lore. I went looking for the Kas upon Rammouthe, long ago – and I found no trace of them, or of their fabled citadel. And now Karine finds a truth I could never... never have dreamed..." At the word, his own voice cracked, failed. He leaned on the side of the seat, caught one huge, shaking gulp of breath, then another. His knees went, and he seemed to curl in on himself, to shrink away from the memory, from the body on the floor, from thoughts laden with pain and loss and fear. Ecko watched him, adrenaline tinged with a tangle of scorn and pity. Then Nivrotar said something in words unfamiliar, a language that sounded like the cracking of ice, ancient and cold.

Steadying, the Bard inhaled again, lifted his chin. His

shoulders straightened. When he spoke, it was as distant as the white moon.

"Karine tells us that, whatever my reconnaissance told me, there are more Kas than just Vahl Zaxaar. And they walk here among us, in whatever strength and form. They may lack their commander, Ecko, but I fear you're right: there is *purpose*."

The word sent a chill through the room.

"Which is *what*?" Ecko said.

"Sadly, that I can't answer." As he spoke, his amethyst eyes seemed to flicker with a hint of his old humour. "Ah, Ecko. You wanted your epic victory, your Final War – perhaps the Gods will yet grant you that desire."

"Perchance Vahl wanted Fhaveon as a bridgehead," Nivrotar said sharply. Her finger tapped her cheek. "And if so, it would mean the Kas are indeed still upon Rammouthe, and that they will come – or have come – over the water. Perhaps they stalk already the streets of the Lord city." She looked at them, one face after another. "This foreknowledge may be enough for us to face them."

May be enough. The words sent a chill down Ecko's spine.

"But – what about the blight?" Amethea said. "We need to be finding a cure."

"We must comprehend before we can cure," Nivrotar said. "But our lore is lacking and as yet, we know nothing."

"And that's a longer problem," Triqueta said. "Look at the damage one daemon caused – if Vahl's family are playing range patrol, then we need to know. And now. We need to know where they are, and where they're going." She looked back at the Lord of the city. "We should scout…"

"There may be a better way." Nivrotar stood looking at the shrivelled Karine. "A way to bring them from hiding, to bring them to us and all unready. To draw them to a place and a time of our choosing and to assess and defeat them. It is a gamble, but a fierce one. And we should show no doubt or fear." She looked up, held Triqueta's eyes for a long, considered moment. "Roviarath holds to her freedom, does she not?"

"Yes, my Lord." Triqueta smiled, a flicker of sunshine. "As far as I know."

Nivrotar nodded. "Larred Jade is a strong Warden and a good man. You will bear him a message. Are you stalwart enough to ride the winter roads alone?"

"Ride…?" Triqueta blinked, realised the Lord was serious. She snorted.

"Good." The Lord glanced sideways at the Bard, but his gaze was cold and he didn't return the look. She said, "Ecko, Triqueta, Amethea, you have earned the gratitude of Amos, and of the world entire. In destroying Maugrim, you saved Roviarath and thus we stand not alone. In destroying Aeona, you halted the crafting of Amal's creations, and forced Vahl into the open. If and when we come to confrontation, these are victories that will count in our favour. Trust in yourselves – you have might unrealised, and wisdom unseen."

"Let's damned well hope so." Triqueta scratched at her flaking hands. "Or we're all in the rhez together."

With a flicker of a smile, Nivrotar came to stand by the broken Karine, the corpse's dry, open eyes staring empty at the black vaults of the Varchinde's oldest building.

"Once before, we discussed Amos finding the fighting freemen and women of the Varchinde, and this I have done." Her eyes flashed. "I have a strong force here, enough to leave the city secure and to muster for a march."

"A march?" Ecko said. "Can you say 'overreaction'? Christ, we dunno what or where the Kas – Kiss – even are—"

"No." The Lord met Ecko's gaze. "But I know the one thing they cannot resist, the lure that will bring them to our gaze and our weapons both. And by that thing, so they can be led, like a furious child with a favourite toy." Her smile was amused, pure and cold. The Bard was staring at her now, his eyes burning with question. "We have much knowledge – gleaned from The Wanderer, from the Library, from your own struggles and triumphs, from the Bard's long returns of seeking, and from my rulership of this city. And I trust it will be enough."

She turned her hand like a street conjurer, and released a single white feather that drifted gently to the stone floor.

"We have one chance to do this, and if we fail, the Kas will take us all."

The Kas will take us all.

Triqueta stood alone, fighting a fear that seemed to wield many blades.

Outside the Lord's audience hall, the archway was cold; the winter wind came through it hard from the empty terrace. Rain stung like flung stones.

Nivrotar had outlined an impossible plan, an insanity, a wager bigger than anything Triq had ever taken, ever dreamed of. It was crazed beyond words, hung on one single and critical assumption – but she had met Vahl Zaxaar and it made immediate sense. It thrilled her to the core of her soul.

Her message to Larred Jade in Roviarath, that was the easy part. The others—

Behind her, Ecko's voice said, "This is fuckin' bullshit."

Triqueta hugged herself against the chill, tried to work her chapped hands into her sleeves and failed. She'd left her cloak inside, and she was cold; her hair was everywhere, scratching at her face. Without turning, she said, "We don't have a choice – the Kas are coming and that's all there is to it. Face it, it's not the most stupid thing we've done."

"It's fuckin' *insane*." Ecko paused, as if looking for the words for something, then ventured, "So, now we go to Fhaveon and we tell this 'Rhan' motherfucker he has to down tools and leg it across the plains with a host of daemons right up his ass. An' you – you get to go *home*."

"To Roviarath, to where the centaurs run." She glanced slyly sideways, and her smile was humourless. "That's not why I'm going—"

"You're still lookin' for him—"

"I *want* to go home, Ecko!" She dropped her chin, rounded on him. "I miss my family – should never've left in the first place. You led us on some Gods-damned dance—"

"Led you?" He bared his teeth. "What're you, helpless now? You're a big girl, you made your own choices—"

"Did I? Did *you*?" She snorted, anger and grief, ridicule. "We should never've gone to Aeona, whatever Nivvy just said. The terhnwood blade I was given in the pub, that damned brimstone – that alchemist wound us in like fish so he could have *you*. And you near damned us all, our whole *world*. And Redlock..."

The word choked her. She expected, *wanted*, Ecko to fight back, needed him to rise against her raw torrent of words, but instead he backed up, spreading his hands.

"Look, I didn't come out here to pick a fight."

"What?" Startled by his lack of resistance, Triq lost her momentum, staggered. Unsure, she sniped, "Makes a change."

He pulled a face at her. "Put a fuckin' sock in it willya, I'm tryin' here. You wanna go home – like, I get it, y'know? I..."

"Yeah, I know." It was Triqueta's turn to back up. She shrugged, not sure where this was going. "I'm not used to you being... well, like that, I s'pose. Sorry."

"Me too."

For a moment, they stood there like kids, neither of them quite knowing what to say. Then Ecko lifted his chin and looked straight at her, black-on-black eyes like pits, expressionless.

"I don't..." He paused, seemed to gather himself, to make a conscious, concentrated effort. "I don't think you should go... ah... alone."

I don't think you should go alone.

It was just about the last thing she'd been expecting. For no reason, Triqueta found her pulse jumping, and she stared at him, his ill-fitting clothes wind-tight against one side of his lean body.

He said, "You came after me." He seemed to be struggling, and, like staring at some deep fear, she was compelled to see where it would end. "You said, 'We're your friends, we came here because we love you, because we won't abandon you, because we don't walk out on family.'" Flickers passed though the colours in his skin. "I don't want... I don't think you should. Not all that way. Not with all the... y'know... critters an' stuff..." His argument tailed into an awkward silence, but he held her gaze. He seemed fixed to the spot, tense.

"I don't need an escort." She mustered a laugh, before realising that really hadn't been the point.

He was asking to come with her.

Asking...

Don't be ridiculous, Triqueta told herself, *you're imagining it...*

Something in her laugh had cowed him, and he dropped his gaze and stepped back out of the wind, into the shadow of the arch's wall. He shrugged, backed away further. He seemed embarrassed, flickers of anger chased impossible blue lights in his empty black eyes. Muttering, he went to turn away.

Triq heard herself say, "Ecko, wait!"

"What?" The word was a lash, cutting, a knee-jerk reaction to hurt.

She said the first thing that came into her mouth. "I needed to ask you about something. Back there, when we were going into the wood and the soldiers caught Amethea..." Now, she found the words were falling from her, easing a weight on her heart she hadn't even known she was carrying. "Would you... would you have let her die?" Her voice caught and she was crying again, unable to help herself. "Let all of us die?"

Would you have killed all of us in order to save yourself?

The question wasn't about Amethea – it was about the choice he'd made on the alchemist's table, the choice to damn their entire world in order to save his own skin.

Shame was one fucking ugly emotion.

"I'm gonna help you." His rasp came from the wall shadow, softer now, almost gentle. "Goddamn motherfucking program. I'm gonna *do* this. You fucking see if I don't."

Triq drew a ragged breath, crying, almost laughing. "I believe you, I *believe* you." She bit her lip against the sobbing and the words were lost.

"Jesus." It was a confession, a realisation, a breaking. Even as Triqueta turned away from him, hands over her face, she could feel him move behind her, small and slight, taut as terhnwood fibre. As she turned back, she found herself abruptly too close – he was there in front of her, a hair taller than she was. His skin was flecked with the warm yellow of hers, the shine of the opal stones in her cheeks; his eyes were huge, featureless and terrifying. A glitter of black showed between his lips.

Hesitant, his hand touched her face. When she turned into it, almost as an excuse not to have to look at him, he caught his breath...

Stopped.

Her colour seeped into his skin.

She expected him to pull away, to snarl denial, to deliver some blistering retort, to hurl her back by word or gesture; she expected to have to fight. But there was nothing. He simply stood there, his hand on her cheek, breathless, unmoving.

Warm.

And something in her began to tremble. That touch was calling an answer from her belly, a spread of anticipation through her body that made her shake with the strangeness of it.

So many faceless lovers, grapple and sweat, attentions just to fill the holes in her soul. Rough relief or momentary comfort, all forgotten with the birth of the sun. And this...

Somewhere Triqueta heard an echo of Tarvi's fire-crackle laughter, taunting.

The heat in her flared in response. His face was almost desert-shades now, warm and normal. Only those limitless, bottomless black eyes...

Neither of them moved. They stood there as if the Count of Time waited breathless, was watching them as they watched each other, transfixed, to see what they would do.

He said, his voice a whisper, a question, "Triq..."

But it broke the moment, and the cold sky lurched into motion. She stepped back, swallowed, unsure what had just happened. His arm fell back to his side as if it were lost.

"Sorry," she said, not even sure why. "But I'm going alone. I don't..." She'd been going to say, "I don't want company", but she realised that was a lie, and instead she trailed into an awkward silence. His closeness, his strangeness, had been so intense they'd made her shiver, made her skin thrill and her heart pound. She wanted...

No, that was just crazed.

She was going alone, and that was all there was to it.

Before she could do anything else, anything foolish, she took another step back. Then she turned and walked out through the archway.

He called after her, and it took an effort not to stop.

It took all the effort she had to turn the corner, and walk out into the cold.

4: MERCHANT MASTER FHAVEON

In a small, high window at the aching heart of Fhaveon, there sat an old man in a red robe.

He wore pince-nez glasses, new and slightly too big for him. They slid down his nose constantly, to be retrieved by the reflexive shove of a finger. In his other hand was a pure white quill, tip dark with ink, and on the cold windowsill lay a heavy ledger, pages yellow and crackling. The book was covered in tally markers, bundles of fives and tens and days and distances. In the outermost corner of the open page, the old man was absently crafting a doodle, a humorous little sketch that might have been a stylised warrior.

But he was not really paying attention, either to the sketch or to the tallies. He was watching the grey street below, the scurries of dead winter leaves tumbling one over another, or stuck like fabric to the roadways; the hanging signs of craftsmen and traders now forlorn as the buildings they marked had been abandoned.

Occasionally, he heard voices, distant ripples of sadness and anger.

Merchant Master Mael was safe up here. Phylos's old rooms

were high and clean, reflecting the city's zenith, and tucked away from the shatter and tumult that Fhaveon's streets had become. Like his title, the rooms were too big for him, but they had one thing in common with his little tent in the marketplace – they were detached.

Though now, that detachment felt strange.

There had been a moment when Mael had been the pivot and lynchpin of the great city's crisis, living and breathing it, vital and alive. In that moment, he'd not been an observer, he'd really made a difference – he was an old man and it had almost cost him his life, but he'd *mattered*. Now, some part of him craved that validation – wanted to be out there, understanding, living, feeling what the city was feeling, and helping. Mael was an academic, certainly, but these allocations of cycles and balances and craftmarks... they were cold. And frankly, the Cartel's sigils and maps and endless equations were making his head hurt.

He glanced back at the little doodle, at the comical, heavyset warrior that grinned up at him from the paper.

You daft old bugger, what have you become!

Mael snorted, and pushed his glasses higher up his nose.

They'd named him a hero, a knight, a member of the Order of the Something or Other – there was a real white-metal medal somewhere with his name on it. He wore the decorous red robe of the Merchant Master – though he feared Phylos had carried the colour rather better – and he had the life-sworn loyalty of...

No, that was one thing he still wasn't ready to think about. It creeped his damn skin every time he remembered it.

More shouting came from outside, faint with distance; the leaves eddied in the roadway.

Mael looked back at the long page of numbers, blew the moisture from his doodle and closed the page. Try as he might, he could not balance the figures and there was real fear coiling in his heart like some smirking, sliding creature.

You're not going to do it, the creature said.

Fhaveon was facing another battle – and there would be no blazing and heroic win to get them out of this one.

No food, no grass, no terhnwood, no trade. The city's in ruins. We won't last the winter.

We're going to starve.

Mael put the book away. They would be coming for him at the birth of the sun, and he had to be ready. Knight of the Whatever-it-was or not, the streets were not a safe place to be alone.

Since Phylos's fall, Fhaveon had become almost nocturnal – the pirates had coalesced into factions, they worked from hit-and-run night markets, heavy with muscle, and they warred merciless beneath the broken awareness of both soldiery and Cartel. The lower levels of the city had disintegrated into rages and ruins and raids. With his still-limited strength, Tan Commander Mostak had little hope of re-establishing control. His forces were split – many had sympathised with Ythalla and Phylos, and many more had simply fled.

Selana's illness worsened, and she lacked both authority and experience. The Council had been disbanded; many of its members fled or vanished. Of those who remained, Rhan was too tainted by Phylos's pedagogue might, Valicia, Selana's mother, wouldn't leave her daughter and Mael, new to his robe, had the mind but not the presence. Mostak had his hands full already, and, lacking leadership, Fhaveon convulsed like a headless serpent.

"Nervous?" Mael's despatched guard grinned at him. "You don't need to come for this."

"I know." The guard had not offered him his title, but it was too heavy for both of them. Mael shrugged, tripping over the hem of the robe and reaching for his winter cloak. "I want to."

"Course you do." The guard winked. "You've got a sack on you, that's for sure. Hope this works."

They crept noiseless into the soft grey light. The air was sharp and cold and their breath steamed.

About them, the street noise had faded to a tense quiet; echoes of shouts hung in the air like figments. A soft mist stole silent from the empty plain and the rocklights hung spectral and sinister, pale blurs of white.

Mael tightened his fists, nails biting his palms. He peered from doorway to archway to corner, from darkness to darkness. They moved cautiously, sensing unseen eyes sliding over them like wet fingers, voices almost heard, lost somewhere in the mist.

Mael coughed, smothered it, offered, "We've made a real mess of this, haven't we?"

A rustle made him start – a hungry creature, grey fur and sinew, fleeing from the unexpected visitors. Under a pile of crafthall debris, several discoloured, swollen bodies lay stinking. One of them twitched, though Mael suspected it had more to do with scavengers than it did with a struggle for life.

He swallowed.

"The fighting here's almost constant," the guard said, voice soft. "Every area has its own petty Lord, and they scrap like greedy children." He nodded at the rotting pile. "This is the result. Keep your eyes open, Merchant Master."

Mael shoved his glasses higher up his nose, then he stilled his heart, covered his mouth and moved on.

They turned a corner, another. The city's striated stonework offered holes, maws of darkness and damage; its carvings were shattered, and piles of rubble loomed peculiar through the mist. The skeletal trees angled like claw shadows, distorted. The guard had drawn his blade and was poised, tight as a bowstring.

Merchant Master.

If this guard chose to kill him, they'd never find what was left.

Then Mael felt a draught, a breath of open air. The white fog eddied, thinned, and for a moment he could see, through a gap where a building had been, and still far below him the dawn-lit plain, brown and black and grey and vast. A bird cried like a skirl of laughter.

He shivered, and shrank his nose into the collar of his cloak.

"Mael."

In the mist, Rhan was there, too much and too close; his presence made the old man uneasy and he drew back. The Seneschal was huddled in some great grey cloak, his head bare, his face drawn and worried. A tan of guards formed a loose ring, all of them spear-armed and watchful.

Mael tried to peer past them.

"You found it. Did you find it?" He tried to be calm, but his voice squeaked with tension.

Rhan jutted his chin at the building beside him, a looming square shape in the fog.

"We know Phylos was hoarding food and terhnwood." His deep voice was quiet, a rumble of threat. "Now we know where. Let's hope this is good information – there might just be enough here to make the difference." The sentence ended in a shrug that spoke for itself. The cool air from the plain shifted the mist about them, confusing. "Ready with the tally markers, Merchant Master?"

"Yes... yes." Mael's cold hands pulled a series of knotted cords from a pouch. He pushed up his glasses and peered at the building. It could have been anything – a church, an old tithehall – its sides were decorated with angled mosaics now shattered like the city herself. He could have leaned forwards and picked at the individual tiles.

At a nod, the closest of the guards eased a heavy, fibrous bar down the side of the door and applied pressure, pushing his shoulder into the lever and grunting with the effort. The lintel was heavy over him; upon it, a sightless beast raised a clawed foot in salute.

As the remainder of the tan closed tighter to defend them, Rhan stepped back to Mael. "We've been speaking to Scythe," he said, conversationally. "He's proven very… helpful."

His skin crawling, Mael stammered something and made himself stay where he was.

The door creaked, the protest loud in white stillness. The soldier swore. It creaked again, then gave way with a sudden sharp bang, a spit of soured dust. The soldier staggered back, his fellows coming forwards with spear points ready. But even as Rhan's bass voice sounded the warning, Mael knew it was too late.

He's proven very… helpful…

The guard had something on his face, something at his throat. Something that wriggled in a crazed, half-starved frenzy; something with big claws and yellow teeth and a fleshy tail. A roll of stink followed it out of the door.

The smell was familiar.

"Down!" Mael's guard hit him like a bweao and he found himself on his face and in the wet and the cold, coughing, his glasses lost, a knee in his back. Struggling to see, he was aware of guards at the doorway, ordered boots as four of them skirmished carefully into the building.

He saw the injured guard stagger back, his hands still clawing at his face. He was shouting, half-muffled, pained and furious; the creature squealed and clawed. Then Rhan blocked Mael's view. The guard gave a brief cry, and there was the slam of something living hitting stone, cracking and screaming with the impact.

Hitting stone again, with a sickening crunch.

The injured guard swore, shook himself. He was bleeding profusely, deep scratches in his face, but he was moving, going for weapons.

"Esphen," he called, "big one! And pretty damned angry!"

Mael rummaged for his glasses, couldn't find them. He tried to push himself up. Scents eddied in the air: terhnwood, rich rot, dying moss, things that had perished from fear. He still couldn't place that smell.

Saravin. Something...?

Then, the guard commander: "The building's secure, my Lord. Scythe was telling the truth. There's terhnwood here, though perhaps not as much as we'd thought." Beneath his disciplined tone, his voice was oddly tense. "My Lord, some of it's... tainted."

"Tainted?" Rhan's question was barbed. He shoved past the guards into the building.

Mael's guard let him up, and he scrambled after the Seneschal, needing to see...

Tainted.

He still hadn't found his glasses, and the light in the space was slanted and dusty though boarded windows. He could see the terhnwood, long canes in regular stacks, piles of worked strips, great furry rolls of fibre. Some of it was darker in tone where it had been steamed. But the stacks were stained, blotched with lichens like rot, flowering with blemishes. And that *smell*...

From somewhere outside, there came shouting.

Ahead of Mael in the dim storeroom, Rhan cursed and turned, but the commander's voice came from outside, calm and clear.

"Seems we've woken the watchers." He barked orders. "Give me a defensive ring. If anything moves, I want to know. Now! No, not you, Ghar. Stay where you are, and take this."

The air tightened, went quiet.

Inside the storeroom, it was thick and cold. Murky with undefined threat.

You old fool, Mael cursed himself. *What are you even doing out here?*

In the gloom, Rhan was a heavy, square shape, his cloak thrown back. He picked up a cane and turned it over. "The Gods and their damned sense of humour." He dropped it with a clatter, picked up another. "This... I know this smell. North of here, Foriath... Samiel's *bollocks*!" Frustration slammed from his movements. "Look at this. Look at it!" He spun on Mael, brandishing the long cane like a weapon, and Mael blinked, still not understanding. "What the rhez am I supposed to do with this?"

And then the smell hit him like a fist, and the memory with it. It was so sudden, so real, that it robbed him of breath. He trembled and his face flushed – Saravin, the market, the woman in the ale tent. It seemed to come from another Count of Time, and yet the memory was as precise as if he'd drawn it.

Rhan shook the cane, pulling at his attention. The thing was caked in moss, in moss that was already dying. It had grown in the cracks, furred the outer edges, but it was brown, flaking into the dust even as Rhan spun the thing like a staff and threw it back on the pile. It rolled down the edge and struck the stone floor, rattling as it settled.

Outside, the injured guard swore.

Mael went cold. His heart laboured in his chest, scaring him. His previous, nebulous nervousness had been replaced by a sharp tang of real fear...

I know this smell.

North of here... Foriath.

But the guard commander's voice came sharply through the doorway. "Whatever you're doing, make it quick."

"We're coming now," Rhan called. Then to Mael, "We need to secure this store. We need the Cartel down here, Merchant Master, get this counted and moved. More guards, porters, whatever you'll need. Take it to the Priest Gorinel, the Cathedral, and the catacombs. It should be safe enough—"

"Wait, *wait*," Mael muttered almost to himself, trying to catch up with his thoughts. "We can't just—"

"We don't have a choice," Rhan said. "We'll take what there is and sort through it." He touched Mael's arm. Caught off-guard, Mael snatched the limb back like he'd been stung. "We still have a long way to go, and we need everything we can find. Now, let's move."

They stepped out of the store, blinking in the rising morning light. The street was quiet, and the mist had thinned, slipping back down towards the water. The injured guard stood back from his fellows, ruefully holding a folded piece of tunic to his face. His skin was reddening, already swelling with infection, and one of the claws had rasped dangerously close to an eye.

"Ghar," Rhan said. "Let me see it."

"My Lord." The guard lowered the fabric, lifted his chin.

Coming close, Rhan placed a hand on the man's sweating face, looked at him with a peculiar, familiar intensity.

An intensity that Mael knew only too well.

Like being lit up from the inside out.

He *knew* how that felt. Mael was not a believer in Gods, but the Count of Time had come for him, his heart had been squeezed in that long, chill hand. He'd known it was over, and it had been all right.

He was an old man, he missed his friend, and he'd done enough.

Lit up from the inside out.

Rhan's inhuman touch had healed him – but had left no part of him secret. It was the light of a truth unwilling, of a whole life revealed in an instant. It had driven that chill hand from him, brought him from death, back to Fhaveon... but what else had it done?

Ghar was shaking, flushed. The wounds in his face were gone – red scars in his tanned skin. He was spluttering, trying to voice incomprehension, thanks, disbelief, but Rhan said only, "Your tan bade you guard the perimeter."

With a fist-on-chest salute, the soldier obeyed the order.

Mael shuddered. "You can do that with a touch." The

question was painfully curious, like tonguing a sore tooth. "Why can you not just—?"

"Not just what?" Rhan snapped back at him, sounding oddly stung. "Cure the blight? Make it go away? Wave my hand and just... conjure it all better?" He snorted, bitterly humorous. "Samiel's balls, Mael, you think I haven't tried?" He made a noise of frustration and disgust. "I wish I could! But I can't even understand it – it's too big, somehow, too much. I can't see its origins or its edges. Even the fragments – it's like they're a part of something else, something huge." He shook his head. "I've touched only its outside, and by the Gods, it terrifies me." He tailed into a frown, looking at the pile of canes. "I can't cure a... a disease when I don't even know what it is."

Mael nodded. He had no more comprehension than Rhan as to the blight's cause or content – it ate its way inwards from the Varchinde's outer edges, destroying the terhnwood at the coast and the forests at the feet of distant Kartiah. And they had nothing – no hope, no cure.

"Enough talking." The guard commander was edgy now, and the shouting was closer. "We need to move."

The sunrise swelled around them. If Mael turned, he would see the rising zigzag of streets climbing the hill; the ascending rocklights, glittering with the hopes the city had lost. At the city's zenith, the sky was streaked with pink.

The shouts grew louder. Hands tightened on weapons.

The guard commander said, "My Lord Seneschal, you shouldn't be here. Take the Merchant Master to safety. We'll stay. When the area's secure, I'll send a runner for you."

Rhan tensed for a moment, then acquiesced. To Mael, it seemed like he was ashamed.

The closest safe house was a dark and tiny cellar, cold and damp. The building above was little more than a shell, but the refuge beneath was untouched; in moments, it became layered with tallow-smoke and tension.

Rhan paced the stone floor, four paces one way, four the other, setting the candle flames to flickering as he passed. His shoulders seemed to fill the room; his face was a thundercloud. Mael ran his tally markers though his fingers and tried to do the maths.

Whatever else one could say about the departed Phylos, the bastard had been truly gifted with managing numbers.

But Mael thought he was getting the hang of it.

Rhan stopped, spun, paced back the other way, the tiny flames tracking him. He said, "Well?"

Mael had so many things he wanted to ask – the smell, the woman in the market, the tainted terhnwood, the vastness that was the encroaching blight...

He cleared his throat. "I didn't really get a proper look. But if the figures Scythe... ah... Scythe gave you are close, then..." he halted, then finished tentatively, "...we may even manage. If it's not too badly damaged."

Rhan stopped his pacing, raised an eyebrow.

"Is there enough? Merchant Master?"

"There's enough terhnwood to equip Mostak's command." Mael took a breath, could almost feel the hulking shape of Saravin behind him, there in the dark, strong and oddly comforting. "But not enough to trade. And the food situation is dire—"

"Dire?" The word was a jab.

Mael wanted to protest – this wasn't his task, wasn't his life, wasn't what he wished to do, or what he had ever trained for – but this was where he'd found himself and he'd better damn well make the best of it.

He owed Rhan his life.

Mael's hands tightened on the string, feeling the knots.

He said, "Even with rationing, and even if we can enforce that rationing..." He shook his head. For a moment, he could visualise it like a picture, the layers of complexity to the decision – what to cut, what to keep, the juggling of priorities. Panic clamoured, but he held himself still.

Rhan said softly, "Can we last the winter?"

Mael sighed. "It's a little more complex than that, my Lord. We'll need to be careful. Once we equip the soldiery, the Cathedral's the right place for the rest of this – at least what we have will be safe."

The Seneschal exhaled, sagged, clapped Mael's shoulder. The old scribe forced himself not to flinch.

"Sorry," he said. "All this – it's outside my experience as well. I need your eyes and your ears, your insight. Whatever happens, we must hold the city."

Any answer was interrupted by a rap on the trapdoor above them. There was a creak, and Mael's guard ducked his head downwards.

"My Lord. Sorry for the intrusion, but—"

"What?" Rhan said. "What's the matter?"

"It's the Bard, my Lord. He's at the outskirts of the city. And he's asking for you."

5: SAVE POINT TRADE-ROAD, FHAVEON

There was a stray, furry thing, all big eyes and radar ears, huddled alone in the winter cold. There was a black blade, carbon fibre and mono-edged, a silent and accurate throw that downed the puffed-up critter without a squeak.

Ecko shivered. He eyed the Bard's knife as it peeled the furry thing and spilled its guts – his own stomach turned over. Chrissakes, this shit he still hadn't gotten used to – food came in sealed packages, processed, labelled, barcoded, unrecognisable. It had safety information, corporate caveats, logos. This thing? This thing still had eyeballs.

Nope – he really wasn't fucking hungry.

Unfazed by the skinless thing, Amethea offered suggestions on herbs and flavours. Christ on a shovel, outbound fucking cookery class was just taking the piss, okay?

Eliza? You even listening anymore?

The Bard cleaned the blade. He banked down the fire, then carved strips of muscle off the dead thing and laid them out on long stones. Slowly the raw meat blackened, fibres breaking and peeling back. Rich smells writhed in the evening air.

Ecko huddled closer to the fire.

Over him, the sky drew in low. The wind was cold down his back. He had a sore ass and stiff legs, his shoulders were damp, and there was a crick in his neck where his fool fucking horse had started at some burrowing critter. Watching strips of beastie slowly char, he found himself in a foul mood that was getting uglier by the minute. He wanted nothing more than to ditch this Adventuring Party shit, an'...

An' *what*?

Strike out alone? Save the world? Win the war? Cure the blight? Pull a white rabbit out his butthole?

Ta-dah!

He couldn't be a hero; he'd lost his fucking cape.

Yeah. I'm funny.

But it wasn't just his stealth-cloak he'd lost, his footwear and his flamethrower and Lugan's fucking lighter – in agreeing to play nice, eat his greens and go to bed on time, he'd lost a fundamental necessity.

His freedom.

He was Ecko, fucksake, he was the 'me' in team. He was gonna do whatever the hell he wanted and no bastard was gonna stop him...

Not even his friends.

Chrissakes.

He held a hand to the fire as if he could hold out the thought and let it go, watch it rise like burning paper, and spark into nothing in the gathering dusk. Friends were a responsibility, something that had to be worried about and taken care of...

Freedom, for chrissakes.

But what could he do? Ditch these fuckers, do a runner? He might make a day, two. But in this barren, almost-lifeless nothing, this wind, this cold... he'd get lost. Or starve. Or break his neck. Or catch fucking dysentery or something. Cities, he could do, but this crap?

The embers popped, laughing at him.

Somewhere under them there was a flicker of blue, of real heat, compelling. Heat like Maugrim's Sical, heat like his own breath.

His freedom had gone, his independence was over. He'd surrendered them both when the others had pulled him off of Amal.

Family, Triq had said.

The fire leaped and crackled.

Yeah, an' y'know what? His thoughts flared in symmetry. *If I'm gonna do this, I'm gonna fuckin' own it. I'm gonna win every trophy and every fuckin' side quest. You peel back my layers all you want, bitch, but when these Kiss Vahl Thingies rise in flames or whatever, I'm gonna kick their fuckin' asses.*

You just watch me!

After Amos, their first few days had been bright, sunshine-cold. The trade-roads had been violent and lawless, dirty. Yet the Bard had ridden through them and the people had fallen silent – he was a maverick, a knife-slinging outlaw, dressed in black and reeking of liquor and reputation. Ecko'd half expected Wanted posters to appear on walls, and for the reward to be higher every time he passed one.

Yeah, you don't mess with Wild Bill Bigcock.

But no one had voiced a challenge. Roderick had shown no sign of emotion, no flicker or falter of doubt. His black horse was as lean and mean as he was – in his scarf and hoodie he looked like some comic-book manifestation of villainy, some doom-bringing monster from the world of anywhere-but-here...

Finally, they'd passed beyond the town's ending, the buildings fading to dilapidation and garbage, and then failing altogether. Beyond, the plain was black and grey and windblown; the whole damn thing was like some fucking rural dystopia, a ruin that followed Vahl Whosit's release.

Chris*sakes.*

The heat from the fire's embers was growing and Ecko

leaned back, opening his soggy wool cloak to let the warmth reach his body.

Roderick passed him a waterskin. Without lowering the scarf, he said, "What do you see in the fire?" His voice was very soft, as if he didn't want to *unleash* it.

"Corn," Ecko replied.

The fire burned shelled corn, an easily portable fuel they carried with them – Ecko had been almost tempted to ask if it popped. The slices of meat spat and sizzled.

The Bard chuckled. "It's called paow, but close enough." He glanced sideways, then said suddenly, like the jab of a blade, "Are you ready for this?"

"For what? You quit bein' Wild Bill to be Bozo the Clown?" Ecko took a swig from the waterskin, then spluttered something that tasted like cinnamon-flavoured meths. Gasping, he croaked, "What the fuck is that?"

"Heating," Roderick told him. "Drink it." His tone was all mirthless smirk. "You don't seem to realise where we've finally found ourselves."

"The ass-end of beyond?"

"Look around you," Roderick told him. "We're here." He gestured at the fading light, at the trashed remains of the range patrol campsite. "Fighting the fucking Final War. Pits of fire and mountains of ash. Well, maybe not quite," his grin was wicked, "but Nivrotar has given you what you wanted. You should be *happy*."

Amethea watched them both, one face then the other, said nothing.

"Dancin' a fuckin' jig here." Ecko took another swig from the waterskin. For a moment, he thought he'd made a ghastly mistake and was gonna empty his guts in the corn-burning fire – but the churning receded and the booze was shimmering-warm, uncoiling like a serenaded snake. "Where you goin' with this?"

"You've been given a second chance, Ecko." Roderick's voice had a mocking edge, savage. "You almost failed, brought my whole world to ruin, despite—"

"Christ, don't you fuckin' start," Ecko said. "You're the one who sat around for a hundred years with your thumb up your ass. Oh, there's a bad guy, but no one knows where. Oh there's a prophecy, but no one remembers what." Ecko raised the waterskin to take a third swig, lowered it again. "You clueless motherfucker, you don't get to blame me for this—"

"*Everything* Nivrotar has planned depends upon this message, and Rhan's reaction." The Bard's gaze fixed Ecko like a blade through the eye socket. "Rhan is an old friend, inhuman in his loyalty, and extraordinarily powerful – but often he sees no further than the end of his own nose." The Bard gave a grim smile. "And he doesn't lose well. Nivrotar's gamble is less that the Kas will follow him, and more..." he paused to make this sink home "...more that he will agree to go."

Amethea still watched them both, silent.

"So – what? You need my help?" Ecko grinned, mocking. "Truss him up an' drag him." He grinned. "Who's your great shinin' hero now?"

"I need to know," Roderick said, "that you're onside. That I can trust you."

Across the fire, his gaze cut like an amethyst blade.

Caught, Ecko bared his teeth. He wanted to get up, fume, throw his toys out the pram – shout back that maybe Roderick was the one that couldn't be trusted because, hell, he'd been to Mom and had his fucking soul ripped out – but this was the loss of his freedom tagged exactly, as precise as a pin in his fractal map.

That I can trust you.

As precise as a Save Point.

"So – we gonna get these often?" His grin was savage. "Love to know where they were at. Reload, get my cloak back, rewind, get Salva's rifle. An' hey, maybe if you fuck this up, we can jus' do it over—"

"We get one chance at this," Roderick said. "If Rhan refuses, we can't force him. There won't be enough left of us to make a greasy smear."

"Yeah, right." Ecko snorted. "Mom loaded us both. Like he can fuckin' bring it."

"You're not listening to me. If we get this *wrong*," Roderick said, "Nivrotar's gamble will all be for nothing. The world will die with you still *in* it."

The word "nothing" went across his shoulders like a skitter of claws; it raked his back and belly, left him staring at the fire. *The world will die with you still in it.* For a moment, he remembered the image he'd had of Eliza turning the program off, him still plugged in. That empty horror of endless nothing – like being on Doc Grey's pacifier drugs, like being stuck gazing at the inside of his own head until the end of fucking time...

"*Kazyen.*"

It sent a shudder down his spine. For a split-second, the overlap of the two worlds chilled him to the absolute core – if Roderick had been in London, had the London he'd been in been real, Ecko's London, or just another, deeper layer of code?

Reality within reality.

Mirrors facing mirrors, reflecting endless...

His stomach turned over again.

Calming and cool, Amethea said, "You really think the Kas are coming?"

The Bard glanced round. "Yes, I do." Whatever else may have changed, his conviction was still absolute. "My body is altered, not my heart, or my calling. Not what I saw in the waters of the Ryll. And I can feel... the world, the Powerflux, more strongly than I've ever done. I—"

"She's waking up, isn't she?" Amethea's question was pointed. Ecko glanced up at her, oculars flicking. "The world,

I mean. Right from the beginning, from when Maugrim…"
She coloured, looked at her fingernails. "He started something,
that's what I mean, he was like a… a catalyst. I think he's the
one that woke her. Maybe we should thank him." Her voice
caught, and she fell silent, frowning.

Roderick said, softly, "You woke her, Amethea. Maugrim
had power and passion – elemental focus that brought the
Powerflux from somnolence and legend – but the love and
courage were yours. We should thank *you*."

"We blew a hole in the world—"

"And with it The Wanderer and I found a world anew." He
glanced at Ecko. "That has saved us once already—"

"Yeah, keep rubbin' my fuckin' nose in it—"

"Saint and Goddess." Amethea glared at Ecko, checked
an irritated sigh and then turned back to the fire, her fragile
confidence lost. Roderick watched her, his gaze glittering,
calculating. She said stubbornly, not looking up, "This is the
end, Ecko, the end of all things. And if you'd stop being so
cursed snarky all the time, you might just feel it as well. Maybe
you should talk less and listen more and then maybe you'd learn
something." The Bard's gaze flickered, amused or surprised. He
watched her for a moment longer, and then went back to the
cooking meat.

And Ecko did feel something. Not the knee-jerk urge to hit
back, though that was there as well – something else, something
strange enough to pull him up short, yet something familiar.
Like that flicker of recognition he'd known in The Wanderer,
or the faintly satisfying snap of the right key in the right lock.

What the…?

It stopped him cold, made him stare at the fire as if the
world – the program, whatever – had really lost it this time.

*What the hell was that? A hint? Extra points, unlocking
secret treasure, now?*

Was *that* how he knew he was on the right track – that faint sensation of something fitting, something falling exactly where it should?

Was he winning this shit now?

Well whaddaya know. Fifty fucking experience points and I'll take plus-two on my perception stat...

He shivered, the gusting wind cold, but the moment had passed – like his flash of the void, it was there and gone, too swift to be really understood.

Roderick reached for the stones at the fireside, checked the now-blackened creature. He lowered the scarf, flexing his chin as if his neck was stiff. Warmth pulsed and flared along the line of his throat, in his jaw and into his ears.

"Make no mistake. Nivrotar gambles all on this roll of the die... but I think, *feel* that her path is the right one. Rhan..." he paused, as if he could pull his fears from the firelight, "...I hope he comprehends."

"He'd better," Ecko muttered.

The Bard held out a strip of burned critter. "Will you eat, both of you, while I beg your indulgence? Perhaps it will help you understand what we walk into."

Ecko took the meat, held the shred to the flame and let it crisp.

Flesh, burning.

"When you first came to The Wanderer," Roderick told him, "I was going to tell you a tale – a saga pieced together from the thousand broken fragments of memory I'd spent my life unearthing. Here, we have a fire and the open evening. A better time for tales, don't you think?"

Amethea said, "I want to hear the tale. I need to understand this."

The Bard took a swallow from the waterskin, said, "I've spent all my life gathering information. This is what I know."

And he began.

"Once within the time, when the great Tusien was still a

seat of high learning, there lived a maiden of the Red Desert. Her hair shone as the dusk-lit sands and her eyes had the depth of the oasis. She had a swift mind and a ready laugh; she was loved well by her sire and those of his Banner.

"This is the first thread of many, the tapestry beginning. It's the song of Tesrae-Mai, the Mother of Mayhem. Other threads tell that, charmed by a dream, she bore a son and she named him Vahl, meaning 'might'. And Vahl grew to vast power, unifying the scattered Banners of the Desert into a single warrior force.

"Other threads tell how Vahl marched north into the Varchinde. He drowned the Soul of Light, and the very Powerflux trembled. It withdrew from mortal ken. He cursed the grass to die in the winter. He destroyed Tusien, seat of highest learning. He ripped the great city of Swathe stone from stone, and used its remains to build a citadel of his own, high upon Rammouthe Island, thus pronouncing it accursed.

"And there, he waited.

"In time, Swathe was forgotten, and the Archipelagan Saluvarith came to build a new city, naming her Fhaveon. Samiel, Godsfather, was pleased with the city and he sent Saluvarith a Promise, his manifest word that Fhaveon would never fall, no matter what assailed her.

"And her assailant came. Rising from Rammouthe, Kas Vahl Zaxaar rained war and death upon the First Lord Foundersson Tekissari, barely more than a boy. Steam and flame bathed all.

"But he was repelled.

"Samiel's Promise rose in flesh and power, a creature of pale might and terrible warfare, and it upheld the word of the God. It wielded the Element of Light; it threw back the assault and it triumphed, white fire and glory. And with that victory, so came peace.

"And here our own tale begins. Guarded always by the Promise of Samiel, Fhaveon brought us prosperity, and peace... and stagnation. Terhnwood became our passion, and our purpose. The Elementalists, Priests of the People, were forgotten, charlatans and conjurers. The damaged Powerflux faded from memory and was revered no longer."

He glanced at Amethea. "Until Maugrim found its centre. You, Amethea, were his catalyst and his focus and his lynchpin, and you destroyed him. And our peace is ended—"

"Hold!" The word was a bark, startling all of them.

Adrenaline hitting like a jackhammer, Ecko was on his feet and moving, back and out of the light.

Amethea had the time to look up, her mouth falling open.

As the Bard had woven his tales, so the sun had died upon the far Kartiah and the air had thickened with cold and shadow. Outside the warm ring of firelight stood a loose scatter of soldiers, their kit battered and scruffy. Eyes and teeth glinted, sharp and spiteful, though no weapons were drawn.

Ecko knew enough to recognise them as Fhaveonic, but saw no tan commander.

Now this, he figured, *can't be good...*

Smoothly, Roderick rose to his feet, his black hood still up, his scarf covering his chin. Ecko wondered if he could sing some note that would blow them all to gory smithereens, but the Bard only gave a graceful, slightly ironic half bow – a gesture very reminiscent of the man he had been.

"And what can we do for you?" he said.

One stepped forward. "By order of the Lord Founders daughter Selana Valiembor, anyone caught damaging range patrol property will offer compensation: trade-goods, terhnwood if you've got it, food." He glanced at the fire, at the roast beast, and grinned. "You got any booze, storyteller, we'll take that as well."

"Will you now." The Bard's tone was dangerously affable.

Amethea was on her feet, watching their backs.

"And if I told you the site was in this condition when we arrived?" Roderick said. "Lawless times, you know how it is."

The grunt didn't lose his grin. "Don't waste your stories on me."

Ecko watched, adrenals spiking. Part of him longed to see what the Bard would do, but another part wanted to do it himself, to prove that he could handle this shit, and alone. Carefully, he began to ease through the damp and the dark, circling the posse of goons.

Roderick chuckled. "Somehow I feel the Lord Selana won't be seeing the benefits. You should walk away now."

Amethea glanced sideways.

Ecko trembled as he moved, eager, poised with anticipation. Oddly, he found himself with a peculiar and unexpected sense of kinship – something in him wanted to see what Mom had done, like for real. What she'd given the Bard, and *why*...

The grunt stepped forward, laid a hand on his long belt blade.

"Insulting the Lord—"

And Roderick laughed at him.

It was a hollow laugh, an open throat of deep bass noise, a speaker-boom, a sound that made the vast sky shrink back, made the dead ground shake. It wasn't loud, but the reverberation of power stopped Ecko dead, staring; his chest almost hurt with it. It was as if a sound could invade his lungs, make his skull rumble with a drumbeat hangover. Chrissakes, he could've been at the front of a metal gig, moshing it fucking old school.

The grunt paused. One of the others whispered something to him; he gestured for them to shut up. Rain gusted, cold.

Roderick said, "We carry messages for the Lord Seneschal in Fhaveon, sealed by Nivrotar of Amos. Perhaps you'd offer us escort, and we can... discuss the matter of damages?"

"Who are you?" The grunt had his blade halfway out of its sheath, and was backing up. "You're not a messen—"

"You don't know me?" Now, Roderick's laugh shimmered

with mischievous humour and was almost more chilling than the bass-speaker throb. Ecko found himself wondering if Mom had driven the man right over the fucking edge – hell, he'd been a coupla marbles short to start with.

But he was still speaking, weaving words and air and cloud and light. "You know me, Talyen of Fhaveon. You've known me all your life. I've seen you work, play, fight, drink. I've picked you up when you've fallen; I've restored your weapons when you've been too ruined to find them for yourself. I've traded for your beer, and your stories. I've sung with your tan, I've clapped you on the back and called you brother. I've commiserated with you when you lost your love and I've helped you when your heart called for someone new. And at the end of the night, I've pushed you from my door in the last moments before the birth of the sun. I'm not a messenger? I'm the Grasslands' final messenger, Talyen. I'm the messenger who knows every face, and every name, every voice that the wind has ever carried. Do you not know who I am?"

He spoke like the sky itself, like the touch of the wind. As he raised a hand to push his hood back, to lower the scarf and expose his throat, Talyen could only stare, his blade still half-drawn.

"You're the Bard, you're the cursed Bard! What the rhez *happened* to you?"

The bass laugh sounded again, but only for a moment. "Everything."

And that, Ecko realised with a shiver, was what Mom had given him – was why his throat, his ears and the fuck knew where else had been wired to buggery. He had a voice that could pull the clouds right out of the fucking sky.

Whoah.

Mesmerised, the soldiers had given up. Talyen shoved his blade back into its sheath and muttered that of course he'd escort them into Fhaveon, and how was he to know that

Roderick the Bard was out and on foot, and what the rhez had happened to the tavern anyway.

That question didn't get an answer.

As the grunts – six of them in total – began to bring up mounts and kit and pitch for the night, calling one to another in loud and foul-mouthed jesting, so Ecko found himself thinking about his sojourn with Tan Commander Pareus, soldier of Fhaveon. Back in his fireside spot, still not eating the roast beast that gradually went cold beside him, he realised that his thoughts were wandering down a very singular road. Past Pareus to Tarvi, a soldier herself at first, and on to the wild living fire of Maugrim's Sical.

And to the tale that the Bard had told.

It triumphed, white fire and glory... Guarded always by the Promise of Samiel, Fhaveon brought us prosperity.

There won't be enough left of us to make a greasy smear.

And he began to understand the severity of what Nivrotar had asked them to do.

6: MONSTERS TRADE-ROAD, ROVIARATH

They caught her at the edge of the Great Cemothen River, in among the angles of the trees that clung to the edges of the water. She'd known they were there for the last half day, loitering like mischief at the limits of her awareness, but she'd been sure she could outdistance them – she was Banned, by the rhez, born in the damned saddle. They were no match for her.

But the afternoon had come like the long slow death of the sun and the trees stood silent, twisted to bones by the ceaseless plainland wind. Their last leaves clung desperate; their roots spread wide and angled into the brown river, swollen now with the rains from the Kartiah Mountains to the west. The water was angry, churning at roots and banks alike as if to pull them down and never let them go.

And Triqueta realised she'd made a mistake.

I don't think you should go. Not alone. Not all that way...

As the fat red sun sank towards its shadowed mountain death, its last light dazzling as the sky ignited to a glorious burning, streaks of lavender and pink, Triqueta contemplated the flooded ford.

"Bollocks." She said the word aloud, though there was no

one to hear her. Only her mare, the skewbald gelding laden with tack and kit. Only the ever-present aperios.

Not with all the... y'know... critters an' stuff...

She'd been trying not to think about Ecko – his awkward concern, his touch on her skin, her reaction...

Not the time, idiot!

Behind her, there were five of them, filthy but well armed, still hanging back out of bow range – her single shot had arced up into the winter sky, then spiralled lazily down to fall short. Perhaps they were just waiting for a passing bweao to do the dirty work for them.

She was going to be robbed, raped and her throat slit – and very possibly not in that order.

I'm going alone.

By the rhez! Stop it!

The water was impassable, certainly with the kit she had – the previous tributary had been less flooded; she'd been able to cross by looping briefly north. This one came southeast from the Scar Lake itself and was full and furious.

She was trapped, and her pursuers knew it.

She could see them out there, lingering, shadows in the rising dark. Her hand on her bow was white at the knuckles.

Come on, then, you bastards. I've faced worse odds than a bunch of damned thugs!

They'd fanned outwards into a loose line, curving at the edges like an arqueus's horns, pushing her back towards the water. She strung a second shaft, waited.

"What're you waiting for? Spring?" Her challenge was loud, clear and fearless.

They waited, five silent shapes. A leaf lost its fight for life and was torn free, turning over and over in the wind.

The first shaft that came for her was wide – she knew it would miss. She made no attempt to move – then realised she'd misjudged as it hit the gelding solidly in his shoulder. He snorted, stamped, tried to back away, but his lead rein was tied to the pommel of the mare's saddle and for a moment, Triq thought he would pull it – and her – completely free. The mare stumbled, whinnied her displeasure.

A second shot missed, skimming the gelding's ears.

Triqueta held the mare tight with her knees and, sitting down hard in the saddle, she loosed the shaft.

With a sharp cry, one figure toppled to the dirt.

"One!" Her hands were nocking another even as the first had left the string. "I can get at least two more before you get close. Want to risk it?"

An easy laugh answered her. "I've got three shafts on you, girlie. Leave both mounts; leave your packs and bags. I'll let you take a waterskin. You behave, you might even make it."

Her reply was another shot.

The light was poor now, but her hands were sure and she heard the shaft thunk home. The speaker groaned, started to say something else and toppled slowly sideways.

"Two. Anyone else?"

The remaining three shifted uneasily. Triq turned the mare this way and that, her own aim not flinching, but nothing came her way – there was no telltale slice of air.

"You'll leave me be," she said, her grin clear. "And when I get to Roviarath, the Banned won't—"

She was cut short by a thin, high-pitched wail.

What…?

Chillflesh shivered down her arms and back. It was a horrifying, terrifying noise that curdled her blood and closed a fist about her throat. She'd never heard it, but she knew exactly what it was.

Oh dear Gods.

Every person in the Varchinde was taught the sound as a child. Taught it meant fear.

No, it can't be…

Her hammering heart redoubled, her mind scrambled in disbelief. For a moment she heard Ecko again, *critters an' stuff*, and she thought in a crazed wheel of denial, *This can't happen, not to me, not here, not now...*

Ahead of her, the remaining riders called to one another, suddenly a lot less sure of themselves. The wail had been close – too close – and they knew, too, that the creature would tear all of them to tiny, bloodied shreds. Breathing hard, genuinely scared, Triqueta looked over at them, their mounts now panicked, spooked and restless. She was vaguely aware of the injured speaker hauling himself back into his saddle, calling to the others to come away *now*.

Her own mare was rigid, ears forward and body trembling. She snorted, agitated, throwing her head. The skewbald stood with his head down, unresponsive to the creature's howl. Triqueta's mind spun loops. The beast was downwind – the horses couldn't smell it – and it must be tracking the rich blood scent coming from the men she'd shot...

Surely that was enough of a distraction?

Gods, who was she betting? She had no idea what the damn thing would do.

She was still backed against the flooded ford. The mare might swim it, but the injured and laden skewbald didn't have a cursed hope. The only way...

By the Gods.

Her solution was apparent, and gruesome.

For a moment, she looked at the gelding – he was brown and white, a strong and solid little runner. He'd whuffled at her hands, been a warmth in the plains' emptiness... Triqueta was Banned-born, and these weren't just animals, pack-bearers, burdens – they were friends, and all of them had characters of their own.

The noise came again, closer.

The thing was moving – it was this side of the river,

somewhere to the northeast. In the dying light, she almost imagined she could hear it breathing, closing, its heat and teeth and savagery right behind her, crouched and waiting, wanting her to run.

Shuddering, she made herself turn to look.

But if it was there, she couldn't see it – the trees were twisted shadows upon the bloodied sunset of the plain.

The riders had gone, a clatter of hooves and voices. If she looked that way, she could just about make out the man she'd shot – an unmoving rock on the barren ground.

Had she heard somewhere that these beasts preferred the chase; that they liked to hunt?

Hunt human prey?

By the Gods, this was no good; she was scaring herself out of her wits.

Triqueta turned to the skewbald, pulled a couple of packs from the back of his saddle. Then, biting her lip, she untied his lead rein. He raised his head to look at her, snorted almost as if he would speak.

Mouthing, "I'm sorry, I'm sorry," as if he could understand, she backed the mare away from him and turned her towards the ford.

The sun was a diminishing red spear; the light silhouetted the mountaintop to a jagged black tooth biting at the air. If she was going to cross the water, she had better cursed well do so now.

Before the bweao caught her.

It was full dark when she realised the beast was still behind her.

The mare was tiring, shivering from the cold of the water – but she had caught either scent or fear from her rider and she was running still, her hooves slashing at the grassless plain. Starless, the moons narrow and like fingernails, the dark was utterly swallowing and Triq had only the noise of the river and the mare's instinct to guide her. She watched the blackness ahead for the faintest glint from Roviarath's lighthouse tower, for any hint of the light of home.

But there was nothing.

She'd heard the cries of the pirates, and the scream as the skewbald died – a single, awful noise that had torn the sky from top to bottom, torn through her ears. She'd gasped, guilt and horror, almost screamed herself. The mare had heard it too and her speed had increased, shudders of panic coming from her shoulders. Triqueta could smell horse sweat and terror.

She'd slung her bow – there was no movement in the blackness that she could see – and drawn her blades, but they felt tiny, the incisors of some smaller predator, faced by the might of the plains' greatest terror.

And they ran.

The mare was labouring now, her gait uneven and her breathing hard. If she missed her footing, if her hoof found a burrow or hole…

The wail came again, the terrible hunting cry.

Triq laid her chest on the saddle pommel and whispered to the mare, "Come on, lovely. You can do this. We can do this together."

Then, there it was, the faintest glimmer of white in the blackness. Like the Fhaveonic legend of the fallen star, like the tiniest glimmer of hope, it gave the pure night focus and scale, made everything diminish to its normal size. The wail was still there, but the light pulled both of them like an elemental rising, like some—

The wail deepened to a snarl, right behind the mare's heels.

The mare leaped, kicking, and something went past her; there was a sensation of heat and teeth. Neck lowered now, the horse was running in a flat-out bolt, homing in on the light as if it were the only point of sanity in the smothering dark.

Triq wished she believed in the Gods she was praying to, and her hands tightened on the blades.

Okay. I can do this. Redlock faced one of these bastard things single-handed. I can do this.

Now.

With a fluid motion she'd learned as a child, she turned in the saddle and stared out over the mare's rump, out into the featureless black.

Were those eyes? Teeth?

The bweao was close, she knew it. There was something right there in the darkness, right—

Then she became aware of another noise, something else between her and the river.

Nearly choking on her own fear, she strained to see, but there was nothing, no movement, no hint of what it could be.

It was big, bigger than she was, its breathing heavy. It seemed to be closing behind her, as if it too was going to chase the little mare to the very outskirts of Roviarath itself.

Triqueta's heart was screaming in terror. Her breath was sobbing in her throat. She was muttering, over and over, *I can do this. I can do this...*

In a flash decision that surged ahead of any kind of sense, she slung both blades and reached for the panniers on the mare's rump. She scrabbled in the darkness; things were falling and being lost and she didn't care and she knew what she was looking for and then her hands found them and she was striking, striking for that spark...

There!

A wash of light was in her face, suddenly blinding her and she blinked as a tiny circle of plain came into view. Red flared, shadows were edged in malice, and concealing horrors danced without name – but she saw it, just for a moment.

Bweao.

Smaller than she'd realised, a low, lithe body that seemed slung between its high-kneed legs, claws like scythes, needle-teeth that gleamed in the light. Its eyes were glittering red. It blinked at her.

And it grinned.

She hadn't thought that the little flame would chase it away, but—

Dear Gods!

Then something else was between her and the crouching bweao, something unfamiliar, something huge.

And her thoughts froze cold, as if she couldn't understand what she was seeing.

It was bigger than the bweao, bigger than she and the mare combined. It was chearl in body, massively powerful but misshapen somehow, as if a human body had been crammed onto the creature where its head should have been, some bare-backed and muscled warrior with his hair knotted and filthy and *red* in her little light...

He was facing the bweao, his heavy chearl body bigger than a horse and rearing, his great foreclaws twisted...

For a moment, he turned, his human teeth bared and filthy. He had no words, but he knew who she was. He met her gaze with a single, searing look, and then turned back to the bweao.

No longer caring if she was screaming or not, Triqueta fled.

CityWarden Larred Jade came to his feet at the sight of her, reaching out a hand, as if to catch her before she fell. But she stood there in his wooden hall on her own two cursed feet. She'd made the heart of Roviarath with her skin intact...

Just.

Triqueta clenched her fists, knowing she was shaking – from exhaustion, shock, from the long loco run across the empty winter plain. From the short walk through the city, from the wide eyes of the frightened people.

From the damned centaur.

Had she dreamed him, for Gods' sakes, out there in the dark?

"Get Syke in here." Jade flung the command like a knife

and he was gripping her shoulders, searching her face with a gaze that asked her every question, demanded every answer. He looked tired, older; there were long lines down his cheeks and he was too close, too intense. She pulled away, holding up her hands... only to be hurled to the floor by a shout and full body tackle that she knew all too well.

"Oof! Get *off* me, you damned thug!"

Family.

Syke bounded back to his feet. He was grinning, helping her up and hugging her to his chest, thumping her on the back hard enough to make her cough.

"You dozy mare, where the rhez've you *been*?"

For just a moment, she wanted to throw herself into his brotherhood and forget it all – Redlock, Ecko, Kas, blight, everything – just let the whole cursed world go away and fend for itself...

Family.

But Aeona's nightmares had cast an unexpected darkness across her heart, and the memory tasted sour, like doubt. She pulled back.

The blade in her cheeks, the blood from beneath her opal stones. Her sire. Kicking and spitting.

No. Not going back there. Not ever.

She found her voice, her grin. "I've got messages, cargo – well, some." She'd scattered mud and filth and the Gods alone knew what all over Jade's polished wooden floor. "Nivrotar sent me with... things."

But Jade brushed filth and concerns aside, held out a steaming tankard of something spiced and herbal that a curious youth had slipped into his hand. Syke was still slapping her shoulder, all insults and ribald concern.

"You pick your time, girl. How'd you get here with your skin still on?"

After the empty plain, the desolation of the winter Varchinde, the cold sky, it was too much. They were too close, the smell was too strong – she was finding it hard to think, to draw breath.

She stepped away, exhaled. Tried to stop her cracked hands from trembling.

"For Gods' sakes." She found a laugh, but it sounded more broken than humorous. "I've fought a cursed bweao on the way here, no jesting. Just... just give me a moment, will you?"

"Bweao?" Syke mouthed the word at Jade, who shrugged, then firmly handed her the tankard.

"Sit your backside down, and drink this. Roviarath isn't going to fall to bits while you get your breath back. In fact," he gave a brief grin, "she's just about holding her guts in, which is more than can be said for most."

"Did you pass the Monument – the hole – on your way in?" Syke was pacing now, a coil of energy – he wanted to know everything, every tale, every update. "By the Gods, Triq! What happened to Ress? To Jayr? That hefty grunt of a boyfriend of yours? And – a *bweao*?"

His restlessness was familiar – an old friend.

Family.

Kicking and spitting.

Overpowered by all of it, she found herself biting her lip, turning away, searching for words but unable to speak.

And Syke came to one knee on the floor, looking up at her. He said gently, "Triq. I'm glad you're home. You look like you've been through a war."

"You've got no idea." It was barely a whisper. "Whole world's gone loco."

"Yeah, we know it." He patted her arm. "We've been here trying to fix it."

"Roviarath's better than some," Jade said gently. "On your way through the city, did you see—?"

"I saw queues," she told him, "people with barrows laden with produce, some of it rotting. Bringing animals, livestock, Gods know what. They were in lines outside the tithehalls. I don't—"

"They want terhnwood." Jade shrugged, helpless. "Literally, they can't last the winter without it. They bring everything they've got into the city in the hope of securing even a little. They can't even craft it properly without help. The crafters I've got remaining, they're here, with me. The terhnwood, the same – what little there is left. We craft, we ration, we distribute, but it's hard to maintain control. The people clamour and riot for it, waves against the walls. Syke—"

"We're keepin' stuff balanced, much as we can." His grin was cold and eager. "For as long as we can eat, we can hold."

Jade added, "The blight hasn't reached us – only the terhnwood shortage. And people without food get a lot angrier, a lot more quickly. In some ways, we've been lucky."

Triqueta shook her head, inhaled steam. "You've had a harvest." She looked up at them, her belly churning. "What about the…" She didn't say it, but they knew what she meant.

The hole. The wound in the world. The place where the Monument had been, where we threw down Maugrim, but changed the world forever.

She'd passed it on her way, of course she had, but she'd not stopped or gone close – she'd not dared. The place was layered with memories of monsters, of the centaur stallion, of Feren and Redlock and Ecko and fire, of the Bard and The Wanderer – of a time when an enemy was a solid thing that could be faced and fought and defeated.

Syke and Jade exchanged a glance.

Jade said, "Yes, we had a harvest – just about. You really want to know?"

To give herself a moment to find her resolution, she rustled in a pannier for a leather message tube. It was sealed with Nivrotar's craftmark, and she handed it over.

"Here. Read this while you tell me."

Syke passed the tube back to Jade without even looking,

said softly, "The hole's all wrong, Triq, all wrong – the whole damn thing's like some half-healed sore. Soil's poisoned, black cracks spreading like – I don't know – rot or something. It…" His hands reached for explanation, insight, a way to express some formless horror. "It's like some cursed canker; it's scabbed over like it's trying to heal, but the infection's still there. Eating away."

"I didn't go that close," Triq said. She shrugged, admitted, "I was afraid."

"Smart." Syke patted her knee like an affectionate uncle. "So, tell me. You really kill a bweao?"

"No, I ran like the rhez." She looked up, almost grinned for real. "But it didn't kill me."

"That's good enough," Syke told her, patting again. "Good enough. Now, are you drinking that or not?" He made a playful swipe for her tankard, and she snatched it back with a mock glare, splashed herbal on the floor, spreading the winter dust into a muddy pool.

There was a rustling as Jade pulled a roll of parchment from the leather sleeve, flattened it. He read, his face slowly congealing.

Syke leaned in, dropped his voice to a conspiratorial whisper. "I'm glad you're back, Triq, I need you, we need you here. We're holding Roviarath – but with no trade and the Great Fayre destroyed, we haven't got long. There's been one assassination attempt already – messed it right up, as it turned out – and out on the trade-roads, people're claiming that Jade's withholding goods, arming up. If the tide of the people turns, we'll have nothing – no terhnwood and no damned food either."

Triqueta watched his expression, drawn and weary. She'd never seen him look old but there were white threads in his dark hair, scattered through his beard. The skin under his eyes was shadowed with uncertainty. He flickered a frown, his face furrowing at nothing.

In the sudden lines, she saw Karine.

She shuddered.

"Triqueta." Jade dropped her name hard onto the wooden floor – its impact seemed to sound from the rafters. "This message – it's genuine?"

"Nivvy handed it to me herself. Ecko…" she stumbled over his name, but recovered "…Ecko took one like it to Fhaveon."

"Then she's serious." The CityWarden lowered the papers, still stubbornly rolling into a tube around his hand. He rubbed his other hand across his eyebrows. "Do you know what this message contains?"

Something in his voice made her stare, made Syke turn and come back to his feet. They spoke almost together, "What? What's—?"

Jade held up his hand, cutting them dead. "You fought Vahl Zaxaar?"

"It's a bit of a saga, but—"

"Yes, all right, I've got the basics – but Vahl Zaxaar himself – itself. By the Gods, this whole world becomes more damned crazed by the day. You really fought—?"

"Yes." Triqueta stood. "Remember, we came to you before, asking you to believe in something and you wouldn't – didn't – and your city—"

"All right, don't rub my snout in it." Jade paced the floor, tapping the rolled parchment in his hand like some sort of baton. "Fhaveon was attacked, but she beat the monster?"

"Make sense, for Gods' sakes." Syke was watching the parchment like a hungry…

Like a hungry bweao.

But Jade seemed not to notice; he pointed it at Triqueta. "I've got my hands full. I cling to my city by wit and will alone. I throw back dissenters every day, rumours, voices spreading lies – and, frankly, spreading truths I'd rather not have known. The blight's crippled us, Triq – we're out of terhnwood and we've got no fighting force to speak of. Without Syke and the Banned, I'd be a corpse many times over. I can't spare... I can't..." With a curse that sounded more helpless than angry, he threw the parchment down, and it rolled in sheaves across the filthy floor. "You read it, you tell me what the rhez the Lord of Amos is playing at."

Syke gathered a handful of the rolls together, tried to make sense of the markings, passed them to Triqueta. She shrugged. "What do they say?"

Jade looked at his filthy, plains-stained floor.

"They call me to a winter muster, Triq. Amos calls Roviarath to war."

7: BLOOD AND RUINS FHAVEON

Rhan.

The Uber-Nasty. The Promise of Samiel. Captain Greasy Smear. The ready-built-in superhero that'd led Ecko to flee The Wanderer rather than face the Council. Reflexively, Ecko had been expecting the old guy with the long white beard, but if this bloke was a superwizard, then Ecko was a fucking ballerina.

Rhan had the white hair, but that was where it ended. Rather than a beard and a long and manky robe, he had a jaw that would cut glass and shoulders like a museum statue. His face was carved in lines like long years of severity, and though he didn't have the Bard's height, he looked like he could pulverise rocks with his grip alone. Chrissakes, he didn't look real – not that that was ironic or anything – he was some sorta bodysculpt, or he'd walked off of a plinth in the fucking V&A.

And if all of that wasn't shock enough... it fucking happened *again*.

Ecko recognised him, *recognised* him. The light was poor and the air thick with smoke, but it was like being jabbed with a taser-baton. Just like Roderick, just like the earlier flash with Amethea, Rhan was already there, neatly pre-programmed into the back of Ecko's head. He was a phantom familiar, the residue of a half-watched movie, a brain-rig performer whose name he couldn't quite remember...

Eliza must be pissing herself.

Bitch.

But Rhan wasn't looking at Ecko. He was staring at the Bard.

The tiny cellar shrank round them, stinking and airless. There were black smoke stains on the beamed ceiling; the cold air was thick with panic and tallow.

None of that mattered.

Consumed by the Bard's arrival, Rhan had come half to his feet, his expression changing from a friend's greeting into something else, something transfixed, horrified and unnameable.

His deep voice barely a whisper, laden with a complex grief, he said, "Roderick?" He shook his head, disbelief or denial. "Dear Gods. What did you *do*?"

The Bard lifted his scarved chin, stepped back.

"What I had to." His voice was pure power.

For just a moment, the look on Rhan's carved face was so confused, so utterly lost, that it broadsided Ecko completely. Something in him had wanted to hate this fucker – this overpowered-fallen-angel-whatever-the-hell – but he found himself oddly and unexpectedly touched. The look was so broken, the expression of a man who'd lost a friend, something he needed and loved.

A man shaken to the core of his soul.

What's this, now? Empathy? Fucksake!

That another level-up skill?

Rhan said, his voice soft with horror, "Samiel's *teeth*."

As Ecko found a corner of the small room, the colours in his skin were blotching with a pale, sourceless light. Amethea had stopped almost halfway down the steps from the trapdoor – she was staring at Rhan as if trying to see the superbeing that lurked under his skin.

"Your city's in blood and ruins," Roderick said, cold as a blade. "And worse is to come. I bear you a message from Nivrotar in Amos. And you need to listen."

Still guarded by the scruffy tan of soldiers, Ecko's first sight of Fhaveon, Lord city, ruling might of the Varchinde, yadda yadda, had been a bit of a fucking let-down.

He and the Bard and Amethea had trailed all the way across the plains in the freezing, fucking cold, carrying their message like good little children, and they'd fetched up at the city's outer walls, being eyed like bugs by a scatter of archers. Here, their self-appointed escort had left them, apparently satisfied with duty done.

Long since pissed with winter travel, Ecko had been bored, and hurting, and quite a lot of other things. He'd been thinking only of food and heat, of shelter from the relentless and glacial plainland wind. His butt ached like hell. Once, long ago, Pareus had taught him the trail trick of sitting on one ass cheek and then the other, but he'd still been sat on both of them for far too long. Stiff as a corpse, he'd cursed the Bard for losing the tavern, cursed the cold ground and the hard wind, cursed the beast under him for a lumpy spine that threatened to saw him in half... He'd *so* been looking forward to a smoky, stinky pub, a bowl of lukewarm mulch and a bit of petty larceny...

Christ, he'd been looking forward to a fucking *wash*.

Apparently, though, what they'd found was a warzone.

Great. Just what we needed – a fuckin' bonding vacation.

The morning air was bone-deep cold, ribboned with a thin mist that crept soft up the city's flanks. Through it, he could see the broken buildings, the empty streets – and this so wasn't the picture he'd carried. Hell, this was some sorta post-apocalypse fantasyscape – could there even be such a thing? Where was the star city, the striated stone, the rising roadways lined with crystal trees? Where were the statues, the falling waters, the glittering pools? And where was the handy fucking merchant with the end-of-level restock?

This... this reminded him of Aeona.

Pits of fire and mountains of ash.

Above the mist, Fhaveon's heights were untouched – a stark tessellation of roofing, black against the paling sky. The sun was behind the city's rise and from somewhere there came a pinpoint gleam of deep colour.

Roderick paused, a wraith in the white. "The Cathedral." He pointed at the tiny colour mote, even as it faded and was gone, lost as the sun moved. "Beside it, the Palace, the main tithehall of the Cartel, and Garland House. It seems the rioting has not yet reached that far."

"Rioting?" Amethea looked along the grim, dark line of the Bard's outstretched arm, though there was no longer anything to see. "How do we get up there?" The mist swallowed the fear in her voice.

Ecko gave a sulky snort. "Why can't you people just teleport, for chrissakes? They do it in all the—" The Bard shot him a glance, cold as stone. "Yeah, all right, whatever." Silenced, Ecko seethed. How the hell had this fucker gotten so powerful? He could just *look*, now?

Yeah, you wait 'til I get you home...

"Fhaveon is changed, certainly." As Roderick turned back, his grin was a fleeting impression of Ecko's own. "But I don't think we'll have any trouble."

"You're jesting."

In the tiny, smoky room, Rhan was reading Nivrotar's letter; black ink like squashed spiders crawled across its surface. His other hand pinched the bridge of his nose between thumb and forefinger – fighting incredulity, or detonation.

"This is *crazed*." His deep voice was a full bass-boom, heavy with disbelief. "You even *dare* bring this to me? You even dare *ask*?" He threw the letter down and rounded on Roderick with a speed that made it flutter like a dying thing. "I ought to pull your damned insides out."

The Bard's tone was flat. "It isn't a request."

Rhan spun back, picked up the curl of paper, brandished it at him. "You know where you can shove this."

Roderick shrugged. "You'll do as she says."

"You're barking loco." It was a statement, hard as nails. "You can't begin to imagine what I've seen, what I've done, what I've fought, what I've *killed*, to regain my city. I've braved the waters of the Ryll, defeated Phylos, thrown down my brother not a stone from where you're stood." There was no irony in his voice; he wielded words like weapons. "We've got food, terhnwood – enough to stabilise. You don't tell me what to do, and neither does Nivrotar. I've cast down Kas before and I'll do it again. Whatever you *think* you've become."

The barb made the Bard smirk, brief and humourless.

Ecko made that one-all. His adrenaline was boosted, his targetters kicked. His oculars cycled scanning modes. If this fucker kicked off, Ecko was gonna hit him there, there and *there* before he could start flinging lightning bolts or whatever—

Rhan's body temperature was noticeably rising.

A blink and a second reading showed the same thing – this joker had a core temperature that'd melt gold fillings and he was emitting a hefty whack of UV.

What the…?

Lacking a bucket of ice, Ecko shifted, eased fractionally away. He had no plans to wind up as an ash pile and a pair of smoking shoes.

But Roderick was on his feet, narrow and black. He had the height, had every bit as much presence.

He repeated, "You'll do as she says."

"Oh, will I?" Rhan snorted, his temperature spiking. "This is ego. You just want your predictions to have been true. All that time waiting, searching, moping and you weren't even here – your final foe manifested in Fhaveon, and you *missed* it. And now, what, you want to play it again, just to prove that you were right?"

"Vahl is not the—"

"*Shove* it."

Ecko changed position – reflex, keeping in stealth. Without reading the letter, he wasn't entirely clear as to what was going on.

Roderick said, "Rhan, you know the truth of the world's enemy. You've fought a battle, and a brave one, but this isn't over—"

"You patronising bastard!" Rhan's words were white, aflame. "I *won*."

"Did you? Games are Vahl's lifeblood, manipulations and betrayals." Ecko could hear in the Bard's voice the death of Karine, his grief. "Did you think it would be that easy? We'll lose everything unless you listen to me."

"I've beaten Vahl once, I can do it again, army or no army. As many times as it takes. Nivrotar has no hold over Fhaveon – no hold over me. This is my city, my purpose, my family, my Gods-given charge. You *know* all of this. Dammit, Roderick—" Overcome, Rhan seemed almost to be fighting tears of sheer fury. His temperature continued to climb, and Ecko wondered what the hell he was going to do – explode, or manifest as Something the Fuck Else...

Daemon. Dragon. Slumming-it Deity. Oh c'mon, give us a clue here...

Amethea, unnoticed by all, had reached for the letter. A frown ghosted across her pale, dirty face as she read down the page.

Then she said, "It does make sense, if you think about it." The knell of inevitability in her soft voice brought stillness to the room.

Rhan turned; his voice was a whisper, incredulous. "Samiel himself charged me—! I've never relinquished—!"

"You don't have a choice," Roderick told him. "Think about it, Rhan, *think* about the city." His voice was strong, but there was none of the force that he could have put behind it. Ecko realised that he was withholding whatever coercive might he had – Rhan's agreement had to be genuine. "Think about what you've been left with. Even with the terhnwood you've found – can you fix this? Can you make Fhaveon live again? Arm her for war? Enough to face the Kas? I understand your pride, Gods know you know that," his hand rested on Rhan's arm, "but please, for the sake of the world herself, please at least think this through."

"Samiel's *bollocks*." Rhan was all shoulders and towering fury. For a moment, Ecko thought he'd really detonate. But then he sagged in resignation, his temperature falling like a sigh. He snorted, ironic and rueful. "You accursed bastard. Only you – *only* you could even bring this to me. And Nivrotar knows that. Bitch."

Roderick chuckled, the expression still wary. "She certainly can be," he said. "But if it helps, I think she's right."

The streets of the great city were devastation.

Leading their mounts through the scattered rubble, bristling with wariness, they'd made cautious progress, watching as the white mist thinned and the sunlight swelled behind the city's black heights.

Here in the shadow of the cliff, the streets were cold and the rocklights failing. Fires glimmered in the shells of buildings; the crystal trees stood bare and harsh, fingers splayed and frozen. Ecko found Amethea walking close – apparently less afraid of him than she was of the Bard – and he took a strange comfort in her presence. She was warm, and she had more fucking sense than the rest of them put together.

A long grey creature scuttled in front of them and was gone.

Ecko let his gaze rest on the Bard ahead of them, oculars cycling like questions, endless. He wondered somewhere in the back of his head what the hell else Mom had done to him.

Are you faster than me, now? Stronger? Smarter? Or can you just bring fucking sky down on my head?

C'mon, Eliza, was his London real, or is it just all still in my head? Do I still have to unravel this to get the fuck outta here?

But there was no answer to that one – and the route'd drive him batshit. He dragged his thoughts, kicking, back to the broken streets.

Then a cold drip shuddered down his back and he paused, turned to look about them.

They were being *watched*.

He knew it, even without the ocular scan – he could feel them, all around, eyes in the mist. Just like on the trade-roads, though, the watchers were waiting; they were eyes-only, cold trails of gaze like wet fronds across his skin.

As he moved forwards, intent and silent, they seemed to gather closer about him. He found himself wanting to shout, to exhale, to turn and run at them like they were London pigeons – just to break the tension.

The air was crisp, like frost; it felt like it would shatter. His breath steamed.

And the watchers closed tighter, flickers of motion, scuffles and whispers.

Slowly, skin crawling like contagion, they rode higher. As they climbed, hairpin-bending up the inside of the city's long hill, the sky grew lighter, the air less cold.

Amethea had pulled even closer to his side. Ecko's adrenaline trembled right under his skin, in his mouth, eager for release. It had been too long, far too long, since he'd raged free and he craved it like an addiction.

Ahead of them, Roderick walked as though stripped of sense and senses alike.

They came to an open plaza with a tumble of glittering water. The square was empty, the flagstones cracked and daubed with some sort of sigil. Just as Ecko was wondering why they'd been herded here, and what the fuck they'd be sacrificed to summon, the shadow of people behind them paused.

Waiting.

And there, in the square itself, was a figure – an older man, his silver hair tied back in a ring. He leaned against a headless pillar and he had the look of a fighter about him, but he was cricked in one shoulder and his face bore a recent, angry burn.

A scan showed nothing, no concealed monsters, no daemons lurking.

Yeah, an' I trust that shit about as much as a suit with two lines of coke an' a big fat smile...

The Bard stopped, his black horse stamping. The noise echoed dully back from the walls, making the air shudder. Ecko and Amethea pulled to an uneasy halt.

The man said, "Roderick of Avesyr. It's been a long time since we've seen you in Fhaveon. Your tavern's missed, but you're very welcome. We need your help."

Rhan said, "And you'd be the 'Ecko' I've been hearing so much about." It was a statement, not a question, and he raised an eyebrow in curiosity.

His temperature had fallen, was almost human-normal.

Ecko said, "Glad I didn't hafta kick your ass there."

The other eyebrow went up. "You think you can?"

"You wanna try it?"

"All right." Roderick cut across both of them. "Ecko, make yourself useful and read this." He lunged for the letter, then rolled it across the bench-top.

Rhan's face flickered a faint, bitter smile. "I'll save you the effort. The letter tells me to leave my city." There was rubble in his tone – he hadn't agreed, not yet. "To take what militia I can muster, and what of the population will follow me, and to retreat across the plains like an esphen with a pronounced *limp*." The word was acid. "Nivrotar tells me there is one thing the Kas cannot resist, one thing that will lead them by their cock-ends into her choice of confrontation. And that thing," his smile was grim, "is my personal downfall. So tell me, dark champion from another world," his sardonic humour was a bass thrum of Ecko's own, "do I look like *bait* to you?"

"Bait?" Ecko was scanning Nivrotar's black writing. He rattled his fingertips on the table and grinned. "I know one thing: the bad guy always comes back. Bigger. An' with more tentacles."

Rhan gave a short, humourless snort. "And you, little priestess. Do you believe Vahl's playing? That his greatest assault is yet to come?" His voice twisted. "That I must relinquish my city to the very enemy I've always guarded her against... having already *beaten* him?"

Amethea stared at him, her answer caught in her mouth.

"This is..." She swallowed, gave a faint shrug. "Look, I think... I think this is about more than just your city. What Nivrotar's doing is about the Varchinde entire – everybody, every*thing* will die if we don't get this right. It isn't about what you want, or your mandate, or whom you've beaten. This is about *survival*."

"What I want," Rhan said. Something in the way he said the words told Ecko that Amethea had touched him to the core.

Hurt him.

Rhan spread his square white hands on the bench-top as if cuffed there. Ecko reached the bottom of the letter. Amethea continued to stare at Rhan, her face flushed, perhaps afraid she had overstepped her boundaries. Roderick leaned against the soot-stained wall, his face still mostly covered, unspeaking.

"Gods *damn* it!" With a detonation of heat and light and fury, Rhan was on his feet, turning the bench over, sending it smashing onto the flagstone floor. Then he took it by one end and hurled it bodily at the cold stone wall, shattering the wooden shelf, sending the candles tumbling. He turned, put a fist into the stonework at the side of the Bard's head, cracking it hard enough to send dust billowing from the ceiling. Roderick didn't flinch; one of his hands grabbed Rhan's retreating wrist and for a moment they stood, eyes on eyes, close as lovers and seething with outrage.

"This is madness – and you know it, *she* knows it." Rhan's snarl was vicious. "If you want me to do this, then you'd better have some damned *proof.*"

"We're glad you've come," the silver-haired man said to the Bard.

Roderick handed back the rein of the black horse and stood like a streak of the fading darkness, silent.

The man gestured, as though searching. "You knew this was coming – you tried to tell us. Before." It was a statement – a need to bestow responsibility. "The Council didn't hear you—"

"Phylos was already in the hands of Vahl Zaxaar, even then. Why would he heed me when his victory was coming?" Roderick's tone was soft, lethal. "What do you want?"

Around them, the watchers closed tighter, listening. Ecko quelled a desire to shudder, to scratch at his sacking shirt as if the damn thing had fleas. He also made sure he stayed well clear of the sigil in the stonework – you never knew when the big nasty was going to erupt skywards out of one of those fucking things, propelled by farts of blue smoke and Armageddon.

Amethea stared all round them, her navy eyes wide.

"Baeru," the Bard said, "what do you want?"

The man started at the sound of his name, but came forwards, his tied-tight hair shining like metal in the rising light.

"Your help," he said. He gestured at the plaza behind him, at the wall at its far side, at the rise of the great city that still loomed over them. "This hasn't ended, Roderick, the city hasn't won, isn't safe." His voice rose, urgency and hope. "Rhan may've beaten Phylos, but they're still here – the monsters, the things that came out of the walls. Ythalla gathers them, they rally to her flag and her cause – and not just the monsters..." He ended the sentence with a gesture indicating all around them. "Rhan can sit up there in the height of the city and pretend it's all fine, but there's been no end to it, not down here. We run and we hide and we die. No one knows who to trust, where to go. We live in the Rhez itself, Roderick, we're damned in its very fire. Please, help us."

Ecko watched the man intently as the crowd pressed closer. His scans were foiled by the mist's lingering chill, but the speaker's body temperature showed genuine passion, movements of emotion and colour in the skin of his face and hands. In the mist, shapes shifted, but he could barely see them.

We live in the Rhez itself...

Amethea said softly, "Monsters. Creatures that are half-beast, half-human? Crafted from flesh?"

"Some, yes." Baeru turned to her, seemed to latch onto her words with something like relief. "And some are... golems, crafted from stone and soil. They're old death, as if lost Swathe herself were rising from her past. And others are creatures that I have never seen, never dreamed of."

"Tell me," Roderick said.

"Sometimes, you can see them. If the day's clear enough." He pointed across the sigil to the far side of the plaza, but the mist was still lingering. "They're down there, below us, past the city's northern outskirt. If your eyes were long enough, you could watch them gather. They come across the water, from Ikira and Teale, from the towns that died." He turned back to the Bard, his face burning. "I think… I think they're *waiting* for something."

"Christmas." Ecko was beginning to wonder if this guy had a marble shortage – hell, there was a lot of it about. Baeru placed a hand on the Bard's black-clad chest in appeal – or as if he would tear his heart out.

"You may be right." Roderick placed a hand over Baeru's, held it to his chest. He watched the man's face with a peculiar intensity. "Tell me everything you know."

If your eyes were long enough…

Sod waiting for a game of soldiers, Ecko had a quicker way to do this.

Ecko said to Rhan, "You wanna know? I'll fucking show you. Whaddaya need? Scars? Dog-tags? Alchemical Haynes Manual? What?"

Rhan's peridot gaze fastened on Ecko like he could turn the little man inside out.

"Numbers. Deployment. Proof. Show me. *Show* me why I should abandon my city."

Roderick said softly, "Not abandon—"

"Don't play your word games with me." Rhan's face flickered, but his voice was hard as rock. "You don't get it, do you?" He glared from one to the other. "Does Nivrotar think I'm that weak, that foolish, that I wouldn't fight to the last drop of light in my blood to hold this city and everything in it? We are the bastion, here, we hold the Varchinde in our walls! Roderick, please…" His voice cracked and he fell back, looking at the scattered pieces of bench across the floor. "I've never doubted you, never questioned your vision. But if you want me to do this, then I need more than a gamble – I need truth."

The Bard rested a hand on the Seneschal's back, and said, "Trust me."

"Save it." Rhan's voice was age and weariness. He turned back, and his gaze was like a fucking laser, boring into Ecko's head. "You said you had proof. Show me."

At the plaza's edge, Ecko peered into the last of the mist, spun his telescopics to see.

The hairpin-bend roadway dropped downwards from his vantage, skated around the lip of a slope of scree, and skidded into a sizeable drop to the next loop below. As the white shroud thinned, Ecko's telescopics could just make out where the city's scattered outskirt of manor and farmland met the barren expanse of the dead plain. Down there, he could see a long stretch of ruin, of buildings hollow and dark-eyed, of soil drained and grey.

And *movement.*

We live in the Rhez itself...

His adrenaline shivered.

They were down there, all of them, waiting. They laid among the buildings as if they'd been crafted there – Amal's monsters, creations of nightmare flesh. The centaurs, the mwenar, the vialer – half human, half creature, half nightmare. They seethed among the stone as if eager to begin their assault.

But there was more beyond.

Holy fucking shit.

There were other things down there, further back. Things that looked like ancient stone, blunt-faced and overgrown, crumbling at their edges but with hands that could crush buildings. Smaller things, swift and almost unseen in the mist; things that had blind eyes and curved claws, that turned on each other in frustration and restlessness.

Trying for a headcount, for some sort of calculation, he remembered the army that had been crafted by Maugrim, deep under the Monument – had that, too, been destined for this fight? If it had assailed Roviarath, and Roviarath had fallen, then Maugrim would have left enough troops to garrison, and the rest of them would have been here.

And if they hadn't stopped Amal...

Jesus Harry Christ in a bloody fucking bucket – he remembered what Nivrotar had said about their successes. If they hadn't fought Maugrim and Amal, would the Grasslands already have fallen – would they already have failed?

He stared over the drop, his adrenaline shimmering.

Patterns, always patterns, everything affected by everything else... tiny ripples that change everything around us...

Chrissakes, maybe we really *haven't* fucked this up!

The insight was a tiny one, but it burned very bright. Ecko suddenly realised that he understood the choice that Nivrotar had made, the gamble she was taking...

...and fuck him ragged if he didn't actually believe they could do it.

But he didn't have time to dwell on the fact.

The thing that came over the lip of the drop, right in his face, was a sudden and pixelated blur to his distant ocular focus – small and fast, teeth and eyes and reaching, stretching claws. His adrenaline was boosted, his reflexes kicked so hard he didn't even know he was moving; his hands caught the thing, but not before the gash in his throat spewed breath and scarlet onto the stone.

Ecko pulled down the neckline of his stupid hairy shirt, showed where the creature's claw had slashed at windpipe and collarbone – a mark straight across the scar that Amal had given him. Only his speed and reinforced skin had saved him from a gasping death; only his increased healing rate had stopped the gush of blood from finishing what the fucking clawbeast had started.

"This what you want?" he demanded.

The mark was a white flash like his insight, another line in his mottled skin.

"The critter was some sorta scout – fuckin' fast and gone before I got it. But I saw enough about where it came from."

Rhan watched him.

"You gotta party on your northern border, dude. You got monsters, crossbreeds, stone beasties from times past – you fuckin' name it, it's gotten an invite. It's a muster point – an' it's gettin' bigger."

"Prove it," Rhan said.

Ecko grinned at him. "That's not all. You wanna know what's happenin' to your population? Your homeless, your jobless, your dispossessed? Someone down there is handin' out hope. *Purpose*. I saw *people* down there, asshole, *your* people, an' they're queuin' to get in."

"This is some sort of jest." Rhan reached to touch the scar and Ecko pulled back. "Why would they—?"

"Take your fuckin' paws offa me and listen." Ecko jabbed a rigid finger. "You're done here. You stay here, an' all them people who lost their homes and loves and jobs an' little kitty cats, they'll find a flag to wave. They'll find themselves a cause. They'll go join that army – you familiar with the phrase 'cannon fodder'? You're fucked six ways from sundown and all the big shiny noble hero shit in the world ain't gonna save your ass this time. You gotta get the fuck outta here. Take your people with you, rally what forces you can, and git." He grinned, black as the starless night. "I've met your brother, asshole. Let him have the fucking city – that way he hasta clean it up."

Rhan stared at Ecko for a minute, pale green eyes blazing. Ecko had no idea if he was gonna laugh, or punch his fucking lights out.

Or try to.

Then he turned and swore, and slammed one fist into the

wall hard enough to make the little house shudder.

"I need to know everything," he said.

Ecko grinned at him. "That's kinda what I do."

8: ACCURSED RAMMOUTHE ISLAND

Ress was not crazed.

His clarity was sharp and painful; he *knew* everything more clearly than he ever had. Even as he breathed, he could feel the winter, could smell and taste it. The island's air was cold and crisp, its scrub-grass was hardy, untouched by the blight; its health was tangible as Jayr's. The creatures that watched them, wide-eyed and unafraid, their spiral horns impossible and beautiful, were tsaka, found only here on the island. About them, everything was beautiful, unscathed, clear as bright sunshine. Inhaling filled him with a vast and wordless ken, a feel of crackling wonder like the Powerflux itself.

Ramm-Outhe, the Island of the Accursed.

He was *here*!

Beside him, he could sense Jayr's sheer strength; her scarred arms were still bared to the cold, but her scalplock was lost in her new hair. She seemed younger somehow, her face lit with a rare and delighted smile as she looked about them. The other one, Penya, was hard-nosed and wary – she prowled, hand on belt-blade, refusing to trust the beauty that surrounded them.

Beauty that should not have been here.

Ramm-Outhe, forbidden and forsaken. Untrodden by human feet since the Bard's disastrous scouting, some forty returns before. By Fhaveonic legend, home to the exiled Kas Vahl Zaxaar.

And it was glorious.

"Look!" Ress would say, pointing at a tree behung with fronds like banners, at the bright mouth of a winter flower. "Can't you see it?" But his words came out jumbled, and his arm would not point where he told it. He wished he could show them, tell them; wished he could wrest this incredible elation from his heart and say, "Can't you feel what I feel, know what I know?" But though his mind was growing with every pace, his words were guttering as candle flame, lost in the winter sun.

Fhaveon, Ikira, Teale – they were all gone now, lost. If he turned, there was no route home – Rammouthe's ring of cliffs obscured any view of the mainland. It had taken all of Penya's skill to bring them safely through the rocks.

She had said it at the time – she was unlikely to be able to take them out again.

But Ress didn't care – he didn't *care*! What was behind him was gone; he was being pulled onwards, relentless as a lead-rein – he could go only forwards. There were words in his head, they were always in his head. Like a choir, like a chant. Like bells. From the lost depths of the Great Library in Amos where he'd first seen them, they now rung at him constantly, restless, in rounds, over and over.

"Time the Flux begins to crack.
To rage becomes a crime.
And Nothing is more powerful
At last, than Count of Time..."

So often he'd tried to give them voice, but they always came out the same, that single solemn toll...

"No time, no time, no time, no *time*..."

Ress found that he'd stopped, was plucking at the sleeve of his overshirt, at the place where he'd tried to write the thing down. Perhaps, he'd thought, if his mouth couldn't form the words, then his fingers could. But like his mouth, his hand had betrayed him and in his determination – his desperation – he'd covered the garment in writing that the others couldn't read, in drawings that made no sense to them.

Drawings of some peculiar, stylised imp, like a little man, with mottled skin and black-on-black eyes.

Ecko.

Thinking about Ecko was like pulling stitches from a wound – it thrilled and hurt and scared him. Meeting the man had been a shock, a flash of hope like black light, like the soul of dark itself. Ress could still feel Ecko's colossal energy – but it made him unpredictable, terrifyingly so. He was just as likely to damn the world on a whim.

To guard him and guide him, Roderick needed to be strong, stronger than human. He needed to surpass himself. He needed to...

Needed to what?

A faint wisp of memory touched him – a taste of a thought not his own, of something bigger than he could grasp. He could see the Bard, younger, wearing the lamellar armour of Fhaveon, a tan of soldiers with him. They were there on the hillside pointing at the tsaka, laughing at their strange horns.

The image wavered and was gone.

Ress blinked.

Since their arrival upon Rammouthe, this was happening more and more frequently, like fog rolling back from some lost horizon, a dream returning to the dreamer. The images made him shudder – sometimes the memories weren't clear, they were figments of figments that caught him for a moment and then were gone. They left him staring breathless at something that wasn't there; they were the faintest after-echoes of a recurring nightmare that he knew would recur again.

Time the Flux begins to crack...

In the Amos Library Ress had found the pieces of the world's forgotten puzzle – they rang bells in his head, wrote words on his shirt. All he needed to know – to *remember* – was how they went together.

Time the Flux begins to crack...

"Ress." Jayr's hand on his arm. "Pen says we need to move – it'll get dark soon. Ress. Did you hear me? We need to move."

"Move." He blinked. Jayr's face was a blur, he could only really see her out of one eye at a time – but that was all right, her solidity was like the rock itself, straightforward and utterly dependable. "Movement?"

"Yes, movement. Us. Now."

The black-eyed sprite on his sleeve winked at him and he found himself in motion, hands under his elbows. The air was darker now and the landscape was changing as they headed uphill, further inland. As they moved, Jayr's delight slowly evaporated into wariness; Penya grew more and more concerned. Ress could feel their tension like a shout. Could you feel a shout? He supposed you could, if it were loud enough.

Time the Flux...

Behind them the sun slowly tumbled, dying in red light upon unseen mountains. Clouds rose against the wind, streaked with darkness and fire. Around them, there was stillness; the mad-horned tsaka had faded into the dusk. And Rammouthe became stark and bleak. Rain began to scatter across rocks scoured harsh by the wind, across high moors and scree slopes.

It began to patter onto the sleeve of Ress's overshirt, making the ink spread to a blur. The black-eyed sprite, the words of Amos, dissolved slowly into the warp and weft of the fabric.

No. He must remember. He must *remember*!

He freed a hand, tried to cover his sleeve – only to see the other sleeve was also fading. Panicked, he tried to pull himself out of the hands that held him. He couldn't let this go, he had to keep this!

The Amos Library had told that the island was the home of the Ilfe, the Well of the World's Memory, sister to the Ryll, the waterfall of her thoughts...

Yes. The Ilfe, the thing that will make all of this make sense. And I'll find it – as soon as I remember where it is!

The irony of the thought made him laugh, high and brittle. He struggled against his captors. The sound split on the loose stones and echoed, jagged, in the half-light.

The rain grew heavier, cold across the wind.

"Shut up dammit!" Jayr put one hand over his mouth. His breath was hot on her fingers; moisture glittered like ice on her skin. She tasted like pure, clean might. He tried to tell her about the ink on his sleeve, but she wasn't listening. They picked him bodily off the ground and carried him, his feet kicking.

But now, Ress could remember more – as if the images were dissolving into his very skin...

At the island's heart, a labyrinth of rock – a citadel. The home of the Kas. He could hear Roderick's voice, that fragment of saga that had brought the Bard here, forty returns before: *...carved into the island's living stone, delved and built into gullies and walls. The street-maze gleams. The Count of Time beats through the rock, granting the citadel life. Suppliants beg upon its streets, traders call wares in its shadows. The people of this city age swiftly. Vialer pace the towers.*

Nothing is more powerful...

But there was only the rain, the high moor. As Roderick had witnessed once before, Vahl Zaxaar had never been here. There was no citadel, no maze, no ruin.

The sky lowered to darker grey.

Jayr said, "Where the rhez are we going anyway? There's nothing here."

"Yes." In Ress's madness and clarity, failure had no place – endless moors or not, he would find what he sought. Would remember. Ignoring Jayr's question, Penya's shrug and mumble, he kept walking uphill, the scree of the slope now sliding under his boots. His feet were sinking into it, and it was becoming harder to move.

"Yes *what*, for Gods' sakes?" Jayr was tired and petulant. The rain had scattered and stopped, but the wind was cold. "Yes, you know, or yes, there's nothing here?"

He paused to blink at her, to show her his sleeves, now a smudged blur of everything he'd needed to know. She rolled her eyes.

"Nothing," he said. "Nothing." The joke made him laugh again, high and shrill. It wasn't really his voice, but it was all he had.

"Shut up!" Penya had her blade out now and she prowled the gathering dark, bristling with suspicion. The stones skidded under her and she lost her footing then steadied herself, legs parted and knees bent.

Monsters. The idea made him laugh, and he lurched onward through the deepening shale, his head thrown back and the strange, angular laugh still cutting free from his throat.

"I swear," Penya muttered, "if he doesn't shut the rhez up I'm going to drug him into the middle of next halfcycle."

But Ress walked on, drawn by certainty. As each foot sunk into the shale, so the memories came to him from the island itself – they seemed to rise from the sliding stones, as if they'd lain there, waiting for his feet to release them.

He could remember now: on the mainland, the ancient city of Swathe, overlooking Rammouthe itself and burning with the wrath of Vahl's victory. He could remember: the bargain Vahl had struck with the grass of the Varchinde – if he allowed it to grow in the spring, then it would die in the winter and offer him its time.

He could remember: the almighty rocklight, the soul of light and the eastern point of the Powerflux, cursed to sink beneath the sea. The Flux had been critically damaged by the imbalance, and its power and memory waned.

And something…?

He groped after a realisation, but it faded even as he reached for it – a wish denied, a dream forgotten. Vahl had cursed the Flux so he could not be challenged, but there was something more, something he'd not yet remembered…

Ress held up his sleeve, pulled out the front of the overshirt to look down at it, but the images there were as lost as everything else. The ink had smudged into his skin.

Beside him, Jayr spat a sudden curse, staggered, went to one knee on the stones. Studying his stained flesh, it took a moment for Ress to realise – the ground was moving, the whole slope was sliding from under them. Penya lost her footing and fell, swearing.

"Go sideways." She was shouting at them, even as the stones began to slide faster, to roar with their own increasing motion. "Go across!"

But it was too late. As though the very rocks had heard Ress's thoughts, the ground beneath them opened like a mouth. The entire slope slid downwards with a rumble and a rise of dust.

And the island swallowed them whole.

They slid.

Swearing and tumbling and bruising, garments tearing, noise deafening, they slid down into confusion and cold, down into a rock-pale glitter that made their skin white as nightmare.

Jayr was on her feet in a moment, crouched and tight, scratched and scarred, bristling with the need for combat. Penya lay still, her temple bloodied.

Ress had skidded helpless. He had bruises at his knees, blood in his mouth where he'd bitten his tongue. He came to an untidy and hurting stop at the bottom of the slope.

Panting.

Time the Flux...?

His smudged shirt was in tatters. Above him was only a tiny strip of almost-dark sky and the faint light of the yellow moon. His hands bled where he'd tried to slow his descent, but it had all happened so fast. They had been eaten alive by Ramm-Outhe.

He thought about this for a moment, then looked at Penya.

"She sleeps. Why?" They had to move; they had no time, no time, no—

"You're the damned apothecary." Jayr's tone was affectionate, but she didn't take her attention from the ghost-lit gloom that surrounded them.

Apothecary.

Yes, he knew that – he was supposed to make her better.

Ress's knees were water, his stomach churned. He couldn't stand. So he shuffled on his backside over to the fallen woman, the stones scraping, sliding. The line of blood came from a contusion on her temple; it seeped in among the roots of her hair, spreading to a crust. The pale light made it black as despair.

He reached out a finger, touched it.

Nothing is more powerful...

Another memory flash. Ramm-Outhe. Island of the Accursed. In blood and wraithlight, he could see the ink smudged on his forearms and it spread into images – the citadel, black against the sky, rage like fire across its crenulations. He could see the people huddled beneath it in fear, their time draining like rainwater down the gutters of the streets...

And he understood something.

There *had* been Kas here. Not Vahl himself – his punishment had been more subtle – but others, his kin. Cast down by Samiel...

Damned.

Time the Flux begins to crack...

He touched Penya's blood again and he shivered – elation, terror, hope – he was so close, he was bright with real urgency, his clarity stronger with every breath.

He said, "Must... get up... walk..."

But Jayr hissed at him. "Shhh. Let me listen. We're not the only things down here."

At last, than Count of Time...

Ress laughed, a softer echo of his previous shrill humour. The sound was garish in the gloom. He should be afraid, afraid of the Kas, of what lurked here in the dark, but his focus was pure, and he had got only one answer – they must go forward.

He said again, "Must... get up... walk..."

Jayr glanced at the fallen Penya, took a step forwards to defend her.

"Who's out there?" Her voice had echoes of her Kartian training – it reeked of challenge.

Could a sound smell? To Ress, it smelled like eagerness.

Then something said, "Go? Ah, young one, this is Rammouthe. There is no egress from here."

And Nothing is more powerful...

Ress pressed his back to the stone behind him, cutting his own shape from the ghost-light. The voice seethed with smoke and shadow. He couldn't see the speaker, but there were footsteps, weary and dragging, sliding hard across the pebbles.

The presence felt... like age and hunger, like patience beyond the Count of Time, like power. Like *eagerness*.

Jayr said, "Hold. You move again, I'll take your damned head off." Whatever it was, her courage was as absolute as his certainty.

"Will you now?" A different voice, from another angle, received a series of supporting chuckles. "And how will one *young* as you," the word was pure appetite, "manage that?"

They were surrounded.

Ress found he was trembling, somewhere between exaltation and need. *Must... get up... walk...* They had to move onwards, and yet the memories were there, telling him what now stood in their way.

The word Kas meant *fallen*.

Into the darkness, Ress said, "You're prisoners. Fallen in ruins. *Caught*."

Jayr was a silent blaze of question: *What are you doing?*

"The Gods punished us twice." The words were a sneer. Ress couldn't see the speaker, though the presence was like smoke on his face. More voices joined the litany, a chorus of ridicule echoing from the rock.

"We fell for pride, but were trapped for warfare. Have you come to free us, old man?"

"Tease us? Tempt us with the light?"

"Poor madman, thinking he can speak to us."

"Maybe he brings a message? A call to arms?"

"He's too late for that."

"Are you our scout, mortal, here to lead us at last to the sky? To a final victory? To freedom?"

"We'll carry you to a new glory, little man, the Varchinde will be ours by midwinter."

"By midwinter!"

The words rebounded, whispers upon whispers, crowding the dark space and pushing under his skin like burrowing insects. Whatever else the waiting Kas had lost, their fear was still smothering, choking. *Are you our scout, mortal?*

Jayr took a step forward, scree sliding. "I'm Jayr the Infamous – and I know where you are and I can take you to pieces. Back up, and leave us alone."

They were playing with her. "Ah, such energy!"

"Such *youth*!"

"Give us your time."

"We hunger, we've waited so *long*."

"We must have time, time to revel in the new destruction."

"And then we'll take all the time we need."

Laughter came from the walls like steam, like the touch of thin hands.

Beside where Penya lay, a single gleam of yellow moonlight had fought its way down to the floor. It was weak, but it touched the fallen woman with a hint of forgotten promise – far above, the sky was still there. Ress lifted his face to feel the wind, but the space about him was sullen, and the air was still.

In the gloom, a shadow moved. Shapes shifted beside it. Ress looked back at the darkness.

And recoiled.

The Kas that came towards him was not the monster he'd been expecting – not some vast saga-beast of wings and flame. It was aged, tired, gaunt-faced, crack-skinned and thin. Its muscles were wasted, and hung from its withered frame like old rope. Its hair was a smoulder, a wreath of smoke that moved about its face, and its eyes burned cold with starvation.

Behind it, he could see the vast stone ruin that was the citadel – the thing the Bard had come seeking, and had failed to find.

Ress spewed words, as if he were flailing. "No time! No time! Must... *walk...*"

But the creature curled its lip. "Do you defy us then, little man? Do you pity our condemnation? Our damnation? Vahl promised us, and we will be free." It came forwards until it could lean over him, overpowering, face to face, eyes of hunger and madness. "We are strong, now. You should envy us!"

"Envy?" The creature's body was so parchment-thin Ress could've reached out and crushed it, even with his old and scratched hands. "We must walk, we must!"

Behind it, others were moving. They came close, began to spread out. Jayr stood like a tower. Penya lay like death.

And the Kas *hungered*.

Unassailable, Jayr snorted at them. "I'm not afraid of you. Whatever you are. Get any closer, you'll lose an eye."

"Ah, little warrior." The creature leaning over Ress crouched down and touched Penya where she lay, its smile merciless.

"You can't threaten what you don't understand." Around it, they closed in tighter, their hunger smothering all light. "We need the time – we're almost free!"

"The time comes again."

"Every desire sated – we've been promised!"

Ress watched as Penya shrivelled, aged, and was dust.

He shuddered in horror, wrapped his hands over his mouth.

Then there was another creature somehow behind them. Its bone-thin hands closed on his shoulders. Hands were reaching for Jayr too, greedy and clawing – the creatures were everywhere, draining the strength right out of their skin.

No time.

Ress felt his bones shrivel, felt his skin dry and crack, felt his hair thin and wisp away.

And the creature's voice was soft, sensual, on the creasing skin of his face. "Our time comes at last, little man. Samiel no longer cares, the Gods have forgotten us. No more exile, no more starvation. We will be free.

"And then we will rage across the sky."

9: ANSWERS FHAVEON

The streets of the Lord city fell downwards into desolation.

In many places the roadways stood empty, bereft of life and hope, torn to devastation by the stone creatures that had ripped from the walls, and by the fighting that had come in the wake of Phylos's rise to power. Garbage blew though empty marketplaces; the fountains stood silent, their water fouled, the crystal trees dark, their branches broken.

At the city's outermost limits, Death was looting the corpses.

Uncaring of his surroundings, the figure of Death was smaller than you might have expected, and lacking the traditional cadaver beneath his black wool cloak. He had no scythe – instead, he bore a single terhnwood blade that glistened at its edge.

It seemed though, the Grim Reaper's luck had upped and done a runner.

"Chrissakes, the vultures've been through here. These guys're picked cleaner than a Saturday night pisshead."

"Then perhaps we should leave?"

Death had a companion. A tall man, austere, clad head to foot in peculiar black garb with a hood over his head and his face covered. His voice held an odd thrum of subdued power, like the strings of an instrument.

The smaller figure cackled. "Yeah, right. Like we don't know what's waitin' for us – we've seen it already." He moved onto the next fallen corpse, this one a woman, her throat slit and gaping and crusted, her skin bloated and pale.

"We need numbers, deployment." The thrum grew louder, a hint of annoyance. "You can line your pouches another time."

"Sure as fuck can't line 'em out here." The woman's belt was empty: anything she'd been carrying had long gone. Besides, something had been eating her and she was starting to really stink. "Okay, okay, we're outta here – though I gotta question before we go." Under the cowl, Death's eyes and teeth were black as nightmare. "If I'm Death, now, then which one're you? You ain't exactly Famine and you sure as shit ain't War – reckon you're Pestilence's little brother, Annoying Personal Itch."

The cloaked figure turned back to the empty roadway, his grin unholy. "Okay, let's get this over with."

Carefully, they moved onwards though the lower streets of the broken city.

Down here, the roads were dark. There were no rocklights remaining, and the moons didn't penetrate the rough patchwork of roofs. Leaving the Bard at ground level, Ecko went carefully up the side of a building and began to run the rooftops, his cloak moving with him, though sodden with rainwater and heavier than the one he'd lost.

Heavier, his mottled ass – the damn thing was clumsy as a drunken teen, but it wasn't like he'd gotten a choice.

Up here, the moons made his progress awkward – their cross-hatching meant that no side of a roof was completely in shadow – but hell, this shit was like being at home. There were chimneys to crouch beside, flat roofs to race along, sloping tiles to make him slip, narrow gaps over alleyways that must be leapt. There were occasional flashes of native wildlife;

crumbling walls that powdered under his feet; unexpected washing lines, now empty, that nearly took his head clean off like some cartoon piano wire...

But he saw the second one – *thank fuck!* – and ran low and fast, keeping one eye on the faint blur of ground-level warmth that was the Bard.

Bastard had insulated clothing. He was difficult to see – and Ecko knew full well he was getting a kick out of it.

Shithead.

Hell, since when had Ecko ever had to do a stealth run in fucking *company* for chrissakes?

Frankly, he was more than tempted to piss off and leave the Bard behind – insulated clothing or no – but he remembered about his freedom of choice and all that "friends" shit and he held himself back, skittering low across another roof.

As he came to its far side, he found an empty plaza and a now-abandoned barricade, a place where some sorta showdown must've taken place. Scanning, Ecko had a peculiar frisson, realised something that was needling him...

When they'd come through Fhaveon, the battle-torn streets of the city had been scattered with people. Less than he'd expected, true, but they'd been there like he could tick the boxes – the homeless, bereft, lost, injured, aggressive... A population dispossessed and looking for answers, food and opportunity.

Now, the streets were empty; there was almost no one left.

He had a nasty fucking feeling the stuff he'd told Rhan was truer than he'd realised.

Amethea stood upon the dusty remnant of an elaborate mosaic, craning her neck to see the wonders that arched over her.

Behind her, great double doors stood open, letting in the breathing winter cold. Debris was scattered under a huge doorway, carven into an elaborate and abstract design. Ahead of her, the rising building was exquisite, wrought with detail – it had might to reave her of both words and motion. She was here bearing messages, but she'd stopped as if she had no courage to go further.

Her breath rose in a soft grey coil, her soul escaping for a closer look.

This was the Great Cathedral of Fhaveon, Samiel's heart upon the world, his eyes and love. Once, as a lowly 'prentice, she'd dreamed of coming here.

Now, she came as it was dying.

The thought made her shiver, rubbing her arms. Despite the echoing beauty, the place felt empty, cold with more than the wind from outside. And she had the oddest sensation of fatality – as if she was also here looking for something.

Answers? Direction? The manifest presence of the Gods?

Her own faith had been shredded by Maugrim – she remembered each word like a cut: *You're no saint, little priestess. In your heart you're just like I am...*

She snorted, striving to drive the memory back, but the open doorway seemed to pull both thought and sound inward and swallow them whole – so she followed, out into the great building ahead of her.

A blaze of stained windows and a huge dome of decorated roof – all the colours and dances of the Gods.

Forgiveness?

In the Great Cathedral of Fhaveon, the mosaic floor was worn into grooves, the damage of generations. About the angled walls, silent statues stood faceless. Rising over them, the huge coloured glass of the windows scattered the sunset light like gemstones, tumbling over the floor.

Ten walls, ten angles, ten statues, ten windows. Ten equal sides like the days of the halfcycle, and all of them rising into a single rocklight that hung at the dome's apex, a pattern carved into its surface like Kartian scarring. It splashed walls and floor with a soft mottle.

Absolution?

She rubbed her cricked shoulders with a rueful hand. If there had been seats for the faithful, they'd long gone now, weapons or firewood. The central dais was unoccupied, bereft of promise or leadership. Dust drifted from where she'd walked. The statue nearest to her seemed to be nothing but voluminous cloak; above it, the tenth window – or the first one – was blank. This was the window that faced north, and it glittered in myriad shades of yellow and grey.

For no reason, her chillflesh prickled again.

Saint and Goddess, stop it!

She could still hear the after-echoes of the dying city – yet the Cathedral seemed to stand above it all, silent and uncaring. She found herself almost angry – this building, this wonder, this heart of Fhaveon, this presence of Samiel, this – whatever it was supposed to be! – had its gaze on the Gods as if the people were no longer its problem. If Amethea ever went home to her teacher Vilsara in Xenok, she could tell the tale of the Great Cathedral, oh yes, standing remote at the time of crisis, lifeless and deserted by all...

Well, maybe not quite.

"Good evening. Would you mind shutting the doors? It's freezing in here."

Amethea blinked at the rotund, grinning man as if she'd been caught doing something terrible.

"Sorry... ah... yes of course." She shut the double doors with a boom, turned back to explain, "I was admiring the window."

"Course you were." The man wore breeches and tunic and dirty apron, and he carried a brush and an old wooden pail. He was sweating and round-bellied; he had a great barrel of a chest and hands as large and dirty as shovels. "Personally, I think it could do with a bit more colour. As north windows go, it's rather drab, don't you think?"

Confused, Amethea fumbled, "Surely... there should be something there?"

The man shrugged, still smiling. "Stands to reason – they say there's a God for every day of the halfcycle, so that one..."

"Yes, I remember that." It had been in Vilsara's early teachings, somewhere lost in the back of her mind. She looked at the faceless statues, then around the rest of the windows. "Then these are our Gods?" She counted them, trying to fit it together.

"So they say." The man chuckled, a deep roll of humour. "But forgive me, my manners! It's a strange dusk that brings people to the Cathedral's doors, though they stand always open."

"I'm Amethea, once of Xenok," she said. "I trained with Vilsara—"

"Vilsara!" The round man chuckled louder, a sound so marvellously infectious that she found herself grinning back at him. "How's the old girl doing?"

"She's very well." The response was guarded. She'd no idea who this man was, or why he had the right to ask the question.

"Good, good." The man wiped his hands on his apron, winked. "Glad to hear it. Now – how can I help you?"

"I was looking for Gorinel, for the Father-Protector? I bear a message."

For a moment, the man eyed her, then he began to laugh, a bass rumble from his round belly, a sound that lifted the building with a warmth all of its own.

"I suppose I look like the cleaner?"

More baffled than ever, she said, "I was looking for His Reverence. I can come back in the morning?"

Holding up a hand, he said, "Please, 'Reverence' isn't something I've ever been any good at. I'm Gorinel – and you, lovely, look very lost. What can I do?"

Holy shit on a stick...

At Fhaveon's most extreme northern limit, Ecko now watched, silent.

Below him, the sleeping thing was huge.

In fact, "huge" didn't fucking cover it. This was the thing he'd seen from the plaza edge high above – and now, close up, it was colossal, like some long, dark monster that'd swallowed an old farmhouse and most of its grounds. It was patchy, dense in the centre and scattered about its edges; in some places it was rigidly structured, in others it sprawled undisciplined. Here and there among the darkness of its bulk there were flickers of flame, faint as if the whole thing was hiding.

It was way, way bigger than Ecko had been expecting.

Watching it, he was crouched upon the sloping roof of a deserted chapel, the building covered in fragments of stone and shell; in many places, the tiles had been ripped free, leaving scars like little mouths. It was a perfect vantage, its tower all sticks and bird shit.

Below him, Ecko heard the Bard catch his breath, and wondered if he could see that far... but the wondering didn't last long.

The clouds peeled back like a picked scab, the white moon a cold eye, high above them. And the sleeping thing slowly took on its full form.

Ecko repeated like some loopy mantra, *Holy shit, holy shit, holy motherfucking shit...*

He couldn't wrap his brain round it.

Monsters that he'd seen from above flanked the thing, ragged musters of nightmare that slept scattered, or prowled its edges. There seemed to be no leaders, no ranks or orders; they wandered loose, guards or guides or both. His telos strained trying to focus on faces – hell, at least on numbers of legs – but it was too far and too dark.

He knew he should go down there, get a closer look. He was *wired* for this shit, for chrissakes.

But...

Further in, the sleeping thing was made up of tents, dark fabric almost invisible against ruined and overgrown walls. He'd not seen this from his previous vantage – some of them bore symbols, food or medicine; the smaller ones were racked in rows, suitably military and identical. *That* shit, at least, hadn't changed.

His telos searched in systematic strips – found more.

The sleeping thing had kitchens, latrines. It had corrals, chearl and horses. It had occupied cages of smaller critters, piled high. It had wagons, though he'd no clue what they were carrying – some looked big enough to cart artillery and he didn't like that shit one bit.

He had to get his ass down there and check them out, find out exactly what the bad guys had to throw at them – hell, some of it probably literally – but he was stuck to the spot like the broken bits of shell had penetrated his feet, nailing him down.

The thing stirred, restless and shifting. Lights flickered; sounds of shouts came across the night. Below Ecko, Roderick muttered something softly.

He continued to scan.

After a moment, he found what he reckoned was the command tent, pitched slap-bang in the middle of the ruined manse. It was a big square thing, decorated with some sort of repeated symbol, and with a pennon that hung limp from a spear. Minions surrounded the tent, cloaked shadows that guarded its flanks. They patrolled silent, stopping to speak, or to study the darkness around them. As the moonlight grew brighter, his telos sharpened and he could see them clearly: their back-bent legs, their bared, tattooed chests, the layers of thonging about their throats. Chrissakes, they looked like Tumnus the Faun all growed up and with a steroid problem – and they were armed to the fucking *teeth*.

Whatever they were – were they called vialer? – they were the beasties in charge and they didn't miss a trick.

Holy...

Transfixed now, Ecko couldn't've looked away if a hole had torn though reality and shown him the Bike Lodge, acid-hazing just off of his right shoulder...

Down there, across the darkness and the glittering highlights of yellow and white, down there, in among the ruins and the overgrowth, the flickers of flame grew brighter. In among them was the muted glow of rocklights, and the whole damn thing was shifting now, like some stretching sewer monster, some spreading pool of oil.

Holy shit. Holy shit. Holy...

Ecko made an effort not to breathe the words aloud; he clung hard to the edge of the tower. *Jesus H Christ. I was right, Nivvy was right – the big baddie may've gone, but his whole fuckin' army's all still here.*

An'... how the hell did it get this big?

Below him, the Bard was silent with anticipation or fear. Or perhaps he'd had his throat slit.

Down there was not the loose scatter of critters that Ecko had seen from the plaza. What he could see now was the entire force gathered, a manifest fucking host. It was every monster that'd ever crawled out of Amal's twisted asshole – every centaur, every half-breed, every fucked up crafting of human flesh that mimicked what Mom had done to his own.

So – what? Was I s'posed to call him "Dad"? Was that the point?

Yeah, Eliza, you're funny.

Down there was every soldier who'd followed the bad guys' flag, every damned critter that Kas Vahl Whosit could throw at the dying Varchinde.

But even that wasn't the end of it.

Ecko continued to scan, strips of extreme moonlit close-up, as much detail as he could get.

And then he realised something that scared him right to the fucking core.

* * *

"Your Reverence," Amethea said. She'd taken a step back and was lost for the proper etiquette. Faced by the Father-Protector, by the worldly representative of Samiel himself, her memory had baulked – it was refusing everything but her apothecarial code and lectures on herb-tending. Was she supposed to kiss the hem of his embroidered overshirt, his jewellery? He wore neither.

And then, somewhere under that confusion of awe and disbelief, more memories of Maugrim crowded close to surface, unwanted and unwelcome, rising and bobbing like waste. She could hear his words, *Get to you, love. The whiners, the needers, the hypochondriacs, the neurotics, the weak-willed and the desperate...*

She was a healer. She was supposed to help people, be there for them – she'd been working in Amos, and had felt much better. Useful, needed. Now, with Maugrim haunting her, she realised what she'd come here to find – that feeling of fatalism, the answer she'd come seeking...

Not just purpose.

But *faith*.

Oh, you're jesting...

She almost laughed at herself – at her own ludicrous predictability. Standing there, surrounded by nameless and forgotten Gods, Amethea found she was shaking, trying to muster something like denial – *Don't be ridiculous!*

Faith.

She swallowed, bit the inside of her mouth; if he saw it, the old priest said nothing. Instead, he put down his pail and stretched his back with a pop and a grimace.

"Your Reverence indeed. I'm far too old to be doing this myself. I really should have minions or something." He winked, wicked and infectious.

Unable to face his clean humour, she looked at her own

hands, stained with worse things than soil, and searched for something to say.

But then she remembered what she had to hide behind, and said, "I bear a message for you."

Above her, the empty window glimmered, mocking. Maugrim was loud now, striving to make himself heard. His words piled one upon another, all of them clamouring at her, laughing. But she couldn't face them, couldn't admit her own part in what had happened.

What had the Bard said? *Maugrim had power and passion – elemental focus that brought the Powerflux from somnolence and legend – but the love and courage were yours.*

Bitterly, she fought the clamour down, but it was too late and the truth leered at her, its teeth bared and bloody.

The truth: that the hole in the world had been partially her fault.

Faith.

Purpose.

Or absolution?

Gorinel though, had followed her gaze to the window. He said, "I don't know why that one's empty. Like Xenok's, our records are long-rotted, unreadable, but we still remember some Gods – Samiel, the moons." His back clicked again and he winced. "In a world with no memory, they've become less than legend, more like comforters. It makes what we do... a social necessity, more practical than political, but I'm sure you know that." He grinned, went to sit on the edge of his pail and then thought better of it, standing back up with another clunk. "Seeing the Gods is easy – if you wish for comfort, you can see them in the birth of the sun, in the beauty of the world, or in her pain. Moments of passion touch us all. But sustaining their presence, without knowing their names?" He looked at the windows. "That's a different beast entirely."

Sustaining

Amethea felt herself reddening. He was answering the question she hadn't asked and she heard him with her entire skin, her whole being. It frightened her like truth.

The fat man chuckled. "Ah, Amethea. How can we trust in Gods with no names? Deities we've forgotten? We learn to sustain ourselves, and to help others to do likewise. They," he waved a work-callused hand, "won't do it for us – they don't grant our wishes, or absolve us of our misdeeds. They won't manifest at our command. You're an apothecary, you were taught this as a 'prentice. Falling to your knees and pleading for Samiel to save a life is one thing – but the dying man beside you needs you to stop his bleeding." He raised an eyebrow; his smile was like soft fabric over old rock. "You are the one that saves his life. Your faith – and his – can be found in action."

Action.

Amethea said, her voice faintly bitter, "The Gods help those who help themselves?"

"That's about the size of it," Gorinel said, shrugging. "I don't have the Gods in my pockets, or in my windows, and I can't parade them for you. But here, sit on my pail – and perhaps I can answer the question you've not asked me."

Holy shit, holy shit, holy...

Ecko spun his telos to a wider focus, now watching the site as a whole. And as he did so, he realised something, something that had been bothering him in the empty streets of the lower city, that'd tickled tentacles at the back of his neck like some lurking Lovecraftian horror...

Almost one third of the army camp was made up of bedrolls scattered almost randomly across the cold ground. They had no tents, no kitchens – they were just huddled bundles of desperation and poverty and garbage that slept near the faint glimmers of the fires. Almost one whole third of Ythalla's force was made up of the city's homeless, the people who'd had nowhere else to go.

He stared.

That was why the streets were empty – Fhaveon's population had abandoned her, and they'd come here. Pulled by Christ-alone-knew-fucking-what. *Cannon fodder*, Ecko had said mockingly to Rhan – but even then, there were too many of them. Why the hell would any force need this many untrained troops?

Holy shit...

For no reason he could name, his blood ran cold. Like he'd stuck his head under some fucking broken shower. He couldn't get goosebumps, but he fought down the urge to rub them away anyhow.

Holy...

Below him, he could hear the Bard's rubber-soled boots shifting on the pieces of shell. *Gawky fucker. Like he could see this far.*

Carefully, mindful of the clumsy wool cloak, Ecko slipped into the hollow tower itself and through to its other side. He crouched low in the archway. Sticks and shit were everywhere, but just for a moment, his gargoyle grin was entirely deliberate.

And he was just that much closer.

He focused his telos again, watching the bedrolls, trying to work out what was freaking him out so much.

Come on, you fucking bitch, let's see what you really got goin' on...

Eliza, Ythalla.

Whatever.

As the clouds parted to reveal a piss-bright glimmer of yellow, so Ecko's telos slowly explored the civilian encampment, length by length. He was trembling with impatience, with the effort of holding himself in place – he needed to go down there, to steal though the bedrolls themselves, to get a real feel for whatever the fuck was going on – but he was sans his decent kit and just didn't dare risk it. And if the Bard came galumphing after him…

Yeah, that's my excuse an' I'm stickin' to it. Sue me.

Fucksake, they'd both be roasting over a slow fire while Ythalla shoved things in places not designed for the task. And that was *so* not how this was gonna go down.

Holy sh—

Shut up, asshole!

Ecko stopped himself, annoyed. His heart was thundering, his adrenaline roaring in his ears. He'd cut his hand on a piece of shell and hadn't realised it; his skin was split and bleeding. Sucking at the wound, he focused his telos here, there – on the centaurs stretching their human and animal limbs, on the things with the human faces like the one that'd accosted him in Aeona, on the controlling vialer, now walking among the bedrolls themselves.

Across the clear night, he could hear them shouting.

As the sleeping population began to stir, Ecko fine-tuned his telos as far as they would go, looked from waking face to waking face, seeing desperation, need, seeing the new blaze of hope…

And seeing one more thing, the thing that curled him with a horror he'd never before experienced. His mouthful of his own blood nearly made him sick.

Not one of the faces was over thirty.

And almost a third of them were children.

"Once," Gorinel said, "there was only Kazyen, the void, timeless and dreamless and alone. Into that void there came the first mother – and so it knew life and movement, and so began the Count of Time. The first mother bore Time children – Gods whose names and roles we've long lost, forgotten to lore and mythology both."

Sat on her bucket, Amethea was looking round at the windows, one at a time, a chill shivering her spine. "The days of the halfcycle…"

"A great irony," Gorinel said. "So much lore lost – names of Gods, the beginning of the Count of Time itself. Yet pieces, we remember – Samiel was one of those children, and he sired twins. The Gods crafted a plaything for them from their own flesh, a toy that shone with light and laughter. In wonder, the children took to the skies of this plaything, circling and admiring – but as they grew older, so their eyes became consumed, not with the toy below, but with each other."

Amethea said, almost a whisper, "I know this, *know* this – they had such beauty that they had no control; they became lovers in breach of all that Samiel had taught. And Samiel condemned them to fly the skies always – unable to touch, faces turning toward each other and then turning away. But the world...?"

"Is a toy – crafted for the children. Such a little thing." His smile was gentle. "But remember, like any child's favourite toy, they have never parted with it, and it holds a place in their hearts still – a place that may yet surprise you. Put your shoulder to the wheel, Amethea, and know that you are not abandoned."

His tone was gentle, his expression quiet. But there was stone in the old man's voice, a strength to match his girth. Not quite sure why, she held out a hand to him, asking for a blessing that she had no words to frame.

Faith.

Purpose.

Put your shoulder to the wheel.

When the old man took her hand in both of his, she found that she was shaking, but that she had the strength to look up at him. Something in her heart had shattered and was now settling, and she wasn't even sure what it had been.

"I'll try," she said. "I can only promise that much – I'll try."

"And that's all we can ever ask," he said, patting her hand and letting her go. "Now. What can I do for you?"

"I came to give you this," she said. She held out to him a white feather. "And to ask for your help."

CHAPTER 10: MUSTER FHAVEON

Ecko and Roderick left Ythalla's camp as if the monsters would uncurl and come after them, as if every generation of Amal's crafted nightmares would coalesce in the cold winter dawn, slavering for victory. Gathering his cloak hem like some shrieking girlie, Ecko lost dignity and cynicism both, and he just fucking legged it. His feet ran to a silent tattoo, as if they recalled his earlier thoughts: *It could've been worse. Jeez, it could've been so much fucking worse. If we hadn't've kicked Maugrim's ass, if we hadn't've fucked up Amal...*

Somehow, though, the plus side had packed its bags and caught the first flight outta there. Whatever his thoughts were trying to tell him, he reckoned the whole city was up a very shitty creek indeed.

Around them, the streets and buildings were all but empty – where were the *adults*, for chrissakes? – and Ecko didn't bother fucking about with rooftops. Silent as horror, he kept pace with the long legs of the Bard, running through the cold like a shadow.

Running like Ythalla's entire army were off the leash and after them, torches and pitchforks and all.

Chrissakes.

As they skidded round a corner and began to head upwards, away from the outskirts, it occurred to him to wonder why the force was just sat there with its thumb up its collective asshole. Hell, that lot could rise up and trash the place any time they wanted. What were they *waiting* for?

But he had a nasty feeling he knew the answer to that one already.

Nivrotar had been right.

The Kas. The Kas were coming.

And then all the merry Rhez would break loose.

They ran.

Around them, the buildings were silent, sagging, broken, their black eyes empty, their rocklights dimmed. Street stalls were overturned and picked clean; there were jagged great holes in the walls where *things* had torn out of them. Critters scuttled in moon shadows; scavengers slunk with low shoulders and bared teeth.

Some fucking fantasy utopia this was: garbage and corpses and stink, oh my. Oz hadn't only fallen, it'd been kicked to shit and pieces. The Yellow Brick Road had been torn up and the bricks were down there, right now, with eyes and claws and fucking *teeth*. How'd it go again? *There's no place like...*

But the word "home" caused an odd pang – it was somehow nebulous, and he veered away from it like a body in the road.

Running beside him, apparently oblivious to their surroundings, the Bard was muttering to himself. The thrum of his throat seemed to make the abandoned buildings shiver – yep, this time, he'd really fucking lost it.

Ecko wanted to rail – this whole thing was batshit. It wasn't *fair*. Here he was, in a world of fucking wet-eared novices, now facing the inevitable World-Ending War... *Yeah, I asked for it, I know.* They were outnumbered, outmanoeuvred, outmonstered. Outflanked. They didn't even have metal *weapons*, for fucksake.

Score fifty points and a cookie for one superhero who could presumably blast lightning out his asshole and nostrils, but he was only one and the other side had all his *brothers*.

And pitched battles? Tic-tacs and strategy? Military shit? These guys knew less about this stuff than he did. What army they had was in pieces. They were so gonna get their asses handed to them on a fucking polished plate.

And then what? If they didn't win the war, would that mean he'd failed after all? After he'd capitulated and *everything*?

Fucksake. In the rhythm of the Bard's feet, he could hear Eliza laughing at him, echoes of nightmare.

Whatever! Stack the fucking odds, why don'tcha? I'm gonna kick your smug ass, you bitch. I'm Sir fuckin' Boss an' I'm so gonna do this. You wait an' see!

They ran on, breath pluming. The Bard's muttering grew louder.

Dude was a certifiable loony.

Over them, the sky was paling now, starless and grey. The air was crisp and bitterly cold. Frost glittered, slicking the roadway underfoot. Despite the dawn of the dead feel to the empty streets, Ecko could hear birdsong.

Wacky.

As long fingers of cold sunlight began to steal across the broken stone, they at last came to a small square. Like many others, the fountain here stood stagnant. The crystal trees had been hacked down and their stumps burned – flakes and ash still blew in the dawn wind. But here Roderick stopped, turned. He'd pulled the scarf from his mouth and throat, and now revealed the snake nest of warmth and steel and carbon fibre that his voice box had become.

"You ready for this?" His voice was velvet and gravel, taint and taunt and temptation. Wondering what the fuck he was about to do, Ecko stayed exactly where he was and let the cloak cover him.

Chuckling at his reaction, the Bard walked out towards the silent fountain, kicking at the last of the fire as he passed. His black Converse brought sparks from the embers.

Ecko got the impression he was grinning. He flicked his scanners warily, and wondered just what kinda dragon he was gonna sing down from the clouds...

You ready for this?

Roderick turned, leaned on the fountain's edge. He began again the strange rhythmic mutter, a bass thrum that seemed to reverberate from the stone, from the square itself, from the surrounding buildings. His voice was soft and dark, but something about it was undeniable, the touch of the tip of a blade. The steam that came from his breath curled upwards into the morning; Ecko half-expected it to make pictures.

You ready for this?

The Bard lifted his chin. Over him, a line of birds was perched on one of the semi-lethal washing lines; as Ecko glanced up, they rose and whirled and settled again. Their song was clear now, a counterpoint to the Bard's mutter – it was painfully pure, liquid and crystal.

And then he realised that the song was not coming from the birds.

Oh you're kiddin' me...

The Bard's throat was aglow, of course it was. Warm, warmer. Ecko's telescopics could see it: the steel cords in his neck were moving, swelling, each cable oiling round its fellows in some sensual and sinister writhe. From his mouth and ears and lungs came a sound of wonder and opal and sunlight, a sound of pure glass and singing steel, a sound that made Ecko stand and gawp like he'd scored front row tickets to a BiFrost gig.

There was no way that sound, *both* those sounds, could come from a human throat.

Mom? What the hell *did you* do?

Bass-thrum and glass-shard music swelled slowly in volume.

Despite the sound's sweetness, its painful clarity, something in Ecko shivered – it jagged at his nerves like the old fingernails-down-a-blackboard trick. It was pure power, some ma-hu-sive engine that was just turning over, warming the fuck up. He wondered what the hell would happen if the Bard put his foot to the floor... Then slapped himself round the head and fought to *think* through the onslaught of noise...

What the hell was the fuckwit actually doing? *Summoning* something?

Oh, this *so* wasn't gonna end well.

His nerves itched. His ears popped. He wanted to put his fingers in them and shut out the song, the bass, the lure, the call, the morning, the whatever the hell it was supposed to be.

Then he saw...

The other side of the square, there was a figure in a doorway – an older man, greying and slightly scared. He was glancing back and forward, then leaning inside to speak to someone Ecko couldn't see. As the Bard saw him, he raised his volume – only a little – and the pure song curled into the paling dawn, sent tendrils of sound across the openness.

No fucking way.

The man took a pack from a woman behind him, helped her through the half-barricaded door, and slung the pack on his shoulder.

They came across the square to the Bard, picking their way carefully through the debris.

Jesus fuck, you're the fucking Pie-Eyed Piper now?

Ecko rubbed his shoulders, chilled to the core.

He'd no clue why he hadn't seen this – *realised* this – before. The man was supposed to be a bard, for chrissakes, a bard with no memory, and Ecko'd heard him play instruments in The Wanderer. The music thing had been inherent all along. So, was this what'd been lurking below the surface of that slightly feckless, starry-eyed idealist? Was *this* what Mom'd brought out of him?

Wasn't that what Mom did – grant your greatest potential, at the cost of your…?

Oh no you fucking don't.

Like "home", "soul" was another nebulous, bullshit word he wanted nothing to do with. He stopped himself, administered another mental slap. It was all crap anyhow, all this sentiment and whimsy – and why the hell was he wasting his time…

For just a moment, there in the char-mark in the square, Ecko saw a ghost – a thin kid, pale-skinned and red-haired, a loner in his room with his imagination and his games. A kid rejected by his parents, picked on by his younger half sisters, a kid whose viciousness and anger were the barriers he'd built to keep people away from him – but a kid who'd craved attention nonetheless.

A kid with a lighter in his hand.

Ecko stopped, his fists clenched as if he could pummel the image physically out of his brain, pound that bit of the program away, stomp it to pieces. What was Eliza doing, looping him now? Haunting him with his past? *Yeah you go for it, you fucking clever bitch.* He might've agreed to kick the bad guys' butts, for chrissakes, but now she was taking the piss with her poor-Ecko-he-was-bullied-as-a-child fucking flashbacks…

What's this now? Cognitive therapy? Childhood issues?

Get a fucking grip, for chrissakes!

The Bard's song dropped in note, a minor key change that sent further shivers through the crisp, cold morning. The sunlight was swelling now, and Ecko shook himself, looked back across the square. Behind the greybeard, there were others, shadows lingering. They came forwards slowly, like some shambling zombie horde…

No, not quite. Their movements were cautious, curious – but they were coming because they wanted to. Needed to. Whatever that song was, it wasn't simply summoning them to a brainless follow – hey, now who's racking cannon fodder? – it was some sorta *call*.

Ecko shook his head, trying to get the sound out of his ears. However pure the Bard's vocals, he could still hear that bass-thrum undertone, and it just sounded like Mom.

Like being flayed alive.

Like having your throat torn out.

Down there in the dark.

Shuddering, he was on the verge of going over there to shut him the hell up already, when he realised the song had stopped – and that the Bard was surrounded by a group of some twenty slightly wide-eyed people, all of them glancing about them, at him and at one another.

Ecko slipped forwards, cloak covering him, until he could see clearly.

The Bard put his hood back, to a ripple of gasps.

And they knew him; of course they knew him. The Wanderer was legend – one of those bucket list thingies that everyone'd probably wanted to do at least once. A whisper of bemusement rose from the small crowd, and a whisper of hope. One of them called out, "Where is it? Where's the tavern?" and the others took up the cry – need and desperation. Like they wanted the amazing teleporting cab ride to get them the hell outta there – and who could blame them?

"Fhae, Jharath." Roderick greeted the people by name. "The Wanderer, like Fhaveon, is no more." Cries answered him, and for a moment he lowered his face, raised his hands as if to hold them back. Ecko could see his expression was clouded, a look that almost resembled out-of-his-depth panic – like he had all these fantastic new toys, but no real idea how to use them, or what they did.

Another memory flash – the streets and rooftops of London, like some fucking newborn superhero, all klutz-like because the radioactivity had just kicked in and he didn't know what his super-powers did yet...

The Bard raised his jaw and his face was cold, carved in

determination. As the people pressed closer, demanding that he save them, he raised his hands again. He was searching for the trigger, the on-switch, for the whatever-the-hell was supposed to conjure the vocal magick...

But the people were close now; curiosity was shifting to aggravation, aggression. Ecko knew enough about crowds to feel the mood change. One last look at the Bard, and he realised they had a mini-mob on their hands who were about to take out every bit of frustration—

"Where's the tavern?"

"Why can't you tell us?"

"What the rhez is going on?"

"Where the hell d'you think it is?" The savage rasp of Ecko's question cut the morning like a serrated blade. People spun, hands going for belt-blades. "Chrissakes, Phylos tore it down, stone by stone, brick by brick, Yth-whatserface blew the shit out of it. Does it matter?" His challenge – such a contrast to the molasses charm of Roderick's tone – slapped the crowd into wakefulness and they glanced at one another, unsure. "Chrissakes, the tavern's a goner, an' unless you lot listen the fuck up, you're gonna go straight after it. Remember all those beasties? Runnin' round, tearing the heads off of your mates? Well they like it here so much, they're comin' straight the fuck back – so you lot get your shit together if you wanna keep your assholes intact."

The comment was pointed – and not at the crowd.

He felt, rather than saw, the Bard shake himself, stand taller. His eyes caught Ecko's, just for a moment, with a flash of humour – like the man he had been.

Then he started to speak.

His voice was as layered as his throat, a wealth of richness and influence and subtlety that Ecko's ears couldn't even hear. It compelled and fascinated him, it made him strain to hear more – even as his own brain berated him for being an asshole.

What the Bard even said Ecko couldn't afterwards remember, but he could remember the paean, the call, the ray of hope that slanted through the city's streets like the long gleam of the rising sun. He could remember that more people came, and that more people came. He could remember that the Bard was like fucking Santa Claus or something – he knew them all, every one by name. And then they walked, speaking and singing and calling to one another, in something that wasn't exactly a procession and wasn't exactly a march, but seemed to be somewhere between the two. And twenty became forty, and forty became eighty, and eighty became a crowd, a flood of people from the broken city, all following as the Bard's voice led. Some of them were soldiers, he thought, or freemen, bearing their arms with them. They moved upwards along the ruin of the great zigzagging road, more people emerging to join the song that called to them.

Even Ecko himself, his own bitterness buried far, far too deep for him to ever access consciously, found tears in his eyes as the song hit a sudden, powerful rhythm. The people were all singing together, a courage and defiance like nothing he'd ever heard. He bit his lip, furious with himself – what the *fucking* hell was happening to him? – but the Bard showed no emotion, only the pure call of the song that led them, roadway by roadway, all the way to Amethea and the high walls of the Great Cathedral, to the last of the crates being loaded through its doors.

It was their last refuge – the only safety the city could offer them.

Banked for the night, the fire had dwindled to a wine-red glow.

His pale skin smouldering sullen in the half-light, Rhan looked at his companions. Both wore clouded expressions.

"You'll stand with me on this," he said, arms folded.

Neither warrior nor scribe looked up.

In Garland House's huge kitchen, the air was chill with the early dawn. Rhan had left the chair that Phylos had placed by the fireside, though more for potential firewood than as a place to sit. To one side of the huge stone setting, Mael stood cleaning his glasses, a dark and troubled wraith in the poor light. He didn't meet Rhan's eyes. To the other was Mostak. He glanced up sharply, his gaze flickering scarlet.

"If you're wrong, Seneschal, then I'll have your head." The warrior's voice held blades.

"If I'm wrong, Commander," Rhan said, "I'll give it to you." In response to the threat, his honesty was savage.

Mostak's foot tapped a sceptical tattoo, more eloquent than any vocal response.

Rhan watched him, trying to measure what the man was thinking. He realised so much of this rested on the shoulders of the Tan Commander – on his trust, on his ability to support and carry out the strategy that Nivrotar had proposed.

Mostak snorted, pointed a rigid finger. "I should slit your damned throat now and be done with it. What Amos is suggesting is treachery. Worse."

Mael nodded, but said nothing. His face flickered with unvoiced fears.

Rhan picked up the white feather that had been laid on the mantel, spun it through his fingers. "Do you trust me?"

"Maybe you did murder my brother, you conniving old bastard. Maybe you are the damned daemon. Maybe you have been all along—"

"Maybe Samiel will manifest in person and we won't have to deal with any of this." Rhan brandished the feather, his sarcasm blistering. "Maybe I'm right – Nivrotar's right – and we need to do this, whatever the cost." White softness glowed red in the fading firelight. "Gods know this is crazed beyond words. There is an *army* on our border. And if Vahl is where I think he is, then we've got only one course of action... and it's against everything I am, everything I was charged to hold, the family I've protected, the babes I've watched grow – you and your brother among them." He looked from face to face. "But if we don't do this, then it's every head that'll be lost. Mine. Yours. And Selana's too. I just hope you live long enough to watch me fully and finally damned."

He let the feather go, into the smouldering fireplace. It hovered for a moment, the heat bearing it up, then it flashed into vicious flame and was gone.

Watching it, Rhan remembered the little priestess, the girl who had shown him his lifelong selfishness, his refusal to care about the rest of the world.

Survival.

Mostak held his gaze for a long moment, the small man wound tight as terhnwood fibre. His resemblance to his brother was uncanny, unnerving. Rhan willed him silently, *Whatever is past, you must trust me.*

After a moment, the Commander grunted and turned back to the fire, the gesture somehow approving, but also giving no ground.

Mael said softly, "You know I can't condone this. She's become... like my daughter. What you're suggesting is—"

"You have a better idea, Merchant Master?" Rhan rounded on him, merciless. "Her nights get worse – nightmares live in her skin. You've seen this for yourself. Will you tell me I'm wrong?"

"She's a *child*, Rhan." The old man frowned. "You talk of babes – she's the last of her line, you're sworn to her protection and she's never even had her chance. How do you know Vahl's in there – how do you know he isn't in me, here, now? Or in the Tan Commander?"

With a faint and humourless chuckle, Rhan touched his fingertips to the old scribe's arm, felt him shiver. "There's no touch of Vahl in you, Merchant Master – I'd have known."

And I'm nothing *like my brother.*

Mael withdrew his arm like he'd been stung.

"And Mostak? I'm not sure even Vahl would dare." Rhan's sharp comment was only half in humour. He looked from one man to the other. "Look, I understand what I'm asking is beyond redemption or reason or forgiveness, but I need you with me, both of you." He faltered, kept going. "The Bard's new strength is… outrageous. And before I can lure my brother and his army across the plains, I need to call him out."

Mostak nodded, though without surrender – he had calculated the odds as a warrior. "I hear you."

But Mael's face was lined with sorrow, and he said nothing.

Mostak said, "We'll need to time this carefully, Seneschal – all of this. Once Vahl is loosed, we'll need to ensure that he brings that army directly after us – that he doesn't make *side* trips." His voice was vitriol.

"Nivrotar's right about one thing – he'll come after me," Rhan said. "I've beaten him once and he'll want to tear it out of my hide – when he can catch me. We just have to make sure he catches me – us – in the right place."

"That might be harder than it sounds," Mael said softly. "We're deserting the city completely. It means we'll have no supply lines – we'll be taking everything we need with us." He settled his glasses on his nose, rubbed at an old ink stain on a finger. "We'll be slow."

"Not that slow," Rhan said. "Our supply lines can stretch to Amos – they'll be ahead of us, not behind, and as we get closer, they'll get stronger. When we arrive, Nivrotar will be waiting for us."

"One last question," Mael said. "What about the Cathedral? Are we hoping… what… that Samiel will step in and help?" The old scribe blinked at Rhan in a faintly sarcastic fashion.

"You might be," Rhan answered him, with a hint of a grin. "Gorinel's agreed, he's taking the people, and all the supplies we can spare – he's got enough down there to stand a siege and those damned catacombs go on 'til the end of the Count of Time. All the way to Swathe, or so I'm told. He's a practical man, he'll manage – and he'll also have help."

Mael settled his glasses back on his nose and peered through them, his old eyes as sharp as arrow-points. "Help?"

"You're staying with him, Brother. You're in no physical shape to be crossing half the Northern Varchinde in an orderly military panic, chased by monsters. You and Amethea both – I need you to stay with the city."

Mael said nothing; Mostak nodded.

Rhan looked from scribe to warrior.

"Then we agree: let the final war begin."

PART 2: WAR

11: THE DECISIONS OF LARRED JADE ROVIARATH

Larred Jade was restless.

Since the fall of the Monument, the Warden of Roviarath had been haunted by the loitering guilt-tails of the things he should have done – things that may have saved the Monument itself, and spared him the yawning canker that swelled upon his border. Anxious, unable to sleep, unwilling to eat, he'd taken to wandering the wide streets of his troubled and overstuffed city, hooded against the eyes of her people.

He watched, and he tried to understand.

Roviarath was a wealthy city – or so she'd always been. With her central location and the Great Fayre wrapped about two-thirds of her wall, her trade had been assured, and her people well fed and comfortable. If her City Warden was canny, he could watch the rise and fall of her controlling merchants, play them one against another, and ensure that none became too powerful – lest the complex wheels of the trade-cycle unbalance for good.

But that trade-cycle was gone now, kicked to bloody pieces and lost in the winter's mud. The critical supply of terhnwood had dwindled, the responding loads of wood and stone no longer reached the city's walls, and the Fayre was a scattered and skeletal ruin, combed clean of debris. The merchants that remained had seen their livelihoods ruined and now they squabbled for pieces, or vanished beneath the seething struggles of their fellows.

Jade needed to know what had happened to them – information that would not reach his halls without help.

And so, he walked.

This evening the cold was bitter but the streets were busy, layered with noise and signs and stalls. Overhead balconies were hung with flags and colour, and the dusk light made them shimmer like desperation. There was a throng of people still out here, people moved by need, outcast from the Fayre or come in from the farmlands and trade-roads, seeking answers the city could not offer. Many were homeless, or hopeless; they'd taken up begging and panhandling, turned to trickery and thieving – anything to secure trade-goods and a roof for the night. Others had struggled to set up new livelihoods, and had been swallowed by the morass.

The blight had not reached Roviarath, but she had still become a jumble, her streets streaked with want and worry.

Jade walked, watching.

Even in the fading half-light, he could see the tension that swelled beneath the haphazard trading. His soldiers were prowling, wary. There was no outright violence, not yet, but the city was writhing with an excess of manipulations – underhanded pressures, intimidations and demands – an ebb and flow of street-strength that had little to do with the Warden himself.

He had to control it, and he wasn't sure how.

As the dusk slowly thickened into darkness, Jade's mind turned his choices as a chearl turns a stone millwheel.

Methodically, and in circles.

Nivrotar had called him to muster, to cross the winter Varchinde to a battle-site semi-legend, there to face an impossibility. Larred was a merchant, he could tally odds – Nivrotar's summons contained the weight of the Varchinde entire.

Though Phylos had failed at the last, Fhaveon was in ruins and the plains in chaos. If Nivrotar was right, and the Kas really rose, they would all die.

If.

Nivrotar's message was an assumption. It had said *when*.

But Larred had failed once before – he hadn't listened when Ress and Triqueta had first come to him. Now, he could see the full tale and he understood the Lord of Amos's ploy – but his people were huddled and scrabbling for what they could hold... he could no more leave them than he could gouge out his own heart.

Over him, the sky was dark now, clouded and rain scattering. Though he could not see the lighthouse itself, the white shine from the tower still proclaimed hope; somewhere the moons shone brilliant.

So many times, he'd wished that he'd listened – so many times. But Jade was a practical man, and though the regret taunted him he channelled and managed it, used its energy to seek solutions.

Ahead of him the streets narrowed, their stones smooth or carven with leafed faces. The buildings were taller, their roofs pointed hard against the sky. In stripes of shadow, layers of balconies lined the roadway; walkways stretched from one side of the street to the other. The street was hung with lanterns, though their rocklights were long gone.

What...?

With an odd shiver, he paused. He could hear the shouts of the street-bazaar, trading even in the darkness, the hooves and the arrival of the Banned. Following an odd impulse, he found himself looking to both sides of the main thoroughfare – at side streets heavily shadowed, bereft of market stalls, and silent as the plains' cooling corpse.

His heart pounded, though he'd no idea why. Jade stopped. Listened harder.

And then, a distance away but coming closer by the moment, he heard running.

Fast running.

It was upon him more swiftly than he realised – it was right *there* at the end of the side street. It was the sound of panic, more feet racing after. Shouting, raw and distinctive. Jade glanced back down the roadway, then ducked in close to the wall – ahead of him, at the end of the street where the lighthouse shone free on an open plaza, he thought he saw movement, a flicker of fear.

He held his breath.

A moment later the flicker came again, then a long shadow, stretching down the roadway. The figure paused, the walkways dark over him, the curving balconies layered with light. It waited for a moment, the pursuing feet coming ever closer, then it turned and ran down the road towards where Jade waited, its long shadow running with it.

The pursuers rushed, scrabbling.

Jade could hear voices, though he couldn't make out what they said.

Then, at the far end of the road, more shadows as the other runners paused, searching.

Pulling back as far as he could, hand on his belt-blade, Jade waited.

Close now, the fleeing figure slowed, looked back over its shoulder. It stumbled, tripped and fell headlong, swearing as it went down on its elbows on the stone. As it – he – picked himself up, he paused, leaning over to draw huge gulps of air. Jade wondered how long the man had been running for.

At the far end of the road, the others were laughing, coming forwards now with slower steps; confident, as if their prey was caught.

The runner stood upright, brushing dirt from crumpled street-clothes. With an inhalation that sounded like resolve, he turned to face his pursuers.

Now, Jade was curious – by the rhez, he was almost *avid*. The road was not a dead end, there was an angled laneway between the back buildings that would take a walker through a series of cobbled archways and eventually out to the riverside. It was a maze, but navigable if you knew it and an ideal place for losing pursuers.

But the runner crossed his arms as if he didn't know it was there.

Or as if...

Almost without thinking, the CityWarden glanced at the half-dark walkways over his head, the lanterns like shuttered eyes – some open, some closed.

Oh, you clever bastard.

Jade realised he was endangered – but he couldn't have moved, even if he'd been able to leave without the man seeing him.

There was no way he was going to miss what was coming next.

The pursuers advanced down the street, jaunty and mocking. "You can't run any further, Roken. We'll just chase you 'til you can't breathe. Then you'll be swinging free."

Roken. Jade knew the name – a roustabout, a troublemaker, one of the smarter thugs of the Great Fayre. A man of some influence, if he remembered it right.

Silent, he watched.

Roken's breathing was easing. He was stood in the middle of the roadway, the criss-cross of walkways like some great black sigil over his head. Watching the incoming goons, he said nothing.

His pursuers came on, laughing at him. "You're done, sunshine. We're everywhere – streets, alleys, roofs. We've taken it, Roken, the manors bring their stuff to us now. We got the food, we got the grass harvest, we say what goes. Jade's finished, he's got no damned clue what goes on out there. You too – no more street wars."

"Come on, then." Roken's voice was less a challenge and more a wheeze. "If the city's yours... you come and prove it."

We got the food, we got the grass harvest.

Jade's finished, he's got no clue...

Really.

Every word made Jade's skin sing, his blood roar in his ears. There had been an inevitability to the Fayre's scuffling factions moving into the city – but for them to have mustered this much influence and intimidation, this swiftly...

No more street wars.

...He wondered what the rhez he was going to do about it.

Then, as he watched the attackers come closer, Jade found there was an idea taking shape in the back of his head – an idea that made him tremble with sudden excitement. Breathing steadily, he tried to build it carefully, to observe it from all sides to ensure that it would work.

It was crazed, but it might – *might just*! – be the solution he needed.

Briefly, he wished that Syke was here – the Banned commander was streetwise and shrewd and would be a far better person to execute this madness – but Jade was alone, and he would have to manage.

He was almost shivering, his palms slick and his skin sheened in sweat. The CityWarden of Roviarath let out a long, steadying breath, as silently as he could, and he waited.

The pursuers approached with weapons bared, their resin blades gleaming with the light of the tower behind. As they passed under the first of the walkways, Jade felt himself tense – but nothing happened.

Sudden fear spiked cold.

By the rhez, what if I'm wrong? What if...?

Roken stood still, his head down. His empty hands were scratched where he'd fallen; he looked abject and beaten.

What if...?

"We'll hang you from the walkways, Roken. A final message – anyone else who tries to take us, they'll see it and learn. No more trading 'less we say so; we're like Roviarath's own cartel." The grin was audible. "You'll be the last warning – the streets are *ours*."

Three, four, five of them neared; others loitered further back. As they closed on Roken, they fanned out across the street. Jade saw loops of rope in someone's hand.

You'll be the last warning.

Perhaps not quite the last, Jade thought. *If I've got this wrong, they'll be stringing me straight up alongside the thug lord.*

But Roken said, soft as a breath, "Come on then. Come and put me out of business, you bastards. Come and use me as a damned message."

The pursuers took the last two steps to reach their target.

The clouds broke for streams of moonlight, and the walkways exploded with violence.

The fighting was brief, and ugly.

Jade made no attempt to move, not when a gagging youth stumbled to a dying halt at his feet, his hands scrabbling for the blade thrust sideways through his throat; not when Roken took the noose that had been meant for his own neck and strung his lead pursuer up with it, watching as the man's feet kicked until he died.

Hidden by his cloak and cowl, and by the shadow of the balcony above him, Jade watched as Roken's defenders walked among the wounded, silently slitting throats and emptying pouches, watched as the golden moon came fully into view at the far end of the street, decorating the roadway in slants and hummocks of shadow.

As Roken clasped wrists with his closest warriors, slapped

them on the back, Jade did probably the second most crazed thing he'd ever done in his entire life.

He stepped out into the yellow blaze of the moonlight.

"Roken." His voice was clear; he raised his hands to his cowl and revealed his face.

People tensed, spun. Several faces were blank – they'd never seen the CityWarden close-up before – but enough of them came forwards, hands on weapons, or turned, looking for the tans of soldiers, the incoming Banned.

Roken himself was an older man, lean-jawed and clean-shaven. He bore a series of what looked like Kartian scars down one side of his face, a heavy white stone upon a thong around his throat. He raised an eyebrow at Jade, checked both ways down the street, and held up a hand to stop the incoming threats.

"CityWarden," Roken said. He spat to one side, a gesture more thoughtful than insulting. As his face turned, Jade could see that his Kartian scarring was clumsy – it lacked the intricate perfection of the race and looked almost self-inflicted. "Evening stroll?"

"Insomnia." Jade gave an affable shrug. He refused to be cowed; he met the man's gaze with a faint grin. "You know how it is."

"You been hanging with the Banned too long." Roken's response got chuckles. "Drinking that rotgut'll keep you up 'til the end of the Count of Time." His grin showed teeth brown and stained. "Alone, are you?"

"Absolutely," Jade said. "Alone, and no one knows I'm here." He spread his hands, his cloak parting to reveal the belt-blade still sheathed. "I came to speak to you. About... business."

Roken's goons glanced back and forth. They were unsettled by his confidence, which made Jade feel a whole lot better. Roken scratched his scars.

"No business here, CityWarden. The Fayre's all clean now. Nice job."

Tense now, Roken wasn't stupid – he'd been loitering in the Fayre and the city for long enough to know the playing field.

"The Fayre's moving, Roken, changing. It needs guides and leaders, men and women who know the... ah... ropes." He glanced briefly at the swinging corpse, grinned. "It needs cool heads and sharp ones. I didn't come out here to play games, I came out here with an opportunity – and one I'm not going to offer twice."

"Nice night for a stroll," Roken said. He spat again, a brown stream of fluid. "Will they miss you if you're *late*?" He stepped forwards, his breath steaming, the sweat-stink strong in the cold night.

"Maybe." Jade nodded, calm as he could manage. "You might take the ground, Roken, but have you the force to hold it?" The question was measured, easy. "The goods to supply it, the eyes to watch it, the skills to keep it operational? Running wagons out of the Great Fayre is one thing – but this is Roviarath herself, and she works slightly differently."

Roken said nothing – he watched the CityWarden through eyes narrowed, smart enough to wait.

Jade shrugged, went on, "Let's say we have food enough to feed the people, if we're careful. Let's say that I have all of the terhnwood that the city has remaining. Let's say that I have a fighting force that could almost be described as 'veteran', though that might be stretching a point. Let's say that I need my city safe, that I need to secure her streets against rising levels of chaos. Let's say—"

"Let's say I slit your throat or take you hostage," Roken said, conversationally. "You know, as we're playing the theory game."

Jade belly laughed, deep and genuine. "And who do you think will take command of the city if you do?"

His answer caused muttering and sniggers from Roken's hovering heavies. Roken gave a slow nod.

"You're a smart trader, Jade, we've always known that.

You come out here to deal – I can deal. What do you want for your terhnwood?"

"You. Your people. Your eyes and ears and hands and feet. Your streets. Your safe houses and your bazaar stalls and whatever stock you're holding. Your confidence. In return, I'll give you terhnwood. You'll get the weight of the city behind you. You want to stitch this up, Roken – I'll give you the needle. But you'll use it where I say."

For a long moment, Roken looked at him. The gold moon touched the scarred side of his face with an odd dapple of light and shadow. Then, slowly, the man nodded, seething the brown goo between his teeth.

"One thing."

Jade raised an eyebrow. "Only one?"

"A clean break – anything that's happened before now gets written off. Whatever I've done, wherever you find it, from here in – I'm clean."

Jade eyed the scars for a moment. He had an idea he knew where they'd come from – but that was so much public rumour, something that had never been proven – then he looked the lean man back in his face.

He held out his hand, they gripped wrists.

And Jade wondered, somewhere there in the moonlit dark, if he'd lost his damned mind completely.

"You've lost your damned mind completely!" Syke told him, hands on hips like a scolding aunt. "Roken's a slaver – where d'you think 'e got those scars? Made his name tradin' flesh – and not 'ow you'd think. And you've just promoted him to goon-in-charge? How you planning on makin' *that* work?"

The warm wooden hall of the Warden seemed to shudder with Syke's sarcasm. Outside, the morning sun was pure and brilliant, lighting the windows to a bright-white dazzle of mica.

"I'm not," Jade replied, grinning like a fiend. "You are." He'd not slept – been too overwhelmed and excited and terrified by the deal he'd just pulled. Beside him, his breakfast and herbal were going cold.

Syke said, "You're *shitting* me."

But Jade was after him like a bweao. "Syke, I need you with this. I can spin logistics, juggle numbers, ensure the right things reach the right places – but I need you to watch him, play his game and bring him onside. You need to make that handclasp a guarantee. He's a greedy little shit and we can't trust him as far as I can spit. You need to make him play nice."

Triqueta helped herself to Jade's leather mug. She looked over its rim at the CityWarden as if he were two panniers short of a travelpack.

"You've gone loco," she said.

"Possibly," Larred said. He grinned at her, his expression like the sun coming up, and the lines round his eyes creased with mischief. "But I've been thinking this round in circles ever since we had Nivrotar's message – how I can muster and still watch the city? – and I think I've damned well solved it."

"You think *I've* solved it," Syke commented darkly.

Jade chuckled. Outside, a flurry of birds rose from the building's eaves, settled again. The CityWarden paced his wooden floor like a man possessed, his mind turning over and over with the new possibilities.

Triqueta drained the herbal, pulled one of her scrrated blades and inspected the tip. As she carefully began to clean under her nails, Jade stopped his fidgeting and met Syke's flat, grey gaze.

His unspoken challenge.

"Look, I can play figurehead," Jade said. "If I'm going to hold this together, the people need to know I'm still here. But I need—"

"You need someone to do the shit you can't." Syke picked up the mug that Triqueta had discarded, ruefully inspected its emptiness, and put it down again. "Kick arse where your boots can't go. An' Roken in control of the streets—"

"Means I want you in control of Roken," Jade said. He jabbed a finger at the sunlit window. "And if the city's out there fighting some damned war, it needs secure supply lines. No gambles, no mistakes." His expression was intense, thinking. "We can't get this wrong."

"I hate to piss on your parade," Triqueta said. "But you've missed something."

Jade raised an eyebrow.

"If you're sending the city to war, you need a commander," Triqueta said. "Not just some goon from the garrison, but someone with experience who knows this stuff nose-to-tail, who can win not only a fight, but a battle. Strategise. And you know Taure can't keep his nose out the ale jug—"

"I know exactly who's taking command," Jade told her. "Can't think of anyone better."

Syke chuckled, catching something that Triqueta had missed. She folded her arms and glared at the pair of them.

"Share the jest?"

"No jest," Jade said, spreading his hands. Syke was grinning like a loon.

Triqueta tapped her foot, raised an eyebrow. "So go on, who gets the short straw?"

"You, Triq," Jade said, his grin as wide as his ears. "See yourself promoted, Tan Commander. You're taking Roviarath to war."

Triqueta said, with some feeling, "Shit."

12: FOUNDERSDAUGHTER FHAVEON

And then the time came when the talk was over, when the strategy was complete and the city's final moments were before them.

When they could stall no longer.

Rhan stood on the balcony of the Palace, the sky before him as grey and cold as drifting ash. He was sheltered by the window, a pace back from the edge – as if reluctant to take that last step into inevitability, to begin the end.

Down below, glimpsed through the balcony's shaped stone supports, lay the city's heart, the open square once as familiar as the backs of his hands. A place of festivity, ceremony – a celebration of the city's life and history. But its elaborate mosaic was shattered now, melted and blurred – just as if Vahl himself had been thrown down upon that very spot. Just as if a war had been won there.

Or lost there.

Immortal or not, Rhan felt sick.

Below him, standing silent about the mosaic's remains and looking like some final jest of the Gods, was Mostak's mustered soldiery, the remnant of House Valiembor's might. Roderick had brought them, as he had brought the people, their ranks and lamellar armour ragged, ruinous like the city herself.

Some of the units were missing completely; others were represented by a lone man or woman, standard in hand as if they were the last fighter in the world. Some bore injuries, many untreated. Most had dirty, ill-fitting kit, though some had repaired and cleansed in an act of pure defiance, and stood with chins raised, their pride puffed like dust.

It was a brave attempt – but by the Gods, it was a mess.

Rhan swallowed, blinking.

So many times, he'd watched their drill – precision and polish, demonstrations to illustrate the city's hegemony, performances to honour House Valiembor, or visiting guests, or days given to harvesting or feasting. Combat tourneys and range patrols and parades and decorations...

He swallowed again, and counted them.

He knew full well what the tally should be – nine warriors to a tan, nine tan to a flag – at last muster, there had been thirty-four flags, eleven of them cavalry. Plus fifteen flags of archers, seven on foot and eight mounted; the latter swift and light-armoured to skirmish, flank and bear messages. In all, some four thousand warriors. A tiny number for a land area the size of the Varchinde, but after four hundred years of peace, why would they need any more? They drilled to perfection, trained endlessly, and earned their pennons by winning games and chasing pirates.

Down below, their standards should have been flaring as the morning breeze caught them – pride and colour.

Instead, the mosaic's dust stirred, mocking. The flags themselves – the battle-standards of each unit – flickered and failed.

Almost two thirds of the force was missing.

We can't do this, we can't...!

He caught himself. Stood firm, looking at the soldiers below.

Many, mostly the conscripts from surrounding farms and families, had simply deserted. Others had been garrisoned at the

Varchinde's cities and had never returned. The heavier cavalry had mostly gone with Ythalla; Ecko's scouting had put their number at seven or eight flags. What remained were mostly skirmishers, both foot and horse, and the older rank and file of spearmen, perhaps those with the experience to have served as range patrol, or with the age to have learned the meaning of loyalty.

What Rhan could see was not an army. It had no artillery and very little horse, and much of its allegiance was carried on the immediate winds of pure and vocal charm.

Thank the Gods, Rhan thought, that he was not actually in command.

Tan Commander Mostak faced his mustered force.

His back was to Rhan, to the Palace and the balcony. He stood rigid, seeming to burn with vehemence in the cold air, as though he could make his warriors follow him by sheer force of will. With him was his command unit – herald, drummer, flag bearer, personal guard – all of them in laminated terhnwood and bearing the Valiembor sigil.

Only Mostak's own armour was different. It was older in styling, had belonged to the First Lord Foundersson Tekissari, and it was ever so slightly too big for him. The irony of *that* realisation had not been lost on anyone.

This is all madness, Seneschal. Mostak's last words to Rhan had been like a warning, a barbed reminder of what he'd once said in the Council. *You and that damned storyteller...*

But Mostak, perhaps even more so than Rhan, understood Nivrotar's strategy, and the necessity of the gamble they played.

Whatever it was going to cost them.

Over the ramshackle force, a glint of sunlight penetrated the heavy clouds. It caught the tips of a thousand upright terhnwood spears, flaring them to life like torches. Like hope.

Rhan caught his breath, the thought coalescing out of the light...

Calarinde, Lady...

But the Gods were not listening.

Am I the daemon, Rhan?

Below him, Mostak raised a hand. His voice cracked, sharp and echoing, "Listen up... *Stand!*"

The scruff of assembled tan came to upright stance with a single, unified click.

Their discipline eased Rhan's breathing, allowed him to uncurl somewhat, somehow giving him confidence in this whole crazed undertaking.

Then, from behind him, came Brother Mael's voice. "Please don't do this."

Not taking his gaze from the force below, Rhan said, "Did you leave any horses?"

Mael gave a short sigh. "No horses or chearl left in the city – other than with Ythalla. You can herd what you can't ride; they're tacked up for portage. Well, most of them." He gave an odd, sad smile. "We've been through the records, everything Scythe told us – we think we've tracked all of Phylos's remaining hoardings. If you can't carry it, and the Cathedral can't take it, it's gone up in flames."

Flames.

Then there's really nothing left.

The thought almost made him stagger. *Nothing left.* Then he took a breath and said the words he hadn't wanted to say, the final tolling of the city's death bell. "Then please bring my Lord Selana to the balcony. When this is done..." He swallowed, grief and complex dishonesty. "She should be free. We should all be free."

Free.

The word was bitter, a slap to the cheek like an insult. Mael watched him for a minute in a final plea, begging him to relent, but Rhan said nothing.

The old scribe slumped, shaking his head, and turned away.

Rhan returned to the shattered mosaic, to the shadow in his own thoughts. *Four hundred returns, my estavah, and I yield my family, and my city. But victorious though you might be, you know you don't dare let me live.*

Come and get me. Come and get me and tear me to pieces.

As if the Gods bore witness, the great drum in the Cathedral tower began to thunder, the sound defiant. Rhan couldn't remember the last time he'd heard it. At the edge of the mosaic the building's great doors stood open – he could see Gorinel, and with him the slight form of Amethea. They'd taken what was left of the city's populace into the depths of the building's crypts, taken the last few helpers at the hospice and whatever supplies had not been loaded or burned. Leaving the people here was a risk, but a necessary one – the fighters had to have speed.

He'll come straight after me, Rhan had said to the old priest. *Chasing you through the catacombs could take cycles – he hasn't got enough trained forces to spare. Once the city's quiet, perhaps you can come out...*

Perhaps.

The drum boomed, like a dare. And now, Rhan had one last thing to do, one last manoeuvre before his abandonment of his city was complete...

Mael came back onto the balcony, Valicia at his side.

And with them was Selana Valiembor, last Lord of Fhaveon.

The sight of the girl, haunted and shadow-eyed, nearly made Rhan's knees fold. He wanted to speak to her, to beg her exoneration, but he had no words for what he was about to do.

She was pale, her face dark with figments. Her eyes jumped from place to place; she shrank from Rhan as though he'd slapped her. Mael held her upright, his hands gentle. He'd removed his glasses as if his old face fought not to crumple round them.

Finding his last reserves of courage, Rhan gestured at the balcony.

"You should speak, my Lord. The city awaits your voice."

The Cathedral's drum stopped, the silence was huge.

Selana raised her head, blinked at him. There were marks on her skin, like scars. Perhaps he was imagining them?

"Speak?" she asked. "Why... why didn't you say...?"

Her voice was soft, afraid. Rhan's heart began to tremble – maybe he *was* wrong, maybe she *was* just the young Lord of the city, maybe this mad endeavour would all end right here—

"I told you, my Lord, your final speech," he said. "Make it a good one."

Baffled, she turned to the balcony, to the warriors gathered below. The sun had risen further now and the mosaic glittered with the cold winter, its broken edges shattering the rising light. The horses were restive, shaking their heads against the terhnwood brackets that held the soft corners of their mouths, thumping wide, splayed hooves against the tiles. Their tack rattled and their breath steamed. The wind had risen, and the pennons on the spear-points were flapping now, agitated, the larger flags stirring to life. Mostak's drummer sounded a blood-pulse tattoo, and silenced.

The sound, like the light, reflected in pieces from the walls.

Selana stepped forward, faltered, looked back. Rhan nodded, encouraging her, found he was holding his breath. *Don't let this be for nothing.* A formless prayer, desperate.

Mael's face was etched in pain.

"I..." She cleared her throat. "My... my people, people of Fhaveon!" Her voice was tiny in the morning air. "Heed me! Our final..." She stopped, started again, "Our final dawning is upon us!"

And a rich, dark voice in the shadows said, "Do you know what you're doing?"

* * *

Rhan remembered.

A young man, Tundran and slender and burning with idealism, a starry-eyed fanatic who was going to change the world. The first Guardian born in Avesyr in numberless hundreds of returns, heralded as a hero, the saviour of his world and his people. He'd had a vision, he'd said, the Gods had spoken to him. He'd touched the very waters of the Ryll and the world's thoughts had been shown to him, her greatest foe and fear...

Rhan had chuckled at the upstart's presumption, fed him a goblet of the Cellen, and told him to calm the rhez down.

How many returns? Eighty? Ninety? Tundrans had a longer lifespan than Grassdwellers. Taught he was extraordinary in his earliest youth, Roderick had carried that conviction all down his returns. Beyond sanity, beyond the Ryll, beyond The Wanderer. Misguided arrogance or genuine vision, it had given him a sense of pure purpose that Rhan had always envied.

His own long returns had bled one into another like mud in water, become vague and pointless until he'd lost them and forgotten them...

Like he'd lost lovers, friends, family.

Stood beside him now, that starry-eyed youth was cold and savage, brutalised, damaged beyond all redemption – Samiel's teeth, perhaps he'd lost even more than Rhan had done. Yet his conviction burned within him still, tempered now, lethal, as cold as the waters of the Ryll itself, as the cutting-ice air of the Khavan Circle.

The Final Guardian.

The only one of his people remaining.

The man who'd been Roderick the Bard met Rhan's eyes. For just a moment there was that shock of old recognition, so many returns of friendship – he was the Bard still, no matter what had been done to him – and then the moment was gone and the stranger with the metal throat turned away.

Mael was crying, a silent run of tears.

Rhan felt like joining him, wanted the comfort – but Selana was finding her voice now, talking to the people below.

"My friends – people of Fhaveon! This is a moment of history, a moment the Count of Time himself will hold to his heart. This is a moment my mothers, my fathers, never believed would come – but a moment in which we can take solace. We are not defeated, warriors, ladies, gentlemen – we still stand proud!"

The soldiers stood silent, watching her. In the Cathedral doorway, people surrounded Gorinel and Amethea, come to see the sunlight for the last time.

Rhan swallowed. *I've got this wrong... oh Gods, I've got this wrong! What've I done?*

He watched Selana, watched her face, her lips, the expression in her eyes.

Come on, show me, tell me I'm right... Tell me this isn't for nothing!

But her voice was alight with love, her expression fervent. "This is the stone that was wrought by my forebears, by the hand of Saluvarith himself! This rock where we stand is immortal, and it cannot be defeated – not by man, and not by monster! As Tekissari once fought to defend Fhaveon, so we will return, my friends, my people – we will come back here with our blades aloft and our hearts afire, and we will take it *back*!"

Mostak's drummer had begun again, his bass thump soft like the shivering rise of adrenaline. Mostak himself stood like a statue, as hard as the stone face of Rakanne herself, unwilling or unable to turn and look at the balcony.

And then Rhan heard the Bard.

"*E Vahl Khavaghakke. E Vahl Sashar, yaedhkka, khava. Khavaghakke.*"

The words were Tundran, cracking like ice. It was an older language than that of the Varchinde; Rhan knew "*Khava*" as a greeting, or a calling, but that was all.

He shivered.

He had no idea if Roderick's newfound vocal strength was powerful enough for this. The Art of Summoning was primal, unused, mostly forgotten – something for fireside tales, not for the balcony of the Palace itself. But the Bard knew enough of the wording, and now had the strength to use it...

Rhan saw Selana shudder. He saw Valicia, her mother, start forwards, her hands to her mouth. He saw Mael turn away, shaking his head as if to free himself of all of this...

And then he saw the surge of ink through the young woman's skin, the power pulse from her shoulders, rising like heat, blistering.

They were right.

By the Gods, Vahl was really in there!

Relief raged and the drum throbbed again, brief like a heartbeat; the sun gleamed from lines of lamellar armour as the ranks of warriors stood watching.

Selana trembled, teeth bared. She stood with her hands on the balcony's edge, ink and heat and rage and power. She shuddered, cried out.

The Bard's voice was thundering now, undeniable. "*E Vahl Khavaghakke. E Vahl Sashar, yaedhkka, khava. Khavaghakke.*" He stood like a streak of darkness, his face concealed, his words a pulse, a demand.

It called to Rhan too, to something dark in his very soul. It pulled at him, hurting, but he strove to ignore it.

The air twisted, struggled.

The girl's face contorted, light and shadow, pain and terror and savage eagerness. Vahl's presence burned. He was in there, Rhan could *see* his brother's expression.

"*E Vahl Khavaghakke!*" Roderick was calling to the concealed creature, pulling him forth, daring him. And if it was hurting Rhan...

Selana spasmed. She started to turn to her protectors, asking them for help, for understanding. The look was the last one she ever gave, and it would haunt Rhan for the rest of his days.

"*E Vahl—*"

And everything happened at once.

Her skin tore, ragged and bloody rips in her face and arms. Steam poured from her, rose like morning mist. Valicia screamed, ran to her daughter, but Selana, laughing, backhanded her mother hard enough to stretch her on the stone floor.

She didn't move again.

Vahl threw the game down, and he laughed though Selana's mouth. His voice held that same double layer that had been heard in Phylos. It laughed at Roderick and his summoning, at Rhan and his horror, at Mael and his grief.

You've got me, it seemed to say to them, *so what are going to do with me?*

Below them, Rhan could hear movement, the tight discipline of the military wavering. He heard voices, demands, cries of alarm, panicked horses. He heard Mostak barking orders, heard the drum repeat them. He heard Gorinel – the old man had a boom like Samiel's own. Gods alone knew what the people were thinking...

But they had to see this. They had to know the truth, the whole story – know who could be trusted to lead them. Their loyalty *had* to be absolute.

And then Selana spoke, and everything stopped dead.

"Oh well done, my brother. Well done indeed." Her voice was Vahl's – it reached every corner of the plaza below. The soldiers would know it; they'd heard it before, in Phylos, at the city's ending. They would know what it meant.

The Count of Time had stopped utterly still.

Roderick's expression was still as stone, his eyes compelled by Selana's new stance and power. Mael stared as if at a figment, some nightmare from his artist's imagination. His hands were shaking. Valicia lay like a tumbled statue, motionless.

Then Selana spoke again, and the instant shattered. "But in your rush, I think you've forgotten something." The tears in her skin were closing, edges melting together like tallow in the steam, and Vahl was smiling with her face, his mouth somehow wider than hers. "Have you become so besotted with your mortal family that you forget your estavah, those with whom you were promised privilege until the end of the Count of Time?" The smile grew wider, showed teeth. "Samiel damned us all, little brother. Not just you and I."

Rhan tensed, trembling.

Samiel damned us all.

Not just you and I.

That endless, shrieking plummet from Samiel's halls, the cold, dark waters that had caught him. But the others...

Not just...

Roderick may not have been able to find them, but there were Kas on Rammouthe, as damned as Vahl had been and curled deep in the island's belly. And they had been waiting long, waiting patient, waiting cold within their citadel of dark stone. Vahl was their eldest and their vanguard. They had forced him to reveal himself before his army had manifested – but manifest it would, and soon.

Not just you and I.

He knew them by their older names, the names Samiel had given them, and then taken away – Tamh Gabryl, Ghan Rafyl, others. And without them, Vahl was not ready.

Not ready – *yet*.

But Vahl had gathered in Selana's skin, in her face – he was a writhe of ink, a smear of blood, a rise of smoke. He was manifest over her like some vast shadow. Now they could all see him.

The mosaic was utterly silent. Whatever tan had broken their ranks, they had stopped dead, transfixed by the tableau on the balcony.

By the thing that had brought the city to ruin, the thing that was even now in the skin of their Lord.

Vahl laughed, enough to make the clouds recoil. He turned on the Bard. "So – what now? You can summon me, Tundran, but can you expel me? Dismiss me? Are you some sage of old, wielding forgotten magicks?" Eyes of vapour crawled over them like insects. "I think not." The smile spread, steam rose in waves from the young Lord's shoulders. "Perhaps your skin and skills are better suited to my needs? Did you think I could not take you, Roderick of Avesyr?" She chuckled. "Or perhaps I should just do this: *E Rhan Khavaghakke...*" She let the threat go, even as Rhan doubled over, gagging – the words were like a fist in the belly.

She laughed again.

Mael stood up, wiping his eyes on his sleeve like a child. "Selana," he said. "Please. Please, come away from all this, come away..."

But she – they – laughed at them all, laughed like a roll of thunder, loud enough to fill the plaza below with sound.

"Muster your troops, Rhan, fight us if you will – if you *can*." Vahl's gaze, two sparks somewhere in Selana's eyes, held Rhan's own. The voice was now half in his ears and half in his head. "Ah, little brother, you're more brutal than I'd ever realised, more merciless." A chuckle drifted. "I'm proud of you."

For a moment, Rhan could see it all in the smoke – the cold of the citadel, the fall and the water, the welcome of his lost siblings, the sense of family that no mortal could offer him, the ultimate fulfilment of his long, lingering loneliness. For that moment, he wavered.

Then a fist like a rock hit him across the jaw. Roderick was bellowing at him, though all he could hear was the roaring of his ears. He shook himself, tried to focus, snarled denial and wordless rage.

Vahl was laughing at him, had always been laughing at him.

Selana's face was tearing at the edges of her mouth; her smile was widening, widening as if to swallow the world.

"Very well," she said at last. "Enough games. We will return for the city soon enough, and teach this feckless Tundran a lesson of power."

Roderick, refusing to be baited, said nothing.

Rhan managed, "Please—"

Selana rounded on him. "I promise you this: we will tear your city to pieces. We will tear your world stone from stone. You will be its last living thing, crying and alone, and I will come back and remind you of this moment." She was burning now, beauty and glory. "Mael understands – he won't leave me. My mother understands. And there are others – Halydd, Ythalla, Adyle." She gazed at him, her beauty breathtaking. "You can come with us, Rhan – exalt in the power and freedom we offer!"

Like the last snapping of his lifelong loyalty, Rhan said, "Come and get me."

Selana stared at him for a moment, then, effortless enough to be scornful, she crouched and picked up the fallen form of her mother. The blaze swelled around them both.

"Then you commit treason, Seneschal. You and Mostak, traitors and deserters." She smiled, almost coquettish. "I'll tear out your soul."

Mael was standing by her, guarding her like a soldier – but he didn't meet Rhan's gaze.

Rhan spread his hands, the gesture a beckoning, a dare.

With a curl of her lip, Selana turned away, taking Mael and her mother with her. Somewhere over him – how had he ended up on the floor? – Roderick was turning back to the sunlit shatter of the mosaic, was raising his voice to a cry that sounded a paean as high as the paling sky.

Wordless, unable to move, Rhan watched him, a dark shape against the winter sky. He couldn't turn and watch Selana walk away through the Palace as though it meant nothing to her, and nothing to Vahl.

And Mael.

The old man's courage had saved Fhaveon; Rhan had saved his life. He had pledged his life – and now his soul – to the Valiembor name.

Rhan had done what Nivrotar wanted, he had no doubts that Vahl would follow him.

But Mael had made it feel like a betrayal.

Standing over his oldest friend, the Bard took a breath. His nervousness flickered like a figment, but he faced the people and he did what he had been born and marked and tortured to do.

And his voice was the fire of the rising sun.

13: MARCH THE NORTHERN VARCHINDE

Ecko was sure of one thing: this long-distance-forced-march shit was no fun at *all*.

He was jogging for chrissakes – jogging! – and he was out on the flank and alone. It was methodical, cold and boring; his rhythm, the sound of boots hitting the dead-cracked ground in perfect unison, his music, the cold wind, the snap of the flying banners and the clacking of the horses' tack. Now if only he could remember the words to "The Duckworth Chant".

But even his acerbic sense of humour was struggling under the pounding. This was tiring shit and, almost unavoidably, his thoughts had turned mechanical, some steampunk machine that rotated ever on the same axis and hissed ire every few klicks. Like the running of the soldiers, his brain was thumping, routine and obsessive.

He missed Lugan.

Yeah, like he knew that bit already, it kinda went without saying. But now, it was more – the vacuum was Redlock, and Triqueta, and Amethea. It was The Wanderer; it was Karine, and Silfe, and Sera, and Kale.

It was the fucking Bard.

Yeah, you know what I mean.

This World-Shaking War shit was seriously not as much fun as it'd been cracked up to be – where were the siege engines assailing mighty castle walls, the clashes of infantry, the strafing dragons?

His thoughts gave another long hiss...

Chrissakes.

...and they ran on.

Unrolling round him, the winter Varchinde was grey and vast and freezing. The wind was chill, slicing down from the rising ground ahead, cutting the skin from his cheeks. It made his fingers tingle, his ears sting; its noise was never-ending. Empty of the grass, of the swathes of autumnal colour, of even the hopeless tumbleweeds, the ground was hard as a slap, and etched in frost. The occasional stubborn tree was bent like an old hag, as grey as everything else.

Pennons on lines of spear-tips snapped whip-like, their colours defiant.

They ran on.

The pounding was compelling, mesmeric – it pulled him into running in rhythm, whether he wanted to or not. Freedom of choice his ass, this shit was just takin' the fuckin' piss...

Lugan would never've stood for this, even Redlock...

Ecko caught himself as the cog clunked into another turn, and he hissed, this time audibly, challenging the cold emptiness.

They ran on.

As the barrenness of that first morning expanded into vast desolation and bitter, aching cold, as the city faded behind them and the winter widened its mouth and swallowed them whole, Ecko's physical machinery clunked, rusting – he'd never had to run like this.

His lungs strained, hauling at the cold air. His chest was starting to hurt.

And they still had a fuck of a way to go.

Yeah, an' like I'm gonna quit. Mom made me; I can so do this.

They paused briefly for water and the compacted ration-pack biscuits that tasted like cardboard, then ran on into the afternoon. For a long time, Ecko's telos clung, fingers-in-windowsill, to the receding city, to the Amos trade-road veering ever further to his left – he couldn't bring himself to turn away. Here and there, they passed manors and farmlands, dilapidated now, their buildings dark-eyed and their lands devastated by winter and blight. In places, black smoke rose from pyres of Christ-alone-knew-what, ash scattered on the wind. Occasional scents of burning flesh were faint but evocative, stomach-churning.

In one place a dark force of implement-bearing nasties came out to eye their chances, then decided better of that shit and vanished again.

They ran on.

Oblivious to the point of tunnel-vision, the warriors ran like robots, their formation flickering but not faltering, their feet never ceasing. They didn't *actually* chant, but their breath steamed, and the horsemen skirted their flanks, armed and watchful. On that first day, no one faltered or missed a step.

Ecko could keep to their speed, his wired body making up for his lack of angry-sergeant training, but he found himself thinking about his travels with Pareus, about the Varchinde's dusty, golden summer – thinking through a haze of idealism that made him grit black teeth. *Fucksake.* He missed that shit too – missed the camaraderie, the affectionate aggression, the hard-edged humour and the vulgar jokes. He missed the tight sense of community. This grim-faced lot had about as much fucking comedy...

Jesus.

His clunking thoughts lurched and derailed as he looked sideways at the faces of the running soldiers, at the dirt that covered them and the short spears they carried, at the flush that was now spreading through the less fit. These poor bastards had lost everything; their future was some lunatic gamble they'd gotten no control over. Hell, they were every bit as fucking lost as he was. He guessed they weren't gonna be cracking gags anytime soon.

They ran on.

As the light thickened, fading to the dirty red of the winter dusk, the wind eased and then faded, a relief to his coldly singing ears. There were rumours of predators – circling bweao. Ecko was really hurting now, his muscles cramping with strain. He was coughing gouts of London's pollution – finding bits of his lungs he hadn't used in years – but he was still half-tempted to skip his cardboard dinner and go see if he could find the marauders. By the time he'd caught his breath, though, the squads of mounted skirmishers had come back with nada.

"Headed north-east, sir," their commander called across the rocklights of the evening. "We'll keep an eye, but pretty sure there's no need to worry." He grinned, feral in the gathering dark. "Job done!"

Job done.

For a moment, the thought sharp-edged and raw against the backdrop of the spreading camp, Ecko found himself wondering what in the ever-loving fuck he was actually doing here.

Job done.

What the hell use was he? Like really? He looked at the mounted riders, sweat and muck and horseflesh, close and stinking – they didn't even know he was here. *Job done.* Chrissakes, in the middle of all this, what the hell did he think he was gonna do?

Fight the ubernasty an' save the world!

Yeah, right.

Roderick and Rhan, Mos-whatsisface the military commander – they'd gotten their roles, their labels. Fucksake,

Ecko should've stayed with the city, with Amethea...

Gone with Triqueta.

That thought was barbed. He wondered where she was, what had happened to her. Then he pushed it away, flickering with anger.

So – now what? I'm as useful as an ashtray on a fucking Bike Lodge custom. I was gettin' it right – what happened? Did I miss a turn? Fumble?

Turn to the wrong fucking paragraph?

In the rocklights, the riders were gone.

Around him, the camp had grown out of the empty plain like a petri-dish culture – soil-coloured bivouacs, the flicker of flame. The fires burned corn and garbage and horseshit, but they gave the same sense of gathered community. Humour returned as the warriors relaxed – Ecko could hear scatters of conversation, genial horseplay. The warriors were tired, but their mood seemed oddly elated.

Almost giddy.

They were making *jokes* about it, for fucksake, like it was the only way they could deal with it – jokes about Phylos and Selana, about daemons and monsters and nightmares. About Kas Vahl Stupid-Name...

Oh yeah, an' I know all about that shit.

Ecko remembered Vahl, the touch of Amal's blade and voice, the bargain he'd almost made how he'd nearly traded this whole world for his own freedom.

Yet he was still here.

And he was fucking *damned* if he was quitting after getting this far, missed a turn or not. *Bring it on, Eliza.*

Whatever you got for me, I'll kick its butt.

By the second morning, Ecko had a growing sense of unease spreading like circuitry up his spine. His cough had receded, but he was wan and shaky and he hurt like he'd dragged himself on his elbows through every layer of hell.

The dawn was slow and the light reluctant, blown back by gusty morning drizzle. Despite the cold, the campsite was spreading into wakening life, and strident shouts across the morning.

Never much of a sleeper, he'd found a vantage – a flat spar of smooth stone, half-thrust from the ground. He'd gone halfway up it, his telos in overdrive, looking out at the enormity of the grey death that surrounded them.

It was hard to wrap his brain round – that this was even the same place. It was all *gone*, for chrissakes, dead as a doornail, dead as a dodo, dead as fucking far as he could see.

It looked like it'd had the life just sucked clean out of it. Some world-eating vampire – *shlup!* – and all gone.

Behind him, fires smouldered into ash and bivouacs crumpled into packs. The soldiers yawned, stretched, scratched, swore, then tightened back into formation. Orders were barked in short puffs of breath, and the running began again.

They warmed up swiftly, ran smoothly and well.

To free the foot soldiers of everything but basic kit, the herded horses carried panniers containing much of the supplies. The flags of mounted skirmishers were formed in a loose cordon, guarding the infantry's flanks. From the previous day, some of them had already turned drover, others hunter, still others message-bearer, tan to tan.

At front and rear, the foot-archers ran light, their formations loose and unconstrained by the regulation boot-pounding.

The Tan Commander himself sat at the head of the force – bastard led right from the front, a choice Ecko respected but was not convinced was wise. The man's voice cracked through the rising morning, and his drummer thundered the pace. At times on the previous day, he'd broken from his unit to ride beside the skirmishers, shouting at them over the noise, listening as they'd shouted back. He was a little man, barely taller than Ecko, but he was wound from knotted cords and bore a constant scowl. As the running began again, he watched the horizons as if the world itself would fold inwards and imprison them all in walls of grey nothing.

In *Kazyen.*

The word hovered for a moment, taunting…

Then Ecko dismissed it, too tired to think, and kept running.

Behind him, mounted on some massive, hairy-hooved carthorse, Rhan roved tireless, watching backwards as if he expected to see the Big Nasty rise like some enormous Balrog, flames and whips and all. His armour was not what Ecko had expected – not shining plate like some book-jacket champion – it was terhnwood lamellar like the others, manoeuvrable and light. He carried no shield, and over his shoulder rested a slender, two-handed blade, the same early steel as Redlock's axeheads. It looked every fucking bit as old as he was. He moved as if he'd personally castrate the first thing that came close.

An order barked sharp through the morning, the drum rippled faster, and the pace picked up.

Ecko groaned, stretched the kinks out of his shoulders, and kept running.

He hurt.

Christ, did he hurt.

Slowly the grey sky sunk to a scatter of rain, and the wind sharpened, vicious. Ecko's muscles eased as he ran, but his cough returned – it left him reaching for air, hacking and spitting until his chest ached from the strain.

He thanked whatever fucking Gods he could think of there were no monsters after them – yet – but as the day passed, a different demon manifested.

Fear.

It slunk through the ranks like some predator, some beast of whisper and rumour. Warriors or not, these people were fucking terrified. They were rootless, restless, homeless, tired.

They had nothing behind them and only questions in front. They were *bait*, for chrissakes, hung on the hook to tempt the big fish out of hiding – and they knew what that fish was. As the weariness set in, and the reality sunk home, they were looking about them and wondering what the fuck they were doing – what'd happened to their families, their homes and dogs and cats and collections of action figures, all left in the Cathedral's basement.

As they made camp that evening, Ecko could see new rot in their armour, patches of green shit all spreading in the wet. It'd gotten into the weapons, and into the supplies – a whole pannier of sodden and mouldy cardboard biscuit had to be dumped.

Dark mutters flickered with the firelight: threats and fears and desertion. Morale was rapidly vanishing round the u-bend.

The Bard began to walk the rocklights.

He'd lowered his scarf to his chin, left his mouth bare, and he carried only a long, curved animal horn filled with some kind of booze. But his presence was like...

It was like blatant subliminal programming, for chrissakes. It was like some damned subvocal itch. As though he could walk from group to group and the ripples of his influence would spread like song and laughter.

It was like he was some fucking fractal in his own right, some pattern within the pattern.

Ecko watched his influence, stunned at what Mom had done.

Everywhere Roderick went, everywhere his voice and music touched, so the fears would evaporate like water in a heatwave and the people would live and love and die for him, promise they'd stand fast. And – Ecko could see it in their faces – they'd mean it, every fucking word. Roderick remembered every one of them – he knew their names, their histories, their families. He told them tales of when they'd been in The Wanderer, reminded them of warmer times gone, and gave them hope for those times to come.

So much for the good guys and the Bard's morals, he was blatantly *coercing* these people. Keeping them on that bait hook. Piping them to their death.

Holy fucking shit.

Like Ecko before him, the Bard'd sold his soul for his new abilities. And, like seeing himself reflected, it was creeping Ecko the fuck out—

From the nearest group, there was a sudden burst of laughter. In the rocklight he saw the Bard stand up, slap the soldier he'd been teasing on the back. As Roderick turned away, Ecko thought he saw his eyes blood-red, cold with their newly inbuilt scan, but he wasn't sure...

The look was like a laser-pointer, a target.

And later that night, Tan Commander Mostak impaled a deserter on his own spear, and left his corpse as a warning to the others.

Maybe it was the blood-smell that triggered the attack.

In the shock of it, Ecko first thought they were bandits – cloaked and armed and manifest like horror, straight out of barren nothing. They were in among the sleeping troops with awful speed, all bared teeth and tattoos and the sharp edges of blades. They were fast, brutal; knives slashing before the exhausted soldiers could even move. Only half-dozing, Ecko was awake in an instant, his stiff muscles protesting at the rush of adrenaline. For a brief, lunatic moment, he wondered why bandits had horns at their temples, but the figures were too tall to be human, and their chests were bared beneath a writhe of blue ink. Then the thought was lost under the screaming and the shouting and the chaos and the pain.

Shit!

Blurs of flesh-warmth, bodies hotter and heavier than human, crouching and slashing, turning and kicking.

Screaming, so much screaming; orders barking and being lost. From somewhere, a drum, suddenly silenced. His targetters were flashing in the darkness, crossing this movement, and this one, and he was moving – faster than the soldiers could see or respond, faster than his own damn thoughts...

Yeah, you fuckin' try an' stop me...

He was there in a moment, and the thing in front of him was too tall, eyes of chaos that glittered cold in the rocklight. It bore a long knife, and it was tearing its way through the just-waking tan, flesh and bivvy and bedding.

Laughing.

Under it was blood and debris, scrabbling. The injured cried out, tried to move. Others were fighting, shouting, going for weapons. Several couldn't get up, were panicking, or calling for help. It was kicking at them, the motion somehow wrong.

The air smelled like copper. Debris billowed, lost in the darkness.

The noises rang loud in Ecko's ears. His adrenaline boosting slowed time to a crawl. The craze of creatures calmed, slowed. His targetters flashed and the one before him was staggering back, blade lost, clutching at a broken arm. It tripped over a body behind it and fell, showing fucking *hooves*—

One of the soldiers buried a spear in its belly and it screamed, hooves kicking.

Oh, *now* he knew what these things were...

Somewhere about him, other tan were moving – there were sounds of horses. But they were too far away to reach them in time. And then he could hear more commotion, coming from further back – this wasn't just a random dare, this was part of a co-ordinated attack.

Shit!

Something in him, a node of stillness in the screaming night, said, *It's started.*

Then there came the sounds of horses screaming.

From somewhere there was a thunderous flash of magnesium-brilliant light. It seared across his vision, snapped his time-sense back to the norm. Monsters screamed in human voices; struggling soldiers reeled and swore.

Closest to Ecko, the chaos was extreme. Bivouacs were in pieces, catching on ankles and trampled into the cold mud. One of the creatures was kicking its way free of entangling fabric, cursing. The dull glow of the rocklight showed figures were struggling to rise, helping their fellows.

Another creature had leapt straight through the tan's site and was moving to the next one; still another had its legs caught in guy-lines and was fighting to free itself. A fourth had come to face Ecko, its almost-human face expanding into an unholy grin, lit hellish by the last of the fire.

Come on then, little man. Ecko didn't need to hear it speak. *Come on then...*

One of the tan came up underneath it, ramming his short spear into its belly and hanging on it for dear life. The beast went backwards, its animal legs kicking – but not before its long knife had slashed the man down the face. The soldier screamed, his legs went from under him and he crumpled in the dirt, his hands pressed to his cheek and flooding with dark fluid.

The creature caught in the guy-lines had been surrounded by upright warriors; noises of fighting crashed across the entire site.

Ecko didn't waste time posturing – the thing in front of him was trying to get up, its insides spilling round the spear shaft. Targetters flashed and his foot came round, took the spear sideways and out of its gut. The wound filled and flooded.

Then another member of the tan hit the thing in the flank. It tried to sidestep, missed its footing and went down in the gore and mud.

The mounted skirmishers were up, voices calling to say they'd track where the creatures had come from – but Ecko wasn't watching, wasn't listening. The downed beast was thrashing now – it was surrounded and it knew it was over. The surviving members of the tan had closed on it, the spears moved with a need for revenge.

These poor, homeless, defeated fuckers had found exactly the outlet they needed.

These beasties weren't even steak, for chrissakes, they were *kibble*.

Close up, Tan Commander Mostak was a permanent knot of anger, tightly controlled and releasing the pressure one disciplined moment at a time. Ecko's scans showed nothing out of the ordinary – hell, maybe this one really was just a bloke doing a job.

Unlike the blaze of Rhan's UV skin through his armour, unlike Roderick's steel-throated severity.

"Twelve attacks," Mostak said crisply. "Thirty men and women dead, and nearly that number injured. We're hurt and we're slow." He turned to Rhan, his fury looking as if it were about to ignite. "Why did we not see them coming?"

"They're vialer," Rhan said. "They're fast as horses, but cloaked, they look human. Probably came from one of the manors. The question is – are they scouts, or is this Vahl's vanguard?"

Three pairs of eyes turned to Ecko.

Frankly, Ecko would rather face fifty of the things all armed to the horns than answer the questions of this lot. He was weary, not only from the march but from a lack of food and sleep, from the aftermath of the fighting. He felt thin, wavering and achy and kinda stretched. He was still coughing, and this was a whole new kinda adrenaline that he really didn't need.

It made him wanna puke.

He remembered the stealth run they'd done on Ythalla's army, though, and thought about what he'd seen.

"My guess?" His rasp made Mostak blink, but the Tan

Commander listened intently. "My guess is you got hounds. Packs of critters – fast on their hooves, in an' out, do one fuck of a lotta damage. An' cover a lotta ground." He glanced at Rhan, who said nothing. "They'll come again, tomorrow, the night after. Your force gets paranoid, gets no sleep, their energy and morale get fucked." He shrugged. "More fucked. One eye over their shoulder, like all the time, y'know? They'll be tired, an' slow. My guess is the main force ain't movin' – not yet – but when they do, they're gonna wanna catch us with our pants down, an' they'll want us tired and broken." He grinned, mirthless. "Hell, they'll want it all over by teatime."

Rhan was nodding, a faint smile at one side of his mouth that had nothing to do with humour.

"I concur," he said. "Vahl's waiting for his brothers – but he wants us within reach."

Mostak nodded, his face still clouded. He was chewing the inside of his lip.

"Then I want these 'hounds' delayed. Find out where they've gone, hunt them down, take them out. Rhan, take two flags of skirmishers. How many of these things can you deal with before dusk tomorrow?"

Rhan snorted.

Ecko expected Mostak's next request to be similar, and aimed at him, but the commander's gaze went straight over him and stopped at the Bard.

"And I want you in the vanguard. Do you drum?"

"And bass," Roderick answered him, without a trace of humour. "I can sustain the focus of the soldiers. And you, Commander, what will you—?"

"Hang the fuck on a minute." Ecko wasn't standing for this. "Don't I get to play? Go beat up Pan? Get a horse an' go scout? It's kinda what I do, y'know. Like – better than every fucker else."

The commander opened his mouth to respond, but the Bard was faster.

"Ecko, you're not a warrior – you don't have the skill, the fitness or the discipline. And, with respect, you can't ride well enough to keep the pace. Scout on foot if you wish, equip yourself with a bow from stores, chase the vialer if you think you can. But if you wish for a real task – something suited to your peculiar abilities – you do one thing better than all of the rest of us combined."

Don't make me answer that...

The Tan Commander's raised eyebrow did the job for him.

If the Bard was smiling, the mask covered all trace. "You can watch. Stop feeling sorry for yourself, pay attention, make sure these bastards don't get close."

Rhan said, "How long?"

The question was ambiguous, but the commander understood him. "We need to pick up the pace, send bretir to Jade, and to Amos. If Nivrotar's plan is going to work, timing's imperative."

"Understood." Rhan tapped a finger against his chin for a moment, contemplating Ecko's silent fume. Then he said, "Ecko—"

Whatever he'd been going to say was interrupted by a commotion outside the tent, by a soldier's flat challenge and a female voice, tired and curt. Whoever she was, she sounded like she'd had enough.

Mostak turned, his thundercloud frown still in place, but Roderick had moved to pull back the tent flap.

The voice had caught Ecko's attention like a hook. He was staring at the doorway, hoping against all fucking common sense...

The woman was Amethea.

Shit.

Rhan was on his feet, his face ashen. His voice soft, he said, "Dear Gods. What...?"

Amethea looked at him, her eyes dark with death.

"You were wrong," she said. Her voice was rock-steady, the tone of someone who'd been there, done that, lived through fucking all of it and just wasn't impressed any more. "They came in after us. The people were dying when I left them." She held up Gorinel's hand-of-Samiel neck chain. "I was supposed to bring you this. Tell you to have *faith*."

Rhan said nothing; his hands and breath were shaking.

Amethea said, "They're coming."

14: HUNTERS FHAVEON

The outskirts of the city were desolate in the rain.

Amethea huddled in a doorway, water streaming down her face, the cold soaking through the shoulders of the heavy cloak Gorinel had thrown at her, soaking through the bag now huddled to her belly. By the light, it was late afternoon, but the death of the sun would come quickly, and the clouds were layered with threat.

She was shaking – and not just with the cold.

Behind her crouched an old storehouse, long empty, this one bereft of purpose long before the blight had come to Fhaveon. Its cavernous cellars led back into the myriad writhing tunnels of the cliffside, back to the Cathedral now high above – but there lay only horrors.

Their gamble had failed. It was over.

The rain streamed down her skin; if she wept, she was past even noticing. She had a single purpose and it was like a light in the grey, a thing to drive her onwards and to keep despair at bay.

She must find Rhan. She must tell him what had happened, that there would be no future, that the darkness had come for them.

Unprotected, abandoned to Vahl's mercy, the last of the city's people would die screaming.

And then night would fall.

The first one had come through the wall.

With a rumble like the groaning of the world herself, it had hammered through the decorated stone near where Amethea had been standing, shovel hands shattering the rock. Panelling split, fell to the floor with a rattle that echoed from the vaulted and painted roof.

The hand withdrew.

For a breathless moment, the dust stood shimmering still, caught fast in the rocklights.

Then the shock had hit her like a fist and she'd sucked in a breath like pure terror. The air was colder, shivering cold; dust glittered, dancing. She thought about screaming, had no voice, stared as the hand slammed again through the hole, shoving pebbles and rubble and debris, widening the gap so the body could follow. She didn't need to see what the thing was, she *knew*.

No...

And then it came through completely, fast, scattering wreckage, tearing the wall to pieces. It had no eyes, no ears. Its blunt head swung back and forth as if it scented the air. Behind it, there was a ruin of collapsed rock, but she could still feel the night, the moisture.

No – crazed denial, pointless and hopeless – *Gods, no, we can't have been this stupid...*

As if it heard her thoughts, the thing's featureless face turned towards her. It looked like some ancient and nameless guardian, some remnant of a city lost...

But this was not some renegade Swathian warden, some animated myth, some saga romance fallen from stone. This thing was *angry* – and it had come straight from Vahl's command.

It took a step towards her. Another. She felt it grinning, though its face remained blank.

For a moment longer, she stared at it, willing it to somehow be mist, some forgotten figment leftover from an old nightmare – but it was as solid as she was, and an awful lot bigger.

Stuff this.

She ran.

Skidding through the doorway, she didn't look back. She told herself it wouldn't pounce, that it was stone and slow and stupid, that she could easily outdistance it. But her heart was choking her and the tally markers were tumbling from her hand, falling forgotten to the floor of the old crypt, lost among the barrels and crates that'd been brought to feed the people. Still not finding her voice, but with her mind repeating *Dear Gods, Dear Gods!* she ran for the main crypt where Gorinel was working.

She skittered, tripped, almost fell.

Outside the chamber, people were scattered though the corridors, huddled in groups, or aimless and wandering, shocked and lost and angry. She gasped at them, gulping at their dejection, then she forced her throat to move and shrieked to them to run, *run!* But they only gaped at her, blinking. One of them grappled for her wrists, trying to make her stop. She shoved, panicked.

Then the stone thing came into the corridor behind her. It thumped onto all fours like a predator, its blunt face crumpled as if it scented the air.

Run! She'd no idea if she'd even said it aloud.

This time, they listened.

Some just scattered, pell-mell, others gathered armfuls of family and whatever belongings they had. They herded each other away from where the thing had paused, head swinging back and forth like a hunting bweao. One man loitered as if to loot discarded baggage – but as the thing crouched, its eagerness palpable, he thought better of it and fled.

Amethea had no idea where they'd go – and right now she didn't care. They were out of its path and that was all that mattered. Her mind was racing, trying to encompass what all of this meant, trying to see too much. Was the thing a lone marauder, a scout? Or had it really come from Vahl himself?

Was the whole damned army on the move?

They had no way to fight – they were soft targets, bereft of any warrior force. Vahl could play any games he wanted – send creatures crafted by Maugrim, by Amal, raise monsters of stone left from old Swathe, come himself if he felt like it – what mattered was that they were defenceless.

They had nothing.

And it was only a matter of time.

As she exploded through the doorway, Gorinel turned from the crate he'd been searching, his round face pale. She opened her mouth to call to him, but the priest was already moving, wiping grimy hands on the front of his overshirt.

He said, quite calmly, "They've come for us, haven't they?"

"Yes." Her response was a whisper. Maybe something in her had known, dear Goddess, had *known* this would happen, that Vahl wouldn't let the chance pass, but she'd hoped...

Hoped what?

That the Cathedral would grant them sanctuary? That Vahl would *respect* it? That the Gods would step down and deign to save them?

Put your shoulder to the wheel...

There was another feeling as well, something in her skin that was faintly familiar – but she couldn't think about it now. Now there was too much fear and her breath was balled in her throat and she needed to know what the rhez they were going to do.

Gorinel hadn't shaved and his jowls were rough with greying stubble. He rasped a dirty hand over them, thinking.

"Is the main force moving? Or is this just a scout?"

"I don't know. The lookout—"

"Two priorities." Unruffled, the old priest was in control. "Find out if it is. If it's mobile we need to get word to Mostak, to Rhan. And... Samiel's *beard.*"

Somewhere outside, in the tangled corridors of the crypts, there was screaming. Then came another rumble of stone, more distant – whatever they were, more of them were coming.

"I don't think that one was a scout," Amethea said softly.

"We'll have to go deeper," Gorinel said quickly. "Carry whatever we can. The tunnels in the cliff go on for days. Every able man and woman, every child strong enough to carry kit, we'll get them moving. We may not be warriors, Amethea, but we don't have to be esphen." Gorinel watched her expression, then said, "And I'll need you to do something for me."

She ran.

She'd never been more scared in her life – and that was saying something – and yet her sense of purpose was absolutely clear, allowed for no mistakes or wasted time. She gripped the paper that Gorinel had given her and ran through the mad tangle of corridors, crypts and storerooms, tripping and missing turnings. She had no real idea where she was going and was trusting in... what? Luck? The Gods? Her own instincts? Whatever it was, she was running essentially downhill and hoping to every God she could remember that the stone beastie wasn't there behind her – rasping and running – that the things couldn't or wouldn't tunnel this far down.

She ran.

The catacombs grew darker as the rocklights began to fade – down here, they couldn't have seen daylight in generations and their elemental energy was spent. She scooped one up, holding it aloft, but quickly her arm grew weary and she passed it from hand to hand, making the shadows dance about her. The walls were decorous; images of lost mythology, sagas forgotten to the Count of Time. Here was a man with three torsos, one flesh, one red and one white; here were hands crafting a gift of flesh, holding it out to twins.

But the images were chipped and broken, and she had no time to stop.

She ran.

Gods alone knew what returns of Protectors had actually kept down here; what they'd needed all this for. There was probably treasure for days, forgotten artefacts, weapons of magick that would glow with forbidden power and spank Vahl Zaxaar's daemon backside... There was probably something that would shatter that stone monster into riverside pebbles... But, turning to glance over her shoulder, she didn't dare stop.

She ran — panting now, her heart and chest straining and her little rocklight sending figments scudding along the walls.

She passed the end of the catacombs and came out into the tunnels proper. Cold and damp, knotted and terrifying, she kept to her downhill heading and ran on, the echoes of her own boots scaring her, as if Vahl's entire army were chasing her down.

Something in the back of her head remembered her saying to Triqueta, "As if I haven't had enough of stone rooms!" and she wondered where her friend was, if she had reached Roviarath safely.

Whether she would see them, any of them — by the Gods, even Ecko — again.

She found that she'd stopped, was leaning on her knees and heaving to pull air into her body. She made herself walk, catching her breath.

Told herself she had time, she did, she really did. That there was no need to panic.

Somewhere now far above and behind her, Gorinel was

mustering the people – not to fight, but to mislead, to delay and harass. They had water – she'd already passed several places where it oozed from the wall – but everything else they had to carry with them...

They were caught, trapped by blight and winter and fear. And now in a game of bweao-and-esphen that would stretch onwards through the Count of Time.

The Gods help those...

She had no idea if they could last the winter – what would happen with the spring. It seemed so far away, impossible.

She walked now, her heart slowing but its sound still loud in her ears. Her little rocklight was a pool of sanity in the rising dark. Sometimes she heard sounds from above her – shrieks, shouts, rumbles of rubble, once a roar of defiance that sounded like the Protector himself...

Gorinel!

She'd grown very fond of the fat old man in the short time she'd known him. He really did rely on himself, shoulder his own responsibilities – and if the Gods helped those who...

She stopped, her attention distracted by a sudden, sinking horror.

That odd-shaped outcrop that threw a peculiar shadow, she'd passed it before, she was sure... She fought to hold down sudden panic. She was imagining it. This wasn't some saga-labyrinth for sacrificing maidens to monsters, it was just tunnelling and there were many exits. She was fine. She had her bag of staples over her shoulder. She had the heavy cloak Gorinel had thrown her. She had her good trews on and her sturdy boots – laced-up boots like Redlock's, like Feren's had been. There was no need to—

Screams sounded, a distant echo.

Her blood ran cold.

Would the monsters find her, all the way down here? How long would it take them?

Somewhere she'd heard tales of the great mouths that opened in the cliff face, endlessly spitting the Swathe River down into the sea; somewhere else, tales had told of tunnels that stretched all the way to forbidden Rammouthe itself.

All she needed to do was head downwards. All she needed to do was get the rhez out.

Reach Rhan.

And when I've done that, I'll take the moons from the sky and wear them as ear-gems...

But her sense of purpose was strong as the stone that surrounded her, as the weight of the city over her head. And she took a breath and ran on, more slowly now, still carrying her little light.

She passed the outcrop again.

This time she stopped, her heart pounding, fighting for control.

Saint and Goddess – she'd be down here until the end of the Count of Time. Until she was the last free mortal left in the city. Until Vahl's entire army had surrounded her and the daemon took her as some damned bride...

Shuddering, she exhaled.

Bride indeed!

Amethea had spent far, far too long feeling sorry for herself, all tangled with her own regrets and fears. She'd called Rhan on his selfishness – how she'd even dared! – on his obsession with his city, and now she must damned well face her own. Why would the daemon even want her, for Gods' sakes? There was no one to blame and no one to help her – she'd broken Amal's visions, by the Gods, and she could do this.

From somewhere now far, far above, she heard the Protector's roar again.

And it made her feel strong, strong as the very stone that surrounded her, as the roots of the city herself.

And then, in the echoes of the noise, the tingle she'd felt earlier returned, a shimmer that she knew. She dismissed the outcrop and began to walk, getting her breath back, and her *feet...*

Stone.

The touch of stone in her skin, in her soul. The blaze of catalytic passion that Maugrim had awoken. The rock that had grown through her very flesh. Touching the walls in the Monument's tunnels, the strength and age that had lain there, untapped.

A confused rush, guilt and confidence.

And knowledge – all she had to do was go downwards.

Falling to your knees and pleading for Samiel to save a life is one thing – but the dying man beside you needs you to stop his bleeding.

She was going to get out.

In the rain-soaked storehouse doorway, she stood shivering, and trying to listen.

The cold was bitter after the ambient tunnels, but she chewed her lips and tried to keep still. She'd no idea what had happened to the Cathedral behind her – if she emerged from the doorway and turned to look back up at the city, perhaps she'd see it in flames, see the Palace and the statuary all finally crumbling as Vahl celebrated with some orgy of gleeful destruction...

But she was free, the fresh air had called to her and she had broken into a stumbling run at last, emerged blinking and nearly crying with relief. Now she stayed where she was, cold biting her skin and watching the grey curtain of the rain.

Put your shoulder to the wheel, Amethea, and know that you are not abandoned.

Across the grey, she saw motion – a shadow, barely more than a figment. It was moving slowly, as if hurt, but the dull thud of hooves was unmistakable.

Her heart thundered.

Fixed to the spot as though stuck by an arrow, she waited,

every sense straining. The shadow paused, one hoof beating restless, but there was no other motion.

The rider was alone.

Put your shoulder...

Carefully, she eased out into the downpour.

The Gods, apparently, were teasing her.

This was not some lone and injured rider – a free pass, offered by the Goddess for good work, or to reward her returning faith. Oh no, this rider was armed and well and truly awake. He was – had been – a courier, by the look of him; his garments were soaked and sticking to him, his hair pasted to his face. He was pale and shivering, young, but very much alive.

"What do you want?"

As she came close, his voice was loud in the drum-pulse of the rain.

Amethea spat water. "I need help! I need..."

I need you to give me your horse.

Like that was going to work!

She wondered what she was supposed to do. She had any number of fascinating herbal concoctions that would make him give her anything she wanted... but she didn't have them out here. All she had was her wit and the blade at her belt.

"I need... help... I..."

Honest by nature, Amethea wasn't a good dissembler. But the lad swung a leg over the saddle pommel and came towards her, his mount stopping to nose the overgrown flags.

"What's the matter?" He stopped a short distance from her, wary. "What's wrong?"

"I need... ah... I've got a message for Ythalla. I must get to her."

Something in his stance felt like relief – like she'd spoken some password that made him trust her. Her mind said, *He's an enemy*, but she shook the notion away – there was no such thing, he was a man doing a job and no more.

The blade at her belt was heavy, dragging at her like a bad decision.

She might have trained with it, but the thought of using it on flesh turned her stomach.

Have you saved a life, little lady? Have you taken a life?

In the rain, she heard the stallion's laughter, cadaverous and deep. Her hand found the haft and tightened.

The courier said, "I can take you. To Ythalla. I can…"

"I can't walk. I need… help…" She was repeating herself and felt ridiculous. Who would fall for this ruse, really?

"Or I can take the message for you." The boy wasn't coming any closer.

"It's important. I have to take it personally. Please! You need to help me up!"

Her knees were folding, that much was true.

The Gods help those who…

The horse was grazing on something, shaking the water from its mane. Glancing briefly back at it, the boy came closer, blowing the rain from his mouth and nose. Snot slicked his cheek. He was barely more than a lad, his voice just changed.

Her hand tightened further, a gesture that was more denial than threat.

She stretched the other one towards him – a ludicrous and theatrical motion.

"Please!"

But as he saw her properly, he relaxed – apparently convinced that something that little and pale and pretty couldn't be a threat. She felt the tension leave him.

She said again, softer, "Please!"

Redlock, in The Wanderer, when she'd refused to kill Maugrim: *Keep it that way.*

The boy caught her outstretched hand, hauled her to her feet. She didn't have to pretend to stagger – she nearly threw up. As she gulped air and rain, calming her belly, the horse raised its head to look at both of them, ears pricked forward.

As if it knew exactly what was about to happen.

The boy turned to it, talking softly.

His back was to her.

She had a moment, a moment only. A moment that would change who she was, how she saw the world. A moment in which she pulled the blade from her belt, feeling it heavy in her hand as if the very terhnwood had become metallic and cold.

You don't have a choice!

And then, watching herself with a strange, slow motion that felt absolutely unreal, she turned her grip on the thing and whacked the back of his skull with the pommel.

As hard as she could.

The horse flared its nostrils and threw its head back, its tack clacking.

She knew exactly where to strike – the boy fell like a sack and didn't move again.

Feeling sick, Amethea blinked at him for a moment, her hands shaking. Then she swallowed a mouthful of saliva, dropped the blade, and knelt, staring. She went to check his pulse – stopped herself.

The horse snorted again, and she picked up the boy's kit-bag, stood to catch the animal's rein.

She stroked its neck, talking softly.

And that, she told the Gods, *is helping my damned self.*

15: TUSIEN THE NORTHERN VARCHINDE

And somehow, the attack made it all real.

There was no time now for indecision, for thoughts of desertion or unrest; their enemy brought them fear, and their fear brought them unity. They pulled together, closed against both foe and winter, and the drums beat relentless in the morning.

Our city is gone, the rhythm said. *Our Lord is gone. Our homes are gone. And those we loved.*

The vialer had killed thirty-one soldiers; thirty-one men and women had died down there in the cold and the muck and the darkness. A further twelve had serious injuries and were unable to be moved. Apothecarial care was limited – and came with some hard choices.

Newcomer to the army though she was, Amethea knew what those choices were likely to be.

Wrapped tight against the grey and bitter cold, her stolen mount in the hands of the supplymaster, she refused both herbal and rest, and went to find what passed as the hospice. As the camp packed up about her and orders puffed like vapour through the dawn, she found the bivouac where the injured had been gathered. They were huddled on pallets on a cold, frosted floor, their faces pale with inevitability.

Eleven of them had been badly physically hurt. The twelfth had no visible marks at all. He was hunched and rocking, his chin streaked with blood where he'd bitten through his lower lip.

Amethea understood all too well – not all harm was physical. She may not be able to call the Gods for miracles, but if she could save one mind, one life, it would be enough. Gorinel had told her: faith was in action, her shoulder to the wheel, and now, she knew her path exactly.

Outside, the soldiers formed into their tans and flags, upright and shivering. Their collective breath plumed over them, dawn mist. They stood in silence, in tribute to those they'd lost – their pennons fluttered like discovered pride. But then the commands rang loud and the damned drums began yet again, merciless and blood-pounding. Goaded by the sound, the skirmishers began to stretch and jump, and the horses shifted, stamping their hooves.

Turning back to the dim and stinking interior of the tent, she knew she had little time.

"Amethea."

The voice behind her was quiet, very deep. Startled, she turned back to the lifted tent flap.

Rhan himself ducked in under the low fabric, blocking the sullen sky. He was grey-faced, dirty and bloodied. In places, his armour was split and filthy, rent to the padding.

He said, "I've come to help you."

Wary, Amethea eyed him. "Help me do what?" If he'd come to slit throats, then she was...

But he shook his head, too tired to fight, and pointed at the young man closest to the doorway whose belly wound had him curling in sweat and anguish, hands across himself as if to hold his guts in. His garments had been cut away from the injury and the wound had been briefly dressed, but the dressing was blood-soaked, darkening like a new bruise. In the poor rocklight, his skin was leeched of all colour and shards of pain were caught between his teeth.

Even if she stopped the bleeding and dressed the wound correctly, the danger of infection was severe. The Count of Time would come for this one, and soon.

Rhan said, "There's no ceremony to this, and no time to delay." He met her gaze and she was surprised how serious he looked – and how old. "Amethea. Do you trust me?"

The wind gusted, made the fabric fold of the doorway slide down over itself. He turned and caught it, threw it back.

She said, "I—?"

"Do you *trust* me?"

"I... Of course."

She watched him kneel at the pallet-side of the injured man. When the man realised who he was, he tried to sit up, speak.

"Lie down." Rhan laid a hand on his shoulder. "I've come to help you."

He peeled back the dressing, baring the wound to the rocklight. The wound had stitches, but they were fast, torn and ragged. She could almost see the infection eating at their edges. As she watched, Rhan laid a hand over the injury.

"What are you doing?" she whispered. Across the bivouac, others craned to look. The uninjured man cried aloud, formless and without words.

Rhan's face flickered a frown, and then, carefully, he took his hand away.

And Amethea gaped.

Saint and Goddess!

The wound had gone. It was an angry, puckered scar, ends of fibrous stitches still peeking curiously from it. Across the young man's abs, a jagged red lightning mark now decorated his skin. He stared at Rhan for a moment, then rubbed his hands across the scar and sat up, stammering and coughing.

Whispers rolled through the tent.

Amethea's mind reeled after them, looked for something to cling to. She heard the Bard's fireside story, the Promise of Samiel, she heard Gorinel, *Know that you are not abandoned.* She remembered Maugrim, attuned to the Powerflux and a wielder of fire – not only of its force, but of its allure, its sense of community, and its warmth.

Heal and Harm. None could learn one...

But this was different. Rhan was *stark* somehow, vastly more powerful than Maugrim had been. She'd felt his sheer energy like lightning across her skin, felt it reaching into the injured man, crackling into his body as if it sought to illuminate his soul. Pure power had shuddered through the dirty tent, touched Amethea and made the hairs on her arms stand on end...

Promise of Samiel.

You are not abandoned...

She didn't get time to follow the thought to its end.

"Amethea." His voice brought her back to herself. From outside, she could hear voices, commands – they were almost out of time.

She found herself asking, "How did you...? How can you...?"

"Not now. Now, we get as many of these people on their feet as we can, find horses for the rest, and then we move before the nasties catch us with our trews down. So, are you going to help me, or are you going to sit back and let me do all the work?" His sardonic tone gave the words a twist of dark humour.

"I thought I might mark you out of ten." Amethea was impressed with her own aplomb. The healed man was scrambling up now, his face flushed, and the others were starting to call out for help. The uninjured soldier cried again.

The man went to speak, but Rhan stopped him. "If you can walk, then take a message to the commander and tell him..." he paused, "...tell him no man or woman will be left behind. Not while I'm here, and I've still got the focus to fight. We've lost enough."

We've lost enough.

Amethea stared at him, at a manifest and complex guilt, like an echo of her own. She was lost for anything to say. He raised an eyebrow at her. "What?"

"If you can do this," she said, "then you don't need me here. You don't need me at all."

We've lost enough.

Outside, the drumming was picking up speed.

"We need you, Amethea," Rhan told her. "You're the most experienced apothecary we have – and you're worth your weight in terhnwood. Now, shall we?"

They ran.

They ran through winter and weariness; they ran through the dead plain and the deep cold.

By the third day, the increase in pace was beginning to take its toll, and the ground underfoot was becoming harder, scattered with angles of sharp and broken rock.

To the north, now to their right, the hard slope fell slowly away. At its foot was the valley of one of the Swathe River's many tributaries, and a dense, usually wintergreen woodland.

Mostak had it marked as a place for potential ambush, but as they passed across the top of the slope and carried on southwest, they could see the woodland in the hollow was dead, like everything else. The trees had slumped into grey resignation, fallen one against another, their needles littering the ground.

The river itself was sluggish and rank. The mounted skirmishers ran as far as the banks but reported that the water was tainted, and could not be drunk.

With a collective groan, they ran on.

Towards evening, they saw the first signs of pursuit.

The threat was far away, but as the force broke for a rest, Mostak issued Ecko a new set of orders.

"I need to know all of it," he said. "How many, how fast. What they're armed with, what they're riding. You saw the encampment – tell me how much of it is on the move."

Hey! Lemme be your fucking intern!

Ecko was knackered, even his sense of humour was outta batteries. Plus, he'd gotten a pretty good idea what was what – if he tuned his telos, he could see the incoming bad guys quite clearly, thanks, horses an' monsters an' all. He could answer the commander's questions without actually having to run that fucking far. Chrissakes, already, he needed a break – he hurt in places he'd forgotten he had. Mom's trickery just wasn't designed for this "hut hut hut" shit...

Before he could win smug points, though, a whole new problem bit them in the ass.

One of Mostak's command tan dropped dead.

What?

Well, okay, not *dead* exactly – but he keeled over and he looked pretty damn sick. The guy was... Jesus Hairy Christ... in the failing evening light, the guy was *green*.

Ecko gawked. Even Lugan'd never gone that colour and his hangovers were fucking legend.

You gotta be kiddin' me...

The warrior was an older man, a proper vet, and he'd come in bearing a message. Now, he looked like he'd swallowed a bottle of Insta-Lawn – despite the cold, he was *growing*, for chrissakes. He was sprouting random vegetation from ears and eye sockets, more at the neck of his armour. Ecko didn't scare easy, but grass popping out someone's eyeball was enough to turn him carnivore for life. And somehow the man was still alive, hands blindly reaching out.

"Help me," he said. "Help me. Please."

The words sounded wrong.

Skin crawling, Ecko told himself to get a grip.

Drums sounded orders.

Rhan arrived at a run.

"Seneschal." The Commander was on his knees in the muck, gripping the fallen man's hand in both of his own. "This man is my friend."

"Samiel's *balls*." Expression contorting, Rhan dropped to his knees on his other side. He held the man's head in one hand, tried to clear the growth with the other.

"Ghar, it's Rhan." The words sounded like a knell. "This is getting to be a habit."

Ghar repeated, like a litany, "Help me."

Propelled by an obscure impulse, Ecko picked up the soldier's discarded spear and turned it over – then dropped the thing as if it'd stung him.

It was *growing*.

Just like the blade from the Amos wharfside, the one that had led them to the House of Sarkhyn – the terhnwood fibres in the resin were struggling for life.

Help me.

What the *hell*?

Glancing back in the direction of the blighted woodland, the symmetry of the two things was unmistakable – but why the hell would one die while the other tried to grow?

Something about all of this made him shiver, right to the core of his being. Ecko had the oddest fucking feeling...

The oddest feeling of what?

So. Do I get a cookie when I solve the puzzle? Or just a piece of veg grown outta my ass?

Rhan was speaking. "I don't know what's wrong with him." He was freaked, Ecko could hear it, freaked right the fuck out of his socks – and hell, he wasn't the only one. Resignation and horror fell from his words like stones. "Mos, I don't think I can help him. Maybe Amethea—"

"Rhan..." Mostak's tone was dangerous.

"I can't tell what's the matter – can't feel it!" It was halfway between anger and plea. "He's not sick! He's—!"

"Rhan!" It was a bark, an order. "You—!"

But the moss-grown man had gone into spasm. His eyeless body was jerking, arms and legs and hands and feet hammering against the cold ground. He was still trying to speak, and green froth came from between his lips. Rhan and Mostak were trying to hold him down. The commander's face was thunderous with accusation. Ecko stared, car-crash fascinated, and saw that the man's body temperature was all over the shop. He was cold at the core, but the places where he was growing were *hot*.

Ecko found he was rubbing his hands like Lady Macbeth.

Jesus fucking Harry Christ and little fuckin' fish...

He managed, "What...?"

"I don't know," Rhan said, baffled, furious. "He's not injured, not infected. It's not a disease. It's like – it's almost like a parasite, but I can't even see all of it. And the *smell*. Like Foriath, like the terhnwood. Like Mael saw in the market. I don't *understand*." His appeal was to the commander, but even as he spoke, Ghar arched his back and gagged a mouthful of green. Then he collapsed like a broken thing, still.

Holy shit. Ecko swallowed, shuddered.

Mostak placed two fingers on the fallen man's lichen-grown neck, then smoothly rose to his feet, his expression set. For a moment, he stared down at the still-kneeling Seneschal.

"Lost enough, have we?" The words were thrown like acid.

Then he turned his back and he walked away.

"I don't... I don't understand." Rhan's response was a whisper. He stared at the dead man, at his own helpless hands, then up at Ecko, his face full of ghosts. He was grey and his shoulders were shaking.

Across the site, the drums had started to call the muster.

"Why the fuck're you lookin' at me?" Ecko picked up the spear again and examined it with his telos flicked in, looking at its odd, struggling growth. He threw it at where Rhan was kneeling. "Get up, for chrissakes. I dunno what that shit was, but we better hope it's not contagious." Green froth trailed down the sides of Ghar's face, oozed into the cold dirt. "Otherwise we're fucked."

They ran.

They ran for real now, ran with the cold night vast over their heads and the winter wind behind them, ran knowing that their enemy was hunting them, right at their heels. Vahl himself was behind them, coming like the end of the world...

Or some such poetic bullshit.

Ecko was tired, more tired than he would've believed possible. He kept going on defiance alone: *Yeah, beat me, willya?* Around him, body heat came off the soldiers in waves, like panic.

He was still thinking about Ghar and the spear, about green froth and growing things, and about the dead woodland. Life and death, sides of a coin, philosophical shit maybe – but he was so gonna work out why.

As the moons set, though, he realised that he could see the pursuit – a red shimmer at the horizon, a distant warmth coming closer. If the curve of the earth – *yeah, okay, funny* – was anything like normal, then they'd be about twenty klicks away, and hell, they were closing *fast*.

Faster than expected.

He couldn't do the math exactly, but he reckoned they might make the morning before the bad guys caught them with their pants round their ankles.

And then they really were fucked.

The drums thundered on, their necessity unrelenting. They sounded like adrenaline. Like demand. Like something that was giving purpose; like not being able to quit.

Groaning, they ran.

They ran through the night.

Behind them, the line of heat closed slowly like the edge of a noose, nearer with every passing hour. After a time, Ecko's oculars could almost pick out individual figures; see the horses coming for them, the roil of monsters. The wind had faltered, and a cold mist rose from the dead ground. Behind them, the red line on the horizon grew steadily, separating out into a blur of shapes – it seemed the Big Nasty wasn't one for kipping either. Moonlight slid slowly across dark soil. Breaths came ragged, hurting; warriors stumbled. Biscuits and water were passed from hand to hand, with warnings about rations.

And then, in the weariness and the flowing fog, they began to hear whispers. Whispers like smoke.

Why do you run? Let me help you.

Let me catch you. Why do you run?

Vahl was speaking to them, in his own voice, and in Selana's.

It was soft, embracing, gentle as a caress. It was rest and sleep. It sounded in Ecko's ear like Amal's temptation, the lure that'd nearly made him give it all up. It coaxed and taunted and tempted, reminded him how weary he was. For moment, he paused, wanting nothing more than to sink down into the soil and let his exhausted body stop...

Why do I run?

Let you catch me...

But the drums answered, loud as thunder and jarring in the darkness. And with them, he could hear the Bard, a jagged and dissonant vocal noise that made him suddenly flushed and angry, made him want to jump up and put his hands over his ears and scream at the fucker to shut up, to shut up now...

The force had come to a ragged and stumbling halt. Their exhaustion was palpable, but somewhere, the Bard was not letting this happen. The drum rolled fury; the noise was huge in the sky, it seemed to pick up the winter wind and throw it at them, filled with grit and the edges of the frost incoming.

Yet the soft voice was not alone. Others wove with it, smoky and faint.

You cannot run any further.

Wait now, the end is nearly upon you.

Give us time, we will be with you.

We will help you.

Time!

In the darkness, the Bard's roar was as vast as the wind itself: "I will give you *nothing*!"

Its sheer force seemed to billow the mist, blow the voices back, weeds rolling before the wind. The taunts faded, but in their faintness they were laughing, soft as ash.

Biding their time.

The drum boomed defiance. The freezing fog eddied round them. The force collected itself, and ran on.

And still, the red line grew closer.

The night seemed endless, stumbling in a half-dream that was full of cold, and numb fingers, and hurting feet, and drum-throb; full of ears chilled and of voices pleading for rest. Hours later as the mist coalesced into a freezing grey dawn, Ecko felt he was wakening from some demented sleep-walk, some endless stagger of exhaustion that'd left him shaking in every muscle, tired enough to fucking cry.

As they paused at last, the pre-dawn chill biting at their faces and ears, some of the soldiers dropped to their knees. The horses stood shaking, their heads hanging low. Steam rose from their shoulders.

The drums rested, as if they too, were exhausted.

And behind them...

As the mist eddied, Ecko found he could see them in glimpses – just like he'd done from the top of that tiny, shell-speckled chapel. He could see the pennons and shields of the city's cavalry. He could see the spears of the foot-soldiers, and the wagons that may be artillery or supplies. He could see the hiss and seethe of Amal's creatures. Like the force before them, they'd stopped.

It was all the fuck wrong – how the hell had they been moving foot and cartage that fast?

But the mist played havoc with his telos – he couldn't see them well enough to even guess.

Then a soldier beside him nudged him with her boot.

"It's all right," she said. "We've done it."

To his left, the sun was just rising. Its first light caught the very top of the slope, the tip of the huge, dark ruin that stood atop it. It shone like some castle tower, some end-of-level promise, some mighty city that guarded the final and forgotten treasure.

"That's it," she said. "That's Tusien. We're here."

16: LAST RIDE THE NORTHERN VARCHINDE

Out in the unprotected winter of the open Varchinde, Tan Commander Triqueta was a tiny, bright figure under a glowering sky.

The wind was vast and merciless. It cut at her skin and harried the dirt in waves, but it wasn't the chill that was making her shudder. Her shiver was one of horror, of absolute disbelief – the cold of confronting something she'd no wish to see...

Something that was making the chapped skin on her hands itch as if she'd already touched it and recoiled.

She'd no words other than, "Dear *Gods*."

But the wind snatched them skywards and dismissed them.

Mane and tail billowing, her little palomino tapped a restless forehoof on the frozen ground. Still shivering, Triqueta stroked her neck.

Beside them, the Banned veteran Taure cupped his hands and blew in them.

"You wanted to see it," he said, with a slightly apologetic half-shrug. "Know what it is? You were the one down there." He rubbed his palms together briskly, as if to somehow keep the exhaled warmth, but the chill had seeped into his skin. The man's fingers and lips were tinged with white like manifest fear.

You were the one down there.

Triq shuddered again.

Before her, like an open mouth in the rising ground, there festered a wound.

It was terrifying; it made her throat rise with nausea. It was poisonous, wide and spreading, caked in filth and *hungry*; it looked like it was somehow sucking the very life from the world. And yet it also looked half healed, as though it were trying to scab over and mend.

It stank.

Triq was compelled by it, unable to look away. Cracks spread through the ground; the whole thing looked like it was spreading, like the mouth would widen and swallow everything, ground and sky and all, down into the hollow below.

Leaving... what?

Nothing.

Triq'd seen her share of nasty injuries – by the rhez, she'd had more than one herself – but this thing, gangrenous and lurking, in the world's very flesh... Gods, it made her stomach turn over.

She realised she was scratching her hands and stopped herself with an effort. She straightened her shoulders and pushed her straggled yellow hair out of her face.

From the wound, and stretching down the slope sides, there spread open fissures, like veins in the soil. They revealed nothing, no clue or hope – they showed only an empty, darkening grey. She thought about dropping something down one of them – thought better of it. One too many market sagas told the end of *that* story.

"You know anything?" Taure asked her. "Anything that might help?"

That might help what?

Yes, she'd been down there – once. A season and a lifetime

ago – on a summer night, in a blaze of fury and fire. That wound, that fetid and spreading fracture, had once been the Monument, the great Elemental Cathedral – Amethea had called it the heart of the Powerflux. Long forgotten, it had lain dormant for returns, until Maugrim had come to claim it. Something catalytic had happened down there – the waking of the world.

Catalytic – and catastrophic.

Everything that'd happened had started from this place.

The wind whined, cold.

"Triqueta!" Taure waved his waterskin at her to gain her attention. She shook herself, looked away. They'd pulled their mounted force to a ragged halt for a meal break, but they weren't stopping long. "Triq," Taure said. "This is some crazed shit. If you know anything…"

Cold rain scattered. She almost expected to see the damn thing hiss as the water struck it.

"No, no… not really." She was scratching her hands again. "Maugrim woke the site. He summoned his elemental – we fled. And then The Wanderer… Well, you know what happened to that." She turned to meet his gaze. "Honestly, your guess is as good as mine. Amethea could explain, maybe. Or the Bard."

The old vet scratched his straggled beard and took another slug out of the waterskin. Triq would've laid a decent wager that it didn't contain water.

"I wish I understood," he said. "Wish this'd never started. Wish I had a giant scaled lizard to fly me to the distant moons." He said something else, shook his head and took another slug. When she cupped a chapped hand round a cold ear, he gave a short and humourless snort.

"It's funny," he said, then repeated it louder, as the wind threw his words away. "It's funny! Just – things. If Jade'd ridden out after Maugrim when you asked, maybe we could've stopped this. Maybe none of this would've happened."

"Maybe," Triqueta told him. "And maybe the cold sky'll fall on our heads and shatter. We're here now, and this is what we're doing. Send the messenger back to Syke with the update – and make sure he sets a watch. We've got a war to fight."

She made Taure grin, just for a moment. "Yes, Commander," he said, sketching her a horseback bow. "Let the arse-kicking commence."

By the Gods, Triqueta had missed this!

Wounded soil behind her, war ahead of her, grey sky over her – however harsh the winter, the freedom of the open plain was what she lived for. The wind in her hair, the feeling of running, the warmth of the mare in the vast cold – by the rhez, she'd been too long behind city walls, held back by rules and boundaries and etiquette. This was *life*! Beside her ran Taure, his grin an echo of hers – for just a moment, they were the Banned again, free to run and with all the plains as their home.

Out here, her age was forgotten – the time she'd lost, the time she'd wasted, the things she'd seen and lived through. Out here, this was all she was, and it was everything she'd ever wanted. She needed to howl, and she threw her head back, lifted her voice in the Banned's ululating cry – for no reason other than she could. The echo from around her made her skin shiver with elation.

But the voices were so few!

Ress's voice was missing, and Jayr's. Syke had hung up his tack to stay with the City Warden. As the Banned's war cry faded, she realised that the missing voices would never come back, that this life was really over now, that everything was backwards, and the whole damned world was twisted up and dying...

Her mood crumpled, like a rag; she swallowed hard, lifted her face to the wind. The vast chill was suddenly welcome, the cold on her skin.

If Jade had ridden out after Maugrim...
Ecko and his damned patterns!

Now, they were the only ones left, for the Gods' sakes, the only ones still fighting. Seventy-two horsemen and women from the Banned; the same again from the city's garrison. And out there somewhere, the other side of the great Scar Lake, Ecko was even now establishing the base at Tusien, holding it until Triqueta could reach him. And then they'd make their final stand for the future of the world...

This was like some damned story.

Well, whatever happens, Triqueta promised herself, *we won't falter. We'll be heroes, one way or another.*

A realisation came out of nowhere, and it felt like hard hope...

This was the Banned's last ride.

And it was damned well going to matter.

The ride was a good one.

It stretched fantastically timeless, empty, somehow fallen down the gaps between one place and another. Away from cities and soldiers and politics, it was a freedom from responsibility, a glorious null-time, and by the Gods it was welcome.

But, as with all things, the Count of Time came for it, and he took it away.

As they rode away from the Monument, the land slowly changed, cresting into a rise and then running slowly downward – and, at last, the mounted force came within sight of the great Scar Lake.

They were northwest of Amos here, and they were taking no chances with random wandering beasties. Triq sent mounted archers to hold the ford site, while the company formed up and waited to cross the water, one tan at a time. The ford was a wide one, she knew, and the water bitter with the cold of the season.

"We'll make camp early, on the far side," she said. "Rub the animals' legs down, take a break ourselves. Double watches all round. There were bandits here as well, but I doubt they'll bother us this time." She chuckled. "Maybe the bweao's eaten them."

"Maybe we should make 'em join." Taure's grin was grubby, gap-toothed and promised a very special kind of violence.

Triq slapped the veteran's shoulder, glad of his support and humour. She was missing too many of her friends, and Taure was like a rock, something she could set her back against.

As they came closer to the lake itself, though, and the mounted archers were deployed to secure the area, their humour thinned and was gone, a wisp on the wind.

"By every God and his arsehole," Taure said, awed.

The air closing cold about her shoulders, Triqueta scratched her hands and stared.

The great lake, too, was dead.

She remembered, the image strong in the winter light, the perfect, sunlit glitter the lake had once been. Now, it was a stagnation of silt and dying weeds, of dead fish belly-up, of the corpses of birds, rotting and floating.

It reeked, the smell oddly familiar.

She pulled her cloak hood across her nose and mouth, but whether to keep the smell out, or the sob in, she didn't know.

Carefully, they eased their mounts down the slope.

As they reached the water, she gave Taure a nod and he dismounted. He went to crouch on the shoreline, his boots making scars in the scum. He picked up a fingerful of weed, lifted it, sniffed it, then flicked it back with a curse. Wiping his finger on his trews, he called back, "Smells like rot. Just like the you-know-what."

That was the familiarity. It smelled like the fractures, like the wound at the Monument.

Gods.

"It's not been like that long," she said. "The lake feeds into the Great Cemothen River. The tributary was clean when I crossed it..."

Just a halfcycle ago.

Panic rose and closed her throat, her hands itched like fire. *How had it got this bad, this swiftly? How the rhez do we face this?*

"Is there another way?" Triq asked. "Can we go round?"

"Too far." Taure's practicality was blunt as a fist. "No time."

Triqueta shook herself, curled her hands into fists and tore her attention from the awful rot. They had to cross, and that was all there was to it.

"We'll need smoke," she said. "Keep insects away. One tan at a time." Watched by Taure, she squeezed her knees and walked the palomino to the edge of the water.

At the shoreline, the little horse stopped. She lowered her head to sniff, then raised it again, her ears flat back against her skull. When Triq squeezed her thighs again, urging the creature forwards, the mare baulked, backed up.

Triq tried again, and the animal put a tentative hoof on the surface. She knew the creature's moods – the horse was her friend, trusted companion through too many adventures – she didn't push her further.

"She'll cross," Triq said, "but it'll be an effort. She doesn't like it much."

"Who does?" Taure commented. "You know we can't stop here, Triq—"

"I *know* that." She snapped it at him, then shrugged an apology. "Sorry. I'm scared – and I'm not damned well ashamed to admit it. Every time we see things, they're worse – and the rot is getting *quicker.*" She could see that damned wound like it was in her head, in her flesh, swollen with grief and horror and hunger. "I know we've got to fight – but then what? Even if we win—"

"Put a stitch in it," Taure said. "You got a force to lead. You got to cross this lake and reach Tusien, and that's all there is to it."

"But we can't just *leave* all of this." Triqueta loved the open plains; the little death of winter had been a natural thing, part of the cycling of the Powerflux and season. This was something else, something bleak and ravenous. "Even assuming we beat the snot out of the bad guys—"

"We come back," Taure said. "But first, we cross this water, and before the death of the sun. And then we'll have a council. And some food. And I need a refill." Ruefully, he shook the waterskin.

"That'll be smart when the bweao catches you," Triq answered him, grinning.

"Then I hope it's pissed enough for you to catch it and wear its fangs as a hat," Taure said. "Let's do this thing."

They did that thing.

No bweao came for them, but the horses hated the rank water, lifting their scum-covered knees and side-stepping, white-eyed. By the time they were all across, and the perimeter established on the lake's far side, the sun was falling towards the distant Kartiah and the air was frosting with sharp cold. The moons were blurs behind thinning cloud, and the company was shivering in its filthy and collective boots.

But the Banned knew their mounts, knew that every animal had to be cleaned down, and checked for bites or wounds – knew that even if they'd not been harmed, there were chances of infection and worse. As the city's soldiers set up the camp – the last one before they reached their target – the Banned did everything they could to ensure the mounts were safe.

Her palomino in good care, Triq sat by the fire, one chapped hand outstretched to the heat. Something in the back of her head was telling her that she'd never do this again – that these were the last fires, the last evenings, the very last days' rides ahead of them. For a moment, she missed Ress's wisdom more than she could bear – yet she almost couldn't remember the man he'd been.

When she'd ridden out with him and Jayr, a thousand returns ago.

It didn't seem real.

To one side of her, Taure sat on the cold ground, his knees drawn up and his arms wrapped around them. The fire made his face glow red, though his eyes were clear and cold.

Triq passed on the offer of the waterskin, and began to sketch in the dirt with a finger.

"Right," she said. "That's Tusien – there – on the top of the hill. It's got two major walls remaining, a tall tower at the corner, plus a scatter of broken outbuildings, statues and other bits." She was sketching it as she spoke. "There's an old long barrow out to the back, grave of the builder, by legend." The map wasn't to scale, but it would have to do. "Amos should already be there, supplies and defences set up; Fhaveon's force'll be coming southwest and it'll form here." Another line. The soil was cold. "There's a sort of an outer wall which should hold Vahl's forces at bay long enough for the defence to form up and for the fun to really start." Her grin was brief and savage. "As long as they can hold the hilltop, they'll have the big walls at their backs and they're good." She sketched another line. "We'll come in this way – if the timing hasn't gone all belly-up, we should hit the bad guys right where it hurts. If the timing's off..." Her sentence ended in a shrug. "Well, maybe everything'll be already dead and we won't have to worry about fixing the damned blight."

It was meant to be humorous, but the jest lost its force before she finished speaking and she lapsed into an awkward silence. The map looked so simple – she found herself wondering if Ecko was really there, if Amethea had survived, if Nivrotar's loco planning could even be fireblasted trusted...

Taure said, "What if they split their force? Do they have the numbers to fight us in both places?"

"Nivrotar didn't know. But no commander'll willingly fight a war on multiple fronts, you know that."

He snorted. "Fair point. We'll stay as out of sight as we can, quiet. We'll be safe enough."

She was going to respond, but she was interrupted by the cry of the archers on watch, by the sudden clattering of the camp-wide alarm.

Shit! Now what?

Her heart hammered, she was on her feet.

Bweao? Bandits?

Surely neither would be loco enough to tackle a force this size?

Her hands went to the blades at her belt, but her feet were already moving. She was running before she thought about it, running for the little mare and for the muster point that they'd marked earlier in the evening. She was shouting, could hear Taure echoing that shout – the call to arms, the command to form up.

Triqueta was Banned, had no need to go after saddle or bridle; still shouting, she was mounted and running for the camp's centre, her orders sharp and clear. She reached the square even as the messenger from the archer tan caught her.

"What is it?" she demanded. "The bweao? It must be damned hungry to—"

"Not the bweao," the man said. He was gasping and pale-faced – she could see the fear clawing at the insides of his throat. "Not the bweao. Centaurs!"

If there was one damned misfit creature Triqueta'd had enough of, it was the centaur. From Baythunder's posturing death to the craftings of Amal, the fireblasted things had been with her from the beginning – they were like bad luck, everywhere, and accursed of the Gods.

And now they were here.

Not going to split his forces, my arse.

She wanted to go out after them, to scout and to see what the rhez was going on, but apparently some thoughtless sod had left her in charge and she was instead standing at the forefront of a forming line – the Banned, like her, minus tack and wanting to go, the city's garrison slower, but drilled to efficiency.

It didn't take them long.

As the line took shape, a second messenger reached her; in her haste the woman's words fell over themselves. There was a whole herd of them, she said, some bore weapons and they were carrying lights like they didn't care who saw them. They were laughing, shouting, like some road-pirate gang out for trouble. Triq asked her a few more questions, making sure she had all the details.

Then she turned back to the formed-up force, almost trembling with excitement as a plan began to take shape.

You've made a mistake now, you bastards.

Oh yeah. I know how to stop this...

Stifling a grin to rival one of Ecko's, she gave the order to advance at a trot.

...if this works.

It might've been the biggest gamble she'd ever taken.

The creatures were easy to see. They'd made no effort to conceal themselves, and their lights blazed as they came on. There were about forty of them, younger than Baythunder had been, and raucous, kids out for trouble. They carried torches or rocklights or both, and they were oncoming in a gaggle, a ragged advance, their claws tearing and their mouths wide with threat. They were outnumbered seven or eight to one, but they didn't care – their long manes flew like flags, and though they bore no colours, pride and ego blazed from their skin. Triq wondered if they'd been sent – or if they'd come by themselves.

I know what you're thinking.

She was trembling, but her hands and knees were sure. For her plan to work, she needed them to stop, to pose and posture and to make all the threats. As they came closer, she rode out ahead of her own troops, her little mare arch-necked and stalwart.

The palomino was tiny compared to the great beasts that faced her. But she'd seen these monsters before, and she showed no fear.

And, as Triqueta had thought, they saw her challenge and stopped.

That's it, good beasts. You know you've got to play this through...

The one that came to meet her was among the oldest. He had Baythunder's look about him – powerful muscles and dark hide. His arrogance was loud as a shout in the night's deep cold.

"Go back to your city, human," he told her, baring his teeth. "Turn round, go home. This fight, this soil, this future – they don't belong to you."

Triq snorted, wanting him to face her, needing the confrontation. "I killed your sire, creature. Not too far from here." She'd no idea if this creature had been sired by blood or alchemy and didn't really want to know. "What're you? Revenge, now? You're a bit *late*."

"Fortune only," the thing said. He even sounded like Baythunder, his voice rich and dark, and now angry. "He was old, his time was almost done." He came close and towered over her, sneering. "Another, younger, stronger, would've taken his place." He bared his teeth, to show he had no doubt whom that "other" would have been. "Turn round."

Triqueta said, "Make me."

Behind her, the garrison's soldiers were crashing spears on

shields and shouting encouragement, the cacophony gathering volume and pace. Over it, the Banned's war cry rose and gathered force, and then fragmented again. In response, the young stallion flushed, the skin of his face and chest darkening.

"I'm not going anywhere," Triq told him. "I'm staying right here. And if you think you're big enough for your sire's claws, come and prove it. I'll take you down just the same."

Behind her, she could hear the combined forces of city and Banned chanting her name. The sound brought a rush to her blood like nothing she'd ever felt.

"Tri-quet-*ah*, Tri-quet-*ah*!"

I'll take you down…

By the rhez, she'd tear this beast to damned and bloody pieces.

The young stallion raked the dirt. He bore no weapons other than his spread hands and huge claws, but he was close enough to blot out the rising moons. Sweat made whorls on his human skin; he smelled like musk and heat and fighting.

He spoke down to her, softly, "Come on then. *Human*."

She was aware of a stirring in the centaur line, but her attention was ahead of her. The centaur grinned, whickered at the mare. The little palomino put her ears up, and Triqueta had a moment of absolute, white-cold terror…

Then the mare snorted, as scornful a noise as Triq had ever heard her make.

And in that moment, she loved the little creature more than she had ever loved anyone or anything in her whole life. Her confidence swamped her, and she laughed at the beast, taunting it. She was going to tear this thing a new arse.

Possibly more than one – seemed fitting somehow.

The young stallion curled his lip, but whatever temptation or command he'd given the mare, he wasn't stupid enough to try it again. Behind him, his own line were calling taunts, sniping sharp comments, but he ignored them.

Triqueta's knees gripped hard, and the mare stood straight up on her hind legs, her forehooves flashing at the creature's human chest. He made no attempt to evade the move, instead reaching as if to catch them, but they were too fast. As the beast swiped with a clumsy hand, the little mare dropped and whirled, lashing out with both heels. Triqueta felt the impact, heard the stallion's breath leave its body with a *whumph*.

Around them, there was an utter silence.

Then her own side started to cheer, wildly calling her name. The sky filled with noise.

Old, am I? Banned over, is it? Never doing this again?

As the mare swung back around, Triq could see that the creature's human ribs were broken, jagged under his skin. The mare put her ears back, bared her teeth. Her blood was high and Triqueta could feel her heart through their shared contact. It felt like thunder, like lightning, like a fusion of flesh to flesh – like she was a centaur herself. Even as the mare moved, she knew what the horse was going to do, could anticipate and move with her.

The stallion was laughing at them, cavernous and belittling. His force was shouting again now – they were jostling something, but Triq didn't get time to look. The mare was pacing forwards; she came up again on her hind legs, her hooves now flashing up towards the centaur's chin.

Triq held on, one hand in the mare's mane and her legs gripped tightly. Her other hand held a blade and as the centaur lashed out with his hands, trying again to catch her fetlocks, Triq opened a gash in his arm that welled instantly rich-red.

Slash! Like the wound in the world!

The beast recoiled; hot, rich blood slicked both of them.

Come on then. Come on then!

She was going to kill this thing.

Furious, the centaur raged forwards, one foreclaw slashing downwards. The mare danced back, light on her hooves.

But not light enough.

Triqueta felt the shock as the huge claw caught the horse, four long gashes, straight down the base of her throat. She felt the animal shake and her front legs give, felt her stumble and go down, struggling to right herself again.

No!

And the beast was there, right over them. Triqueta let go of the mare's mane, had both blades in hand – but she didn't quite have the reach. As the mare struggled to get back up, Triq was on her feet on the little horse's shoulders, slashing at the monster as it closed.

The mare jerked herself back to all four feet, but it was too late. Blood was streaming down her chest and forelegs, she was sagging and her breathing was wheezing tight in her windpipe. Torn between fury and grief, shrieking defiance, Triq slashed one blade sideways across the stallion's chest, and, as he winced, she slammed the other one to the hilt between his broken ribs.

Ha!

It wasn't in his human heart, but it was damned well close enough.

As the mare faltered and fell again, her body beginning to weaken, Triqueta was on her feet on the dead ground, going after the stallion as he fell back.

She was going to cut him to bloody *pieces.*

Behind her, she could hear people running – Taure, probably, come to see to the mare. She trusted him, knew—

Then something huge came out of the rising dark.

She knew what it was, of course she did. Something in her had been expecting this from the moment they'd stopped here – maybe from the moment they'd set out. The thing had been stalking her like a hunter, like the damned bweao itself.

The bweao it – he – had saved her from.

This time, her shock was less and his presence made her angry. She knew this odd, misshapen form that Amal had crafted, his chearl body and his axes that glittered in the hazing moonlight – but she didn't want him, not here, not now. She wasn't some damned damsel that needed rescuing, for the Gods' sakes, she was Banned and she was going to kill this fireblasted thing herself.

Ignoring the incoming creature, she went after the injured beast on foot, her remaining blade strong in her hand. The stallion was staggering, coughing gore, his claws rending great gashes in the soil underfoot. As she watched, pitiless, the creature went over on to his side, kicking in protest.

The Redlock-centaur stopped, seeming to understand her anger.

Triqueta ignored it and knelt beside the injured monster. Meeting its eyes, she spat in its face. Then, with a gesture as hard as it was deliberate, she cut its throat with the remaining blade.

She felt the ripple go through the centaur force as she did so, and she held her breath.

This was the moment she'd gambled on, her life's last bet. Herds followed the stallion, and if another defeated him, then they would follow the victor...

Would these? Was there enough horse instinct in the human mind? Or would they just...?

She felt the Redlock-centaur's flank beside her, the warmth both familiar and discomforting. She wanted to turn to check on the mare, but her attention had to be on the herd in front of her. If she showed a moment's vulnerability...

Across from her, as the darkness closed about them, the centaur force laid down their weapons.

Behind her, the cries of her name rose to a roar of fever, voices of Banned and city alike.

But her little palomino mare died on the empty soil of the Varchinde.

17: FIRST ATTACK TUSIEN

Tusien.

Once a speck on the wall in the cellars of The Wanderer, now rising out of the ground-level fog, huge and jagged against a paling winter sky. Its lone tower caught the first light of the rising sun, and blazed as if already aflame. Halfway between the now-abandoned Fhaveon and the ruined remnant of Scar Lake, Tusien's black and broken walls still held massive strength – they seemed unassailable, defended by the long slope of the hillside, and by an outer curtain-wall that crumbled forth about halfway down. Once, the ground would have been all grass and wildflowers – now it was lifeless, shrouded in winter mist.

Nivrotar had designated the great ruin as their target, their last stand, and they'd crossed half the Northern Varchinde to reach it. And, if her scheme had gone to plan, the forces of Amos should already be there; set up and waiting for Rhan to draw Vahl into the battle he could not win.

In theory.

But the Bard could see no sign of the camped Amos force.

He turned in his saddle and looked backwards, out across the plain.

And so: the final battle begins.

Out there, dawn mist seethed over dead ground. There were dark shapes in the fog and the cold: Vahl's army, straining to get at them, writhe and eddy and slaver.

A thrill of anticipation went though him.

It's all so close now! Everything I've been waiting for!

Around him, the warriors were weary and shivering, shadow-eyed and haunted. The voices of the Kas had called to them, touched them. The tan and flag commanders were numbering their soldiers, counting to see if any had been lost in the night's run. They barked orders, puffs of steam and instruction. Drums sounded, the sharp sounds muffled by the fog. Runners took tallies to Mostak's flag.

High above them, the sun slid slowly down the line of Tusien's tower. The air began to warm, and the mist to clear.

And out across the plain, Vahl's army began to move.

Roderick could hear them – shouts that grew in threat and volume, cries like echoes of bloodlust, now rising with alarming swiftness. He turned to the commander, but Mostak already knew – he was turning in his own saddle, barking orders. The drums changed tempo, stern retorts that brooked no delay. The warriors got up with a groan that felt like the hillside coming apart.

They formed up, flags and pennons fluttering like a last flare of hope.

From below them, there came a roar. A promise of death. A surge of eagerness and horror.

Fearless, Roderick answered it.

Boom. Ba-ba-boom. Ba-ba-boom.

There was power in the vibration, in the very sound. He could feel the heavy bass drumbeat in his chest, his throat; he could match and echo and rebroadcast it. He could call it forth, make it shake the air, the ground, the bleak ruins of the standing walls – he could make it shiver in a thousand bloodstreams.

The sound was pure courage. The heads of the exhausted militia came up, their chins raised and their eyes burning.

The drumbeat took them up the hillside, up towards where Tusien waited.

Below him, the snarl of the incoming forces rose in response. It grew louder, defiant – it rolled the last of the mist back with its hunger and rage and fury. It came closer, fast now. Vahl had heard the drums and now he came in at a run, his creatures racing reckless. As the fog rolled back, they were bright figments in the early morning, flashes of shields, a seethe of multi-hued fury, a rush of anger against the backdrop of the rising sun. The army had no formation: it seemed governed only by intent.

It *slavered*.

And he dared them: *Boom. Ba-ba-boom. Ba-ba-boom.*

The hillside rose before them. Behind them, the roar grew louder, pure lust. The mist had burned away; the sound rippled the winter-cold sunlight and the bright morning air.

And then, all at once, it became too much. The soldiers were strained to breaking point; they'd been pushed beyond their limits in the last days, and the hunger behind them was overpowering – they broke their ranks, and they ran.

Mostak swore, wheeled his mount, shouted orders. His banner flapped hard in the wind. The drums echoed, sharper now, the tan commanders shouted, but the fear was an infection and spreading fast. They were too little, too late.

Roderick stood in his stirrups, opened his throat to the air of the plain. He could feel it in his lungs, like he was attuned to it, like he could wield the very sky like Rhan wielded light—

The commander's gesture was sharp, cutting him dead. For whatever reason, Mostak was letting this one run.

Perhaps it was the only way they could reach the heights in time.

As they broke, the shriek became a ragged, mocking shout, and the pursuit came even faster. The very ground seemed to shake with it – as if Tusien herself would come down upon their heads. Vahl's force was closing the distance with terrifying speed.

The Bard let his kettledrums fall to silence, let his shoulders rest. He touched his heels to the big mustang, and they, too, ran.

Like Ecko, he was all but immune to fear – one of the gifts Mom gave her children.

While they were screaming.

Down there in the dark.

But sometimes, flight was the only rational choice.

The mustang was powerful, running hard to the top of the hill. The wind was chill in the Bard's ears, laughing at him. Around him, the drums had stopped. They'd become so routine, he'd almost stopped hearing them – now, their absence was deafening.

Behind him, the militia were running scattered, ragged and panicked, packs thumping on backs already sore, spears and shields in hand and breath short. Shouts carried one to another, cries of alarm and encouragement. Soldiers staggered, fell behind, were picked up. Shouts rose, cries. Roderick looked for Ecko in the morass, couldn't see him. The skirmishers were still out at the flank, though their horses were flagging. One of the mounted warriors had pulled ahead, bearing their presence to Nivrotar.

If she was here.

Behind them, the gap was closing with terrifying speed. Vahl reached the bottom of the incline – his forces were snapping hard at their heels. As the sun fully crested the dying remnant of the distant Fhaveon, so it streaked the sky with colours of pink flame. It lit the incoming force with rage and brilliance. They were close enough for him to see individual riders, faces stretched in hate.

They howled at their prey with a hunger that made him shiver – a hunger without humanity.

Mostak's force was reaching the hilltop now, staggering

but determined to keep running. Here and there, as wariness overcame panic, the warriors stopped and rested, hands on knees, leaning over as though they were about to throw up.

Judging flawlessly, Mostak's command was perfectly timed – the drums began again and, under the sound, the formation found its feet, and its courage.

The mustang slowed to a walk, blowing hard now, placing his great hooves carefully. Roderick picked up the beaters for the kettledrums. He began again, the drums' thunder answering the howl from below.

Boom. Ba-ba-boom. Ba-ba-boom.

His arms and shoulders hurt, but they didn't matter. The sound steadied all who heard it.

They could not afford to slacken.

Below them, the enemy's cavalry, once part of their own, had outdistanced the rest of the assault. The Bard could see now – eight or nine flags in total, though in disarray. Over all of them flew the white-feather banner of Fhaveon. The feather had been defaced, coloured blood-red.

The drums thundered loud, complex rhythms that echoed from the ruin's walls and reissued the commander's deployment orders.

But surely, Amos is here…?

Below them, the incoming force reached the curtain-wall.

The old wall had been long-shattered, rubbled to the ground in many places, and Vahl's army simply spread about its outside like an infection. It surged over and past it, swelling up the hillside like bright dye in water.

Laughing.

Where is Amos?

Mostak bellowed; his flag bearer swung a flash of colour through the morning. The drums picked up speed, each of them resounding until the noise was colossal, a rumble of desperation that echoed belligerent, back from the walls. Commanders were shouting, the militia were running to their directed places like cornered esphen – without Amos they had to turn and fight, they had no other choice. The Bard joined the movement, his heart thumping out the rhythm.

Boom. Ba-ba-boom. Ba-ba-boom!

In the cold morning, orders snapped, sharp and brittle, like sticks underfoot. As the running militia reached the edge of the flat ground, the rearmost tan, those closest to the pursuit, parted and ran for the flanks; the tan at the front stopped, did a sharp about-turn, and stepped forwards, shields slamming tight together into a wall facing the incoming riders. At their edges, the archers turned, arrows nocked and waiting. The mounted skirmishers peeled to the sides and paused, hooves thumping at the cracked flagstones.

The shieldwall was just at the outermost edge of the wide and overgrown courtyard, keeping what height advantage they could.

The Bard, too, turned to face the incoming force, his kettledrum still thundering, striving to give the fighters courage. He could feel the ground shake beneath the incoming hooves as if the walls themselves would come down; he could see muscle and armour gleaming as the attackers came on through the sun and the dirt. The gap was narrowing by the moment – as the spears thumped into place on the top of the shieldwall, so the command came from the archers' flanks, "Loose!"

Shafts arced across the morning, thunking hard and home. The incoming assault faltered, stumbled. The lead riders fell, tumbling over and over in tangles of legs and arms and reins and kit. Horses whinnied, riders thrashed, a plume of dust followed several of them, skidding, down the hill. Behind them, other riders jumped by instinct alone.

From the defenders, there came a ragged, vicious cheer – a first blow struck.

The archer commander called again. "In your own time. Loose!"

A Fhaveon archer could put twenty shafts in a fist-sized

target in less time than it took to tell, but the riders were close now, almost upon them. They were huge in the morning, walls of plunging muscle; their horses' eyes were ringed with the demented white of madness.

As the archers began to shoot again, picking their targets, the Bard desperately scanned the courtyard, the rising ruin.

Hot tension pricked in his throat, behind his eyes. *Where are you?* He aimed the thought at Nivrotar, though she couldn't hear him. *Where have you gone?*

A final look, a very last shred of hope...

You must have come!

You must!

And then there they were – their dark armour and their black aperios banners...

Amos had come after all.

As he saw them, his breath escaped in a cry. He let the beaters fall, the great kettledrum silence. He watched them run from walls and cover, knew the fighting style as well as he knew his own.

As the exhausted Fhaveon troops held defiant shield and spear, so three ranks of foot-soldiers ran across to close in front of them, snapping to a spear-bristling rigidity even as the surge of cavalry came on. Behind them and to their flanks, the archers had reinforcements now – all along the tops of the walls there stood figures, silhouettes against the sky. They were not all in Amos colours – some of them bore the road-ragged garments of Varchinde freemen, increasing their numbers.

They outnumbered the incoming cavalry, now, more than two to one.

Yes! Elation rang through him. *By the Gods, we will do this!*

The Bard saw the arrows that ripped across the morning and came down like black hail, devastating. Riders screamed and fell, others tore the shafts from their shoulders and kept coming – but the charge was faltering, now, stumbling in the dirt.

He heard Mostak shout again, heard the Commander's note of savage defiance, of utter relief.

And then the Bard heard something else.

The rushing of fabric. The creaking of ropes. The rumble of stone.

Amos had brought artillery.

And *levers*.

Tusien's outer walls were towering huge; they climbed into the sky as if nothing could touch them. But the ruin had statues, loose walls, room walls, rearing creatures of stone – and all of it was ammunition.

Stunned, the Bard watched as one of the statues tumbled, hit the overgrown paving and shattered, its face broken in half, its blank grey eyes open. The tan were upon it in a moment, but behind them, the covers had been pulled from the engines and the cups were already loaded.

The commander barked a single word, her voice like a whip.

Pegs were knocked from their housing.

And two huge arms swung, up and over, crashed hard into their stops.

Both cups were laden with a scatter of smaller stone pieces – fragments of the Varchinde's past now used to secure its future. They soared overhead, shadows scudding, and the scattershot came down on the centre of the cavalry advance.

There was a thunder of rock hitting terhnwood, screams of both humans and horses. Riders and mounts fell. The Bard watched as the arms were creaked back, the cups refilled with the broken fragments of Tusien herself.

Mostak's voice came across the morning. "Wait! They're too close now! Hold your shooting!"

Roderick heard the command, "Brace!"

The surviving enemy cavalry, bruised as it was, hit the shieldwall with a detonation like the side of a mountain coming down.

The shieldwall staggered, shattered under impact. Belatedly, the Bard picked up the beaters, began to thunder again at the great kettledrum. He found he was shouting, his steel throat raw as flesh. Under him, his horse thumped a forehoof on the old cobbles, shook his mane almost as if he wanted to go join the melee – but the wall of shields had crumbled now, and the cavalry were through...

Dear Gods.

From his mounted vantage, Roderick could see that the second wave of the assault was coming up the slope – this inhuman, a wave of monstrosities. But the archers had seen it too and the volley-shooting began again, two cities unified, showering shafts onto the incoming creatures. The catapults shifted aim, scattered more shots.

But the next wave was not upon them – not yet.

In the courtyard of the ruin itself, chaos ebbed and roared as the incoming horsemen rode rampage through the defenders. The shieldwall had scattered and the warriors had formed into small, round units, defending themselves and each other with a shield and spear at every side. The cavalry had responded, viciously, turning in tight circles, jabbing and harassing.

Soldiers fell, screamed, bled, ran.

Then Mostak's voice bellowed, and the drum sounded sharp – the Bard echoed the rhythm, galvanising the order.

From the back of the courtyard, the second rank, formed up of warriors of Fhaveon, advanced on the wheeling enemy horses.

They did so at a rhythmic stamp, their rage and homelessness and fear and elation all crystallised now into action. They hammered spear-shafts on shield-rims and chanted defiance, they pushed the horsemen back towards the slope. Mostak sounded the drums again and from the Amos archers, high on the wall, came a single, sharp command.

The next shots came straight down, hard, and at savagely close range.

Screams sounded – pain and fury. They echoed from the wall above. Hooves thudded hard on the overgrown slabs. Riderless now, the horses wheeled and stamped. The last few cavalry, still mounted, wheeled and fled.

Their first attack had failed.

18: SCOUT TUSIEN

The rush of the first fight over, Ecko sat like *The Thinker* in miniature, bored and pissed off. He was worse than useless in the middle of all this – didn't have the training to fight with a unit, and had no fucking desire to be in the centre of the melee. Unwilling to stick his head above the walltop with all the shit going down, he'd cased the artillery instead, curious about the first pieces of engineering he'd seen.

They were onagers, he reckoned, basic – but they did an impressive job.

Now the fighting was over, Operation Homestead had kicked into high gear. Orders rang from damp stonework, soldiers shouted, feet ran, hooves stamped. Barracks were being set up in neat squares and rows; at their centres, rocklights lit tidy piles of kit. There were no fires – not yet – they had too little fuel, and the cold was bitter. The sky had clouded to grey and the ruin's walls were moist and drear. Old buttresses curved over part of it, like giant broken ribs against the sky.

A scatter of rain made him shiver.

Lost amid the fused reeks of righteousness and testosterone, he felt both tiny and inept. He had about as much chance of kicking Big Boss Butt stuck in here as he did of growing a prop out his ass and learning to fly.

Chrissakes.

And to add to *that*, he was cold.

First his clothes, now his insulation? What next, was someone gonna peel off his fucking *skin*? More layers, more stuff lost.

It wasn't *fair.*

His adrenal glands kicked, bringing him to his feet. He booted sulkily at a nearby statue's ankle, and when it didn't go Talos on him, he booted it again. Irritably, he flicked his oculars, and scanned the ruin: the silent siege engines, the expanding camp, the various patterned flags...

Yeah, this is one helluva vacation spot. Lemme just get a thingy of rock and a souvenir keychain.

His gaze took in the walltops, targetters idly crossing on the patrols. The archers' spans were limited by the state of the ruin – there were huge, unsafe stretches of wall that they didn't dare tread. Yeah, like he could fucking show *them* how it was done—

And then, of course, he had an idea.

Well okay, so the idea wasn't new – but fuck it, he was bored, and he was restless, and he was feeling kinda useless in the middle of all this shit. And hell, it wasn't like it didn't need doing.

Grinning now, he shed his overcloak and clumsy footwear, and he left the mouldering Talos to his own devices. Fuck the cold; adrenaline and anticipation were warming him already, giving him a much-needed sense of purpose. His oculars scanned corners, seeking the ubiquitous secret doors, but they found only more stone. Apparently, the long-dead sage, whatever the hell his name'd been, hadn't read the gaming manual.

Gleefully, he slipped across the overgrown cobbles of the courtyard and found the long side wall of the ruin. He passed the remains of the vast stone fireplace, ancient soot stains still visible. He passed the green and slippery innards of what must've been the well – Nivvy had despatched crews of scrubbers to reach down to the water. They'd probably find tunnels, seething with restless undead – hell, he was almost tempted to wait.

But no, that wasn't why he was here.

At his shoulder now, the wall was cold and slippery, growing a reddish lichen, like rust. He eased along its length, his adrenaline thrumming and warming him through – Mostak's silent guards had no fucking clue he was there.

Yeah, I can so still do this.

He reached the front of the defences without being seen.

So, whatcha got for us, Mistress Control Program?

Have a look, my Ecko, she said, though it could've been just his head. *Tell me what you see...*

Beside him, frost crept like death up the dark stone. He crouched at the ruin's outermost edge and tuned his telos to the army below, scanning length by length until he'd seen everything they had to offer.

Come on then, fucker. No surprises, now.

There – the tumbledown curtain-wall halfway down the hillside, the ragged stone length that protected Vahl's force. There – the Lord's command tent, sigils and all, flanked by the horned and hooved vialer. There – the paddocks of the cavalry, the racks of carts and animal cages. There – one, lone stores tent pitched a sizeable distance from the rest of the site. And there – the endless, untidy sprawl of bedrolls that was the homeless people of the city, driven beyond—

No, that wasn't right.

Now, just you hang on a fucking second...

Telos focusing, he looked closer.

It'd taken Mostak's force everything they had to cross the plains – and they were trained soldiers, almost to the last man and woman. They'd also brought no baggage train – their supplies had come from Amos.

Which was why they'd been able to move so fast.

Ecko was no tactician, but he wasn't dumb as he was asshole-looking. Lumbering carts and cannon-fodder-foot simply did *not* shift their butts that quickly. Even the cavalry, armoured as they were...

What the hell? Daemonic magick? Portal power? They've invented the combustion engine? Oh, come on...

And he saw two things.

The first one, he clocked almost by accident, and he had to stop and think – to remember.

He could see the vialer, the beasties-in-charge, and he could see a large glut of Amal's crafted monsters – but he'd swear on his right bollock that their numbers had fallen since he'd seen them in Fhaveon.

And stuff was missing. Where were all the stone things? The golems that had torn themselves from Fhaveon's walls?

He wondered if they were sneaking round the back route, or had gone in through the ubiquitous underground tunnels – but he had a feeling he knew exactly where they were. They'd chased down under Fhaveon and were gleefully stomping the city's population. Amethea had told them this much.

But what about the centaurs? They didn't fit down fucking tunnels. Where the hell were they?

And, more importantly, why would Ythalla split her force like that? Fighting a war on two fronts was fucking stupid enough – but a war on *three*?

What the hell was she doing?

That, though, wasn't even the biggest problem.

As Ecko looked over the lurking force, carefully studying, he found he could see a peculiar, distinctive difference in the faces of the people – cavalry and foot alike. They had a darkness, now, an elation, a seething steam that rose from shoulders and gazes and foreheads. They had a burning sense of purpose, and a sheer, savage glee in what they were doing.

They no longer looked human.

They looked... visionary, somehow, like they were about to experience full-on Rapture. Like their Gods had come for them, descending in tongues of flame or whatever the hell it was; like they were rocking out to bad Norwegian metal as they found the true heart of Satan.

The Kas, whatever they were, had come.

But even that wasn't what caught his attention, wasn't the thing that froze him to his vantage, struggling to breathe.

Holy shit.

He backed up, rubbing his eyes, but it was still there – the image seared on his forebrain like some mental brand. There was the camp – if that's what you'd call it – of the city's jumbled homeless; the scattered bedrolls, the mess and the poverty. The place where the children had been gathered.

It was significantly smaller than it had been.

And sitting there, in the heart of the muck and the cold, there were the shivering huddles of those who remained – those who had once been the young people of Fhaveon.

Ecko had seen their eyes, their expressions.

Those that were left were old men and women, frail and drained, their lined and shrunken faces hypnotised by the blacklight of the Kas.

Nivrotar, Lord of Amos, stood austere in the light of her command tent, perfect and carved in monochrome. She wore soft, blackened leathers and a long knife across her belt, neither of them, Amethea suspected, remotely ornamental. Her expression was severe and her hair in a tight and shining-cold braid.

Flanking her, Rhan had his forehead in one hand, was rubbing his skin as if it hurt. Mostak paced back and forth before the pair of them like he'd never again be still. His outsize lamellar armour rattled and his hands twitched, as if reaching for a weapon – or a throat.

He said, "Why did you delay?"

The bright winter sunlight dappled patterns on the tent's fabric, though the stealing wind was bitterly cold. Amethea quelled an urge to shove her numb hands up her sleeves.

The Lord of Amos smiled. "Your fear gave you the speed you needed to survive," she said. "A good choice, Commander, and a brave one." The smile held no mockery. "Giving up control is not easy. And regaining it, once lost, takes a miracle."

Mostak snorted, unappeased. "This is your strategy, my Lord of Amos—"

"This fight belongs to all of us." In her dark armour, she reminded Amethea of old paintings, of histories lost – she seemed anomalous, somehow, some figment of the past.

"We face our own troops," she said, "our friends, fallen to Vahl's lure. We face the blight; we face the end of the Varchinde entire. Commander, if we fail, we will die up here to the last man and woman. I have stores, fodder, fuel," she glanced at Amethea, "remedies – but we are besieged, and our time is limited."

"Triqueta will come." Amethea's voice held a squeak. She forced it down. "I know she will."

"I believe she will," Nivrotar said. Her face flickered a faint smile, though at what, Amethea couldn't tell. "Larred Jade refused Triqueta once, which is precisely why he won't do so again. Guilt is a powerful thing." The smile deepened. "All things happen for a reason, little priestess. You, of all people, know that."

Little priestess.

All things happen for a reason.

Now, those words and the memories associated with them made her angry. *How dare you—!*

Beside her, Rhan suddenly coughed, a puff of startled vapour, and then doubled over, fingers to his temples. His face was lined with ash and shadow, he was shrunken and shaking, exhausted to a point she'd never seen – but he had a determination to him, was still fighting.

His voice like gravel, he said, "They're taunting me – I can hear them, all the time. Pulling at me: *E Rhan Khavaghakke.* I'm like the odd child left out of the game, the adult that's missing the party—"

"Ironic," Mostak commented, his tone like a slap.

"Oh, shut up." Rhan glanced sideways at the Tan Commander and the response had a flicker of his old, sardonic humour. "If you can't find a way to block them, don't make smart remarks. *You* can't damned well hear it."

"I'm Valiembor," Mostak said. "I can feel it in my very bones."

That brought a silence, as if they all strained to hear the voices of the Kas down there on the hillside, the monsters mustered by the curtain-wall. The creatures below them watched with a hunger that was palpable, even from here.

Amethea shivered.

"So, what now?" Rhan pulled himself back to his feet. "The camp is set up, stores and hospice ready. We just sit here until dusk?"

"We have numbers and ground." Mostak's pacing had an edge of mania, as though the tent were somehow airless. "We should strike back. Send bretir, co-ordinate the assault with Roviarath hitting Vahl in the flank. We can finish this – and we can *win.*"

Nivrotar chuckled, the sound as cold and bright as the winter morning. "It's the Kas themselves that await us, Tan Commander," she said. "I wish it were that easy."

The parley came under the traditional yellow flag. Against the bleak hillside it snapped brilliant, like the final piece of the world's lost sunshine.

Selana Valiembor, Lord of the fallen Fhaveon, ruler of the dead Varchinde; Kas Vahl Zaxaar.

She rose ahead of her two companions, rode with a palpable confidence, a new blaze of righteousness that reminded Rhan forcibly of Phylos. Young though she was, her Archipelagan heritage was suddenly visible in her bearing and demeanour – and Vahl himself seemed to float about her like a cloak, a rising flare of power and strength that she wore only to make herself beautiful. Ink seethed in her skin.

To one side of her rode the military commander Ythalla, the old soldier grey-haired, spear-straight and apparently unchanged. She carried two ink stripes on her cheekbones like war paint, and she bore the truce flag with a certain, silent contempt.

To Selana's other side rode Brother Mael.

The old scribe's presence hit Rhan like a fist. Mael had been the last good man in the city, a man whose courage and insight had saved Fhaveon – Mael had *humbled* him, dammit. Now, the old man rode arrogant, younger, his bearing almost mocking. He'd lost his pince-nez, and his face was sharp and shrewd, cruel.

He met Rhan's gaze with his brothers' humour, daring him.

A long time, my estavah. Tell me, how have you been?

Kas Tamh Gabryl.

The name was like claws in his skin.

His armour burned and battered, Rhan came to the ruins' outermost edge to look down at his family, his brothers – as if he could, and would, defend the great ruin single-handed.

Beside him stood Tan Commander Mostak, Selana's uncle.

Behind them, Nivrotar waited with her maps and her catapults, watching.

But the Kas intended no treachery.

Selana came forwards, Mael at her side. They were tiny against the hillside, fragments under the sky. As Rhan watched them approach, he could see the writhe of the ink in their skin, the slowly circling serpents that moved with their thoughts and needs and passions...

Images tumbled, tangling.

Four hundred years. Vahl screaming in blood and flame and steam and fury, assailing the walls of Fhaveon herself. Fire over the water, death across the plains. Samiel charging Rhan – "If you fail me, you will be as nothing." Phylos on the clifftop. Falling through chaos, rising through water. Fhaveon, House Valiembor, generations of children. Each crying babe in his hands, and his sworn protection. Now the last of the line grown to power and stood there, his brother in her eyes...

The images were bright, vivid, gone in a flash. They left him shaking – so much was layered in this moment, as if everything that had ever happened was somehow focusing *here...*

"I would speak in peace," Selana said. Her voice carried without effort, as though the wind itself did her bidding.

Mostak called in return, the words unreal: "I will hear you in peace." The litany was a human thing, ludicrous, tiny against the vastness of time and ruin.

Selana walked her horse a step, turned her face upwards.

"Then hear me, my friend, my defender, my brother, my uncle." Her voice was her own, clear and sweet – yet under it, he could hear the *E Rhan Khavaghakke* that had been thrumming bass in his ears, pulling at his heart and soul.

"I admire you," she called, "all of you! Your resistance has been strong. You've come far, and fought well, and your courage is commendable. What you've achieved is astonishing." Charm and sincerity wove through her words, were borne on the morning air. She called love up to them, opened her arms and her heart. "But you know this is folly. However proudly you acquit yourselves, this will be your end." Regret distilled from the words. "You cannot face us, and by the death of the sun tomorrow, every one of you will lie *dying*."

The word was like a slap. From his vantage, Rhan could

see the heat in her shoulders, in her eyes. And beneath her earnestness, he could hear something else – the challenge aimed at him alone.

Ah, my estavah, you're so tired, and your attunement so weak. You've been running, protecting, healing, chasing down my hunting packs, defending your kine. I've been keeping you busy, little brother, distracted. I've been wearing you down, and your weariness is obvious. You cannot face me, any more than they can.

Selana spoke with him, the two voices twisting, one upon another, a writhe of sound.

"Yet I don't wish you harm," she said. "I want to offer you what I've always offered you, what my family has always offered you – home, security, wealth, a hand in salvation. Love."

Love. Mutterings flowed across the hilltop, crept around the ruined walls.

"I make no secret as to who and what I've become, but I've done this for *you*, for Fhaveon, for the future of the world herself. I am Vahl, I am Selana, I am Phylos. I am the last child of Saluvarith and I am your friend. You can *trust* me!" The word was a plea, tugging at all of them.

Yet Rhan could still hear his brother. *You know how we live. We're drawn to those with strong emotion – ambition, grief, anger – to those we can understand, work within. You murdered her father, forced her mother, damned her city. What did you think she would do, Rhan? Of course she would come to me, and willingly, at the end.*

His denial was reflex: *Damn you! I didn't hurt Demisarr, or Valicia...*

As if in answer, the Lord walked her horse forward another step, and her voice rose to a paean.

"My people, people of Fhaveon! Of Amos! Of the Varchinde entire! I'm not your enemy, I never was!" On the hilltop, bodies tensed. "Please," Selana said, "you don't need to end your days in blight and starvation, or in war and pain. I can help you. I *beg* you..." and now she rose in her stirrups, calling to them, "...lay down your weapons, your flags, your drums, and come to me." She was their mother, their daughter, their sister, their lover, everything they had ever wanted. "I'll welcome you, I'll embrace and forgive you. All of you who choose to leave the ruin, the old ways, the stagnation and *death* of the Varchinde..." Rhan's name was loud though she didn't speak it, "...if you would have a new life, and progress – come down to me now. You'll be named as estavah, as brother and sister, and a place will be made for you when the world begins again."

On the hilltop, no one even breathed. Shiftings flickered among the gathered warriors, but no foot came forward.

"And make no mistake," she said, "the world will begin again." She sat down in her saddle and gestured at the army behind her. "It's why we saved the *children*."

The word had an edge; under its touch, Rhan flinched and shuddered. He could still hear the soul-call, his brothers pulling at him, but he ignored it and watched Selana carefully.

The young Lord studied the hilltop for a moment, then turned her horse full circle and went to wait beside Mael, her head lowered. He patted her shoulder, the gesture so human, so familiar and ordinary, that it pulled at Rhan's heart.

Ythalla took her Lord's place, armour shining. The old warrior's voice rose dark with an undertone of power – in Ythalla, the Kas were both eager and obvious.

She said, "But the Count of Time isn't going to wait. For now, we give you amnesty. You can come to us, one at a time if you want, or muster your courage and *revolt* against your commanders." She was smiling, cold. "Come down, be reunited with your friends, your loved ones, with those who've missed and needed you. We've got food, ale, fire, warmth and welcome for those who wish it." She turned, making her yellow flag snap, threw the last words over her epaulette. "But don't take too long. At the sun's zenith, anyone left will be beneath my blades and hooves."

And you will be alone, little brother, alone in a world of death. You will come to us, give yourself, because there will be nothing else remaining. The world will be ours and you will have let it happen.

Watching, Rhan said nothing. *Let it happen.* He was grappling with their presence and power, with the voices and the bodies they were using, with an onrush of memories too much to bear. Somewhere in the back of his mind he was railing – *Samiel, why? Why have you let it come to this?* But he knew the answer.

The Gods had bored of the world; it was an old toy, rolled away and forgotten. He had been left – had been set up and cast down – to be its caretaker.

Calarinde, lost love. Why did you do this to me? If you have ever heard me, hear me now...

But Mostak shouted the only answer Vahl was going to get. *"Bollocks!"*

At the response, Ythalla turned and sneered and spat, the gesture specifically aimed at her one-time commander. Selana shook her head, sorrow and regret; she looked up at her commander uncle as though pleading with him. Mael made no move; he watched the hilltop for a long moment, looked almost as if he would say something, then turned away.

As the three of them rode back to the curtain-wall and their own lines, the commander raised a hand for archers, but Rhan shook his head. Mostak's face was flushed, his expression unreadable.

Rhan realised that he, too, was struggling with his family so close.

And Vahl must be laughing at all of us.

By the Gods. Bring me war, brother, bring me something I can face and understand. I want this over!

Behind them, the overgrown courtyards of the ruin were lined with warriors, and they were shifting now, with temptation and unease. Rhan understood: they, too, had had enough. They wanted an end, they wanted to go *home*. Slowly, the whispers were beginning, a susurrus of tension and curiosity; a restless need that flowed from lips to ears, and was rapidly gaining strength...

Selana speaks! And what if she's right? What if her promise is true? What if there's healing offered for all? A future!

Food – and ale!

The zenith of the sun.

The warriors at the hilltop had been through the rhez itself. They'd lost their families and friends, their homes, their city. They'd run across half the Northern Varchinde, feeling it die beneath their very feet. The figure of Selana was like a light, bringing them home. Gone was the memory of the trick Rhan had pulled on the balcony – their Lord was here, and she was warm and real.

Because they needed her to be.

Okay, so he couldn't help it.

The image was haunting him; fucking thing wouldn't leave him alone. It felt like Eliza was ramming the point home – *See, you need to fight for the good guys, you need to care!* – and he just couldn't let it go.

So, fuck it, he went out through the defences, looping out round the edges of the hillside. They were all intent on the parley anyhow, and hell, if they saw him, they could fucking bring it on.

This shit was messing with his *head*.

The morning had clouded over, and the air was drifting with sleet, and bitterly cold. Carefully, well aware of his lack of kit, Ecko came to the outer edges of the Kas encampment.

The chill was sharp outside the protection of the ruin, and it had cooled his adrenaline, made him think. He closed on the site carefully, leopard-crawling through the cold, covering his woolly garments in Christ-alone-knew-what, and then pausing to scan and inching forwards once more.

Nothing saw him.

Nothing raised the alarm, or opened fire.

The place was quiet.

Too damn...?

He waited.

There were no morning muster points down here, no campfires, no breakfast. Neither were there blazing pentagrams, blood-drenched sex orgies or giant idols of goats with too many eyes. Frankly, if you came down here expecting to party, you were out of luck.

The command tent stood obvious; the horned vialer paced out on regular patrols. He watched them carefully – wishing to every fucking deity that he still had access to plastic explosive.

Boom.

Solve the whole mess.

But the vialer paced on, unseeing. And right now, Ecko only wanted the outskirts, the people that the Kas... *chrissakes...* the *children* that they'd used as fucking *batteries*.

Like Triqueta. Like Karine.

Silently, wary of sticking his belly on some giant pit-trap and heading straight for Rhez in a handbasket, he approached the camp.

And stopped.

He didn't feel the cold ground under him.

He forgot that he was in stealth mode.

Ecko had no idea of the last time he'd cried – chrissakes, not in his adult life, not even under Mom's delicate touch – but now he was biting his lip, his breathing ragged. It wasn't just the tiny huddle of the pathetically elderly, all of them curled together in the freezing cold. It wasn't the thin blankets they had pulled around their shoulders, or the corpses, eyes and mouths open to the black sky. It was the memory of Fhaveon, the children bereft of their parents and too young to understand.

Ecko's family had run an orphanage.

A world and a lifetime ago.

These children had run across the dead plain, and they'd been sucked dry, day by day, night by night, drained of their time and youth. What the hell had they gone through? What the hell had they thought, watching their friends age and falter and die? What the hell were they thinking now?

He swallowed bile, and the pile shifted.

In that moment, his resolve was stronger than it had ever been, it was absolutely powerful, sartorial, some fucking fist-in-the-face epiphany. He'd capitulated for Roderick, almost because he'd had no choice, but this... *this* caught him right where it fucking hurt. He'd seen Triqueta drained – ten years, fifteen? – seen Karine as a hollowed-out cadaver.

But this had no words.

Somehow, he'd tear these fuckers to pieces.

He'd make them tell him how to fix it.

Sudden thoughts: if they ate time, did they shit it out again? Could they puke it back up? He wasn't fucking scared of Kas Vahl Whatsit, he'd be quite happy to shove two fingers down the daemon's throat—

One of the vialer was coming his way.

He froze, focused his lowlites, watched.

But the beast veered off – it went past the edge of the people's campsite and over to the lone stores tent, the one that stood a distance from everything else.

It paused as if checking, then it turned and wandered back.

The little huddle of people shifted again. He could almost feel the time being sucked out of them, slurped greedily downwards and inwards, fuel for the commanders' strength.

It made him want to rage, to burn, to fuck everything up, really very badly. He wanted—

Oh, hang on a fuckin' minute.

A lone stores tent?

A distance from everything else?

Silently, somewhere in the back of his head, Ecko started to laugh.

The lone tent had a single guard, and a laced-shut front flap.

Ecko went in at the back, rolling silently under the edge.

And then he crouched in the darkness, almost as if he were right back in the great grey sprawl of London.

He was beginning to grin.

So.

What's the one fuckin' tent you put the hell away from everything else?

In fact, he was grinning like he hadn't grinned in days. He was grinning so much he was making his face hurt. *Fuck*, he'd missed grinning.

Oh, baby.

You know you wanna...

And they were all there, waiting for him. Heavy pottery balls, a fucking mother lode of them, all very, very carefully stacked. And with them all the little spiky caltrops, lovingly made out of terhnwood fibre.

And there, carefully placed on one side, a bucket of white powder. Not Lugan's Best Bolivian, but something just as much fun.

Yeah, an' it's Christmas. New Year. Thanks-fuckin'-giving, all rolled up together. Let's see you deal with this, *motherfuckers.*

It wasn't exactly plastic explosive.

But – gift fucking ccntaur – it was good enough.

His grin grew even wider. Somewhere in his head, his laughter was manic – *Oh yeah, you watch me now!* Somewhere, Eliza was looking at this on her fucking flatscreen, waiting to see what he'd do. Somewhere, at the top of that hill, his own forces were gonna be ground into shit and gravel...

Not if I can help it.

Ecko cut a long slit in the back of the tent.

He racked his boosting through the ceiling, tuned his targetters to the max. His pulse screaming at him, he chose two of the spheres for himself – they were all he could carry. Then he placed the bucket – with all the delicacy his technical wiring could manage – on the top of the pile of pottery.

He didn't bother with the door guard – not like that fucker was gonna last anyway.

He'd no idea what the range of this stuff was – but if it took out the people's encampment, ending the lives of those last poor fuckers that remained, and if it deprived the Kas of the final gasp of their fuel source, then hey, he was gonna take the risk.

Besides, he did fucking love the movie-explosion thing.

Targetters crossing, he aimed a roundhouse kick at the stacked explosives, just below the bucket of quicklime.

And then he ran like fuck, before the world went bang.

19: KHAMSIN TUSIEN

The detonation was enough to rock the ground, shake the sky. The walls of Tusien shivered and ran with dust. Mostak turned a single, savage look on Rhan, but the Seneschal shrugged, his terhnwood armour clattering.

Amethea's heart was pounding so hard she could feel her skin shudder. She'd run out of the hospice and now stood on an old wall, craning on her tiptoes. She could just about see the flare of flame and the huge cloud of smoke that was now billowing from the bottom of the hill. She could smell it – that strange mix of substances burning. The smell was Maugrim, the scent of his heated skin.

Faintly, she could hear shouts, cries.

Something in her heart said, *Ecko*, and she found herself laughing, almost unbelieving that he'd set off his fire alchemy right under the daemon's very nose.

At the hilltop, everyone was running, shouting, trying to work out what the rhez had just happened. Tan commanders bellowed, drummers sounded the cadence for order.

But then a voice cut hard across the chaos.

"They're forming up…" The voice was the Bard's, cold and

clean. The drums changed note – she recognised some of them now – this one was the order to muster.

From somewhere she heard the great kettledrum – *boom, ba-ba-boom, ba-ba-boom.* She could hear Mostak shouting, hear the flag commanders echoing him and the curses as the soldiers ran to their places.

"We were at parley!"

"What the rhez was that?"

"They blowing themselves up, now? Saves us the bother!"

Raucous laughter echoed after that one.

The kettledrum boomed, echoing in her skull. Soldiers scrabbled, tripped over guy-lines, swore. Everything was spears and shields and flags.

Then she heard the drums sound again, and the warriors ran – every man and woman to their place in their tan, and their flag, and their line. Their discipline was startlingly good, their ranked shields and spears impressive.

She could hear Mostak shouting, coughing, shouting again.

And then, there they were – she could see them, now, surging out of the smoke of their own destruction. The leading cavalry was a short line, but four-deep, the formation behind it ragged but furious. Several looked wounded, had taken flying pieces of debris; the horses, too. But they came on anyway, and they burned with righteous fury.

As though their injuries were unfelt, their damage...

Dear Gods!

Her healer's soul shuddered as she understood. Driven by the Kas, people and animals and creatures had no concept of hurt or injury – they would simply fight until they dropped, whatever it took. They would fight through shredded flesh and broken bone – fight until they literally could not stand.

It was a travesty, a horror beyond words. But what could she do?

Put your shoulder to the wheel.

Gorinel's words – and his courage – steadied her. She took a breath, jumped down. Her own struggle started here, and she would just do her damned best.

She spared the fat old priest a momentary touch of her thoughts – wondered what had happened to him – but she'd no time to fret, not now.

Outside the tent, Amethea had several defending flags of her own – not hers to command, but Mostak's reserve, held back from the fighting. Among them, rumour was stabbing back and forth. The incoming were monsters, they said, immune to death, they said, would fight with their claws and teeth, they said. Above her, archers scrambled on the walls, shooting through the smoke. At least one had fallen screaming to his ending, his neck snapping as he hit the ground.

And she could see their own mounted troops, the lighter-armoured skirmishers at the flanks, though trapped and mostly useless in this closed-in area. They were fast-response, waiting to plug any gaps if the assembled shieldwall crumbled.

From somewhere the Bard said, like a sudden rush of courage, "We will win this."

She heard him with her heart and her blood. Her pulse thundered like the drums. The very hillside seemed to shake.

Then Amethea heard the command to volley, heard five hundred shafts slice through the air. She could watch them arcing up, over the smoke and into the sunlight – they seemed to pause for a moment, high above, and then come back down in a hard black rain. She felt the ground and walls shake. Then she heard the command to brace, heard the colossal impact of the horses hitting the shieldwall, of the warriors stepping forward into the collision with a single, unified shout.

And then the mayhem really started.

She couldn't see it – not from here, the smoke had drifted across the field. Fear was making her sweat in spite of the chill air. Yet she could hear the tumult, the clatter of weapons and hooves, the shouts and cries and screams. It took only a moment for the first of the injured to be with her, a young man, his hands over his eye, and blood streaming from beneath them.

But she knew this, this was what she did.

As she clamped her own hands to the injury and helped the man into the tent, she was half watching the blind rage of the incoming horsemen – the defenders' flank was closest to her, and the attackers were pushing hard, striving to surround them, to get past the edge of the shieldwall and in behind it.

They had no humanity in their movements, no flicker of recognition. Injuries did not slow them, fears did not touch them. Something about them was both relentless and terrifying.

Horses and riders both were being hacked to pieces in order to make them stop. She saw one young shieldman turn and throw up.

Memories assailed her, borne by the smoke – Feren, and fighting, and falling. It seemed so long ago. Out there, horse bodies reared, hooves flashed, tearing shields from arms and arms from bodies. Weapons shattered, or tumbled and fell. More screaming, a chant of defiance that fragmented into shrieks of horror. People fell, puking and writhing; they clutched at gashes that would kill them, at dropped spears and spilled guts and courage gone forever.

And behind it all, Amal's monsters ravaged and raged.

"Amethea!"

She'd taken her attention from her patient.

"Sorry."

She was blood to her wrists, with no idea where it had come from. More were coming to them now, some of them hurt beyond words, some of them bearing broken friends. The courtyard was standing tense – she could see past the reserve to the second rank, more tan formed up and ready to plug the breaches, to step forwards and carry on the fight. She heard commands as the shieldwall tried to push back, stepping forwards and slamming shields hard into the horses' chests and flanks – it bristled with spears like some spiked creature – but they were outmatched and had little hope. The horses were driven, loco and demented. They were huge, hooves and teeth and fighting fearless. Before them, the soldiers were simply being ground down into the stones and weeds of the courtyard. They didn't have the experience to face this. The archers could shoot down from the walls, or volley over the heads of their own side, but the shieldwall just could not hold the weight.

It was crumbling, at both edges and at critical points in the centre.

She swallowed fear, let out a breath.

"Amethea!"

Cursing herself, she ducked into the tent proper. Her helpers had their hands full, her supplies were limited, and she had promised Gorinel...

Shoulder to the wheel.

All your training, Amethea told herself, *all your life has led to this. Now shut up and do it.*

"Don't move your hands, don't move your—! *Saint* and *Goddess!*" Amethea shouldered the lad out the way and gripped the woman's upper arm, fingers and thumbs in a circle, clenching as hard as she could. Below her grip, the muscle had been sliced clean through, the artery severed. The woman's elbow and forearm were covered with freshly pumped gore.

Cut like that, she'd taken a blade hard and edge-on. It had probably scraped the bone.

"Give me your belt tie." Amethea pointed with her chin. "Then if the water's boiling, bring it here." Even as she turned, there were more wounded incoming, some of them on their own feet, some of them being carried, on shoulders or on shields...

The horror of it blackened her heart, but she faced it, and she held strong.

Around her, the tent now seethed with shit and fear. All

of her rough sacking pallets – fifty of them, the best beds she could offer – were full. Other figures lay or sat round the tent's outsides, some of them tended by friends, some of those friends getting angry. The doorway was constantly bulging with more people, with hands reaching for succour. She was trying to help the worst ones first – but she didn't have enough *time*.

And it was too warm in here; sweaty and choking, all tangled up with the stink of infection and despair.

The woman's blood was slicking Amethea's fingers, making her grip slide. It had soaked the split-open sacking, and was sinking into the dirt.

"You!" Amethea caught the attention of another helper. "The man with the ankle. Go to the chest, take a cloth and the blue resin bottle at the front. Pour a little liquid into the cloth; hold it to his nose for a count of five. Then secure his leg so it can't move. When you've done that, I need the orisi herb – the one in the packet with the red tie. And where's my water?"

"Here." The lad laid a steaming clay jug by her feet and then handed her his belt.

"Good. Hold here." She directed him to replace her grip with his own. "Hard as you can." Then she took the belt cord and tied the arm off, gripping with her teeth for a tighter knot.

The flow slowed to an ooze. The woman groaned, shifted. Amethea wondered if she ought to dose her with the soporific, but she was only half-conscious and supplies were shrinking fast.

Voices cried out. For mercy. For help. For a bucket. The place was a shack of dirt and misery and she could barely see, the damned rocklights were so dim. Where was the runner she'd sent for more?

"Get more water going. I don't want to see you with idle hands." She was snapping at the helpers she had, but they jumped without question. "The greatest danger is infection. This isn't the treatment I'd recommend, but we don't have a choice."

A burst of shouting came from outside. The bottom of the

tent fabric stirred in a freezing draught.

"You! 'Pothecary!" A solidly built man bellowed at her from the doorway. "Get over here." He bore a belly, and the brassard of a tan commander. One of his hands was clamped to the side of his face.

"Speak to me like that again, you'll lose something personal." Amethea's mutter was under her breath. She made sure the tourniquet on the woman's arm was tight, put a fold of fabric between her patient's teeth, then very, very carefully poured a trickle of boiling water over the cut.

The woman sprang taut, neck cording. Her skin steamed, reddened like meat. She'd blister, but they could deal with that later.

"Now, you, cold water and thread me up a needle," she said. "Enough fibre for six – seven – stitches."

"Thea? Thea?" Another of her helpers was panicking. "You need to come, quick..."

Cursing, she spun round, but it was too late. The man on the pallet two down had soaked though the grubby bandage that covered the stump of his lower leg. There was a pool coagulating under him. Over him, another man crouched and panicked, shaking his shoulder, screaming up at the hovering help. The helper was trying to staunch the rush, but it was too late. Even as they grappled together to stop the flow, the injured man's head lolled sideways and his face went slack.

His eyes stared, empty.

The figure over him cried aloud, rocking, his bloody hands dug in his hair.

Goddess. Not another one.

Amethea felt sick, a rising wave of hopelessness. She swallowed it back.

"Has he gone?" Her voice sounded oddly void, like there was not even grief remaining.

The helper said, "I think so."

"You 'think'," she said bitterly. The flame in her faltered and she sagged.

Like it matters if he dies.

Maybe those who die in here are the lucky ones...

Futility loomed at her, leering and grey. Faith may have been in action, but if those actions were failing...

Briefly, she wondered where Rhan was. Presumably, he couldn't be spared from the fighting.

Shoulder.

Wheel.

"Take him out the back," she said, fighting to find the words. "As soon as you can, free up the pallet. We still have clean sacking – they're bringing it in as they empty the stores." She turned. "Young woman – you – with the kicked ribs." Amethea took long breath, flexed her cold and aching hands, and fought on. "Do you feel dizzy? Are you coughing or passing blood?"

Rhan anchored the left flank of the front line, facing the incoming horsemen, the Kas that burned in their blood. He bore no shield, but the point of his sword was fast as a whip, taking human throats and horse bellies. He could wield the blade one-handed, catching at spears with the other. Where he stood, the attackers flinched and fell back; the defenders formed with him and they held. But the melee in front of him was swimming into a haze, coaxed by the voices that teased him, by the temptations that sounded in his head. *E Rhan...* They knew how to play him – visions of the halls they'd once lived in, the lives they'd all led under the wise eyes of Samiel himself. Visions of Vahl, cast down for pride and rebellion; visions of himself, of Calarinde, of flesh and love and lust and betrayal; visions of his shrieking plummet through Kazyen...

The memories were clearer than they'd ever been; he couldn't think. But he couldn't falter – he had to *fight*.

The foot soldiers were being cut to pieces – the cavalry was over them, trampling them into the ground. It was flanking and round them and Ythalla was laughing, in her own voice and in that of the Kas. She was playing a longer game, pushing at the wall in multiple places – she wanted the whole damned thing to come down.

And it was only a matter of time before it did, and she would be free to bring death to the ruin's last defenders.

Their backs were to the wall, literally. They had nowhere to go.

About Rhan, the death was horrifying. His blade was fast, brutal, taking the throat of one, the belly of another, a lunge into the face of a third. But he was only one, and his exhaustion clawed at him from the inside.

His brothers had played him well.

At the far side, the horsemen had rounded the wall's end and were starting to hack their way through the warriors, hitting them in the flanks as they struggled to face the cavalry line in front. They were being torn down where they stood, trampled into the flesh of those that had fallen before them.

And behind them, Amethea's hospice was vanishing under a tide of injured – a tide he had no way to help.

A tide that would be cut down in its own turn.

The realisation was dire: *We will lose this.*

There will be no future.

Still astride his mustang, Roderick had stayed with Mostak at the command point, watching the battle and awaiting the Commander's orders. With them was Nivrotar, her white face calm and expressionless.

This was the last stand. If they were overpowered here, they had no way to flee, no escape and no fallback position. The walls of Tusien behind them were as unforgiving as the sage in his silent long barrow, now with all of these good men and women to keep him company.

Yet the Bard's absolute faith was unshaken – he trusted in their victory. Everything he'd ever believed was crystallising, becoming true. He could feel the waters of the Ryll on his skin, almost touch the images that the world had once shown him. He was there with Rhan and Ecko, Amethea and Nivrotar. And Vahl Zaxaar stood with them, his many faces shifting like firelight.

He could hear words in the throbbing of the command drums, a cadence like a song.

Time the Flux begins to crack...

The words were spreading like wet ink on fabric, like ink into skin, a blur of colour.

No time, no time, no time, no time...

The images were strong, exultant. The tumble should have overwhelmed him, but Mom's darkness had taught him a pure, almost elemental focus. He could feel a rising, savage shout of exhilaration that would split the very sky—

Mostak bellowed, sudden and sharp. The smaller drum rattled staccato, a call to fall back.

With a shock, Roderick realised that their position was being overrun.

No. Oh, no you don't, you bastards.

Focusing hard now, he concentrated on the crazed and driven force before him, on the arch of the winter sky, on the air that seethed between Tusien's walls. He could feel it – like Rhan felt the Powerflux, felt the light.

And he began to speak.

Once, the walls of The Wanderer had reflected his warmth and humour to the drinkers gathered within. Now he understood how that had worked, and he could take control of the ability – the walls of Tusien heard his voice, heard the power that Mom had given, and they reflected it back at the force below. His words didn't matter, his intent was all – he was their strength, their litany. As he had called the people from the streets of Fhaveon, so he called them now. His voice touched the warriors faltering under the hooves and blades of the incoming cavalry, the archers whose shoulders ached and whose fingers stung, the tan and flag commanders who were overpowered, not knowing even how to follow their own orders...

Mostak himself, the Commander tight as a knotted cord.

Like some war chant from an old saga, so he let the words rise, let them call to the ears and minds and hearts of the warriors that defended the hilltop.

This was Khamsin, the instrument that Mom had given him.

And he could win the battle by the force of his voice alone.

20: THE RED RAGE TUSIEN

Thunder.

Not the grim, grey sky, spitting its scatter of hail, but the dead ground beneath a rumble of hooves, a noise to shake the walls of the ruin itself.

Triqueta was at the front of the charge, the mustang surging under her, its hooves reaching and slashing at the soil. She was upright in her stirrups, screaming into the wind, fired with elation and fury. The red-maned chearl centaur was still beside her, pacing her like some damned guardian, but she wasn't thinking about it now – she was watching the enemy lines, their flanks to her as she raced to cut them down.

Bastards!

Her own force was outnumbered, but the opposition were only foot-soldiers, lamellar and shield and spear. They could hear – feel! – the incoming force and they were turning, shouting, but not fast enough. She heard the commanders start to bark the order for spears, but they were too slow, way too slow. She was going to crush them, screaming, into the mud.

To Triq's other side ran the centaurs, all rage and rumble. If they had any human conscience at charging their own lines, she didn't see it – they laughed like Baythunder had, savage and gleeful, voices thrown wide by the winter.

Hail and dirt stung her face, chapped her cold hands. She slammed the mustang like a battering ram, chest-first, straight into the side of the turning tan of infantry.

The horse was strong; it crashed her clean through the bewildered footmen and into the commander, his face etched in an instant of pure surprise. Spears clattered, screams sounded. Curses.

She was on her feet on her saddle, now, knees bent, balancing as she'd done all her life. Blades in both hands, shrieking, she cut the man across the face and throat and he fell, his expression sliced and shattering.

Chaos seethed and shouted.

Ythalla's forces had seen the centaurs incoming and they'd started to cheer, anticipating reinforcements – it was only as the lines closed that they'd realised the creatures were a cover, and that they'd hidden the lines of Banned behind. Farther up the slope, other fighters had seen the ruse clearly and there was a writhe of confusion as some of them tried to react. Some were barking orders, others were turning, there was shouting and a frenzied flapping of flags – but all of it registered only at the periphery of Triq's awareness. She was sweating, despite the cold; around her was a blur of colour and motion. Her throat was sore but she was still screaming, raw defiance and battle-lust. Under her, the mustang leapt and kicked as something slashed at his rump. She laughed, her footing easy, and turned to slash backwards with her right-hand blade.

It bit, cut, and something swore in pain.

Redlock was still with her, his red hair and tan hide constantly in the corner of her vision. The centaur the other side had been cut off. The opposing tan had found its formation and now bristled with spears, stomping in time and driving the creature back. It reared at them, claws flashing. Orders carried clearly now, and she saw...

Shit.

Below them, almost at the bottom of the hill, the enemy force had a reserve. A flag of lighter cavalry were armed with long spears, and about to hit her straight up the arse.

Somewhere off to her left, one of the Banned toppled sideways from his saddle, keening, both hands raised to the spear in his throat.

Her belly lurched, but she didn't slow down. Didn't think, didn't care.

Surging forwards, she left her own lines behind her.

From somewhere, a voice called her name, "Triq! Triqueta! Tan Commander!" but the words made no impression. She was savage with fury, release and revenge, her body singing, her reflexes faster than conscious thought—

Then, suddenly, she was alone.

The chaos was gone, the noise of the battle retreating. Her ears rang. The mustang stumbled, almost dropped to his knees in the muck, but he righted himself, snorting.

The hail had turned to slush, cold and wet across her shoulders.

When she looked round, she saw open ground, a gap in the fighting. She slipped back to her seat, the elation draining out of her like piss down her leg. Redlock was still there, his huge form fighting to break through a tight, heavily armoured tan that now held him at spear-point, but there was no one else, no one close.

In a rough half-circle stood a grinning gaggle of the horned vialer, all of them bare-chested and heavily armed.

"Clever," one said. "But just as easy to undo."

By the Gods' hairy bollocks – they, too, knew exactly what would turn the centaur herd. If they tore her down, then all of this...

For the first time, she wondered at the wisdom of her idea.

Battle shouts and fury seemed to reach her ears through a seethe of tension. From somewhere, white light flashed savage. She was closer than she'd realised to the top of the hill – but she was caught, the reserve on one side and the responding cavalry on the other. Drums thundered. Tumult raged in all directions.

Here, she was the eye of the storm.

"Come on then," she said, her voice low. "Amal died, you won't last much longer."

Unimpressed by her defiance, they spread out, half-crouched and weapons held low. The mustang snorted again. His front hoof tamped at the ground. Knowing they were showing off, screwing her fear back into fury, Triqueta came again to her feet on the saddle. She stood, knees bent, and aimed her blades at the one who'd spoken.

"Come and get me."

The vialer were swift, mocking; they started to circle her. The mustang stood solid, throwing his head up and down, his shoulders twitching. On her feet, she could give him no commands – instead, she watched, waited. The beasts were taunting her and she knew it. She was going to carve them into gobbets.

But their attack didn't come.

There was a sudden surge of noise, and straight into one of the circling creatures slammed a heavy, misshapen thing wielding two bloody axes. It was savage and furious, injured and bleeding and overprotective and, by every cursed God, it was *unnecessary*.

Gods *damn* him!

Suddenly, she really was furious – not with the vialer, but with Redlock, with this damned shadow that just wouldn't leave her alone. First the bweao, then the centaur herd, now this? What the rhez did he think she was, some housebound seamstress?

She found herself shouting at him, a furious torrent of words, "Go away! Go away! I don't need you!"

But the vialer were closing on her now, their games over.

Then everything happened at once.

Redlock was bare-chested, scarred and sweating, his teeth bared, claws and axes too fast to follow. He was hacking at everything to get to her. She was still shouting, she didn't even know what. The mustang jumped sideways to avoid the first of the incoming vialer – but knocked straight into the second. The horse lurched, and she was off the saddle cantle; the vialer's blade-strike missed her as she fell. She landed on her feet on the ground, but the horse was on his hind legs, mane flying, hooves flashing at the creatures' faces. Using him as a distraction, she cut down the first one, blade slashing it across its belly.

It burbled, hands flailing at its spilling insides, but she kicked it over, right under the hooves of the panicked mustang.

Redlock hacked down another, and a third, merciless and brutal. She'd never seen anything fight like he could – his sheer skill was stunning, artistic and fast and absolutely pitiless, now brutal with the power of the animal he'd become. On his hind legs, he was bigger even than Baythunder had been. He blotted out the winter sky, his claws gashing faces and shoulders clean to the bone. As he crashed back to the ground, hair flying, she found a lump in her throat.

Red!

Had to look away. Had to shout, almost crying, "I don't need you! Dammit! I don't *need*—!"

A cut opened her collarbone, hurting. Blades still in hand, she viciously rounded on another of the vialer, cross-slashing it, shoulder to hip. It reeled backwards, tripped and lay kicking. She went after it, needing to open its throat before it got up again.

But the vialer were smart, and there were still three of them standing. Out of the corner of her eye she saw one of them had got round behind the fighting Redlock. Even as Triqueta turned, spitting her flying hair out of her mouth, she knew what was going to happen.

Saw it unfold, as if the Count of Time himself had slowed to watch.

Smirking, the vialer cut the tendons on both of the huge creature's rear legs. Redlock bellowed, lashed out backwards – he was too smart to rear. He tried to turn, but there was another vialer there, and then there were spearmen, closing on where he fought. Their commander bellowed orders, and Triq realised what a Gods-almighty target he must have made himself. She forgot her own foes; she ran towards him, her whole body charged with denial.

"No! No…!"

She wasn't close enough.

He staggered back and fell onto his rump in the bare dirt.

She was bawling, now. "No! Why did you *do* that? You didn't need to come after me!"

But the spearmen were closer than she was.

From the top of the slope, the searing white flash came again – the Amos forces were fighting to reach them, crushing the Ythalla's army between themselves and the Banned.

But it was too late.

"Redlock! *Redlock!*"

Dust and dirt and cold blinded her. Suddenly there were horses everywhere as the rallying cavalry finally turned.

They were overwhelmed, surrounded.

Struggling through, slashing right and left almost blindly, she caught a glimpse of him – even arse-down, his axes were still savage. Anything that came close died screaming. His red mane was bloody and stuck to his skin; his teeth were streaked with gore. He was bellowing, wordless with rage and pain.

Maybe, if she got there in time, maybe, if the Amos force reached them…

But it was too late. The spearmen were all round him now. There were horses kicking and the damned vialer, and he couldn't stop them all. Even as the Amos force crashed through, she saw the spears come down hard, stabbing over and over, saw Redlock as he crashed sideways, fighting furiously to the very last of his strength.

She saw the wounds torn in his body.

Saw the vialer cut his throat, shouting with triumph and brandishing its blade at the sky.

Saw the blood as if it was the only colour in the winter cold.

It soaked her vision red, and she remembered nothing more.

When her head cleared, she was being held down.

She was on her back, cold and drained, with a faceful of sleety drizzle. Her arms and legs were pinned by crossed spears, each driven point-first into the frozen dirt.

She swore, struggled to rise, but a voice said, "Easy, Tan Commander. It's all right, it's over. For now."

The ground was cold. Cursing, she craned her head, trying to work out what the rhez had just happened.

She'd bitten her lip, and her mouth tasted like blood and metal. She turned her neck and spat.

"What...?" she began.

A heavy military boot came down in her field of vision. The voice said, "You're a hero, Triqueta of the Banned. You've won us the day."

"Then let me up, for Gods' sakes. My arse is like ice."

At a gesture, the spears were withdrawn. She sat up, shivering, looking for her blades.

But her gaze stopped on the slumped figure of the red centaur. *Oh Gods.*

He lay still, a cold lump in the failing light. The air was bitter; her breath clouded away from her as if she could exhale her own life and just lay down beside him. Give up all of this madness, once and for all.

"You stupid motherfucker," she whispered. The word was one of Ecko's, but it seemed to fit.

She tried to stand, failed, crawled on cold, wet knees over to where he lay. When she reached him, she stopped, unable to speak. She made herself look into his face, put her hand on his shoulder, almost as if she could shake him awake.

Redlock?

His axes were still in his hands, his knuckles still white, his eyes still open. He stared out across the freezing hillside, out past ruin and wreckage.

In his face, she saw Feren.

She saw Baythunder.

She saw a Banned party, firelight and ale and boisterous humour, a square of spears laid out in the summer grass. Within them, Taure wrestled a bare-chested mercenary champion, a red-haired man she'd never seen before – they held a fifth spear between them, each fighting to pull the other one over. She remembered clearly how the merc had downed every challenger, to much coarse wit from the watching lines. He was damned good, whoever he was, and when Taure, too, had bitten the dirt, she'd stepped out herself. She'd been half the man's age and less than two-thirds his weight, but she'd picked up the spear and challenged him.

He'd eyed her curiously, but hadn't insulted her by refusing. Syke had counted down, and the Banned had called her name, stamping in time, "Tri-quet-ah!" She'd waited until the mark to start, then had stepped towards him and kissed him squarely on the mouth.

But he'd been sharper than she'd realised – hadn't been shocked enough to lose his grip on the spear, or to let her trip him backwards. Instead, he'd willingly dropped the thing and just kissed her straight back, passionate and unashamed. The fight had disintegrated into shouts and cheers, fragments of thrown food. He'd broken away from her, grinning at trickery and kiss both.

"What do I win?" she'd asked him, the spear still in one hand.

His grin had broadened into pure, whetted mischief. "Anything you want."

But summer and firelight were long gone, and he lay dead on the cold ground, the sleet settling over his skin. Shivering, she tried to retrieve his axes, but his fingers were locked solid – she couldn't prise them free. After a moment's struggle, she found herself yanking in a rush of temper, her body shuddering with something between fury and grief. It was huge and impossible, something that clamoured for this not to have happened, for him to wake up, to turn over, to be back in the warmth of that fire...

Those last shouts – *I don't need you! Dammit!* – rang like bells, like a haunting figment that would never leave her be.

And then she was shaking, raw and hurting, furious at him, at herself.

In a gesture that was pure instinct, she took her belt-blade, dug the point under one of the stones in her cheeks. Blood oozed down her face. She tried to prise the thing out, just like in the dream—

A warrior's scarred gauntlet reached down, closed firmly on her wrist.

The same man's voice said, "He died fighting."

She swore, let the blade fall free. She felt sick, felt like she ought to be crying, but there were no tears. Instead, she wrenched herself upright, her legs as weak as a newborn foal's.

The man said, "You broke one set of teeth and two arms before we managed to put you down." He chuckled, though the sound was bleak. "No one's seen the Red Rage in my lifetime – longer. They sent for me in person."

The comment made her look round, tear her eyes from the centaur's body.

The voice belonged to a small, tightly muscled man, his shoulders strong and his energy palpable. His lamellar armour was odd, somehow archaic, and slightly too big for him. He looked like he'd borrowed it for a pageant.

But his face was lean, stern, the line of his nose almost Archipelagan. He punched a fist against his chest, a formal gesture she didn't return.

She glared at him. "And who the rhez are you when you're at home?"

"I'm Mostak Valiembor," he said. "Tan Commander." It was delivered without boast or inflection. "Your friend, the apothecary, is on her way down. The Lord Nivrotar also wishes to speak to you. For now, we've established a perimeter and secured the area." His eyes were sharp as claws, his energy palpable. "A truce has been flagged, but you'll forgive me if I don't hold my breath."

Triqueta snorted. "Bloody right." For the first time, she turned to look out at her surroundings.

"Dear Gods." The words fell away from her and rolled down the hill like stones.

The slope was a tangle of bodies and weapons and fallen flags, decorated by the black flappings of the hungry aperios. Pain was everywhere, audible, harrowing; in places, hands still clawed for help.

Down among the fallen, there were horses, bloated and injured and broken. One of them struggled to stand on a shattered foreleg, failed. Here, there was a centaur, her hide stained with blood. Beside her was the cavalryman she'd torn down, his chest raked open with huge claws; his organs had swollen and blood soaked his colours.

Among the dead and the dying walked several tan of Amos warriors, in pairs and bearing short blades. The slitting of throats and the salvage of kit were brief and efficient. Every so often, they would stop to help someone, and then point them or carry them to the ruin at the hilltop, to the fires that burned against the walls.

"Dear Gods," Triqueta repeated softly.

"We won," Mostak said. "Today."

And then there was a cry of her name and a flurry of cloaked figure stumbling down the hillside. The hood blew back, and the hair was blonde and the face grubby, familiar, a mote of hope in the rising darkness. And Triqueta and Amethea were wrapped in a friends' embrace beyond fear, beyond life and beyond warfare. Suddenly, Triqueta was crying after all and she didn't care. She sobbed like a child, her body wracked to spasm with the force of it.

"Thea. He... he..." She was sobbing too hard, couldn't speak.

"I know, they told me." Amethea was crying too, her voice was catching. "I'm sorry, I'm so sorry..."

"I know." It was facile, but there were no words adequate, and they both knew it.

The two women pulled apart, stared at each other, streaks through the dirt on both their faces. Amethea gripped her friend's shoulders with hands that were strong and still as stone.

She took a breath, said, "He couldn't have lived like that, you know that. He wanted... he *chose*..."

"I know," she said, again. "But I can't help it. I told him... the last words I said to him..."

"Do you remember?" Amethea's words were calm, firm. "Maugrim's chain, Redlock's cough? He was in my care, do you remember?"

"If you're going to tell me he would've died anyway—"

"Not died, Triq." Amethea's gaze was sure. "Got old. And soon. Been unable to fight, to breathe. Even without what Amal did to him, blood clots in the lungs don't just go away. He died in a battle, weapons in his hands."

"I *know*," Triq said.

Then something else occurred to her. "He... had a wife." Triqueta looked round her, as if the woman would manifest out of the cold. "A daughter – she'd be grown now. They—"

"If we get out of this," Amethea said, "we'll find them. Take them his axes, or something."

"We should move." Mostak's voice was chill, wary. "I've no wish to stay in the open. Gather what you can, and we'll return to the hilltop. And you, Master Apothecary, you're needed."

"Yes, Commander." Amethea nodded, her face bleak. As they turned to look up the hill, she said, "Nothing, in my whole life, could've prepared me for this. They came after us at Fhaveon, down into the tunnels. And I ran here. The only survivor, as far as I know. I crossed the plains alone. And now, I try..." She looked at her hands as if they were strangers, swallowed hard. "I try and save as many as I can."

Triqueta took her friend's hand in her own.

As they went back up the hill, she didn't let go.

PART 3: FRACTAL REALISATION

21: THE ILFE RAMMOUTHE ISLAND

Jayr the Infamous stirred, cold.

Her body was heavy, weak as water. She could barely raise her head. Her arms and legs felt like dead stone. She struggled to focus, but had no sense of how much time had passed.

What the rhez happened to me?

She opened her eyes to darkness as deep as the tunnels of the Kartiah. She couldn't see herself, let alone look to check on Kess. She listened for a moment, then made herself move, careful and silent.

The floor beneath her was smooth stone. There was stone to either side of her, and there was a faint breeze on her face, indicating a very large space somewhere ahead.

She'd no idea why she was still alive.

She remembered, pieces with jagged edges. Rammouthe Island. The tsaka with their mad, curved horns. Landslide and falling. The creatures who had said: *Our time comes at last... Samiel can no longer hold us. No more exile, no more starvation. We will be free.*

As she came more awake, she wondered why they'd not restrained her.

Maybe they'd just not cared.

Jayr had no memory of her life before the Kartiah, no understanding of why, as a small child, she'd been traded away. The dark was all she'd known, and she could navigate it, by the damned Gods, like a Grassdweller could walk down a trade-road.

She touched a hand to the wall. The stone was distinctive, not the hard edges of the Kartiah, nor the softer, sandier stone of the plains. It was flawlessly smooth, but had no feel of being worked. And there was potency to it, a luxurious, moving chill that she had no way to name.

It felt like it was breathing.

Shuddering, she ranged further forward.

She found Ress, his faint warmth slumped by one wall. He was conscious, his breathing shallow and too fast. As she bent over him, he latched a hand into the front of her vest and pulled her down so he could whisper in her ear, "No time. No *time.*"

"Never mind that now." She put her hands under his arms, lifted and steadied him. He felt light, shrivelled. When she went to let him go, he staggered and coughed, then he lurched to one side and almost pulled them both over. She caught him, and he felt like a bundle of sticks.

She thought of Penya, of dust and ashes.

And that was when Jayr realised...

They were going to die here. The Kas hadn't bothered to kill or restrain them, because they were caught – they'd been left alive in mockery, blundering blind like lost and squeaking esphen. Even if they found their destination, even if they were able to return above ground, they would never go home. They would never leave this place; never see Syke or Triqueta or their Banned family again.

Suddenly, the darkness felt very hard, and very real.

Jayr clenched her fists. In that moment, she understood this wasn't a game any more, a jest, an insubordination. They were going to die here, sooner or later. And there would be no long ditch, no Banned fire, no songs to celebrate their lives...

She would never see the light again.

Ress said, almost as if he'd heard her, "We... must walk."

And she answered him, "I know."

Slowly, painfully slowly, they wound through a vast and sprawling maze, a mighty ruin of the breathing stone. The air was always in their faces, and it smelled like something waiting.

But Jayr knew the darkness, and Ress's focus never failed. After a time, the walls faded away. Jayr's senses tingled to a rising whisper of power.

Not the Kas.

Something else.

Something *bigger*.

As they crept forwards, the air began to grow cold, a shiver that was tangible on her skin, a thrum like a slow pulse. She paused, held a hand for Ress to stop.

"Something's here," she said, her voice low. Ress twitched and muttered. "Something... I don't know. There's something in the air. It's like it's watching us, like..." She was no damned poet – whatever it was, she had no words to describe it.

After several breaths, Ress said, "Must... walk."

"I know that." The tickle made Jayr want to sneeze. It was like a heartbeat, or the rhythm of a song.

"The Gods. Made Rammouthe. From their flesh," Ress said, his voice breathy, barely a whisper. Jayr had to strain to hear him.

She shivered, said, "Don't be ridiculous."

He fidgeted. "This is the Ilfead-Syr. The Well of the World's Memory. It was made *first*, made from Godsflesh. Made for the children. It's a toy." He started to laugh, then gagged and fell silent.

Jayr's senses were being overcome by the soft rhythm. It was lulling, deceptively sweet.

Godsflesh. Made for the children. A toy.

This time, she said, "We must walk."

"But they forgot about it," he told her. "There's nothing down here."

A chill raised the flesh across Jayr's shoulders.

Nothing down here.

"Ress..."

He grabbed her, his hand like a claw. The grip was tight, almost painful. He was panting now, as if he was struggling for focus, or to remember something.

"The Library," he said. He shook her to make sure she was paying attention. "'Time when Substance of the Gods.' Do you remember the Library? The words grew. The words I read. They grew in my head. Like a plant, like an infection. They brought us here. So we can *remember.*"

She remembered. Remembered the light draining out of Ress's eyes, remembered Nivrotar telling them to leave the books alone...

They grew in my head.

"Ress," she said. "You're scaring me."

He let her go. For a moment, she thought he'd folded, doubled over with age or pain, but as she turned to him, he spoke again.

"We're close," he said. "The stone here... it warps under the weight of the memories. The walls move, writhe. Or we do. Like the Ryll, like the Bard touching the water... the Ilfe is too much for mortal man to bear. It means everything's *twisting.*"

Twisting.

"Ress..." Her tone was a warning.

His hand touched her skin, traced the line of one of her scars. "Trust me. I know. Can *feel.* We're almost there."

Two isolated fragments of human vulnerability lost in Rammouthe's seething soul.

They kept walking.

They went onwards through a vast passing of the Count of Time. They moved in silence. Several times Jayr was convinced they'd retraced their steps, or turned back on themselves – but something drew Ress like a lure. He shambled onwards, a man obsessed.

He grew weary, and fell often. She caught his elbow – painfully thin – and helped him. He leaned more and more on her strength.

Eventually, he stopped.

"Jayr," he said. "We've come... we're here."

"We're *where*, for Gods' sakes?"

"Jayr...!" His voice was crystallised horror. "It's a tomb, all unsealed." He was really shaking now. "A cavern, goes on forever. The walls just..."

The fear in his voice was making her chest tighten.

"What the rhez are you talking about?"

"You read it, Jayr." His hand clutched at her, desperate. "You read the book from the Library. Tell me you remember?"

Dread crawling all over her skin, Jayr suddenly feared she knew exactly what he was talking about.

The words were as clear as the day she had read them.

How could we have believed that the Substance of the Gods, the Ilfead-Syr, the home of the Well of the World's Memory, could be so utterly chilling to the souls of such as we?

It was coming back to her now, faster as her memory began to pick up the thread.

We found at last the island's inhabitants... their faces were empty – their eyes held nothing but nothing, telling us that nothing had been their deaths...

"Jayr." He was still whispering. "The *floor*!" He shrank back against her. "By the Gods...!"

"It's all right," she said. "I've got you."

But Ress was trembling. "Their *eyes*!"

All were made more terrible by their faces, faces that held not despair, and yet not relief or release... their eyes reflected nothing...

Do not, I beg of you, ever return here.

And, as Ress spoke again, his voice melded with the memory, as though the words had all been his. He said, "This is the Ilfead-Syr, the home of the World's Memory. And its Guardians... they're all still here." His voice was soft with dismay. "They go on, into the darkness, into the endless Count of Time. Their eyes are all open."

Slowly, Jayr became aware that there was light, glimmering in the stone floor. It was faint, but it was enough for her to see.

Around her was a vast underground chamber. It had no walls, and the polished-smooth floor stretched away in every direction, limitless.

Power pulsed softly beneath its surface.

Ress stood a half-pace ahead of her.

And he was *older* – stooped and frail, in the last days of his life. His scalp was wispy and his arms and legs shrivelled and bent. For a moment, Jayr blinked at him – and then she realised what she could see.

Penya. Triqueta.

His time sucked like sustenance.

By the rhez.

Was she, too, older? Did that explain the odd weakness when she'd awoken? The Kas were jesting with them, teasing them like prey – perhaps they would come back.

But Ress was pointing, now, out across the emptiness.

All round them, the shimmering floor was covered in bodies, shadows against the light. Men and women, children, farmers, peasants, merchants. They were unusual in appearance, long-limbed and graceful. Their skins were weathered and their garments preserved.

Yet they were grey, as if drained of all passion.

As Jayr looked further and further outwards, the sleepers were numberless – death without end. Most chilling of all, their eyes were still open. They stared upwards blindly, and their expressions were empty, forgotten and forsaken. Expressions of nothing, eyes like windows into the void.

All were made terrible by their faces...

These sleepers hadn't died; this was no daemon-possessed charnel house, no citadel. This was something beyond. And in each face a terrible truth could be witnessed.

We have lost the Ilfe. The World will die because she cannot remember.

Jayr was tumbling with fears, with words, with a need to put them together – to somehow make everything fit. She could recall the texts they'd found in the Library. She found herself looking at the remains of Ress's overshirt, at the ink that had stained his skin.

Now, she was truly afraid. A vast, bottomless fear, a fear that came with a realisation...

"The Library," she said. Her tone shook. "The Guardians of the Ilfe. Is this what you came looking for?"

"Yes. The words brought me. I came to remember," Ress said. His thin arm pointed, but the cavern was too dark for her to see that far. "We must walk."

His voice had the same determination that she'd heard as they'd left the Palace in Amos – the pure focus of a man who was going to complete his task and not be prevented.

Directed by his pointing finger, they picked their way across the floor.

The light was weak and intermittent.

As they moved through the huge tomb, the space became impossible, stretching back into the darkness as though it had no end. It was bigger than Rammouthe, bigger than the world herself.

Memories came at her out of the emptiness, fragments with sharp edges. She remembered the Amos Library, the look in Ress's eyes as the words had taken his mind. She remembered the Banned and Syke, how they'd welcomed her without rancour or judgement. She remembered the Kartiah, the savage darkness of her pit-fighting past.

Then, earlier still. An image lost – so distant she'd no idea if it was even hers. A mountain city, a mining community, trading openly and in peace with the Kartian priestlords. There had been a hall, and a scarred Kartian trader. Jayr had been very small, her hand held by a young woman. Then there was metal, and the Kartian had taken her arm and pulled her away. The woman had dropped to her knees, given her one last hug, then turned away. She'd been crying.

And there had been a man there. Arrogant and massive of build, Archipelagan. He'd been wearing blood-red like he was soaked in it. He'd pulled the woman to her feet and comforted her, though his face was like stone.

Whoever he was, he faded into the cavern's shimmer. He left Jayr hurting, and she didn't know why.

And then, there came another memory. No, not a memory, this was different. It was a figure, a man, and he seemed a part of the cavern itself. He wore an odd white garment, tarnished to grey – an unfamiliar overshirt that reached his knees. His hair was long and black. There were ink marks at the skin of his throat, his pushed-up sleeves revealed scars at his elbows, like open mouths. And he was looking out at the sleepers as though they held a beauty only he could comprehend.

He said, "It's beautiful. It's everything I need. I can bring peace to the suffering, end poverty, end wars. No one will ever want for anything again."

She stared at him.

He looked right through her. His eyes were full of nothing.

And then he was gone.

Jayr realised that she'd stopped walking and was shaking. And she could remember something else...

All this time, the Bard's been right... Ress's words from

the Library, so long ago and now so clear. *The world had a nightmare, a nightmare that Roderick witnessed... Whatever destroyed the world's memory... that's what the nightmare was about...*

"Ress? Did you see—?"

"We must go!"

"Ress, wait!" The man in grey had scared her, but more than that, she found him oddly fascinating. She wanted to know who he was.

"In the Library," she said, "you talked about the Bard's vision, about the thing he'd seen in the Ryll. What was it?"

"I remember everything." The answer wasn't aimed at her. "I remember—"

"Never mind everything," she said. She stood there in the darkness, surrounded by desolation. She could feel the grey man, pulling at her skin and her soul and her thoughts. *Give up,* he was saying, *just trust me, and lay down and it will all go away, you'll never know pain again.* She thrust it from her, kept talking. "The thing the world fears, it destroyed her memory to stop her fighting back. Yes?"

"Yes," Ress's voice was beginning to tremble.

"Is it still here?"

"There's a hole," Ress said, "sucking the life from the grass. It empties the world. The little man with the black eyes – he knows what it is. Understands."

Jayr's flesh was prickling now.

The little man with the black eyes.

"The Ilfe, Ress, the place we're going. Do you know what we do when we get there?"

"Yes. We remember. And we show the Bard – he's seen it, and forgotten. He has to know how to fight *back*."

In among the dying and darkness, their last walk began.

* * *

There was a light ahead of them.

At first Jayr thought she was hallucinating; she rubbed her eyes and looked again. But it was still there, enticing as a figment, calling them on.

Ress pointed, his thin arm wavering. He started to laugh. Not the high cackle she'd been used to but a sound almost like his former self. It was the laugh of a man proven right at the last, a laugh of wonder and relief.

They walked faster, stumbling now.

Across the smooth floor, there were still fallen bodies, shadows stretched away from them like puddles of pure dark. Ignoring them, Jayr and Ress came to the thing that the world had lost, the thing that the Bard had needed and sought, the thing they'd crossed the Rhez itself to find.

The Ilfe.

The Well of the World's lost Memory.

It was an underground lake, small and curved like an oxbow. And it was utterly stagnant, grown over with a thick skin of green.

It didn't smell good.

At its centre was a single stone statue. Jayr could only see its head and shoulders above the slime-filled water. It was pitted with long returns, stooped like an old man, and its face was twisted into an expression of both humour and great cruelty.

It, too, was overgrown, stone eyes and skin slick with weed.

Ress stumbled forward and stopped, teetering, on the edge of the water. He looked almost as if he would jump.

"We come – to the face of the Count of Time."

The Count of Time.

"Apex of the rule of Heal and Harm. Time heals all wounds, yet Time takes all things from all beings." Ress was taking off his ink-stained overshirt, laying it on the rock. The ink had smeared into his skin, covering him in symbols, in words. In the odd light, he looked like some ancient, saga-bourne priest, some aging prophet of the God before him. "In the beginning, there was Kazyen, the void. And into that void came Cedetine, first Goddess – and so began the Count of Time. Cedetine bore Time three sons, the Gods of one birth, red and white and flesh, and their names were Asakat, Dyarmenethe and Samiel. When Samiel bore twins, the Gods made the world as a plaything for the children. And this island was crafted first, from their very flesh."

Jayr was staring at Ress, and at the statue.

"You know the rest," he said. "The two children, Calarinde and Alboren, loved each other, and so were destined to turn their faces away forever. In time, they each took a mortal lover and so we have our ten Gods. Our ten days of the halfcycle."

She barely breathed; she was staring at Ress's strangeness, at the odd sense of power that he now radiated.

"Jayr." Ress turned to look at her. "You must go home."

The word sent a shock up her spine. "Home?"

"You must go to Fhaveon and tell them who you are."

"They know who I am." Her snort of humour was brief. "I'm staying with you."

"I won't be here much longer." Ress turned back to the water and looked out over the green. "Find the Bard. And find Rhan. Tell them who your father was."

"I don't know who my—!"

"Jayr." Ress eased further forwards. She sensed him trembling, but it felt like elation, an eagerness to be free. "Your father was Phylokaris Valiembor, Merchant Master of Fhaveon. You were traded to the Kartians in your fourth return. You are the direct descendent of Saluvarith the Founder. Rhan... Rhan will know. As soon as he sees you."

"What the rhez are you talking about?" Jayr wondered if his mind had gone again.

He didn't look at her; the water compelled him. He took another step forwards.

"Ress..." She knew what was coming, but he was her friend

and dear Gods she *couldn't* let him do this...

Ress, please. Don't leave me...

The statue watched the pair of them through stone eyes older than the world herself.

Ress eased forwards again, until his toes were over the slick green.

"Jayr," he said. "You're the bravest person I've ever known. You've faced the Kartiah, the Banned, every warrior the world could throw at you. You've faced the Kas themselves, bare-handed, and been fearless." He looked back at her, smiled. His pupils were focused, the same size. "If I can trust any one person with the words I've carried this far..." He passed her the ink-stained overshirt. "The Bard will remember everything, and soon. It will show in his skin, in his heart, in his mind. But take this, keep it. I don't need it any more."

She could see some of the words, faded though they were.

Time the Flux begins to crack...

"Ress, please..." Jayr had never known panic in her life, but she knew it now. "Please, don't leave me down here, I can't find my way back through all of that, the sleeping army, the citadel, everything. And I couldn't leave the island, even if I did. Please..."

"You can, and you will," he told her. "You'll *remember*." He was still smiling at her, at thoughts only he could see. "And one last thing – the last thing of all."

She was crying. She, who'd sworn as a child that she would never shed another tear, she was cursed *crying*. "*Ress!*"

"I understand it now," he said. The statue was staring at both of them as if it were listening to every word. "At the very beginning, when Cedetine came into the void, then it lost itself. It was a void no more. It's been longing to regain its emptiness, its grey perfection, ever since. This is not about 'good' and 'evil', about Rhan and Vahl, and their endless war. This is about the end of all life, all existence, all passion, the end of

Time itself. A return to Nothing." His gaze was mesmeric, the most powerful thing that Jayr had ever seen. The sheer focus that had carried them away from the Palace in Amos was now aimed at her, willing her to understand.

"Take my words, Jayr, and go home," he said. "The future is more yours than you know."

Ress's last smile was like the sunrise, the rebirth of hope – it burned into her head and her heart. The ink-stained shirt in her hands, she watched as he waded into the Ilfe and was gone.

22: MASTER APOTHECARY TUSIEN

As Triqueta and Amethea reached the hilltop, the campsite ahead of them surged into life.

More than four thousand tired warriors rippled to their feet; four thousand ragged throats gave a cheer that challenged the sinking night.

Triqueta stopped. She found a lump in her throat, more water in her eyes. They shouted her name, a blur of faces and flags and bodies and voices. They cheered her almost frenziedly, blades crashing on shields, spear butts thumping on the frozen cobbles.

The noise gathered into a rhythm, gained speed to a rising crescendo, and then scattered again.

Her heart swelled to breaking, and she lowered her gaze.

"Welcome to Tusien," Amethea said wryly.

"Thanks," Triq muttered. "It's everything... everything I was expecting." The sentence started as a jest, but finished in pain.

Amethea squeezed her hand, then let her go and stepped away.

"Go on," she said, with a shove. "This is all yours."

Triq could see, stern above the shouting force, Tusien's damp walls looming severe – as if they asked her what the rhez she thought she was doing. Through the dead windows, the air was a clouded grey and it glittered, sleet-cold.

Amethea poked her again. "Go *on*," she said. "You're a hero. A warrior of legend, with your Red Rage and your centaur lover. The Bard'll be making up sagas before you can squeak." Her voice dropped slightly. "Besides, these people need this, so you're not getting out of it."

"Shit." Triqueta wanted to deny all of it. She didn't *want* to be a hero, didn't *want* everyone's hopes resting on her shoulders – but still, some part of her thrummed to the shouts of her name. She'd led her force here across the dying Varchinde, she'd tamed the centaurs, she'd fought a battle and won. By the bloodied Gods, maybe she *could* do this, could lead this force to victory. Maybe...

She turned to Amethea, but the girl had gone, her grey cloak lost against the neat rows of tents.

Your Red Rage and your centaur lover.

Triqueta wished he could have seen this moment...

What do I win?

Anything you want.

She scrubbed her chapped and bloody hands across her face. And she walked, alone, to the top of the hill.

Tusien's two remaining outer walls stood at right angles, cornering the remainder of a moss-grown, raggedly cobbled floor. It was wide enough to cover the hilltop, stepping down in places, and it bore broken statues and a few half-height remnants of inner walls. It also housed neat rows of barrack tents, their pegs dug into the soft ground between the stones.

Down the steps, Mostak came to welcome her. And the Bard came with him, his odd garments swathed in a cloak the colour of dried blood.

They looked like they intended ceremony.

The commander took her wrist. Then he turned to face the assembled troops, warriors of three cities, and he raised her hand to the sky. The cheers redoubled. Drums sounded, echoed. Howls came from the Banned.

"We live in an age of legend," the Bard called. "This is Triqueta of the Banned. Master warrior, wielder of the Red Rage, blessed by the Gods themselves. She has faced bweao, defeated the centaur herd, battled the vialer and won. She has fought Vahl Zaxaar himself and *beaten* him down!" The shouts rose again. "She brings us Roviarath, the fighting men and women of the Banned. And today, she brings us *victory*!"

The speech was predictable, perhaps, but the cheers came again, an emotional rush that all but knocked her on her arse. And then they were all there, down the steps and all over her – friends and hugs and back-slaps, shakes of her shoulders, and the Banned's ribald jesting. And so many questions – no, she'd never had the Red Rage before, no, she hadn't killed a bweao. Yes, she had faced Vahl Zaxaar. *And* beaten him, dammit.

She found herself lifted onto shields and shoulders and paraded about the courtyard like an icon of the force's victory. It was overwhelming. It made her feel giddy, and slightly sick. With one outburst of fury, she'd become some creature of great deeds...

A symbol.

These people need this.

Some part of her wanted to scramble down and run and run and *run* until she found the summer again, until she could hide in the long grasses of her youth.

Where Redlock was waiting for her.

But another part understood, now, those days would never return. As if her younger self had finally died out there with the axeman, she found – at last – that she welcomed her age and the strength it brought with it.

There was darkness to be faced, and fought, and beaten.

"You've high courage, Tan Commander." Out of the lines of tents, the voice belonged to Nivrotar.

The warriors carrying Triqueta muttered, "My Lord." They set her down and backed off like naughty children.

The Lord of Amos hadn't bothered with a cloak, and her arms were lean and pale and bare. A silver band encircled one bicep, and her white face seemed thinner, almost hollow. "And brave wit, and flawless timing," she said. "And I am sorry for your loss. Faral ton Gattana was a good man, fierce and high-hearted. We will remember his victory – and yours. No warrior will wish for a greater monument."

"A monument?" Triqueta said. The word sounded like a wound. "I did as you asked, my Lord. I brought you Roviarath. And the Banned. And some extras, just for *fun*. And apparently a hero, to boost your morale." She swallowed the bitterness, scratched at her flaking hands.

"We're going to win this," she said.

It's going to be worth what it's cost.

The Lord of Amos smiled, and Triqueta tried to remember if she'd ever seen the expression on the woman's face before.

"Let us hope so, Triqueta of the Red Rage," she said. "Or your monument will stand beside Redlock's, headless upon a plain of death."

Dusk swallowed the walls of Tusien, stretched sullen shadows across the courtyard.

As the light died upon the peaks of distant Kartiah, the clouds gathered close. They clustered as if they awaited the outcome of the world's fate, bulging heavy with the threat of new snow. Lost somewhere in their bellies, the unseen moons glimmered, rippling highlights, hinting at the cold sky beyond.

Secure beneath their cover, fires had been lit at last, and the warriors' mood was lifting. They'd all come far, and fought hard. They'd won the day, and a party was rising now, a swell of necessary laughter against the red and flickering stone.

New friendships were being celebrated, toasted with leather mugs and exaggerated with tall tales. Hands gripped wrists, and faces gleamed with battlefield recognition and drunken embellishment.

Triqueta went looking for Taure, and for his waterskin. She wanted to find Ecko, too, but not just yet – her memories of their farewell were odd and out of place, in this cold where Redlock had died.

Right now, she wanted family. Needed to remember why they were fighting, what all this was for.

As the party rose into the night, the beaten force at the base of the hill remained motionless, curled up and sulking like some wounded nartuk.

But Tan Commander Mostak never left the wall.

Amethea rested her back against the heavy tentpole, then slid wearily downward to the cold and filthy floor. She wiped her hands down her trews, said, "Is that all of them?"

"For now." One of her helpers smiled, passed her a cup of nvuri tea. "Though the patrols are still out. They say the retreat is always the worst."

She shook her head and sipped at the restorative, then wrapped her hands around the cup's heat, and let the warmth of it spread through her. It was less cold in here, but her breath still rose like she'd exhaled her soul.

Put your shoulder to the wheel...

I've tried, she told Gorinel silently, as if he stood behind her in his grubby apron, with all the nameless Gods ranked at his back.

Around her, the murky light of the hospice resembled some

outer chamber of the rhez – bodies slumped on pallets, reaching hands that flickered shadows on frosted fabric walls, echoing cries of pain and hopelessness. They'd come in here in numbers, in panic, in suffering and in agony. They'd come to her crying out, and bleeding out, cursing and staggering, carrying those who couldn't walk.

Triqueta had fought her war, and won. In here, Amethea had fought a war of her own – a war of tight and endless focus, a war without the release of naked rage. This war had been fought against hurt and grief and infection, against filth and stench and injury. This war against antagonism, against the curses of those she hadn't been able to help, or hadn't helped fast enough. This war against the Count of Time, against inadequate facilities and dwindling supplies, against increasing numbers and rising desperation.

Against death...

...and against her own despair.

Faith is in action.

She realised she was shaking, and put the tea down. She wanted to cry, but didn't dare let herself go. If she opened the gates, it would never end. Instead, she closed her eyes, and took several gulps of the shit-stinking air.

She wondered what Gorinel would have said about her failures. About the bodies, those she hadn't been able to save. About those who had died in agony, cursing her with their last breath. Were they symbols of faith? Of *purpose*? Were they the shoulder-to-the-wheel forgiveness that he'd guided her towards?

Or were they just Gods-damned *dead*?

Her mouth jumped, fighting the flood.

Then something moved in front of her, blocking the rocklight.

"Amethea." Rhan was a cold colossus, all armour and shoulders. His long blade was sheathed across his back, and he was covered in gore as staining-dark as pure dismay. His helm was off, held under one arm, and his face and sweated hair were smeared with other people's lives.

At the sight of him, her heart recoiled – she wasn't even sure why. She scrabbled to her feet, tripping over her tea. It sank into the muck, steaming.

"Come to make yourself feel better?" she said. It was uncalled for, but she didn't care – her weariness was spilling out of her like her tea into the ground. She understood why he needed to help – his need for absolution was the same as her own – but his presence made her uneasy.

Promise of Samiel, he was as close to the Gods as anyone could ever get... and somehow, he undermined everything that Gorinel had taught her about her faith. He made her *unnecessary*.

But he said only, "I came to see if you were all right."

In the looming shadows, the statement lurked, a figment in a corner – as if he knew full well that he could have helped these people, sent them back to their tents and tans and commanding officers with nothing worse than a red scar and a tall tale.

Like she was so much extra baggage, useless to him and the battle both.

But I was trying! she told Gorinel, the gathered and frowning Gods. *I was trying so hard!*

"I'm fine," she said.

"I don't doubt your courage, Master Apothecary. Or your ability."

He pulled off a gauntlet, one finger at a time, dropped it into his upturned helm. Then he touched his hand to the side of her face, smiled at her, and kissed her forehead like a father, a benediction.

With a shock that stood her hair on end, she felt his light in her skin.

Amethea had been unconscious when Maugrim had healed her; she'd had no memory of his elemental touch. This time, she could *feel* it, all of it, feel the Powerflux as it flowed through her body – a seething, sparking crackle. It was tremendous, ludicrous and elating. The light was in her head and heart and mind and soul, pure and brilliant. It illuminated all her secrets, everything she was, or had ever been, or had ever hoped to be. Every success, every failure; every life she had saved, and every life she hadn't. It made her feel exhilarated and wild and sick... but there was something more, something familiar, something like—

Recognition.

It stunned her like a slap, and she pulled away. She staggered backwards into the tentpole, shaking her head like she'd been stung.

"What did you just...? Why did you...?"

"Easy," Rhan said. "You need help too."

"I'm *fine*," she snarled at him, then coughed, retched bile and spat. She was dazzled. The light was everywhere: in her eyes, in all the cracks in her faith, in every question she had ever asked herself. It was in the Bard's fireside tale, in Gorinel's warmth and humour. It was in the face of every soldier who'd lost their life because of her.

Faith is in action.

Every soldier that Rhan could have saved.

No.

That first ripple was small, like a rattle of stones that foretold a hillslide. *Master Apothecary.* He was damned right she was, trained with solid and practical formality; she was worth her weight in terhnwood, the best they had. And she had to prove her faith and forgive herself with *purpose*, with...

But I tried!

"Amethea—"

"No." She said it aloud this time. "You don't get to do that. Promise of Samiel, whatever you are, you don't get to just *do* that." She was shaking her head, words falling out of her borne on the day's howling horrors. "I've been in here. Saving lives.

Losing lives. Taking lives. Taking abuse. *Watching* people die because I couldn't save them." She was angry now, shuddering with reaction. "And you can't just... light me up like a Gods-damned rocklight. *Fix* me. Heal mind and body by just..." She waved an arm, scornfully casual. Her forehead was stinging, and she knew that there was one of those odd red marks where he'd touched her.

"Amethea," he said, softly. "You're exhausted beyond words—"

"No." She couldn't listen to him. His light had shown her the truth, the churning in her belly that was curling round the failures of the day. Gorinel had shown her faith, and had died anyway. Redlock had been her friend, and had died anyway. She'd struggled to save the lives of these people, and they'd died anyway.

Her presence, her training, had failed.

Her need for absolution had failed.

She had put her shoulder to the wheel and fallen anyway.

"I should've stayed in Fhaveon. Died with Gorinel. He understood – at least I *mattered*."

Everything she'd done – was for nothing.

Cracks in her new faith.

And then shattering, falling.

She was backing up towards the cold draught from the doorway. As he moved, went to reach out to her, she turned and almost fell out into it. Anything to be away from him, away from the Gods, away from everything she'd failed to be.

Master Apothecary.

Uncaring of him calling after her, Amethea half ran and half staggered out into the darkness, and into her own loss of hope.

Ecko scuffed an awkward foot against the overgrown cobbles.

In front of him was the biggest of the circles of firelight; it radiated warmth that made the colours of his skin shift as if they ached to give him away. In that circle sat the warriors of Roviarath and the Banned. It was a circle of boasting, booze and laughter.

To one side of it, the stones in her cheeks glittering, sat Triqueta with a leather waterskin in one hand and a bared blade in the other. She'd been given one of Fhaveon's blood-feather pennons and was holding it on the blade-tip out to the flame. She let the fire dance up its edge and consume it.

As the pennon flared and died, the circle around her cheered, and thumped their fists on their thighs. They raised drinking vessels and shouted her name. Ecko couldn't take his eyes from her – he wanted to speak to her, to say *something*... some awkward gesture of sympathy, some "wish it could've been different" comment on Redlock's death...

But his fucking useless social skills spiked him to the spot. He'd no clue how to approach the circle, let alone his feelings about the loss of the axeman.

Chrissakes. Grief: tick. Two outta ten, could do better.
What's up next, table manners?

Savagely, he twisted a foot and ground a weed to death.

Redlock was *gone*. Assertive, bluff, wicked, Redlock had been exactly who and what he appeared to be. And Ecko... *Yeah all right, I miss him, okay?* He couldn't get his head round it. He wanted to rail at Eliza that it wasn't fair, that he hadn't signed up for no Tragic Hero shit, that no one should hafta die like that. That if he'd been there, he could've stopped it. That it was his program and his – what? Responsibility? That if one pixel in this stupid bastard fractal had been in a different place, if the butterfly had flapped its wings in a different way, then everything after it could've been changed...

Chrissakes, he might be able to hand a major daemon its ass on a plate, but this shit? Stupid tests. Beat the bad guy – check. Emotional growth and learning – check. And Triqueta...

Her face danced in the firelight and with it his memories of Tarvi. He turned away, angry and baffled. He'd no bastard *clue* how to walk into that circle of light.

His oculars caught movement across the campsite: a figure running from the ruin's sheltered corner. Amethea, uncloaked, fleeing in a stumble from the hospice.

What the hell?

Fearing the worst, he tuned his telos and saw Rhan standing under the open tent flap. Suspicion flickered, the images it conjured unpleasant.

Almost glad of the excuse, Ecko gathered his heavy wool cloak and headed out after the doc.

Triqueta left the fireside and went to find somewhere to piss.

As she headed, reeling slightly, towards the tower at the corner of the ruin, she became aware that she could see moonlight through the wall. Only a chink, but enough.

And that wasn't going to end well.

Steadying herself with an effort, she checked her weapons and headed that way.

Tusien's walls contained several cracks, splits where the ground had moved with the intervening time. The Amos force had blocked them with piles of shattered stone. Now, one of them was open.

Somewhere, her wine-addled mind said, *Oh shit*.

Struggling for sobriety, she reached the tiny gap and crouched to look through it. The back of her neck prickled.

But there was nothing there – no sneak attack, no creeping beastie. Only a long, pale grey curve against the darker grey ground: the graceful stone stairway that had once decorated Tusien's gardens. In places, its creatures still stood guard, each with one claw raised. Monuments over a field of death.

She crouched, watched, then told herself it was too damned

cold and she should just pee and go back to the fire.

Then she saw a slim figure in grey, all but invisible.

Amethea?

Carefully, Triqueta eased through the tiny gap, crept down to the top of the broken stairs. The sharp chill outside the wall woke her up pretty damned quick. Her breath steamed and she rubbed her itching hands.

She still needed to piss, but that would have to wait.

Amethea was not alone.

Betrayal? No...

As she came closer, she realised that the other figure was Ecko. He was cloaked, but making no effort to hide.

Her heart jumped; she wasn't even sure why.

"...everything I've ever been," Amethea was saying softly, her voice aching with pain. "It doesn't matter now. Nothing matters. We can try our hardest, but we'll fail in the end."

"Will we fuck," Ecko said. His voice was firm but hushed, lacking its usual rasp. "We do this shit. Whatever it takes."

"Why?" The word sounded like heartbreak. Amethea held up a hand, looking at it in the faint light. "Why bother?" Her voice was empty, echoing like loss. "I can't do this any more."

"You hafta *fix* this," Ecko said. "You're the fuckin' doctor."

She looked at both her hands, turning them over and back as if she'd never seen them before. "It's not a disease," she said. "It's *growing*."

Ecko put his hands over Amethea's and closed them, stopping her looking. "You gotta *fight* this. You—"

"It doesn't matter," she said again.

"Everything matters," Ecko said. "You most of all." His voice was warm, human. It touched Triqueta to the core, made her bite her lip.

And, as Amethea slowly shook her head, a gesture heavy with resignation, Triqueta knew, like a cold stone sinking in her heart, she *knew* what had happened.

It's growing.

She crept closer, fear clamouring in her throat. She tried to find something to say.

Growing.

In the darkness, Ecko turned. "Triq?"

"Yeah." She moved forwards, knew he could see her.

Ecko's black gaze held so many things, all of them unsaid. Then he turned away, and voiced the thing she'd been most afraid of.

"Amethea..." he said. "Amethea's caught the blight."

23: ELEMENTAL TUSIEN

The winter night was smothered and still, silent on the edge of the end of the world.

They sat, their backsides freezing on cold stone steps, Amethea in the centre and sheltered by the cloaks and closeness of the other two. Under low cloud, the darkness was almost complete, but they didn't need the light to see the discolourations that were already flowering in her skin.

She coughed, as if her lungs were filling with moss.

And she was talking, lorn and lost. "Do you remember the House of Sarkhyn?" she said. "There was a man there. He kept saying, 'Help me, help me'." She coughed again, her shoulders hunching. "I feel like that. It's like... it's like I'm nothing."

On the far side of the jagged ruin, Tan Commander Mostak stood unflinching. The clouds had lowered, dark with threat, but the Commander paid them no attention. He watched his sleeping enemy as if he'd never blink again.

Behind him, Nivrotar stood in the command tent, pieces of knotted cord in her hands. With Roviarath here, their food and fuel was running dangerously low.

"Six days." Her words were soft as she untied another knot. "Maybe seven. And then we starve."

Rhan stood in the entrance to the hospice. He was ashen, hollowed out, far beyond exhaustion. *E Rhan Khavaghakke.* A final stagger of confused patients limped past him, back out to their glinting campfires. They thanked him, some slightly awkwardly, others in tears. He nodded at them as they left, couldn't manage anything more.

As they faded into the darkness, they seemed to take the very last of his vitality with them.

Ghar's death still rode him like a figment, and he wondered what had happened to Amethea.

The night grew deeper, and the warriors' party petered slowly out. The clouds bulged in ominous threat and the fires flickered low, forgotten. As it curved towards morning, it grew colder, and flakes of snow began to drift across the hillside.

The world, what was left of it, lay sleeping.

And then, in the stillness, there came music.

It was a single voice, wordless. It brought an ache to the emptiness, to the dead plains and the ruin's desolation. It turned the snow into something enchanted, something perfect and timeless.

Those on watch felt chillflesh prickle their skin. The voice gained volume, now ranging to more than one note, its harmony perfect but faintly unsettling. The song lifted with the cold wind. Sleepers stirred and turned, then awoke wide-eyed and trembling in the dark.

The walls themselves seemed to be listening.

In the hospice doorway, Rhan raised his head.

Over the great ruin, the heavy snowclouds were parting. As if somehow leashed, they rippled with force as they withdrew, their underbellies showing tumbling curves of moonlight. As Rhan watched, transfixed, a fissure began to show, an opening through which poured pure hope.

Moonlight lit the campsite, spreading like a pool. It was warm, blissful and confident. The walls stood black in contrast. The clouds blazed.

And the song rose still, a power and reach both almighty and inhuman.

His skin tingling in response, Rhan stood, his eyes now closed, lost to the touch of the light. Calarinde was up there, his Goddess – she was in his face, in his hair, her fingers on his pale skin. He could almost hear her, her voice more warmth than sound. *Oh, my lovely. I'm so sorry.*

The water on his face caught the light, and glittered.

Out on the steps, the spreading light had another effect entirely.

Ecko said, "Oh, you whoreson mother*fucker*," and he was on his feet, unbundling himself from layers of cloak.

"What?" Triqueta huddled more fabric round the now-silent Amethea. "What bit you?"

Ecko grinned like a fiend. The yellow light made his skin seethe, as if the moon were setting him afire. It turned Triqueta's face and hair the colour of molten gold.

"Oh c'mon," he said. "Who the hell d'you think that is?"

He didn't wait for her answer. He was adrenals-boosted and away, back up the long steps, two at a time, and heading for the gap in the wall.

Above him, the fissure was wider now – some Parting-of-the-Cloud-Sea trickery. He was impressed – okay, so he admitted it already – the cloudbreak was a helluva thing to pull. Now, it was showing the yellow moon, fat and full, lighting the snow-covered campsite to a piss-coloured glitter. And above it – looking almost like the very first time he'd seen it – the smaller white shine that resembled the moon of his home.

"Golden showers," he muttered. "Yeah, funny."

But the light made him *happy*, giddy, insanely so. The song lifted his heart and made him want to giggle like a kid. It filled him with wonder, and pride, and courage, and it flickered dreams of hope and future…

You whoreson fuckin' bastard!

Ducking in through the gap, he flicked ocular modes, scanned the site. In a moment he found the upright figure of the Bard standing at the entrance to the tumbledown tower. He'd shed his cloak, and he sang at the sky in his London jeans and leather. And above him, like some fucking movie effect, the clouds parted further and the brilliant light made the old walls shine. It bathed the campsite in glory.

Ecko appeared at his side like a daemon in miniature.

"Cut it the fuck out, willya?"

The song fell from the air. The wind was cold, crying like a lost thing.

The Bard was trembling, his chin raised and his throat fully stretched. It glistened in the new moonlight, coiling through and under itself in a way that made Ecko's skin fucking crawl.

"Ecko!" he said. It was a whisper, but metals slid with the power it held. "We can do this. We can win!"

"Mom musta turned you inside out, you're mad as a box of frogs."

"Trust me." His grin was unholy. "I can lift every heart, every man, every woman, every warrior. Every name is known to me, and every one of them matters. As the confrontation comes, every voice and blade will be raised. And we will tear down everything that comes at us. We are the grass, and the light, and the world's strength and soul. Not even the Kas can stop us. Now…" he held up one long hand. "…listen!"

Across the silent ruin there came the sharp, clear screech of an instrument – a horn, high and grating. It wasn't a musical noise: it was a warning, a wake-up call. A noise to bring warriors to their feet.

A moment later, there came the sound of echoing drums.

The Bard laughed, the noise layered and reverberating as if the walls themselves would come down. "Let them come," he said. "We are standing ready. This is it, Ecko. This is endgame."

And so came the final morning.

The sun rose from the sea, streaking the parted clouds with yellow and pink. It burned the dusted snow away, almost as if Samiel had decided to give his children's toy one final polish before the end.

At the top of the hill, the defenders waited. Commanded by Mostak's single focus and unbending courage, by Triqueta, upright and on horseback, they had formed up in their tan, and stood tall against the threat. Flags of three cities flew proud, colours bright.

At the bottom of the hill, a seethe of nightmare lurked beyond the curtain-wall. If ever there had been human faces among that mass, they'd been lost in the writhe of the monsters, in the daemon-driven run across the dead Varchinde. Lines and tans and flags no longer defined them; they were obsessed beyond reason, beyond sanity. They were demented, unarmoured, and clamouring. In among them were the last of the Fhaveon heavy cavalry, and men and women who had never been warriors – those who'd followed Phylos's politicking and had been caught up in the madness.

About the force's edges paced the horned and tattooed vialer, watching the fervent mass, keeping it in check; watching the sky as if for some unknown signal.

Of Selana herself, there was no sign.

Triqueta watched them, gauging numbers, routes, counterattacks.

Mounted on a Roviarath mustang, she'd taken command of the two hundred Fhaveon skirmishers as well as her own force. With her, too, was the centaur herd. Her gauntleted hands itched, and she watched the swarm below her, waiting for their attack.

Told herself, *I can do this*.

At the front of the ruin, facing down the hill, the shieldwall had formed anew. It was noticeably smaller than before. The freemen and women of Amos and Roviarath were skirmishers rather than infantry, and they'd been divided to the flanks. On their outsides, Triqueta had formed the cavalry on the extremes of either edge – fast retaliation and response.

The catapults were loaded. Archers from all three cities lined every wall.

On the top of the tower, the Bard stood alone, like an icon.

Somewhere behind Triqueta, Mostak bounced on his toes, agitated. Still heavy with exhaustion, Rhan commanded the reserve, saving his energy.

The clouds were almost gone now, the early winter sun surprisingly warm. The force at the base of the hill was all but throwing itself against the curtain-wall, eager for release. They were hungry. She could feel it.

But there was one more thing.

She'd noticed it only as the sun rose – it had been hidden, perhaps, because so many of the hilltop weeds had been ground under foot and hoof – but now she could see it was everywhere.

The moss, the grass, the rust-coloured creeper that grew upon the walls – they were fading to the grey of everything else, to dust and emptiness.

As if Amethea had been its herald, the blight had come to the ruins of Tusien.

* * *

The attack came as the sunlight reached the base of the walls.

As the long shadows retreated, so the force surged up to meet them, released at last.

It came in a rush, figures striving to reach the front, pulling one another down into the dirt, trampling and savage and oblivious.

Triqueta watched them, heard the drums, heard the Bard cry courage and victory, echoes of his song from the previous evening. She knew the drum sounds were orders – she also knew the opposing force would understand those orders. When she'd challenged Mostak on this, the commander had given her a grin to rival one of Ecko's.

"I'm counting on it," he'd said.

Now, though, the drums sounded the order to hold, to interlock shields and to defend the top of the wall.

The catapults cranked and threw, the crews showing a sense of humour as they pelted the incoming force with the debris of the previous night's party. By the rhez, if they were going to die, they were going to do it in style.

Their flash of humour made Triqueta chuckle, and she raised her voice in the Banned's war cry. She didn't need the Bard's damned trickeries to find her courage for her.

The command came from the walltop, and the archers started shooting. They weren't volley-shooting now, arcing their arrows over and down, they were picking their targets and shooting flat, sniping, and their skill and numbers were counting. The first wave of incoming skidded and cried out and hit the floor. It was surged over and ground down by its fellows.

Triqueta swallowed bile as she realised that the first wave had been almost all non-combatants, unarmed but for belt-blades. The lost and displaced people of Fhaveon, the people to whom Vahl had promised a new life, an answer.

Dear Gods.

But the archers shot again, merciless. The catapults reloaded. This time, their load was broken stone and the centre of the advance crashed to a bloody halt under falling masonry. The vialer didn't care, they laughed at the blood and chaos. The creatures bore decorated spears and some of them wore skins – of what, she dreaded to imagine. The image of them killing Redlock had been burned into her like a brand – and she used it to source her rage and her courage. The vialer churned the ground and the fallen to a mass of gore as they came.

The force grew close, and the drums changed note – the archers stopped shooting. She could see faces – ordinary men and women, driven beyond hope, beyond fanaticism. They had teeth bared, many of them bloody where they'd raked nails down their faces or bitten through their lips or cheeks. Their lack of humanity was terrifying, and their age—

Their *age*!

It hit her out of nowhere – how they'd come so far, so fast, what the Kas were doing to the people they now threw at the hilltop. She would have gambled everything she still owned that these fighters had not been in their fortieth and fiftieth return when they'd left Fhaveon.

She swallowed hard and gripped her blades. These people had been *drained*, just like she had been, used as fuel. Who knew how many of them the Kas had already killed?

Or was the right word, *eaten*?

The insight made her shudder – yet it made no sense. The Kas were draining their own force, damaging their warriors in order to gain time, to reach the ruin swiftly. And likewise, they'd deliberately broken their assault into separate pieces – sent one force into Fhaveon, sent the centaurs after Roviarath...

Initially, she'd just thought them full of themselves – they were daemons, for Gods' sakes, better at flinging power than military tactics. But now she wondered: what if their choices were *calculated*?

Triqueta had faced Amal, witnessed his games – by the rhez, she knew enough of Vahl to trust nothing... so, if this was deliberate, then what was he *doing*?

She didn't get time to follow the thought through.

The first wave of incoming hit the shieldwall with a crash of wood and flesh and shouting.

The warriors' response was well-drilled, commanded clearly by the drums. The attackers were all over them, hands like claws and teeth bared and bloody. They were sweating and age-lined and seething and angry, scratching and fighting weaponless, or struggling to bring their blades to bear, and cutting at each other in the process.

Facing them, the defending wall hit back, and hard. And then it parted, very briefly, letting just a few of the attackers through and cutting them off. Behind the wall, the skirmishers made short work of them, grinding them into the blighted cobbles. They did this time and time again. If the attackers faltered or fell back for long enough, Triqueta would despatch the cavalry and counterattack, hammering out from the flanks and into their lines, then racing back before they had time to fully react.

Sometimes, a voice would cry out in the heave of the melee – a name, a plea, a call to someone they had known from their youth, or from the street where they had lived.

But Ythalla's forces were beyond human and there was no recognition.

Nothing left.

They were like Maugrim's stone creatures, they just came onwards, relentless, pushed blindly by those behind. Injuries seemed not to slow them – to put each one down, they had to be hacked to pieces, their legs kicked or cut from under them, their eyes removed, their hands severed at the wrists. Even then they came on; the heat that burned from them was that of the rhez itself.

Triqueta saw more than one defender quail and try to fall back, only to be caught between the press behind them, and the press in front. The wounded and the terrified had no way to leave the crush – they simply fell where they stood and were trampled.

She thought: *I can still do this.*

She lifted her chin.

Oh, she could still do this, all right. For Redlock. For Amethea. For Roviarath. For the wound in the world. Triq was furious and fearless; she shouted defiance back at the incoming force.

Sunlight slid down the hillside.

The line was too spread, not tight enough, and there were too many of them coming. For every attack she anticipated and countered, another would come, further away, eager and unstoppable. And the shieldwall itself, already devastated by Ythalla's cavalry, was heavily outnumbered, outflanked at both edges.

Their discipline was good – they were striving to hold. Archers still shot from the walltops, carefully picking their targets. Many of them shot at the vialer, and the tattooed creatures yowled and laughed and snapped the shafts as they struck.

But there were just too many of them.

And the arrows were running out.

The shieldwall held, but it was being pushed back, and back, and back towards the rear wall of the ruin – warriors' boots could get no traction on the cobbles as the press of bodies in front of them forced their way forwards. From somewhere, Triq could hear a strong and even rhythm, a stamp-stamp-stamp that was making all the attackers stamp in time, a heavy pressure of ruthless forward motion.

Triqueta held the cavalry back, waiting for the chance to get in behind the push of the attackers... if it came...

Then she heard the drums. Somewhere she could hear the Bard's voice, a jarring arrhythmic disruption that was hard on her ears, but was making the stamping slacken, confused. The drummers hammered out a loud and obvious tattoo, a second.

She remembered what Mostak had said about the drumming, just as the pressure of the attackers slowed. Whatever the order had been, the enemy had understood and anticipated it.

And then the big kettledrum hit a single bass note. It echoed from the walls as if Tusien would ripple and fall. And the shieldwall abruptly shifted formation – from the long flat line of the wall itself into an arrowhead, the strongest warrior at the point and every shield locked behind his, slanting backwards towards the flanks.

At the edges of the formation, the shieldmen had suddenly pulled back and the attackers staggered, bereft of resistance. At the formation's point, the warriors leaned hard into the heavy man at the very front and they pushed forwards, aggressive and shouting, moving faster and faster as they gained ground.

Behind them, the skirmishers came to clean up the edges.

Belatedly realising their mistake, the attackers faltered, tried to react but they were confused and too slow – their line was cut clean in half and each half spun sideways, its back to the incoming skirmishers.

Triq wasted no time. Her war cry loud in her throat and ears, she slung her bow, drew her blades and hit them clean in the back, riding them down – warrior and monster and non-combatant alike.

By the Gods, she was beginning to believe that they might even win this...

And then she saw what was coming.

Watching from the hilltop, Rhan knew it the moment it manifested.

It shivered his skin and his soul. Its presence was in the Powerflux itself, in the light and the air. Even as it sparked into being, it was lust and energy and rage. It was growing by the moment, and by every God it was *moving*.

No one on the hilltop had a hope in the rhez of facing this thing. It would char them all to a smoking pile of ash and hopelessness.

Samiel's bollocks.

Scared and angry, Rhan pushed past his drummer, his message-bearer. He shouted for Mostak, abandoning his post to shove his way through to the command tent. They could discipline him later, if anyone lived that long.

Around him, warriors were craning to see.

"What the rhez is that?"

"Do you see it?"

"Too much of the good stuff last night, mate."

No, Rhan thought, *you probably didn't have enough*.

Above him, the sun was setting. It stretched the shadows of the walls long down the hillside. But that light – *there* – that wasn't the sun.

That was the one he could *feel*.

The smoulder was distinctive – it rose and it hungered, pulling energy and life from round it, from flux and from flesh. The Kas were building it, fanning its flames, flattering it, offering it the time it needed...

"*No!*"

He found he was shouting, incoherent and livid. He could hear them still, laughing at him, calling to him, *E Rhan*...

Fuel for the Kas, fuel for the monster, fuel for this Sical, the rising life of the Gods-almighty fire elemental that was going to burn Tusien and everything in it to the ground.

There was no way he could face this thing.

It ended here.

All of it.

Ash and hopelessness.

His soul raged, deep in his chest. He wanted to shout at them, cry denial and helpless fury, but there was nothing he could do. He didn't have the strength. Vahl had played him well, and he was beyond shattered – and with all of his brothers behind it...

He wondered if maybe, just maybe, Samiel would take him home after all.

But the Sical was still growing. As high as the sky, clouds now massing around it. The ground under it parched and cracked. He felt it swell and flicker. He could feel the time, the lives that were thinning and faltering, though he could do nothing to stop them. He saw them in flux-flashes – terrified, crying, burning, watching each other stumble and fail. He could hear their voices calling for help, and family.

And then, suddenly, his anger was ablaze like the Sical itself.

He entered the command tent, calling to Mostak, words falling over themselves.

"You'll need a strike force – the best vets you've got. Older warriors, all of them. They'd better be good, or this is over."

But Mostak was signalling the drummers, shouting warnings, shouting for water, for the reserve to reach and hold the old well. He had his own tactics for the fire beast.

Rhan could hear them laughing at him. *E Rhan Khavaghakke. You can stop us, all you need is time. You have kine all about you, why do you not use them? Feed, little brother. Sacrifice the few to save the many. Is that not what your "strike force" already is? Feed...*

"No!"

He threw himself open, yet again, to the surge of the Powerflux. To the sunken Soul of Light ever-lost below the eastern horizon. Like throwing himself in the Ryll, this was a last moment, a gesture of the end.

If he had but one spark of energy left, just enough to find his focus...

He could hear them mocking him. *Ah, the endless melodrama, little brother. Throwing yourself off the edge of this, and into the pit of that – you don't lose well, do you?* Laughter bubbled, like molten rock. *Your forfeiture is almost complete. Join us, at last. All you need is time...*

And then, he could hear the liquid and crystal voice of the Sical, crackling from one horizon to the other...

Hunger, I.

* * *

Triqueta knew what it was – knew as it rose against the winter sky. It was huge, far, far bigger than the one Maugrim had called. This damned thing grew to the size of Tusien's walls, and still higher. She could feel the heat on her face, blistering. Under her, her mustang snorted and plunged, fighting to flee. Skilled though she was, she was struggling to hold him – and she wasn't the only one.

In the shieldwall, the warriors had paused to stare, to shout questions – but the incoming force paid the thing no mind. They kept hammering, demented.

The heat grew worse, searing. Triq raised an arm to shield her eyes and the horse backed up, resisting the pressure of her knees and barging hard into the animals behind him. He was sweating, frothing at the mouth.

Another animal lashed a bite at him and a moment later, the assembled cavalry was chaos, the horses barging and kicking. The shieldwall was crumbling in spite of itself and still the Sical was growing.

Orders were shouted, ignored. Drums sounded. Archers shot, but the shafts flashed to ashes and kindling. Triqueta saw the catapults being loaded with buckets of water but knew even before they threw that they'd do no good.

And still, the heat rose.

Ecko stared at the thing in the sky. All he could see was the flame-beast from Maugrim's cathedral, only this one was as high as the zenith, as wide as the horizon.

Hunger, I.

Need, I.

The words and the heat made his head spin.

Tell me. Tell me how to burn it down.

It was the option Amal had offered him, the route out, the way home. It was the chance he'd longed for, to fuck Eliza once and for all, to trash the program and protest his freedom, his will and his independence. It was Vahl, it was Maugrim. It was Tarvi. It was lust and flame and—

He blinked, and tore himself away, after-echoes of light leaving coloured flares in his vision. The heat was making him remember something, something about the cathedral, about Maugrim, about...?

About what they'd done last time.

E Rhan Khavaghakke!

The call was distant now, unreal. But the Powerflux was close and alive, its energy flaring and powerful, right under his skin. No Elementalist could wield more than one element – to open your mind and heart to more than one was suicide, it would char you to a smoking ruin.

But Rhan would have taken all of them and more, if he could.

To focus his attunement, he needed energy – and it came from his fury at himself, at all the mistakes he'd made, and everything he'd been, and lost, and lain down. It was his fury at his brothers, at their cruelty and their games. It was his grief, manifested as pure white anger. It was the Bard's music, and Calarinde's touch from the previous evening, giving him the spark he needed to catch light. And it all blazed together, crystallising into something like the purest focus he'd ever known, into an absolute vision of the Powerflux itself.

He could *see* it!

It was everywhere, in everything!

In the sky and in the sun and the shadows; in the ruins and the dead ground and the hillside. It was a crackling mesh of spark and pulse and flame. He could see the elemental souls, the Flux's anchor points – the Tacs volcanoes that housed the

Soul of Fire, the white crystal cave in the Khavan Circle, the home of the Soul of Ice. He could feel the pure darkness at the heart of the Kartian culture, that same darkness that lived in Ecko's black eyes. And he could see the glitter of the water where the Soul of Light had once been cursed.

And he could see something else.

The Monument, a vision or a recollection. The stone below it, like strength; the sky above, like inspiration. And the Flux was there too, flowing element to element across the world.

The force of all things.

Power crackled in his skin. He could feel it now as if he were a node himself and able to throw all of that Gods-might wherever he wished.

Now, my brothers. His laugh was as wide as the sky. *Face me now.*

But they had no fear of his attunement, his light. It was flawed, always had been – Vahl had cursed the Soul of Light and he would never reach it.

Their might would remain unchallenged.

And then... Rhan saw something else.

Something soulless and savage, governed by chaos and passion. It was pure dark, but it was not Kartian, it was something smaller, and closer. It, too, could see the Sical, and it knew no fear.

In a flash like a heartbeat, Rhan realised he saw Ecko – tiny in silhouette against the might of the monster. His rasping shout was pure defiance, and he was throwing something at the fire.

Two things.

Two sealed pottery cases.

Rhan had an instant of utter disbelief: *What?*

Two shapes arced into the flame, momentarily silhouetted. Then two detonations rocked the elemental, one after another. They made it flare and scream, begin to eat itself from the inside out.

Fire alchemy!

They *hurt* it, they made it flicker. And then they started it burning even brighter – almost burning through. The whole sky flashed with fire, the horizon blazed glorious.

Startled, the focus of the Kas faltered, just for the tiniest moment...

And in that moment, that space suddenly bought, Rhan could see it. There, eastwards across the darkening sea, sunken beneath the waves, never to be found again...

Somewhere, he heard Vahl breathe smoke. "No...!"

But Ecko's sheer wit had given him the opening he needed. And they were too late.

He stretched out his hand, across Flux and sea and sky, across land and winter. He could see it now, the single, vast rocklight that was the eastern point of the Powerflux. He could hold it and bring it to the surface. He could touch it, make a new sun with it, change the Powerflux for the rest of the Count of Time.

The OrSil, the lost Soul of Light.

His.

24: SOUL OF LIGHT TUSIEN

From the top of Tusien's corner tower, the Bard saw everything. He saw Ecko dart forwards, a slight, swift shadow. He saw the two missiles describe perfect arcs into the flame of the Sical. He saw the elemental rock backwards as they detonated. And he saw Rhan's resulting surge of power, his perfect attunement to the surfacing of the Soul of Light.

More than that: he *felt* it.

It was a blaze of pure and livid outrage. It surpassed all prior limits, all knowledge. It seared across the hillside, dazzling the fighting warriors to stumbling blindness. Nothing stood in its path – not the defenders of Tusien, not the deranged and slavering army that faced them, not even the Kas.

It took the Sical clean in the chest, igniting it with a white fire that burned brighter than its own, and consumed it completely. The elemental gave a huge cry, a flattening roar of noise that scaled upwards into a shriek.

Burn I!

And the horizon detonated into a thousand fiery shards.

Blinded, his ears ringing, the Bard found himself on his knees. He was laughing, deranged and disbelieving. He dragged his hands down his face, struggling to breathe.

I can see! I can...!

In the whack of light he had seen something – a flash, an insight – some aspect of his vision from the Ryll. It had been brief, explosive, but so strong he could touch it: a snatched sight of the Powerflux, of *how* the elements flowed across the world—

In a surge of furious exasperation, he slammed a fist into the stonework, splitting his knuckles, scattering scarlet. He was so *close*! He wanted to cry out, tear at the sky with frustration and power, demand the world give up its secrets, held away from him so long.

But he flexed his hand and grimaced, looked out over the wall.

Below him, the hillside was a crater, scorched and smoking soil, superheated stone. Burned bodies lay twisted, human and monster and animal, all of them seared black. The detonation had blistered everything, and burned the ground to char.

Ash drifted like snow.

Below, people were picking themselves up. Running, shouting, scattered and scared. And right down at the very bottom of the hill, the tents of the Kas still contained pockets of sporadic fighting.

Did we win?

The thought was unreal, it made him fall onto his backside. He leaned against the stone behind him, held up his split knuckles.

He started laughing, stopped himself.

But winning was fallacy: the war was not, had never been, what the world feared. He had known that from the beginning. Whatever field they may have taken today—

There was ink in his skin.

What?

In a sudden trembling panic, he turned his arms, peering at them. His first thought – that the Kas had somehow invaded his soul – he shoved aside, almost by instinct alone. These were not the marks from Amal's flesh, these were faint, faded, blurred by water and time. Grappling for understanding, he unzipped his London leather and pulled apart the front of his hoodie and shirt.

The words flowed across him like serpents.

Time, one said. *Flux.*

Caught, he forgot to breathe, searched further as if checking himself for lice. *No time, no time.* In other places, he could see the symbols of the elements, running one into another, and an image of a face with pitch-black eyes.

His heart lurched, thumping in his chest and temples. He knew these words – he *knew* them! It was like a drop-key fitting home, a dream suddenly realised.

He could *remember*...

Uncaring of the cold, he shed his garments and bared his chillfleshed skin. He was shivering, but he didn't care. He teetered upon the edge of a moment he had sought his whole Gods-damned *life*...

Roderick had been barely thirty returns when they'd welcomed him to the Ryll – little more than a youth in Tundran terms. Young as he'd been, they'd lauded him, afforded him every accolade, and he'd lost his head to it. Their attention had made him giddy. When they'd explained their rules to him, he hadn't cared – they were aging greyhairs and he was the hope of his generation, first Guardian born in Avesyr, and so on... he'd heard it so many times. He'd thought himself better than their observation and patience. And one night, he'd held out a hand to the water.

Touched his fingers to the falling and forbidden cold.

Now, the memory of that sensation was extraordinarily clear: the vastness of it, utterly drowning him. He remembered the shocking, tumbling onslaught of images, too fast, too big, too many – the thoughts of the world were not meant for mortal minds. He'd tried to catch a flicker like he'd catch the fall's rainbow spray, but it had all just swamped him, pummelling him down into the darkness.

Leaving him unconscious at the water's edge.

In the morning, the Guardians had found him. Their fury had been stern and silent; they'd shut him in his room without food or answers. His right arm had been numb to the shoulder, the skin of his fingers burned like he'd shoved them in a fire.

A halfcycle later, they'd exiled him from his home.

But what he'd *seen*...!

He'd seen the world's nightmare, her nameless fear that had governed his every waking thought from that point onwards.

But he'd seen something else, something that was a part of that fear.

Time.

Time the Flux.

Time the Flux begins to crack.

He'd seen the *Powerflux* – almighty webwork, warp and weft through world and sky; seen it as it touched and governed all things. He'd seen Rhan, the loss of the OrSil, and Ecko, the darkness of his eyes and soul. And Amethea...

Shivering with cold and need and tension and wonder, he struggled to piece it together. He was tight with urgency, with a clamouring disbelief. In the back of his mind, he could hear a voice – *This is not about 'good' and 'evil', about Rhan and Vahl, and their endless war. This is about the end of all life, all existence, all passion...* and he could see a figure, the exact same writing in his aged and shrivelled skin.

Ress.

Roderick remembered him from The Wanderer, from the night Triqueta had found the injured Feren. He remembered the man as practical, dismissing the Bard's talk of monsters, his forgotten visions.

In The Wanderer, Roderick had pleaded with him: *Ecko is* here. *He brings darkness and fire and strength the likes of which I have never seen! He understands my tale, my vision, the world's lost memory—*

And then, with a sudden shock of realisation that nearly made him shout, he made the connection.

The Bard was mortal – he could not encompass the thoughts of the Goddess. In his small and limited way, he'd been struggling to see and remember the parts because the full picture was too big.

But Ress's mind had been blown wide by information. The words he'd seen – they'd changed him, made him crazed. And they'd given him the same damned vision, or something that overlapped it.

The Bard was on his feet, now, elated, excited, afraid. He paced; the wind was ice-cold on his bare skin, but he refused to don his clothes.

He could *see*!

He could see Ress standing on the edge of an oxbow pool of water, stagnant and overgrown. In its centre, there was an old stone statue.

And he knew what it was, just as if the world had shown him.

The water, the stagnant water, was the World's lost Memory.

Ress had found the *Ilfe*.

And he was giving it to the Bard.

So he could remember.

Roderick was still, stunned. Breathless. Prickling with adrenaline. With vision and insight.

The Ilfe – hidden deep under Rammouthe Island, concealed from mortal and immortal alike. No one had been able to get close, because the Kas had been down there, hidden and broken and waiting—

His mind jumping, Roderick understood the ink in their skin. All unknowing, the Kas had been waiting at its side, and it had marked them. Like it had marked Ress, and was now marking him.

Deep below the city of London, Roderick had asked Mom for understanding, for information and comprehension. Now, every horror he'd lived through was worth it – his mind had the speed, and the capacity, and the memory, to finally encompass the thoughts of the Goddess herself.

It would take him time to unravel the imagery completely, but he saw one thing clearly – something the world had forgotten, long, long ago.

The full truth about the Powerflux.

The sun had gone, spilling its last bloody light across the plain. On the hilltop, Tusien's walls stood cold and black in the moonlight, while among the scattered destruction of the enemy camp, the rising dark hid lingering horrors.

In the chaos that had followed the lightning strike and the fall of the Sical, Triqueta had commanded her combined forces on clean-up detail. Her cavalry had ridden to the base of the hill, scattered what remained of the army of the Kas, offered the survivors the chance for surrender.

But what they'd found had been wreckage – the remnants of warriors, now aged and crazed, eyes and minds burned out with the Sical's glory and demise. Many of them could no longer speak, they'd slain their animals and turned on each other. Belly unsettled, Triqueta had rounded the last of them up and placed them under watch while she secured the campsite itself.

Now, the site was quiet, and the moons were rising. She crept silently through the remains of the Kas encampment on foot, her blades drawn. Her back ran with sweat in spite of the cold; she was prowling wary, watching for movement.

Behind her, darkness had swallowed the dead and the dying. Her hands itched like fire, but she ignored them. She tripped, nearly fell. Through the moonlight came spasms of noise – calls to the Gods, cries elated and victorious; gasps of pain and slavers of hunger. In places, there were hummocks on the dead ground and some of them moved, reaching out hands for help.

In a fragment of rocklight, she saw Taure, half his face missing and a last look of shock in his one remaining eye. She dropped to one knee beside him, staring at him as if he were the embodiment of the final death of the Banned.

My old friend.

A memory – she was in The Wanderer, playing dice. Ress and Taure had been propping up the bar, chuckling at her skills. For just a moment, it was more real than...

But then it was gone, and Ress was gone, and The Wanderer was gone, and Taure was there in the cold muck with half his face torn off. She picked up a handful of dirt and threw it over him in a silent farewell.

To him – to her youth – to the Banned entire.

Then, taking a breath, she stood and walked on.

Around her, the shapes became more creature than human. A hand clawed at her leg and she kicked something hard in the face – had no idea what it even was.

She left sick. Her heart thundered.

As she moved onwards, she realised she was coming to the heart of Ythalla's camp – she could see the ruined remains of bivouacs and tents, store carts left to rot. Many of them had been damaged by the explosion of the alchemy stores, and in places, there were huddles of frightened people, all of them in their last returns, frail and aged and dying. Some of them raged at her, shaking querulous fists, most were too weak.

The Kas had drained their own army, everything they had, to fuel the rise of the Sical.

She shuddered – pity and horror.

And then Triqueta saw something that made her stop.

* * *

The command tent was lit by rocklights, each glimmering in a standing terhnwood sconce. They bathed pools of warmth on the ceiling, threw angled shadows on the frosted walls. In their light, the tent was bare of luxuries – purely functional – and the guards had been ordered to stand outside.

Now, the occupants of the tent were gathered in a curiosity that felt like judgement – Nivrotar, Rhan, and Ecko. Amethea was there, but huddled and staring, curled shivering beside the Lord of Amos. Roderick was alive with his new knowledge; he thrummed to a song that only he could hear, and needed – craved – its release.

"I have waited… for so long," he told them. He had replaced his garments, wrapping them around himself. The Bard's gaze went from face to face, stopped as he caught Rhan's eyes.

"The Kas have left Rammouthe, we know this," he continued. He looked at all of them and then opened the layers of garments so they could see his lean frame, the writing that was inking itself into him, even as he spoke. Ecko swore. The Bard stood still for a moment, his steel throat bared and flanked by Mom's scars like its acolytes. "And in leaving, they have left their citadel open. Left the passage through it finally free."

"And you found…?" Rhan asked him.

"Knowledge!" The Bard grinned, the expression pure mischief, an echo of his former self. "All through our history and mythology, there have been four compass directions. Four elements, four souls. This has been the cornerstone of our entire lore, of everything we know and understand."

Ecko was bouncing on his toes. "Jeez, keep us in suspenders, willya?"

Roderick said, "There are not four elements." Wind breathed cold through the entranceway, making him shiver. "There are six."

"Shit!" Rhan's breath puffed out in a curse.

Roderick could see him surging with the information, with so many things suddenly fitting…

Six!

Rhan said, "How did we not *know*...?" He ran out of words. His hand reached for an explanation, came back empty. "Ice and fire, light and darkness—"

"Stone and sky," Roderick said. "The Powerflux isn't flat, edge to edge, horizon to horizon. It wraps us; it runs in the stone beneath our feet, in the air above our heads." He paused, went on. "And we *forgot.*"

"I saw," Rhan said. "I saw it in the Light, in the OrSil."

"The Ilfe has been found, hidden deep behind the citadel of the Kas. It's why their skins are marked, why mine is now. Even Vahl bears the ink, though I don't think he even knows what it is. But I *remember*. And I saw..." His voice caught, trembled. "All those returns ago, in the Ryll, I saw the Powerflux. Its full manifestation, vast and over and under us. In all our returns... Rhan, even you have only ever touched the edge of it. Its might is beyond belief." He was blazing, etched in symbols, his lone prophecy fulfilled at last. "With it, we can do *anything.*"

"Well, whaddaya know," Ecko grinned at him. "We've upgraded to 3D."

Triqueta could see her quite clearly: Ythalla. The thug-in-charge. The commander of Fhaveon's cavalry.

She was defeated and on foot, though still armed, armoured and Kas-possessed. Her metal-grey hair gleamed; the ashes of the Sical had settled over her like a shroud. Blade in her hand, she faced a small, angry man in armour slightly too big for him.

Mostak.

Ythalla was sneering, her chin lifted, her teeth bared. "So here we are again, Commander."

Mostak snorted, scathing as a slap. "You've lost, Ythalla. Lost everything, including your soul. I've got nothing to prove to you."

The woman lunged at him, point of the blade under his

chin. "You damned bastard. I'm going to carve you 'til you can't stop screaming."

He didn't bother moving, only chuckled at her. "Kill me if you like, it won't make any difference. This is over. All those lives drained for nothing. All your bullying and scheming, and look where you've ended up."

"You'll all die one way or the other," Ythalla said. "You've won, but what? You can't go back to Fhaveon – we slaughtered the last of her people. The cities of the Varchinde are charnels of disease and starvation. There's no food, no fuel. No terhnwood. Your world's *ended*."

"Then why?" Mostak said. The last of the sunlight made his armour gleam. "If this world is dead, why fight so hard for it?"

The question made Ythalla laugh, a savage spit of humour. She slung the blade over her shoulder in a deliberately jaunty gesture. "You think we care?"

The commander inhaled a breath, refusing to be baited.

Irritated by the woman's posturing, Triqueta slung her blades and unhooked her bow from her shoulder.

As swift as thought, she strung a shaft, sighted, let fly.

Ythalla never saw it coming.

It took the older woman clean in the throat and dropped her like a felled tree. She gouted blood, kicked for a moment, and was still.

Bitch.

Triq blew on her fingertips, the gesture of a perfect shot – though there was no one to see.

But then, as she slung her bow back on her shoulder, and Mostak turned to see where the arrow had come from, Triqueta realised that she'd made a mistake.

A damned great big mistake.

Oh, shit.

As the commander turned, she saw the blood-light bathe him, saw the slow wash of greed and power as it rose in his face.

And the blood curdled in her body.

Backing up, she glanced about her, but there was no refuge or help. She wondered what the rhez she'd been thinking, realised she'd been tired or showing off or both, realised that it didn't damned well matter now.

The Kas that had been inside Ythalla was now trying to take the Tan Commander.

But Mostak – she had to look twice to see it – was fighting *back*.

When she understood the man's sheer strength, what he was trying to do, Triq froze to the spot. Fascinated and horrified, she watched his face as he ground his teeth. Unbelieving – could he *do* this, could anyone? – Triqueta saw the commander struggle, quite literally, for possession of his soul.

She wanted to help him, felt responsible, wanted to tear the thing out by the roots... but what the rhez could she *do*?

Then, from somewhere in the chaos and failing light, she heard her name.

"Tan Commander Triqueta! I saw her! She came this way!"

She realised there were survivors and they needed her.

Without Mostak, the army was hers to command.

She needed a drummer, dammit, she needed a flag...

She needed not to panic.

Now, Mostak was on his knees, his hands clenched at his temples. In the rocklight, his forehead glistened with sweat. He made an effort, lurched to his feet and staggered forward several paces. She went towards him, one blade ready.

But his hand was on his long sword – Valiembor white metal – and then it was a glitter in the moonlight, and he was Kas and coming for her, laughing like Ythalla had done only moments before.

No! Damn you, fight!

She didn't know if she meant Mostak or herself.

Triq stood still, her stance defensive. She didn't want to fight him, but if he turned into Kas Gash Something-or-other, then she was going to kick his backside, Commander or no.

Mostak stopped, shaking, his face contorting. He was trying to speak, but shudders racked his body.

In the thin light, figures were starting to come into view, shattered and bloodied, but survivors.

Victors.

Mostak didn't look at them.

One of them ran to him – a member of his own command tan. He shouted relief at the sight of his friend, his Commander. But Mostak's face changed again and he snapped round, fast as a whip. He slashed the man's throat and left him kicking on the blood-soaked soil.

Shit.

"Now," he said, turning back to Triqueta. "You, you've been a spike in our sides for quite long enough."

"You come and get me, Vahl," Triqueta told him. "I've faced you before and you *know* I'm not afraid of you."

But the commander, the Kas in him, laughed aloud, harsh with amusement.

"I'm not Vahl, you stupid mare. Vahl's gone, Tamh with him. This – all of this – has just been to keep you busy."

Busy.

It was like a fist in the face.

Busy.

Why fight so hard for it?

This – all of this – had been a distraction. They'd been played. Just like in Aeona, Vahl was games within games, wheels within wheels...

Busy.

She'd wondered why he'd split his forces into three waves of attack, why he'd thrashed his own force to death to cross the plains.

She'd even wondered what he wanted...

Busy.

She said it aloud, her voice hushed, "By the rhez." Then her mind was scrabbling to catch itself up, work it all out. "Then where... where did he go? Dammit, what does he *want*?"

But Mostak laughed at her, the Kas in him laughed.

Furious, Triqueta surged forwards, placed her blade across Mostak's throat. He made no attempt to defend himself. She snarled in his face, at the Kas in his soul.

"You fucking bastard. I don't know what you are, but you're going to tell me where Vahl's gone, and what he—"

In response, he did the very last thing she'd been expecting.

Rather than fight back, score points or sneer, he simply pushed forwards, his eyes on hers, slowly and grimly cutting his own throat.

Thick red leaked down his chest.

Horrified, she saw the Kas command and then leave him, saw the humanity return to him as her blade was deep in flesh and windpipe. She tore it free without thinking, heard the hiss of air, heard him burble, felt the explosion of warmth that covered her face and hands – but it was too late.

Fearful it would try for her, she fell to her knees, instinctually, stupidly, trying to stop the bleeding. But the thing had gone, and Tan Commander Mostak Valiembor said his final words to her alone.

And then he died.

25: POWERFLUX TUSIEN

"We have so much power," Roderick said. "More than we can wield – if only we knew how." The rocklit walls of the command lit his inked skin like some ancient saga shaman, etched in alchemy. He was trembling, fighting to keep focus, to not just let it all loose in a shriek of pure joy.

"And we still face a foe," he said. "Not Vahl..." he caught Rhan's gaze and he grinned, "...something more, something darker and deeper. Something that the world has always feared and that we need to defeat." He closed his shirts and jacket around himself, became again a long, lean figure in his otherworldly black.

Ecko snickered. "Remembered that bit yet?"

The question jabbed at him, sharp like a blade. It was the thing he still couldn't see, couldn't quite make out. He was pacing now, agitated, searching for that opening, that final breakthrough. He was thinking aloud, words tumbling over themselves.

"We will need the Powerflux, all of it, all six elements. We will need all of our knowledge and strength—"

"We'll need to know where it is?" Ecko said.

The Bard spun and glowered at him. "If you're so fucking smart, you tell me."

"Let me Google it for ya."

"Stop it," Rhan said. "If we can't peel answers out of your skin, let's do this another way. Two new elements – must have souls, yes? Anchors and focal points. So where are they?"

Roderick let his breath out in astonishment. "A Soul of Stone—!"

"An' an air-soul," Ecko added. "Sorry."

Without looking, Rhan cuffed him round the back of the head.

"Ow."

But the Bard was thinking fast now, his energy surging.

"Yes, yes, of course." Connections and vision, recollections, information tumbling over itself. His skin sang, his throat was warm. "And the Soul of Stone would be the foundation for the Powerflux. It would be the centre, the crux, feasibly the single most powerful element of all. It must be beneath our feet somewhere." He stopped dead, tapping his fingers on his thigh in a sharp but silent tattoo. "It—"

"Would be the heart of the world herself?" Nivrotar commented softly.

The Lord of Amos had not spoken a word throughout the entire conversation. She stood silent, her face in the shadows of the rocklights. With a slight shock, Roderick realised that the sun had set without him noticing, and that the wind in the tent blew ice-cold.

He suddenly shivered, bundling his garments tighter.

Rhan whistled though his teeth. "And its *potential*—"

"Would be terrifying." The Bard rapped his fingers harder, an unconscious and complex rhythm. "If we knew where it was, then could we—?"

"For chris*sakes*." Ecko's tone was somewhere between amusement and disgust. "Bottom of the fuckin' class, both of ya. There's only one place it can be – we *know* where it is."

"It's the Monument." The words were Amethea's.

By the Gods!

Then Roderick's fingers stopped dead.

The Monument.

Of course it was. Of *course* it was! He wanted to smack a hand into his forehead, curse aloud. The Soul of Stone could be nowhere else – and he'd *known* it, known it all along, known it from his earliest research, from the sagas of the Flux itself. The Monument marked the centre of the Varchinde, the site of the lost Elemental College...

The college that Maugrim had blown into a smoking hole, its cracks even now spreading across the world...

Time the Flux begins to crack.

Oh...

...shit.

The rush of adrenaline made him hot and cold and sick. He opened the shirt again, searched his skin for answers, frenzied.

Come on come on come on...

Ress – what did you see? What did you see?

What are you trying to tell me?

"Aww." Ecko had turned on Amethea, sounding crestfallen. "How'd you—?"

"I *remember*," she said, slowly. Her eyes were unfocused, as if she fought some internal battle that none of them could touch. "When I was held by Maugrim, I *touched* it. I touched the stone of my room, and the wall was warm. It was vast and mighty, and I was tiny and lost, but it knew I was there. It *knew* me." She blinked, looked around at them. "And later, it grew into my skin, through my feet." Her face coloured, but she went on, "It became a *part* of me—"

"You're an Elementalist, Amethea," Rhan said, only half-jesting.

But she paid him no attention, was still speaking. "How else did Maugrim wield that much power? It must've been what he found, how he was able to make the stone guardians of the Cathedral move—"

"Bullshit," Ecko said. "Maugrim threw fire. Like the Sical. We *know* that, we saw it."

Rhan interrupted him, "Maugrim wielded fire?"

"Flame-beastie?" Ecko said. "Pocket version of the big fucker outside?"

"*And* stone?"

"So what?"

"You can't wield two elements at once," Rhan said.

"Or?"

"Kablooey." Rhan's shrug implied destruction beyond his ability to describe.

Kablooey.

Roderick whispered softly, "'Time the Flux begins to crack.' I think," he added, his voice soft with wonder, "that understanding lights our way at last."

Triqueta stood wordless, the body of the Tan Commander at her feet. She could hear voices in the darkness, close now – shouts triumphant and calls for friends. They were coming – and as soon as they saw her, she'd be reliving her Aeonic nightmare, boots and spitting, her stones pried from her face...

I didn't... She couldn't find the words to say them aloud. *Gods, I didn't...*

The shouts were reaching a peak, there were running boots. Somewhere, she could hear hooves, voices calling her name. She wasn't going to wait to see who it was.

By the rhez, if anyone saw this they'd hang her where she stood!

Dropping the blade, Triqueta backed away from the cooling corpse of the Tan Commander. His body was rigid, as if even in daemonism and death, he'd never faltered in his loyalty, or his courage.

Like Redlock.

But she didn't have time for that now.

There were more people behind her, a rise of caustic humour. She could hear voices she knew getting closer by the moment. Heroic monument, her arse, Nivrotar would wind her guts onto a Gods-damned *spool...*

Maybe that was why the Kas hadn't bothered hanging around.

Triqueta looked swiftly about her and ducked into the remains of a campsite bivvy. She hunkered down in the smells of shit and cold and soil, and tried to calm her scrambled thoughts.

The Commander's last words were critical, they circled her like predators. She tried to think where they would lead, but her thoughts were all jumbled. The battle was won, but Vahl—

The Kas had never *cared* about winning the damned battle.

Busy.

From somewhere higher up the blasted hillside, a drum sounded the muster. Rocklights flared, drums and voices bawled commands.

She needed to get out of here. She needed to reach the command tent and tell them what Mostak had told her.

Where Kas Vahl Zaxaar had gone.

"It's so simple when you understand it," Roderick said. "Maugrim had no way of knowing that stone was an element, and he broke a fundamental rule without realising."

"And he stood upon its elemental soul," Rhan said, "at the heart of the Powerflux."

"An' he blew the fucking shit out of it," Ecko finished, with some aplomb.

"Kablooey," Roderick agreed with him. "And so, we have a

dirty great hole, cracks that spread through our life and our world and our soil." He looked from face to face. "But that damage isn't just physical. The Ryll knows – remembers, now – that the damage is in the Powerflux itself. If it's permitted to spread further, then what will be left?"

"The end of the Count of Time," Rhan said. The words started as a jest, but his tone ran dry and he fell into silence.

Outside, something cried, long and sorrowful.

"So, c'mon, visionary," Ecko said. "You're on a roll, dude. The Powerflux is busted, so how do we fix it? Is this my shining moment? Where's this bad guy at?"

The Bard shook his head, spread his hands.

"All right," Rhan said. "Another question. What about the Soul of Air, that one's a bit harder. If the stone is our foundation and strength, then the air must be our inspiration, our creativity? Can we find that?"

The tent doors stirred, laughing at them.

Inspiration.

Creativity.

And the Bard knew the answer. It came with a rush, with a rising, overwhelming sense of everything fitting together. His whole *life*. Something in him was shouting, raw and wild, crying in a voice none of them could hear...

The Soul of Air.

He let his garments fall open. Slowly, he picked up a rocklight, and raised his chin. Metal seethed, shifting and writhing and gleaming.

And Ecko whispered, "Holy fucking *shit.*"

He stood there, letting it move, letting them see how it felt and what it could do, see the scars he'd gained in acquiring it. Then he lowered the light, and looked back at them.

He said, "I saw a world where information was everywhere. Communicated by thought, or so it seemed, free in the very air itself. And I asked to understand. To *own* it." His words were a ripple of motion, graceful and eerie. "This is Khamsin. This is what Mom gave me."

"No," Ecko said. "No, no. Absolutely not, fuckin' *no*. This crossing-realities shit is startin' to do my head in. There's no way that Mom gave you technology that now transforms into magick. Mutually exclusive. You don't get a plus-five elemental whosit of doom in the deep, dark depths of the fuckin' London Underground, okay? It's not a *dungeon*."

"Really?" Roderick laughed, and the sound was like the first whisper of the tsunami, like he wanted to shout forever. His excitement was tingling in his skin. "And what did she give you, Ecko? While you were screaming? Down there in the dark? Did she give you new strength, new speed, new skin, new eyes? Or did she *give* you her darkness?"

"Hell yeah, maybe she gave *me* a loada techno-magick. Maybe I got the Soul of Dark. It's the black eyes, nice symbolism. An' hey, maybe that's why we *recognised* each other." Ecko's comment was vicious, sarcastic. "We got matchin' tattoos. Hell, let's assemble the Avengers and go kick bad-guy butt." He snorted. "When you remember where he is."

The wind stirred again at the tent's doors, a cold breath that brought shivers to all of them. The Bard threw his torn shirt back round his shoulders, and began again his relentless pacing.

"Ecko," Rhan said, his voice like a rolling rock. "Say that again."

Ecko grinned. "You can be Thor if I can be Loki."

"When Roderick left the Ryll," Rhan spoke slowly, as if exploring each word, each conclusion, before he spoke it aloud, "he came first to me. And I *recognised* him." He caught the Bard's gaze and he smiled, his expression briefly gentle. "And you, Ecko, I know you too."

The three of them looked at Amethea, but she made no response. The green in her skin was swelling, lichens flowering like decoration – but her jaw was clenched and sweat glittered on her forehead. Knowing what had happened to Ghar, Roderick wondered how hard she was fighting to keep her soul.

But she was strong – as strong as the stone itself.

"We're the parts of the Powerflux," Roderick said. The tent was alive with the realisation. It was crawling all over his skin, tingling with the connections and why they made sense. "*That's* why the Ryll knew you. Knew you both. It's why we know each other."

And then his knees did go, and he was on the floor and on the rugs, and looking up at the rest of them. His words were breathed in cold vapour.

"You really are the darkness, Ecko, the darkness in which the fire burns brightest. And Rhan is the light, as he has always been." He was shaking, swallowing before he could speak again. "Amethea has touched the Soul of Stone, holds the strength and heart of the world herself. And I have Khamsin, power to lift the heart and split the sky." His throat slid, gruesomely sensual, as he spoke. "And if we can understand what Maugrim did, then maybe, maybe..." his voice became a whisper, "we can set this right—"

He was interrupted by a thump of boots outside the tent's door, a slap as the fabric was slammed back. In the rocklight, Tan Commander Triqueta was cold and bleak and filthy. Her leather armour was blood-soaked and torn, and her face was figment-pale.

There were horrors in her yellow eyes.

"My Lord—!" She stopped at the sight of them all, gathered there and facing her. "Secret meeting?"

Roderick scrabbled to his feet.

"Tan Commander." Nivrotar stepped into the rocklight, diverting her attention. "Report."

"The enemy camp is secured, my Lord." She paused, looking from face to face, went on. "Tan Commander Mostak is dead. Vahl's fled the site, the rest of the Kas with him."

"What?" Rhan surged forwards. "What happened to Mostak? Where did Vahl go?"

Triqueta stepped in, letting the tent flap drop behind her. Her gaze stopped on Amethea. "Dear Gods—"

"*Tell* me about Vahl," Rhan said.

Triqueta glowered at the Seneschal, but answered him.

"This," she said, "all of this. It's been a distraction. This has never been about winning a war."

Rhan's face darkened. "What do you mean?"

"Mostak told me, before he died." Triqueta's jaw jumped; she looked from Amethea to Ecko, and then back up to the Lord of Amos, and to Rhan. "The Kas – they didn't follow you to kill you. They followed you to keep you busy. They've gone to the Monument."

Rhan swore.

And Roderick said, in a voice like flame, "Of course they have."

"I'm coming with you," Triqueta said. "To the rhez with Nivvy and her damned orders. You're not doing this without me!"

They stood outside the command tent, Triqueta and Amethea and Ecko. The walls of the ruin stood over them, black and glistening-cold. Cross-hatched moonlight cast impossible shadows, massing monsters in corners.

Ecko said, "You're the fuckin' *boss*, Triq. Guess who gets mop-up detail?"

"No damned way." Fuming, Triqueta aimed a kick at a tent peg. Out across the ruin's floor, the rows of barracks stood silent and iced in frost.

"Amethea should be staying, not me," Triq said. "She needs help—"

"I have to go with them." Amethea was huddled under layers of cloak, her face blotched with stains of living moss.

One eye was half-closed, now, and the same stuff grew at the corners of her mouth. She had a vague and perpetual frown, as if at some internal search or turmoil. "I have to hold on for long enough... Whatever this is, the Monument has my answers too." She blinked, made an effort to focus. "It's all tied in together, I can *feel* it."

"You *can't*!" Triq turned on her, almost pleading. "I can't lose you too. Please, Thea, isn't there an apothecary who can help you? Anybody? Someone who even understands what this is?"

"Not even Rhan." The word was bitter. Amethea's mouth flickered with hurt, and the movement peeled at the lichen at the corners of her lips. Absently, she scratched at it. "Triq, I *have* to go."

Triq swore, then threw her arms around her friend. After a moment, Amethea responded, but the hug seemed confused, and her gaze stayed half-focused. She patted Triqueta on the back, and let her go.

"I'll be okay," she said.

"You come back, you hear me," Triqueta told her. "We need you. *I* need you."

"I will," Amethea said. Then she seemed to stand up straighter and her focus cleared slightly. "You never know, I might even put my shoulder to the wheel." She took Triqueta's hands. "Look, I'm going back to the hospice to gather what I can. But – first light – you'll come and say goodbye?"

Triqueta nodded. "I still say I should—"

"Ecko's right," Amethea said. "You're a war hero, you're in command, and you're needed here."

"Shit!"

Amethea let Triq's hands go and turned away. She ducked under the frozen guy-line and was gone, her grey cloak dissipating in the cold.

Triqueta rounded on Ecko. "And you? Are you coming back?" The question seemed poised on the edge of tears, or judgement. "Or do you – what? – fade out of existence when all this is over?"

Ecko watched her, trembling, telling himself he was cold. Faced with his own end credits, he was thinking about his score, those numbers racking up in one corner of the screen. Had he completed this task? Or that one? Finished all the side quests? Found all the fucking Easter eggs?

Achievement failed.

Hell, he *wanted* to reach out to her, but he still didn't have a fucking clue...

I'm sorry, hey, I'm here for you. Like, what can I do to make it better?

Asshole.

Instead, he said, "This is it, Final Showdown." His voice was soft, as if he was already resigned to his failure. "I don't get to come back. We gotta save the world, fulfil the prophecy, whatever the fuck. An' if we do, I guess I go home. An' if we don't, we all fuckin' die anyhow." He watched her face, her eyes, the golden shine of her skin. "This is it, Triq, Mount Doom." He made an odd, swallowing noise in his throat, but she didn't get the joke, and it kinda wasn't funny anyhow.

It all ends here.

The line of her mouth jumped, like she was fighting tears. She closed her eyes, raised her face to the moons. Her skin was carved in age and pain, marked with all the things she'd seen. The stones in her cheekbones glittered.

Greatly daring, feeling like a dickhead, he managed, "I... I guess I'm gonna miss you," and then he cursed himself for not managing something smarter. "Y'know, all of you."

But it made her smile, looking back down and meeting his eyes. Then a sudden grin lifted her expression, and she gave an impish chuckle.

"Funny," she said, "when Tarvi took my time, I didn't realise I'd have to be responsible as well as just *older*."

It was only a joke, but the mention of Tarvi was like flooring his accelerator. He felt his adrenaline dump, his heart lurch and then *pound-pound-pound* like an industrial hammer. His knees wouldn't hold him. She was so close, and he was abruptly, tautly aware of how good she smelled.

Under the sweat and the blood, she smelled like a spice market. Like marzipan. Like butter. Like, even in the midst of the dead Varchinde, she had a saffron subtlety of warmth and promise that made him shiver...

You fuckin' loser! He berated himself, furious. *What the hell're you even thinkin'?*

Torn between anger and self-consciousness and a sudden crippling sense of want, he did the thing he'd dared once before – he laid a hand on the side of her face. The warmth and colour of her flooded his arm, and her skin was fine and smooth under his fingers. He could feel it, gritted in blood-flecks and dirt.

"Bein' a grown-up sucks," he said, trying to muster a grin. "But I guess we gotta put our shitkicker boots on."

"I'm all right with it now," she said. "Age brings its own strengths and insights." Her chuckle sounded again, a moment of wicked delight in the darkness. She held his hand in place with her own. "Ecko." She said his name as if she just wanted to find out how it tasted. "This has all been so crazed."

Ohhh, shit...

He was trembling, breathless. Hopeless. Jesus H *Christ*, he was no good at this shit. He was shaking, as confused and as painfully overeager as some inexperienced teen.

And then her arms were round his shoulders, sliding, and she was there against him. She was strong and sweet and supple and he could feel her leather armour and the leanness of her body beneath it and his hands were going around her back as if he'd never, ever let her go. He had a split-second of pure, cold panic, and then her mouth was warm, and wanting, and he could kiss her like he knew what he was doing and just let the rest of the world fall away...

But there was still a shadow between them. Something a lot closer than Tarvi had been.

He pulled back with an effort, needing to know. "Triq..."

"What?" She was still close; she was breathing the word almost into his mouth.

"Redlock..."

"Redlock is *dead*," she said. The word was abruptly fierce, and she pulled back to meet his gaze, her expression afire. "Ress is dead, Jayr is dead, Taure is dead, Mostak is dead, Roviarath is dead, the Banned is *dead*. The world is crawling on her knees." She was whispering, but each word was a slap. "I'm desert-born, remember? Life is sacred. The life of the world, and the celebrations of what really matter. Redlock will never be forgotten: he'll be with me 'til the day I die. However damned close that might be. You," and now her hands pulled him closer, and her voice was in his ear, "you're *here*. And tomorrow, you go too – you and Amethea both – and I have to grow up, once and for all. I have to rebuild a world."

For a moment longer, he teetered on the edge of massive, world-shaking indecision. But the simple urge of *want* was roaring loud, drowning out everything else. It flexed him under the touch of her hands, it pushed him closer into her, it wrapped his arms around her back.

It made her catch her breath in response.

In the darkness, the moonlight caught the opal stones in her face, the blood scattered across one side of her jaw. It caught the gold of her skin.

And it made her shine.

Drenched in disbelief, Ecko wished he could keep this one image, this one moment...

And then his indecision was gone and he touched his mouth to hers. He had no clue what he was doing, but she kissed him back fearlessly, a murmur of pleasure in her throat. And he found himself responding, losing everything else to the sensations and the scents of her.

And later, when she was there under him, a tangle of hair and blankets and rocklight, when her smooth thighs were hard around his hips and pulling him into her, when he was kissing her, still in astonishment and wonder and incredulity, when he was feeling the arch of her back and her slender, callused hands on his skin and her body wrapped all hot and sliding round him...

Then he would have given his entire fucking soul for that world, for that lust and closeness and release, to be real.

26: VISION QUEST THE KARTIAN MOUNTAINS

It was the ruin that finally gave Lugan his insight.

The building was a stone cot, walls crumbled and beam roof half-collapsed, all of it grown over by creeper that had long since dried to desiccation. It looked like the kind of place you'd find some lone Highland warrior, battle-scarred and hell-bent on revenge. And Lugan knew it – or something like it – from the throttle-dropping days of his youth.

The old shell stood in silhouette, guarding the mountain pass.

He reached it as the sun was lowering in the sky ahead, and he paused to lean his weight on his knees, legs and lungs straining from the long, ragged climb. The wind cut like glass, making him cough, and swear, and cough again.

Memories passed him like tail lights: urban desolation, revving engines through abandoned buildings, a sore arse and stiff back, cold hands, ears that thundered with ferrocrete echoes. Then he grunted, half-reminiscent and half-scornful, and straightened up, wincing. He closed his eyes to the sunlight, absorbing much-needed warmth.

His Pocket of Eternal Dog-Ends had finally run dry, old

baccy re-rolled and re-rolled until it was almost pure tar. Even his flask was empty – though he'd stopped to refill it with water at every possible chance. He wondered if there was anything in the cot that he could smoke, or eat.

"Yeah," he muttered aloud, "Fuckin' *moss*."

When he opened his eyes to look down, though, he ran right out of sensible thoughts.

"Bloody 'ell!"

Below him, spread out like some artist's map, was a vista of pure impossibility, immense beyond words. It was a vision, land and time and distance that robbed him of breath and left him coughing all over again. It was plains and rivers and clouds, tiny points of cities, long roadways that unrolled between them. It was distances vast, all of it afire with the setting of the sun. It was...

It was fucking *magick*.

Okay, so he was still tripping his arse off, he *knew* that. Crystal trees and two moons, for fuck's sake, you didn't tell him *that* shit was anything normal. He'd been able to feel it, all through the pale trees and up the toiling, zigzag path – soon now, reality would spike its cold, grey fingers into this... whatever the hell it was. Christ, he'd done his share of psychotropics, once upon a time, and he knew how the story went.

Like that time when—

It was then that the insight really hit him: the broken cot, the memories of his youth. From the days when they could ride as they wanted, racing through derelict warehouses, dropping LSD, mescaline, peyote, whatever they could score. Watching Moorcockian colours rippling fantastic in shattered urban walls. He remembered it so clearly – the insight, the wonder, the worlds they'd seen and built and craved – and he remembered what it felt like as those worlds came apart. As they thinned to two dimensions, burned through, became bleak and chill as a pencil drawing.

As reality manifested once more.

Comedown.

Like the little cot, those broken walls of memory were pure dereliction.

Standing there, cold wind in his face, he looked at the dream spread in front of him, its glow now fading as the sun sank.

And then he saw smoke.

It wasn't ordinary smoke: it rose briefly white, then billowed into a writhe of black and grey and tan. Sparks danced upwards into the darkening sky. And the *smell...*

Rising to the pass where he stood, it was nauseating and sweet, putrid and steaky. It reminded him of childhood barbeques, or of an old leather being cremated on a fire. More echoes – once you'd smelled the stench of decomposing bodies burning, you never, ever forgot it.

Bring on the zombies...

At the meaty reek, his belly rumbled, making him gag. He crouched down by the mossy side of the empty cot, one hand over his nose. Focusing his telescopics, he steadied himself against the momentary head-spin and began to scan the land below.

He needed Fuller, for fuck's sake, needed Collator to tell him what the hell was going on. And he needed a weapon – he wasn't sure he wanted to face Dusk of the Living Dead with only his bare hands...

Arse, bollocks and shite!

The fire was close – less than two klicks away, east down the pass – and it was gutting a cot rather bigger and newer than the one beside him. It was hard to see through the smoke and the heat, but the whole place was apparently ablaze, crops, outbuildings and all. There was at least one figure standing there watching it burn.

Ecko?

The thought made him lean forwards, instinctively trying to see more clearly, but the figure was heavily built, bulky-shouldered, and watchful, neither Ecko nor zombie. Lugan was too far away to hear it if it spoke, but he could see it as it turned, its mouth and nose covered, and its forehead etched with... were those scars deliberate? They were more like tattoos, consciously curving and artistic.

They writhed in the heat-shimmer.

Don't tell me this trip's gonna turn nasty before the end...

He swallowed bile, tried not to breathe. He searched his pocket for the dog-end he knew wasn't there. Combing his telos across the site, strip after strip, he found billowing flame and thick, dark smoke, then more figures, faces covered, several of them bearing uplifted flambeaux.

Looking further, he found their mounts – ugly, slope-backed things that resembled camels more than horses – picketed a distance upwind. He supposed he ought to get his arse down there and nick one, saddlebags and all.

Yeah, an' then what?

The thought made him chuckle.

'Alf a tonne of muscle an' a brain the size of a lug-nut? Even if it don't turn into a giant octopus 'alfway down the road, you're pullin' my bleedin' chain. I ain't ridin' nothin' without an engine.

The picketed creatures nosed the grassless ground, uncaring of his opinion.

Motionless, he watched.

After a time, the masked arsonists threw their torches into the blaze. Leaving the fire, they remounted, formed up into a loose gang. He watched them ride away, turning to shout gleefully at one another with faces now exposed and bad teeth bared in laughter. Only one of them had the distinctive scarring, and her face was covered with it, wrought with careful gouges.

Ritual?

Body art?

Self-'arm?

They turned behind a spur of land, and he lost them from view.

Disturbingly loud, his belly grumbled again.

Great. Now what?

Disappointingly, perhaps, no giant octopuses emerged, the sky didn't erupt with tentacles. The smoke continued to rise and the sun continued to sink, and the clouds glowed, striped with lavender and gold. Lugan sighed.

Onwards it is, then.

His exploration of the ruined cot showed him neither baccy nor food, so he picked up a decent, heavy length of old beam, and wondered if he could make the blaze before full dark.

The sun faded slowly from the plainland, and Lugan used the firelight to lead him through the gathering dusk.

The gang hadn't left much.

On his half-clamber, half-skid down the pass, Lugan had been very conscious of leaving the sun behind him, had felt the mountains' darkness creeping, shadows down the slope.

He'd had bad trips before, and had no fucking intention of letting this one go off the rails.

Instead, he tried to clear his thinking, made an effort to focus – he found himself reflexively asking Fuller to detail the threat. He needed the info-feed, the background, the scans for local populace and security and infrastructure. He needed Ecko to run scout, needed his old Remington, a decent blade, a drone, an aircar with miniguns whirring – hell, don't do this shit by halves – he needed the whole kit an' bleedin' caboodle. The absence of urban sprawl he could do, he'd been enough time on the road to understand space, but the lack of foreknowledge? Right now, he'd settle for a *map*.

The info-vacuum was trippy in itself, messing with his head.

Christ almighty. Lugan searched his pocket for a dog-end,

swore. Fuller and maps and miniguns were a world away, explain it however you fucking liked. He'd got himself and the shit in his pockets, and he'd better get on with it.

At least it meant the baccy craving was only in his head.

As careful as he could, he eased closer, boots scrunching. He paused as he felt the whack of heat, scanned the rising shimmer.

No zombies, no gang, no traumatised and fleeing civilians.

No security. No fire services.

No fast-response, absolutely bloody nothing.

He raised an arm to shield his face. The wavering of the air made the whole thing completely unreal.

Realising he was sweating, he opened the zip of his jacket. His mouth was dry, tasted like ash. He knew he was jittery – if he didn't get a roll-up soon he was gonna—

Do what, pillock? What you gonna do?

He could see more clearly now – the place was larger than the cot he'd left behind. It was almost a hamlet, nestled right up here in the cleavage of the mountains. Drystone walls marked simple farming; there was a tiny storehouse, a single standing stone, a scatter of still-burning huts...

As he tried to count them, one collapsed in a shower of sparks.

Nothing else moved.

Baffled now, increasingly freaked and wary of the heat in the stonework, he began a circuit – seeking movement, outbuildings, anything that might've escaped.

And slowly he began to understand that something, somewhere, was very badly fucked up.

Okay, so Lugan'd torched stuff a time or two in his life – though he usually used more petrol. When the corporations' drones didn't put out the fires, the flames spread swiftly, gobbling their way downwind to take out entire warehouse units, black market stock, squatters, whatever was necessary. As problem-solving went, it was a quick fix.

If you knew what you were doing.

Downwind here, the land was empty – no crops, woods, trees, or fences – and the fire was suffocating for lack of fuel. As Lugan completed his circuit, though, he realised the clearance hadn't been deliberate.

This farmstead – whatever the hell it was – had no life surrounding it at all.

What?

Sweating profusely now, conscious of his own stink, Lugan paused on a slight rise. This whole thing was becoming more fucked up by the moment. Fuller's absence was loud as a shout. Informationless, feeling a rising, formless anxiety, he turned to look round him properly, tuning his oculars to see through the failing light.

To see something – anything! – that would tell him what the hell was going on.

And slowly, Lugan began to understand that everything, all round him, as far as he could see, was barren. Bereft of life. Crops and forests, grasses and heathers – everything was dead. Brown and shrivelled, rotten against cracked soil.

Holy fuckin' mother of God.

As his understanding grew, so his heart shrank in his chest and he stared in disbelief, in rising panic. His vision expanded further, desperate; it roved wider, looked for life, for something still moving. The horror in him swelled, suffocating, leaving him choked and breathless. In the pass, the sun had been in his eyes; now, he could see clearly, and he was surrounded by just...

Nothing.

By emptiness, as far as he could see.

Fuller, mate, if you can hear me, I wanna wake the fuck up right now...

The incredible vista he'd seen was an illusion, a lure. This was the worst bastard trip of his entire life.

Fuller...?

But Fuller couldn't hear him. Collator couldn't find him.

He was still tripping, and he had no control.

No way out.

Oh no you don't. This ain't gonna scare me...

One hand closed over the little red light, the only thing he trusted. The other gripped the end of his beam, as if he needed to swing it at something, to smash and to *smash*, to break his way through and out the other side, to let it all go in violence...

Yeah, bring on the zombies!

But the mountains' swelling foothills were carpeted only in twisted stumps as far as he could see.

Somewhere he remembered the Bard, his reaction to Mom – his craving for information.

And the price he'd paid to get it.

Standing on the rise, like some last surviving icon of humanity, Lugan looked in the direction the gang had gone. They'd probably stopped not far away.

And whether they'd turn into Cthulhu or not, he was going to get some fucking answers.

They didn't turn into Cthulhu, or anything else.

Lugan made no attempt to sneak up on them – like he could – instead he walked in there as if he owned the joint. The tethered beasties snorted at his bootsteps, and the gang was on its feet as he reached their circle of firelight.

He addressed the woman with the scars, the only one who remained sitting, pointing his wooden beam straight at her.

"Ade Eastermann, pleased t'meetcha. And you're gonna tell me where the 'ell I am."

They surrounded him, hands on clubs and cudgels with the ease of people who knew how to use them. No blades, no firearms. Fuller or no Fuller, Lugan wasn't going to have too much trouble guessing their chosen profession.

They sneered at him.

"What we got here, then?"

"Where the rhez did you spring from?"

"Put the tree down, sunshine."

There were five of them, all men of various builds, none of them as big as he was. They were dressed like old school homeless, layers and grot – no bright colours, no tech, no jewellery.

Lugan ignored them. Some sort of roots were roasting round the edges of the fire, and his hunger was suddenly thunderstorm-loud.

He swallowed.

"You're a bit out of your way," the scarred woman said from the far side of the little circle of light. She wasn't young, her face was lined and square, her long hair dirty and greying. Her features flickered unholy in the rising heat. She made no attempt to stand up.

"Local, are you?" she said.

Her cronies muttered, speculation and rumour. A couple of them were edging round behind him, and Lugan shifted, keeping an eye on them.

"Came over the mountains," he said.

The mutters became open mirth. The woman raised an eyebrow and grinned at him, baring teeth that were stained, chewing-baccy brown. She was gauging his jacket, his battered, oil-stained jeans.

"Oddest leathers I've ever seen," she said. "You Banned?"

"From several places."

The men shifted. Lugan went to take a step back, to keep all of them in sight, but a cudgel in his back stopped him. Weapons smacked into palms with that timeless gesture of gleeful threat.

"I said put down the tree," the bloke beside him said.

"You mean this?" With little effort, Lugan cracked the heavy beam straight under the man's chin, lifting him two inches off his feet and stretching him backwards in the dirt. The man the other side of him raised his club. Lugan slammed the opposite elbow into his face, breaking his jaw and sitting him down hard.

The others surged, cursing.

The scarred woman said, "Wait!"

They stopped.

"Stay where you are." She was on her feet now, assessing Lugan more carefully. She said, "You came across the mountains?" This time, it was a question, and it held no mockery.

"Yeah," Lugan said. "Walked all the way. And you're gonna tell me what the fuck I just walked into. What is this? Rural dystopia? There ain't no such beast."

"No one lives in the Kuanne." She nodded at the mountain pass. "They say the Kartians cursed it, that everyone died and that the mountains' shadow was twisted. And then we forgot, like we *forgot* everything else." Her stained grin spread, and he wondered if she really did have tobacco. "You want to know how I know?"

"Not really," Lugan told her. He searched his dog-end pocket, snatched his hand back.

"Where d'you think I got these scars?" She came closer, prowled round the edge of the fire, some aged hag pronouncing hoodoo-voodoo. He had no fucking clue what she was talking about.

"Tell me why everything's dead," he said. "Why you torched a dead village. Tell me what's east of here – down out the mountains."

"We like the Kartians," the woman said. Now, she was close enough for him to smell the liquor on her breath. "We bring them... what they need. Terhnwood, leather, food. And sometimes, other things. People who're lost, or missing their families. Children who've got no one left to care for them. Those who're unwanted, or unloved. The priestlords like their... *help*." The last word was accompanied by a nod at the remaining cronies.

Oh for fuck's sake.

Lugan dropped the first one with a fist in the face, spun on one boot heel and brought the beam smack into the ribs of the second, cracking wood and bone with the force of the blow. The third one, smaller and faster, hung back, grinning with a mouthful of gaps – one pace forward and a boot in the bollocks dropped him like stone.

Everything went quiet.

Lugan rounded on the woman with the cracked beam still in his hand.

"Well?" he said.

"Impressive," she said. She made him sound like a custom chop.

"I ain't goin' to ask you twice." His boot came down on the neck of one of the goons.

The action made her laugh, thin and nasty. "Maybe you really have come across the mountains," she said. She turned to gesture eastwards, at the open darkness, at the cold. "Down there is the Varchinde, the open plain – goes all the way to Amos on the coast. And it's *finished*." The word was a brown spit, hissing, into the fire. "All of it. Dying. Dead. Even our trade's dried up; the Kartians've closed their doors. Well," she eyed him up and down, "almost."

Lugan lifted the beam, placed it under the woman's chin, made her look up at him.

"Why'd you burn the village?"

She grinned, grot seething between her teeth. "Can't be too careful. You know how it is."

Lugan lifted his boot and the fallen goon scuttled away, joining the huddle of others at the fireside. They looked up at him, sullen with hatred.

The woman pushed the beam away, stepped inside its arc. "You ever seen the blight?" she said. "It grows through your skin, like moss. It pulls you down into the ground, eats you alive. Not just people. Animals, plants, everything living. It chokes you, and it lives off you – sucks the life right out of you. And then when you're empty, it dies. And the worst thing? It's not the infection, Ade Eastermann of the Banned. It's the loss of hope. The emptiness. The worthlessness." She gestured at the darkness. "The *nothing*."

Nothing.

Lugan went cold.

The word was a frisson, like a spark-plug jumping.

Nothing.

He stared at the woman, watched as firelight made the scars on her face shift and dance. Caught, his voice was a husk. "What d'you mean?"

"That farm," she said. "They gave up. The blight came, and they didn't fight any more. They just... let themselves rot. Their livestock lay down and died in the fields, right where it was. The people sat in the chairs and just didn't get up again. Stopped caring, stopped fighting. Let the moss grow through them. They had no more passion, no more anger, no more love. No more use for life."

Her voice continued, some archaic priestess in the firelight, but Lugan was staring at her, staring through her, staring at the darkness that rose behind. And he could see – as if his trip was thinning, and the grey pencil lines were returning – something beyond the black. He stood at the bottom of a rise of cells, looking up at bars across boxes, boxes where people were kept. *Stopped caring, stopped fighting.* They were *in* there, quiescent, content with a bed and a fridge. A console. People who lay unmoving, their eyes open; people who'd just... *stopped.*

The woman was still speaking, but her words were a part of the picture – she was describing the disease and it was the pencil that was piercing the illusion, that was greying the colours from the dream.

Not wanting the colours to go, not without him understanding them, he said, "Wait. Wait!"

"Scared you, have I?" she said. "Big chap like you?"

The grey was gone, the pencil vanished. He was back in the firelight, back in the winter cold. He was shivering, there in the starless dark.

He blinked, focused on the woman's scarred face. Not even sure where the impulse had come from, he said, "Where's The Wanderer? It came from 'ere – didn't it? The Bard...?"

He spoke the tavern's name and the breakthrough was like an epiphany. Suddenly he knew where he was going, what he needed to do. Everything fell into place, it all made fucking *sense*. It was symmetrical – all of this had started with the tavern, its manifestation in London. The Bard had known, Mom had known – she had given him the red light for a reason. *The one thing he trusted.* When reality returned, and if Collator wasn't fucked—

Oh of *course*.

Collator's viral infection was all part of the same hallucination. There was *nothing* the matter with the AI – there never had been – it was all the same damn trip.

Vision Quest.

Whatever the hell it was.

The mention of The Wanderer had made the injured goons sit up. They glanced at one another. The scarred woman was grinning like a loon.

"The Bard warned us," she said. "Returns ago he saw this, and no one listened. He spent his life... looking for answers, insight. Whatever happens, dreams mean everything. The Kartians know that – they see more in the darkness than we've ever done in the light. The Bard knows it: he saw it in the water. And I know it, that's why I burned the village. Our passions and visions are what we are. We break down barriers, we see magick, we experience pure illumination. Without it, we're nothing."

Nothing.

Lugan was still motionless, stunned by the sheer force of his understanding. Memories of youthful antics, racing through warehouses while colours writhed glorious in broken windows; the pile of grey cells that rose round him, holding those who'd just... given up...

We see magick.

Nothing.

He was here for a reason. He had to find the end of this vision.

Find Ecko.

He found the little red light, held it in his hand.

And when the woman offered him a small pottery cup, he tilted it to his lips without question.

And he fell back into the vision, and went to find answers.

PART 4: FADE TO GREY

27: KAZYEN THE DEAD VARCHINDE

Grey air, pre-dawn cold.

The world was fogged and bleary, drifting with snow. The wind stirred sluggishly, as if it, too, thought it was too bastard early.

Ecko sat in his saddle, his shoulders hunched against chill and inevitability. He was tired, but gladly so. Wrapped in layers of cloak and a luxury of recollection, in the warmth of her that still lingered on his skin. Around him, Rhan, Roderick and Amethea sat silent, like ghosts.

The horses' tack clattered as the animals shifted.

Only two people had come out to see them leave. Nivrotar, upright and cold, wreathed in the slowly breathing fog. Beside her, Triqueta, smaller but strong and poignantly vital, a touch of sunshine in the gloom. She bore the blade-on-pennon brassard of the Fhaveon Tan Commander.

Ecko was trying not to stare at her, trying not to etch her every movement into his memory like a blade carving cuts into his skin.

She met his gaze, offered him a wicked flicker of smile, a look that could have meant anything – everything – and then she drew herself up and composed her expression, a warrior to her fingertips.

"Fare you all well," Nivrotar said softly, words all but swallowed by the fog. "Fare you all very well. My heart rides with you. You are the world's last warriors and I trust that you carry her life in your hands. I am proud of you all, more than I can say." She came forwards, laid a white hand on Amethea's knee, but the doc was a forlorn and staring huddle and she gave no reaction. "I realise there are only the four of you, but we are all but out of supplies, and you will have to prevail, if we are to survive. Trust in me, and in each other, and I believe you will be strong enough. Understanding will come, before the end."

"You, my Lord Seneschal," Nivrotar said, looking up at Rhan. "Guard and guide these people, hold fast to their protection. Find your brother, and never forget how close to you he really is. And remember, humility is the hardest lesson of all."

Rhan's response was a rumble. "My Lord."

Her gaze moved to the Bard, swathed in his blood-red cloak. "And you, prophet and seer, you that has the world's memories inked in your skin, remember this: everything you have ever learned now gathers in upon you like a storm. Now, Master Bard, *now* you earn your title. You must return, to bear your long tale to the generations of the future. The world must not forget again."

"Yes, my Lord."

"And you, Ecko…"

He tried to come back with something cutting and jaunty about hackneyed final speeches and who the hell was she anyway, but sex and fog had smeared his wits and he had a big fat zilcho.

"…when you come to the last, I will be there with you. Remember that. By my hands was The Wanderer built and the Great Library defended." Her gaze swept them all, lingered longest on Amethea. "I will be there with you all."

She stepped back, leaving Triq standing alone, the commander's white-streaked yellow hair a sodden glimmer and the stones in her cheeks running with moisture like tears. Ecko knew he had to move, say something, but there were no words, nothing his clumsy ass could rescue from the moment.

"We muster at Amos," Triqueta said. "A detachment will be sent to Fhaveon within the halfcycle. Some of the populace must still survive. Meet me there."

"Yes, Commander." Rhan saluted her with a fist against his chest.

"Take care of Amethea," she said, "with everything you have. Bring her back."

"Yes, Commander."

She took a breath, then, "Ecko…"

He thrummed at the sound of his name. He teetered, waiting for her to say the last words that he could carry with him, some final touch that he would never lose – yeah, an' now who's bein' hackneyed? – and then he cursed himself for being sixteen years old.

But she said only, "When all this is over, is it you who fades out of existence?" Her final smile was oddly sad. "Or is it us?"

Or is it us?

It was the only goodbye he was going to get. And as the four of them turned and rode out across the cobbles, hoofbeats muffled by the seething fog, he found himself thinking far too many layers into what she'd said.

They rode though the winter morning, the pale sun thinning the fog to wisps and ribbons. The air grew colder and sharper, biting to the bone.

Before long, Ecko was absolutely bastard freezing. His ass ached and his fingers were stiffened into numb, curled claws.

Beside him, Amethea sat in her saddle like a sack – she made no move to communicate, or to look to either side. When her cloak fell open, she didn't bother to close it. Memories of what had happened to Ghar flickered at the corners of Ecko's thoughts, and he wondered how the hell she was managing to hold on.

Ahead of them, Rhan and the Bard rode knee to knee, talking in low voices. He wondered what they were saying. The Bard's sense of massive expectation came off him in waves, like some vast and jagged percussion. When he looked back, he had a Cheshire Cat grin that was as wide as his ears.

Hell, yeah. We're all mad here.

Rhan was thoughtful, more serious. He rode with his blade in his hand and his gaze half-outward, watching the dead horizons as the fog slunk away.

But there was nothing out there. No frozen bandit or lingering monster. Even the bweao-whatever-the-hell-it-was had given the fuck up and gone home for cocoa with marshmallows.

Muttering, Ecko shut out the cold and lost himself in the previous night – the opal stones in her collarbones, the necessary savagery of her release – but her last words flicked at him, insistent and annoying.

Or is it us?

If he won this – beat the final bad guy, yadda yadda – what would happen to these people? Fucksake, his *friends*?

What would happen to them when Eliza turned them off?

He tangled himself round the question, muddled with memories of breathlessness and body heat. He lost himself so far into it that the thud beside him took him completely by surprise.

"Ecko!" Rhan's bark brought him to his senses.

"*Shit!*"

Amethea had fallen from her horse. She was choking, her body striving for air. As his oculars flashed, he could see that her fight was almost over: she looked like Ghar had done. The moss had closed her mouth, her eyes, her ears – she looked almost half-rotted. He had no idea what to do, but hey, he was off his horse and down on his knees beside her.

The other two had ridden too far ahead. They were turning fast, but they wouldn't get to her in time. What the fuck was he supposed to do?

Rhan's bass bellow: "She needs to breathe!"

Thinking *shit, shit, shit,* Ecko put one hand on the back of the doc's neck, tilted her head, and, grimacing, began to pull green shit out of her mouth. It trailed back into her like some invading jellyfish, tendrils of gunk that stretched down her throat and into her lungs and chest and heart and veins. Pulling at it, fucking strings of it, he shuddered. She was retching as he pulled it free, her face unresponsive, but her body reacting, craving the air.

Fuck fuck fuck fuckety fuck!

The ground was icy cold. Ecko had green shit all tangled round his fingers, slimy and stringy. He shook his hand, trying to get it off. There was more of it in her nose, her ears. He peeled it from her eyes like scabs. He could almost hear her muttering, *Help me, help me,* but the voice was somehow not hers – it was fuller and older.

It sounded like Ghar.

It sounded like Mom.

And *that* shit, he must be imagining.

Not nearly enough sleep.

"Breathe into her mouth." The legs of Rhan's heavy, hairy-hoofed horse, then Rhan himself, boots hitting hard on the dead ground.

"CPR?" It was almost a squawk. "Are you shittin' me?"

But he knew this, fuck knows how – he tilted her head back further, held her nose and breathed into her mouth.

As he exhaled, he remembered Pareus, burning to death, the woman on the bed in Grey's base, the flames he'd had for so long and then lost. His breath was something that took life, not gave it. The images were overlaid by Triqueta, the insistent heat of her mouth on his—

Chrissakes. He shoved all of it aside.

Amethea tasted of frog. He turned, spat, swore, wondered which one of them was the fucking prince. Then he inhaled, gave her another breath.

He got a mouthful of green shit and sat back on his heels, spitting, wiping his lips – but she was breathing, her eyes were open.

He'd just – well hot shit on a chrome shovel – had he seriously just saved her life?

"Well done." The Bard's voice sounded from behind him. A gloved hand passed him down a waterskin and he took a swig, washed out his mouth.

Yeah. Stick that in your fuckin' pipe, Eliza!

But Amethea wasn't coughing, or sitting up. She was breathing, but she lay motionless, her eyes staring empty. Her pale hair was spread about her like a nebula, and her palms were oddly flat against the soil – what was left of it. The lichens in her flesh were still there. And something about the way she lay—

"Ecko," Rhan said, "stand up." His voice was tight as wire.

Ecko's nerves skittered, like bird claws on a roof. He lurched to his feet, soil caking his trews.

"What?"

Rhan's blade was bared in his hand. He pointed the tip at the only thing that broke the flat horizon.

"What's that?"

Cold wind scuttled the debris in tiny tornadoes. A hoof thumped restless.

For a moment, Ecko didn't register – Rhan was pointing at a wagon – two – laying a distance away and on their sides. One of the wheels had fallen from an axle. As his telos focused, though, seeking the skulking nasty, he realised he could see something else. Between the traces, there were the hummocks of fallen beasties, half-slumped, their outlines blurred. Just as if they'd...

...as if they'd melted into the ground.

His skin went absolutely cold.

What the fuck?

He scanned further, found more shapes, smaller and widely strewn. One had a fallen pack beside it, its contents scattered and crumbling.

"What is it?" Rhan asked, again.

He didn't reply, barely heard the question. The closest shape, the smallest, had stains of dead lichen. Like the moss that grew on Amethea. Moss that had struggled for life, and then died.

Help me.

He stood stock-still, rigid with shock. Then he blinked back into focus and stared at the green stuff he'd pulled from Amethea's body. Some of it was still on his fingers. He resisted the urge to shudder, and brush it off him like a spider.

Help me.

A thought caught him, like a hook in the edge of his mind – something she'd said, as they'd sat on the wall at Tusien...

Like I'm nothing.

And the word was there, again, echoing massive as all of the lifeless grey plain.

Nothing.

Nothing, like the dead ground. Nothing, like the emptiness in Amethea's eyes. Nothing, like the creatures that had lain down in their traces and just... given up. Nothing, like—

Boom.

Holy motherfucking shit.

And he wanted to fucking kick himself. He wanted to rage at Eliza, at Lugan, at the Bard.

I don't believe this!

"Like you're nothing." The words were a whisper, like a

question. He knelt down beside her, stroked her hair from her face. He felt her skin with his fingertips. He was making a huge effort to hold himself back, to not bury his face in his hands or turn round and scream at the others, *Don't you see?!*

"Ecko..." Rhan said, again. His voice was dangerous. "What—?"

"It was a travellin' family, maybe two," Ecko said. His tone was flat, blunt, holding the roar in check. "They lay down, and they quit."

Rhan and the Bard exchanged a glance.

"They *quit*," Ecko said, again. He rounded on them, coming back to his feet in a rush. "Amethea – in the hospice – she *quit*. She'd fought so hard and she fucking *quit*." He spat the word at Rhan, remembered seeing him stood in the doorway. "*That*'s how you catch the blight – and *that*'s why you can't cure it. It's not a disease, it's a... a parasite. It invades you when you give up."

"Foriath," Rhan said. His tone was deep and soft, thunderous. "The woman Mael saw in the market. And Ghar— "

"An' it's in the terhnwood, like the blade in the tavern in Amos." Ecko rubbed the green shit between thumb and forefinger, trying to order his scrambling thoughts. "It's been everywhere. Sneakin' in at the edges."

Help me.

Older and deeper, not Mom's voice, but...

"Look, Maugrim made a kablooey, right?" he said, spelling it out as much to himself as to the others. "A great big fuckin' sinkhole that's suckin' the life outta the grass. Two elements, Higgs boson, we got ourselves a mini singularity." He gave a brief grin. "Well, okay, maybe not quite. But *that*'s why the grass died from the edges – it's like a... an event horizon, like water goin' down a plug."

The other two were staring at him. Rhan had sheathed his blade and picked up Amethea. He held her in his arms, tight against his chest like a father holds a sleeping child. His face was etched in horror, in disbelief.

Or was it denial?

"So," Ecko said, "our sink isn't jus' drainin' the grass. It's drainin' people, critters. Terhnwood. *Every*-fuckin'-thing."

Roderick said, "But the moss grows. It grows through people, as it has through Amethea. You said yourself: it's a parasite. It isn't a nothing, it wants to live."

It wants to live.

Help me.

Well fuck him for a brain-dead sonofabitch.

He remembered standing looking down at the fallen woodland, the double vision – the life and the death. In one place, every last breath of life sucked from the soil; in the other, the man dying on the ground, killed by something trying to cling to its existence.

Help me.

Grass trying to grow on the slumped body of a dead child.

A child that had melted into the soil.

"An' that's it," he said, like the light finally coming on. "That's the final step, the last piece of the puzzle." He wanted to shout at the winter clouds. He wanted to rage at Eliza, *Oh, you bitch, you motherfucking bitch!* He wanted to laugh, cry, scream. "You fucking smartass bastard," this at the Bard, "this is it. *This* is what you've been looking for." He was grinning, now, black as an assassin's blade.

The Bard said softly, "The world's fear, the thing she had forgotten..."

"Jeez, this is all like some fuckin' huge jigsaw, some goddamn fuckin'... I dunno... fractal realisation. Like – *kapow!* – an' everything feeds into everything else. If that kid hadn't've died, right at the beginning, Triq would never've gone to Roviarath, they wouldn't've been here to fight – an' we would've lost. If I hadn't've run from the tavern, I wouldn't've met her, we'd never've gone after Maugrim, stopped his forces, found Amethea. Soul of Stone, rise of the blight, you know the rest. It's all some huge fucking pattern. It all *fits*."

His fingers were at his temples as if he was reeling with the onslaught of information, of comprehension.

"An' if we hadn't gone after Amal, Vahl wouldn't be free, not here, not now. Christ on a *bike*, it's like everything, every little fuckin' thing, slots into everything else. Every choice we've made, every place we've been, has brought us *here*. The whole fuckin' pattern has just made *sense*." He was laughing, a sound completely unlike his usual sarcastic cackle. "Like I can *see* Eliza's program – all of it, nodes and synapses, the lot. Fucking *Matrix* shit! Chris*sakes*! If I'd missed one connection, one decision, one *moment*..." his voice faded to awed, "...we'd not be here, like this, like now. Jesus. Like *everything* had to fit...!"

Roderick had lowered his scarf, and his face was like his old self, overwhelmed with feeling.

With more of his vision coming back to him, the thing the Ryll had shown him so long ago.

With the knowledge that he had, indeed, been right all along.

"By the Gods, Ecko..." He sounded like he was nearly in tears.

Ecko spoke straight to him, "Because the hole Maugrim made is a nothing, an absence, a giving up. It sucks all the life away. And the moss is the world trying to live, to grow." *Help me.* "And *that's* what you've been – we've been – lookin' for, all this time. It's what you saw; it's what now lives where the Monument used to be. And it's what we gotta face."

He and the Bard spoke the word together as if they'd been brothers all along...

"Kazyen."

* * *

There was a fissure at the heart of the Grasslands.

The ground was no longer even soil; there was no touch of life to show that anything had ever been here, not an insect, not a blade of grass. It was bare rock and ash, barren and broken. In places fused fragments of crystal caught the light like a cry.

Cracks spread outwards from the central fracture, jagged and widening. From them, unhealthy bands of light bled into the burning sunset sky. They reached almost to the edge of the river – only a precarious grey dam now kept the water flowing to Amos and to the sea. They reached out towards Roviarath, threatening her wharves and walls. They stretched as if they would shatter the world, and send the pieces spiralling into Kazyen.

Once, there had been centaurs here. Bweao. Esphen. Here, Feren had fallen. Here, Maugrim had awoken the Monument, and Amethea had found the Soul of Stone. Here, The Wanderer had crashed. Here, the Flux had been overloaded, and the world riven to her core.

Now, upon the edge of the fissure, there stood a richly dressed young woman. With her, an old man in a plain overshirt. They were alone, incongruous amidst the bleakness and the drifting grey smoke, two tiny figures at the heart of destruction.

Ink writhed about their flesh.

Selana Valiembor, last child of Fhaveon, brightness and colour and beauty.

Brother Mael.

Both stood lost in wonder, as though the wasteland that surrounded them was the finest discovery of their long existence.

And Kas Vahl Zaxaar laughed.

He laughed with Selana's mouth, loud and long. He laughed to fill the emptiness, laughed as if he could bring the dying sun itself to worship at his feet. It had taken him returns beyond number to reach this moment, and its realisation was glorious.

He could be *free*!

Stood upon the edge of nothing, Vahl had little interest in the darkening grey below him or in the rising, bleeding light. He didn't care for the spreading damage, for the world's pain or how she suffered. The Gods' toy could shatter into a thousand pieces, be lost to the Count of Time and never even remembered...

It was the *power* he wanted.

Whatever lay at the bottom of the crevasse, whatever was sucking the life from the grass, Vahl wanted it, wanted to touch and claim and use it. The battle behind him was irrelevant – had been effective enough in keeping Rhan occupied – *this* was his real victory.

Show me, he told the smoke, the drifting ash. *Show me what you hold.*

And his brother Tamh echoed him, *Show me!*

All through his long exile, living behind the eyes of Amal, Vahl had dreamed helpless, raged and longed and lusted and schemed. At the beginning, he'd dreamed of war – of flame and death, of razing Fhaveon to the ground, and Rhan with her. Amal had been a scholar, but their goals had been aligned and their symbiosis strong; Phylos, when he'd come from the Archipelago, had shared Vahl's superiority, his hate, and his dreams of devastation.

Phylos had waited long for Vahl to come to him.

Yet the awakening of the Monument had altered Vahl's dream – made it more urgent, made him hunger for its realisation. Afterwards, he'd no longer dreamed of lengthy and tiresome wars, he'd dreamed bigger – of shattering Fhaveon, of breaking Aeona and Rammouthe, of smashing the Gods' toy and returning to Samiel with pieces of it in his hands, *laughing* at its annihilation...

Damn me, would you?

Ecko would have given Vahl strength beyond measure – but Ecko had no time he could take. Amal had tricked him – and had paid for it. Vahl had turned to Phylos after all, and they'd raged their hate together...

And they'd failed.

But there was another solution.

Selana Valiembor, last of the family his brother had sworn to protect – the irony was glorious. Rhan's victory had been short-lived. The Grasslands were in ruins, Fhaveon had fallen, Saluvarith's legacy was ended.

Vahl's brothers were free – and their release would fill the sky with fire.

Elation rising in him like the hunger of the Sical, Vahl turned to his brother. He raised Selana's arms to the last of the light, raised her chin to look up, to cry aloud at the burning sky. The sun was lingering at the peaks of the Kartiah, almost as if it refused to set on this, the Varchinde's final day...

Standing there beside him, Brother Mael had moss growing in his human skin, in his eyes and ears. And the Kas, for all their might and rage and scheming, could do nothing to stop it.

They, too, had caught the blight.

28: VAHL THE SOUL OF STONE

Half a day after they crossed the rank remnant of the Scar Lake, they finally came to the wasteland's edge.

And there, they stopped.

They shouldered their packs and they let the horses go. Rhan carried Amethea, holding her to him like a wounded child. A complex guilt rose from his shoulders, but he spoke not a word.

The Monument – or the wound where it had been – lay somewhere ahead of them. To their right, the tiny flicker of rocklight was Roviarath's Lighthouse Tower, a lone mote that glittered like a last hope. Everything else was ash, silent and cold.

It tasted like nothing.

If they sheltered their faces and peered through the grey, they could see ahead of them the last approaches, the heart of the Varchinde. But now, that heart was bare of all grass and growth and life – it was rock, scoured and empty. It was a sunset-red sky that glowed sullen on jagged mountaintops.

The Rhamiriae, the western forest, had gone.

Ecko remembered this place. He'd first met Triqueta here, and Redlock. He'd come this way with Tarvi, when there'd been sun, and green grass, and blue sky...

Chrissakes.

He fidgeted, oculars flicking modes. He wondered if he'd changed as much as the others – if his journey of self-discovery now neared fruition, or whatever the hell it was supposed to do.

Did I get it right, Eliza? Didja tick all your li'l boxes now?

Collator: *Chances of success…*

But the voices were in his head; hell, they'd always *been* in his head. There was no scorecard, no trophy, no marks outta ten; there was no flicking forward to read the final paragraph. There was only *ash*, for fucksake. There was only the four of them, damaged and struggling. There was only Kazyen.

He told Eliza, told himself: *You jus' bring it on – it can kiss my chameleon ass. Let's do this thing.*

Tempting her – *daring* her – he was the first to set foot on the cracked, bared stone.

And the ash fluttered upwards from under his boot.

The others followed him, and they moved onwards.

The going was treacherous; the ground was uneven, holed and harsh. It seemed to shift, shuddering like an earthquake. The drifting ash got in faces and mouths, making it hard to see, to breathe. As they moved, they stirred it into tiny whirls that made them cough and had their eyes streaming.

So here we are at last: Pits of Fire an' Mountains of Ash. Well, kinda.

The ground shuddered again, and Ecko stumbled, his adrenaline lurching, erratic. The sky had lowered over them, gathering into a heavy darkness that blotted out the mountains and the bloody sunset, yet there was still light enough to see.

A pale light, sourceless, and bereft of all warmth.

Jesus. Ecko's uneasy adrenaline faltered. He reached for a smart one-liner, came back with nothing…

Nothing.

Shit, I'm funny.

They continued, careful now, watching in every direction.

The ash and the light seemed to haunt them, joyless and unchanging – it was almost as if the Count of Time himself had deserted the dying Varchinde.

Yeah, that sucker's gone down the pub...

They slowed down even more. As they moved, their path grew more treacherous, and the shudders came more frequently, harder. Deep, pained rumbles accompanied them – ground or sky, it was impossible to tell.

Ecko began to feel peculiar.

Skin-crawlingly-belly-emptily peculiar, like he wanted to lay down and rest, and never get up again...

He realised he'd stopped.

Fallen to his knees.

Rhan's bass rumble sounded softly. "Get up. You know what will happen if you don't."

"Tell me about it." This was Kazyen, the world's fear and foe. This inertia, this lassitude, this loss of energy and motivation and passion and *life...*

He had a flash – again, a memory of the woman on the bed, the one he'd burned. The one who hadn't even tried to stop him.

Fight me, you fucking...!

"Can't you sing, or something?" Ecko shot that one at the Bard. "All that power, an' you dunno anything from Queen's Greatest Hits?"

"Keep moving," Roderick told him, flatly. "We approach the place of the Monument, the Soul of Stone." His voice still carried a huge sense of suppressed eagerness. "We must understand this, or everything dies."

"No shit, Sherlock." Ecko turned back to the lifelessness that stretched away from them in every direction and as far as they could see...

Lay down, it said softly, *lay down and rest. There's no need to fight. Trust me, and I will look after you. You will be content...*

Pulling closer together, they walked on.

The Count of Time had left them. After a while, they began to see cracks splitting the rock, the sources of the empty grey light. As the ground shook, so the cracks were spreading, their movement swift enough to be noticeable.

Roderick murmured, "'Time the Flux begins to crack'."

They were fracturing the Powerflux, the Varchinde entire, taking the last of the life of the plains.

The rock beneath them shook. Ecko stumbled and the Bard caught his elbow.

And so they came to the edge of the great fissure itself.

To the rise, the place where the Monument had been.

And Ecko had no words, no sarcasm, no dare...

Nothing.

The Monument had gone, the ditch, the bank. The centaurs, The Wanderer. There was only that final grassless slope, and then the great rocky gape like a mouth, open and hungry, sucking at the Grasslands' life. Its cracks spread further with every shake of the ground.

"Careful." Rhan's warning was reflex, unnecessary.

Jesus Harry Christ in a bloody fucking bucket.

Here, at the very heart of his personal darkness, Ecko stopped. He struggled to find his breath, struggled to find his *balls*, for chrissakes – to man the fuck up and take that final step. To look over the edge and confront Kazyen, to see that final boss staring back at him.

Why bother? the voice said. *You've come this far, only to fail. How can you face me when you don't even know what I am? How can you wield the Powerflux entire, with only four of you? Rest now, and leave everything to me...*

Ecko was a knot of fear and confusion, he couldn't make himself move. As he hesitated, the Bard stepped past him, fell to his knees at the edge of the crevasse. He buried his hands in the ash, stretched his face to the sky. He'd sought his whole life for this, and Ecko could feel the shout building in him.

But beneath him, almost in defiance, the ground shook again, and he put out a hand to stop himself falling. The cracks groaned wider still, spreading the nothing further and further, out across the Varchinde.

It would shatter the world entire, send its pieces spiralling out into the void.

"Samiel." From behind them, Rhan's voice in plea or prayer. "Godsfather. How can you—?"

"The world was in your care, my estavah." A new voice, precise as a fine blade. "I might even say this is your fault."

Rhan swore, vicious and bitter.

Manifesting from devastation, two figures came into view on the far side of the fissure, each lit from below to grotesque parody. One was a young woman, pretty, and exquisitely dressed beneath her covering of ash. She stood slender, absurdly out of place, but her chin was proud, and her stance scornful.

Beside her was an old man, plainly dressed. His arms were folded and his face clouded with moss and shadow.

Serpents of ink curled though their skin.

"My Lord Selana," Rhan said, his words laden with pain and anger. He still held Amethea. "Brother Mael."

Ecko stared at the newcomers, oculars scanning.

This was the Lord of Fhaveon herself, Selana Valiembor, but she was no more a girl than Ecko was a winner of the Nobel fucking Peace Prize. *Yeah, you don't fool me.* He'd been right up close to Kas Vahl Whosit, had a scar in his chest to prove it, and he knew the daemon all right, no matter who he was *wearing.*

Fucksake, he knew the daemon even without the manifest beastie that he now saw, fading hazy through the ash and darker than shadow. A mantled creature of twisted smoke, a figment that somehow withstood the breeze.

The Kas itself.

His oculars scanned, fascinated.

"Ah, my faithful Seneschal." Selana's voice was like Amal's had been – layered with the tones and tensions of that other presence, that rising, oddly solid haze. "Your determination is impressive – though calling on Samiel is surely folly. You should be angry with him, brother. He's hurt you as much as any of us, maybe more." She spoke to Rhan, but looked at each of them in turn, face to face. Her smoke-shadow echoed her movements. "Look at you," she said. "The world's last warriors. How touching. You look like you've lost one already."

Ecko grinned, savage. "Look, you fucked this up once before, an' you're gonna do it again. What the hell d'you think is gonna happen here? You're gonna do – what? – tap the power source, an' destroy the world? Burn the sky? Make out like some bad metal stageshow? You gonna sacrifice your evil zombie runegoats and rule the universe?"

He walked up to where the Bard still knelt, faced human and monster across the grey light of the fissure.

"This is big shit – bigger than you, daemon – an' it's gonna spank your smoky ass."

On cue, the ground shook.

The girl didn't move, but the shadow of the Kas leaned down, right over him, its head to one side and its eyes glittering flame-yellow. It studied him, curious.

He thought he saw teeth.

And what are you here to do, little man? Stop me? Just how do you plan to do that?

In spite of himself, Ecko shuddered at its closeness. He wondered if the thing could jump hosts, and his skin crawled. But it withdrew, and he breathed again.

"It's all over," Selana told him, "I no longer need you to gain my freedom." She laughed and the Kas laughed with her, shadow rippling like Ecko's lost stealth-cloak.

The ground shuddered again, cracks in the world.

And then, there in the ashes, Ecko could see more of them.

Not humans, just drifting shades, the Kas without their mortal shells. They had come – all of them – from the war, and from Rammouthe.

Come to witness the end of the world.

Or to cause it.

"You can't stop me." The Lord of Fhaveon smiled at them. "Look at you, three squeaking fools surrounded by powers you neither wield nor understand. It *ends* here, all of it. I *will* be free."

"You're the fool, Vahl," Rhan said. "What's happening here will tear you to screaming pieces. You can't ride this power—"

"I will be *free*!" The shadow flashed with flame and rage. "My name is Dael Vahl Sashar, and I am first made of the Gods' creatures, and oldest of all." Selana's voice was a lash, savage as a whip-strike, stinging. The shadow with her thickened and rose, its eyes glimmering like the Sical's had done, pure fire. "I watched this world's creation, its crafting at Samiel's hands. I watched the twins play with it, laughing as it rolled across their jewelled floor. And I watched it forgotten, abandoned, gathering dust and *ash*." She spat the word. "The world is insignificant, a lost toy, no more. This…" she gestured at the fissure, "…is the only thing that matters now." The shadow shot through with livid sparks, eager. "I am Kas no longer. I can *take* this power. Use it!"

Roderick said, his throat writhing, "Understand, Vahl: what lies here is *hunger*. This is the heart of the blight, the force that pulls the life from the Varchinde. And if you try to *touch* it…" he smiled faintly, "…your life, all you've known and all you remember… will be *nothing*." His tones were woven with layers of strength and appeal; they made the ash stand still in the wind, made the last of the red light glitter scarlet in the ground's crystals.

Mael laid a hand on Selana's shoulder, and spoke through the moss in his mouth. "Roderick. The Gods crafted us –

made us first and favoured. Rhan knows this. We've strengths unrealised and potentials unknown. We've watched our prison walls for returns unnumbered. We've served our time. Should we not return home?" He turned his plea to Rhan. "You, my littlest brother, my estavah, you *understand* what it's like to be trapped, sealed away from everything you love and understand. From your family. Please." His mantled shadow flickered, paled and swelled. "We care not for anything that happens here – we no longer even wish you harm. Do as you please – heal the world if you can! We only want to go home."

The word rippled back through the shadows of the others. *Home.*

Selana raised her chin and her smile was cold as the rock at her feet.

Rhan said bitterly, "I almost believe you."

"Believe us." The girl came forwards, right to the fissure's edge. "This is our final moment, little brother. And you can come *with* us, come home! Rhan, the world is gone, your mandate no longer matters. Unbend, *join* your family! You're my brother, my defender and protector." She smiled. "I'm the last child of House Valiembor and you owe me your loyalty, Seneschal." The smile spread, all teeth, her face unholy with the light from below. She held out a hand to him and, even as she reached, the ash shook from her embroidered garments and the Kas behind her began to swell, untwisting, flashing through with deep blue flame.

E Rhan Khavaghakke.

As it did so, Ecko could see that its wings were broken – long-since torn from its shoulders.

Rhan stood with Amethea still in his arms, her body covered in moss, her eyes open and staring. He clung to her like some kind of talisman, but his brother consumed his gaze.

You owe me your loyalty, Seneschal.

He swayed, took a step forwards towards the fissure. Behind

Selana, the others were moving, shadow upon shadow, each flickering with new strength and rising power. They reached for Rhan like a dark cloud rearing over him.

The sharp retorts of shattering rock filled the air.

But the Kas paid no heed. They were smoke, writhing, exalting, their broken wings reaching as wide as they could, their figment faces and arms outstretched. Ecko almost expected them to chant, but they were silent, only their shadows shifting.

You owe me your loyalty, Seneschal.

The rock cracked again.

E Rhan Khavaghakke. Join us, brother, we go to face Samiel Himself!

Rhan took another step. He was on the very edge of the fissure, a silhouette against the great rise of his brothers' might and challenge.

The sunken sky began to rumble, thick and ominous. And there, at the horizon's edge, the clouds were pulling down into a monster twister.

Like the wound in the world would suck down the sky.

Holy fucking shit.

Ecko was really scared now. They had to stop this – chrissakes, this was his gig, his world-champion shit, and he'd no fucking clue what to do. The Bard's Powerflux bollocks was all very well – hell, he'd understood the theory – but how they were supposed to...

He realised he was snarling, "Chris*sakes*...!" but it was reflex – he didn't even know why.

Roderick put his hood back, pulled free the scarf – if he could wield the very air, summon Vahl, or control him...

The Bard lifted his face to the rising wind, inhaled. His throat hummed.

He said, "We have to stop this. The more power they manifest, the more the hole will drink that power, and the wider the cracks will spread. They're *feeding* it! We *must* stop this!"

Ecko almost screamed at him. "How? How do we—?"

Rhan moved, called out. "Vahl! Wait! I'll come – I'll come with you! Take me home, my brother, take me back to the skies! We'll pull Samiel from his seat, together – we'll cast him *down*!" His voice rose, was livid with light and power, crackling though the storm. "We'll shatter his throne and we'll tear him to *pieces*!"

The great Kas laughed, stretched out his hands. *Come!* Selana mimicked the motion like a puppet. The sky growled, lowering closer, lightning flashed jagged. The wind was clearing the ash and pulling at hair and garments, a taste of what would come. If this shit didn't stop already, they were all gonna go straight the fuck down.

The Kas raised their arms, opened them to the heavens. "Then join me, little brother. We will be *free*!"

"How the hell do we do this?" Ecko's shout went unheard as the ground cracked again, splintering and juddering. The twister was coming closer and the wind was harsh.

"Free!" Rhan cried with him.

"*Stop!*" Roderick's voice was hard as a slap, clear as a scream. If he really was attuned to the air, then his words were loud as the sky and they carried the might of the storm. Their sheer force made Rhan halt at the fissure's very edge, made the swelling Kas flicker and stare. "The power here has caught you, Dael Vahl Sashar. Has caught all of us. Understand it cares not for Kas or Dael, for good or evil, for order or chaos, for any such storybook definitions. What lies below us is an end of all things – a Kazyen, a *nothing*. It will suck your power from you regardless, and will spread its cracks until the very world shatters, spiralling out into nothing, into the void from which it came. And it will take all of us with it." The Bard sank to one knee on the stone, ash drifting from the movement. "Vahl, I beg of you. This is not your way to freedom—"

"Enough!" Selana's voice was a shriek, a final refusal.

Rhan shook, made no move.

The Kas rose again, but as they did so, the ground rocked hard enough to knock Mael from his feet. Ecko felt the shock, but didn't know what it meant until the Bard spoke again.

"The cracks have reached the Great Cemothen River," he said. "The Varchinde's very lifeline drains away. Stop this, Vahl, I beg you. You cannot free yourself or Rhan with this power. This strength is an emptiness, all it will do is pull your existence from you. You dislike your prison – how will it be if you live an eternity in Nothing? In the void? In the grey that has no passion, in an emptiness bereft of all desire? All my life, Vahl, I have sought this world's foe, and you are not it. What lies at your feet is as much your enemy and opposite as it is mine!"

Selana was screaming now, refusing to hear him. Her face was sliding, flesh and expression, down towards her chin as if the hole were literally sucking her skin from her body. The Kas behind her were flickering out, winking and vanishing as if they had been turned off. Mael was struggling to stand, and the edge of the fissure was close, so close.

"Please!" The Bard's cry was pure storm – but the pull was affecting him too. His voice faltered even as he pleaded. "The harder you resist me, the harder I plead. And the more power is pulled from both of us! Vahl – we have to stop this!"

Something in the cry seemed to reach over the fissure.

Selana paused, lowered her arms. For an endless moment, she stared at the Bard with her face lit unholy and desperate as if searching for another answer – any other way out. At her feet, Brother Mael had his hands at his throat. He was gasping to get air into his moss-grown lungs, just as Amethea had done.

Then the ground shook again, and the sky roared, and the rising twister screamed fury.

Ecko watched Mael roll helpless, watched him grapple, cling for a second, and then he heard the cry as the old man fell down and down into whatever was below.

For just a second, everything was quiet.

Selana fell to her knees, her hands reaching – but whether it was the girl reaching for her friend, or the Kas for his brother, Ecko had no idea.

Roderick said, his voice faint now, "Please, Vahl... We can heal this – but you have to help us."

Kneeling on the edge of the end of the world, Selana Valiembor, Kas Vahl Zaxaar, looked up, tears streaking her face.

Roderick said softly, like a chant, "You are the fire to Rhan's light, the two of you more alike than either of you know. We need you. We need you both."

The mantled Kas had faded now, shrunk back to within Selana's skin.

The ground shook, creaking ominous, as though it really would detonate, and the pieces be gone in the void.

And Kas Vahl Zaxaar said, "Then show me. How can we stop this?"

29: NIVROTAR THE SOUL OF STONE

It was a gesture that defied the Count of Time himself, that healed rifts in worlds. Rhan rested Amethea gently on the dead ground and held out a hand to his brother, his protégé, to the last surviving child of the Valiembor line. He helped Selana cross the fissure down which Mael had fallen, his last words lost to nothing.

And she gripped his hand and came to him, her finery billowing, embroidery and ash.

E Vahl...

As if it stood still to witness the brothers' loss and unity, the sky had fallen silent. Now, though, the air rose again, cold and dark and shrieking, gathering itself to howl its final breaths before it, too, vanished down into the emptiness below. The twister was a pillar of grey that stretched from rock to sky, sucking at clouds, tearing the air into spirals. It flashed with suppressed power, and Ecko could feel answering shocks of adrenaline shooting through his skin. He could almost feel its mottle rippling with storm-colour.

He was fucking terrified, and he was okay admitting it, and he didn't fucking *care*. Maybe he was even more scared than the first time Thera had taken him down to see Mom...

The sky circled and screamed down at him, tiny as he was.

Under him, the ground shook.

"Okay!" Pushed beyond his limits, he shouted back at the shrieking air. "Shazam! Abracadabra! Magius fucking Stryke! Let's break out the plus-ten magickal-whosit-of-doom an' *do* this shit!"

An' start the countdown sequence already, 'cause I reckon we got air for about sixty more seconds...

Despite the howling storm, though, the thought of Thera and Mom stayed in his head, spreading like enfolding arms and filling him with its darkness. It was rich and familiar, wrapping and secure. As it grew in his thoughts, it seemed to have a life of its own, seething in and out of itself, turning over and over. As clear as if she were there beside him, he could hear Mom's soft tones, feel that towering, more-than-human presence. Her darkness was a part of him, had long ago sunk itself into his soul. It made him feel safe. If he opened his mouth, he could breathe it in, and out.

And in. And...

Her darkness. *His* darkness. Something he hadn't damned-well *lost*.

Oh, yeah...

And there, in the midst of the madness, Ecko started to grin – his wide black grin that he hadn't worn in days without number. Hell, he was a lotta things – but he wasn't fucking dumb. And he *understood* it now, how the pieces fit, and the neatness of them. Rhan really *was* the light and Vahl the fire – and he, Ecko, he *knew* the dark, knew how it moved, and knew the things that lived in it...

Adrenaline thrilled, warm this time, a rush.

We can so do this...

They were here, all of them, exactly where they should be – they were on the biggest fucking ride of all, the last one, and it felt like they were hanging, suspended over the fucking great *whooooosh!* below...

Waiting, breathless, for shit to go down.

His adrenaline rose higher, pounding, choking, elating.

He was gonna do this. Sir fuckin' Boss, he was gonna *do* this! Save the world, already, defeat the blight, be the champion.

D'you see me, Eliza? Is this where I was always meant to be?

Chrissakes, now his oculars were on the fritz – he could see *lines* there in the darkness. Maybe he was looking down the rift already, he didn't know, but they were there below him, ahead of him, around him, flickering like laughter, like writing with sparklers in the dark. They were crackling through the rock under his feet, surging up into the twisting sky.

He turned, flicking his oculars, mode to mode, but the lines were unchanged, heatless and colourless, glimmering with energy unknown.

Holy shit. Then what he could see...

Those lines, they were the Powerflux itself.

He tried to open his mouth, ask the others, *Do you... do you guys...?*

But it took a moment for him to realise he couldn't speak, had no words, no way to form the question. Hell, first overwhelming fear, now a sense of wonder like a fucking kid, awe that nearly made his knees fold – it'd been a long time since his emotions'd been this free...

Well, these ones, anyhow.

That thought made him grin wider, the black one, the one like the edge of the blade. Made him grin like he could *feel* that odd electricity in his skin, in his reflexes and adrenaline and blood. By every God, he *knew* this darkness, knew it like his own breath – he'd lived in it, fucking almost died in it, returned to himself in it, been recreated as Ecko. The dark was his cloak and his weapon, his home and his safety. And if he could *use* this crackle of power because of his own attunement to that darkness, then he was gonna fry the ass of this Kazyen Void Thingamajig and serve it up with a mug of tea.

Yeah, you jus' bring it the fuck on, dude!

The flicker of the Powerflux was joyous, exhilarating. It flowed before him as reality juddered, teasing, at the edge of the drop. His belly did flip-flops, but they didn't fall – not yet. The lines were still spreading outwards, ever outwards, and rising to a rage of surging power. Yet something about that surge felt wrong, as though—

His jubilant adrenaline flashed to sudden fear.

He turned to see them – needed to understand how they ran, element to element across the world, up into the clouded sky and deep into the ground. He could see how everything Eliza had created came from this network – sunrise, daylight, weather and season – hell, it even explained why the damned moons could be in opposition. It was like he was seeing the actual core code of the program itself, the very life of the world.

Hadn't Amal said something about Eliza and the World Goddess being the same thing?

Ecko shivered, premonition and energy. Maybe Eliza really *had* made a world – a world that believed utterly in its own existence. Maybe that was the only way it could be complete enough for real interaction.

But then: what would happen to it when he'd gone?

He shivered again.

But as he looked further, searching for more power, more answers, more insights, he began to realise that the electricity was flawed – it was moving wrong. The lines weren't straight, they shifted and eddied, and the power was increasingly uneven. It was being pulled one way, as if by some vast magnet – it was flowing in towards the fissure.

Sucked down by the Kazyen.

An' that's what we gotta fix. We gotta make the power run right. That's why it needs all of us.

It made sense, all right. But hell, he didn't have the faintest *inkling* of a shred of a motherfucking clue…

Like, who had the instruction book?

As his understanding had spread, though, he'd become aware of the others, there in the darkness with him, anchors and foci, part of the flow of the power. He could hear the Bard, his voice the sky, the storm, the rage of the thunder and the touch of the wind. He could feel the moss in Amethea's flesh, the stone strength in her soul, the pleading life of the world. Rhan's light and Vahl's fire, merging at their edges. And—

You're close now, aren't you?

The voice was too gentle to be unexpected; it was cold and soft, there in his ear, in his heart.

Mom…?

But he wasn't sure.

We come almost to the final hand. Be strong, my Tam, my Ecko, my little champion.

The words made his skin crawl. It was Mom, and it wasn't. It was closer than that, insidious and rich with potency. There were layers in its tone like there'd been layers in Amal's, and Selana's…

Like she was *Kas*?

But no, her voice was too cold.

Ice cold.

And then there it fucking was – the snap of the very last tumbler, the click as the box opened and the light bathed his face, that glorious moment when the last piece snicked into place.

The voice was Nivrotar.

When you come to the end, I will be there with you. Remember who crafted The Wanderer, who defended the Great Library…

It was the final corner of the Powerflux, its northern anchor, the Soul of Ice.

And it was Mom. It was Eliza. It was the fucking World Goddess herself, whatever the hell her name was…

It was the completed concert – all six elements fused at last, and melding together.

It was the brake coming off the roller coaster.

And...

Ohhhh shi-it...!

The front went up and over the lip and they followed it, all of them, their hands in the air and screaming as their bellies dropped and their teeth bared and their adrenaline surged. The lines were there, under them and round them and through them and they were a part of the Flux itself, sweeping round the routes of those lines, and utterly at the mercy of the Kazyen below.

It was pulling at them, pulling them down.

Around them was noise and juddering and the howling storm. The air with them twisted and screamed.

Through the pounding of his heart and ears, Ecko yowled, "You fucking *bitch*. You got us all here – now how do we finish this?"

That's "You fucking bitch", my Lord. Nivrotar's voice was cold and amused, and right in his ears. It was a core of unbroken strength, a pure steadiness that underlay the screaming, the raging wind. *Call me Cedetine, oldest mother. I came into the void and so began the Count of Time.* The coaster jammed round a corner, throwing them all sideways. *I bore three sons and I gave my flesh for the crafting of the world.* The coaster fell again, throwing Ecko's belly into his mouth. *Call me Calarinde, manifest love. They gave me the yellow moon as my prison and my chariot.* The coaster paused at the bottom of a drop, was carefully cranked to the top of a second, smaller peak. *Call me Nivrotar, Lord of Amos. You, Ecko, you have your own name for me.*

And over the edge it went again. A second, shorter scream, a second flash of terror and exhilaration. A rush round a bend, a rattle and a clatter.

Still, the Kazyen pulled.

But the others were there with him, blazing. He was closer to them than he'd ever been to anything in his life, to family, his half sisters, Mom's other creations. The lines of the Flux were there, tying them together, blood and fire and sparks and light.

Ah, she said. *We come almost to the final hand. I'm so proud of you. All of you.*

The roller coaster screamed again. It cornered, sharp and swift, voices cried in layered concert. And then Ecko felt something snap, something give and break – something in the soil, in the Flux, something in the world herself...

They clattered into the station, and they stopped.

What the hell...?

He found himself on the ground, shaking, his arms and legs as weak as water. He was coughing, laughing, covered in ash. Fucksake, he wanted to puke.

Roderick and Rhan were leaning on each other in an embrace like years of friendship. Selana stood close, her face pale and her expression oddly, almost childishly, bemused. The great shadow of the Kas was still with her.

Then Ecko saw Amethea lying on the dead ground, the moss still in her skin.

Around all of them, the Flux was steadying, the huge drain slackening. The pull of the fissure was less. As his darkness thinned into normal night, Ecko couldn't see the lines of power as clearly, but he could feel them – faint flashes in his skin, like sparks that tickled on his nerve endings.

"So – what the fuck was that?" His voice was harsh, a serrated cut of reality through wonder. "Did we *fix* it?" He called the question at the Lord of Amos, his tone bitter, edged with savagery. "Did we slay the dragon? Is spring gonna spring out the ground, now?"

The energy in him was fading, thinning out into the air. Its loss was impossible, more than he could bear. To have gone that high, just to come down…!

"Do we get a party?" His voice faltered. His face was sore from its rictus black grin. Somehow, he'd chewed the insides of his mouth to bloody ribbons. "Do we visit the Guild and level up? *What the hell did we just do?*"

About him, the air was settling, clearing.

"To face Kazyen," Roderick said, his voice deep as night, "we had to have the full Powerflux. That's what the Ryll told me, every soul, united and together. It was so gloriously simple – but we'd been made to forget."

Forget.

Ecko could feel the last of the flickerings in his skin, in his wiring and cybernetics. He repeated, almost numbly, "Been made to forget."

Across the broken grey stone, the Bard had removed his scarf. His expression was younger, had lost the weight of its years of lone belief. As he raised his face to the sky, his steel throat glittering, Ecko could see that his face was damp with tears.

Then he met Ecko's eyes and smiled.

The look was warm, genuine; a look of humour and grief and success and loss and wonder, of achievement beyond impossible odds. It made Ecko bite his lip and turn away, refusing to let his own emotion show. Roderick had fought so long, struggled so long…

You've done it, the Bard said, the words in Ecko's ears alone. *The blight falters, and the Flux begins to flow as it should. Truly, Ecko, you're our augured champion, the saviour of our world.*

Ecko's eyes prickled and he bit down harder, hurting his sore mouth. The storm was almost over. Ecko could feel the others drifting backwards, their closeness fading…

You've done it.

Had he?

Truly, Ecko, you're our augured champion.

But then…

Why the hell am I still here?

Nervousness began to crawl down his back, trailing like cold sweat. The others withdrew further, and he shivered at their absence, suddenly alone and feeling his mortality return. Nivrotar had said, *We come almost to the final hand,* not, *Congratulations, dude, you've won, here's a vacation for two in Hawaii.*

But the Bard was speaking, his voice clear as morning. "Memory returns – the words the Ryll showed me, the words long buried in the Great Library at Amos. The words she showed Ress and Jayr." His voice deepened, now almost like intonation, "'Time when Substance of the Gods, has lost its heart of fire. Time when Promised is released, to promise yet more dire. Time shall mastery of light, give up, and lose the will to fight. Time the Flux begins to crack, to rage becomes a crime. Time Nothing is more powerful, at last, than Count of Time. Then Time you bid your world farewell, your Gods, tonight, they sleep in Hell.'" He was coming closer to Ecko as he spoke, his voice getting ever deeper. "'Time when Final Guardian, defeated at the last, time when passion cannot sing, and everything held fast. Time your world farewell be kissed, unless you find the—'"

"Catalyst." Ecko spat the word, hearing Ress's voice saying it, even as he did so. "Catamite, catatonic, catalytic fucking converter. Chris*sakes*." Still off-centre with hollow loss and unease, with his strange and nebulous fear, he couldn't quite believe what he was hearing. "*Now* you remember the ubiquitous prophecy?" It was a piss-take, Eliza having a laugh; he couldn't wrap his head round it. "Oh, this takes the motherfucking cookies. What kind of fantasy gives you the prophecy at the *end*?" He didn't know whether to laugh or punch things. "Oh, you *bitch*!"

Roderick laughed, rich and free, a laugh that cleared the grey of the sky and warmed the air around him. He was sharing

Ecko's disbelief, his humour at the irony – shared the fucking great joke the world had apparently played on all of them.

Rhan knelt over Amethea, his growl like gravel, "All right, it's not that funny."

"It really is." The Bard's laugh faded to a chuckle. "All that searching and seeking and hand-wringing, all that hope and work and struggle, everything I fought for and preached about. For so many returns…" The colour was fading from his voice as he spoke, replaced by perplexity. "The tavern, they used to say it travelled through every point at once, which was how it knew all people, all places. I remember the day Nivrotar gave it to me, and I remember losing it. Karine. My friends. Our long travels. The *cat*…" The sentence tailed into silence, and the air above him thickened. The wind was cold. "All that… all that was pointless. For nothing."

Nothing.

The word hung like ash in the air.

The wind breathed soft, like a threat. Under its touch, the ground rumbled, ever so slightly, like some stirring, sleeping creature.

He could hear Rhan, his voice distant and soft as a smothering cushion. "Wake up. Amethea, little sister, it's over. You can wake up now…"

Whatever it was, Ecko could feel it too. Flickers of disquiet, flashes of unrest in the Flux. Spasms. The pull was returning, subtler now, deep and cold. Mocking. The recovering Flux faltered, sucking back towards the centre, towards the fissure and the pull of Kazyen.

Shit.

Whatever it was down there, it wasn't fucking dead. Hell, like all bad guys, the damn thing had to come back at least once.

Roderick said, "No…" but the word was barely a breath. A wisp of horror that was gone as the wind began to pick up. "No…"

Ecko stared at the hole.

We come almost to the final hand.

Almost.

But it wasn't cigar time yet.

Around him, the others were fading, weakened by comedown. Angel and daemon, mortal and immortal – their elation and energy were spent. Perhaps the Kazyen had lured it out of them, Ecko didn't know, but they had nothing left, and now it was returning, soft and grey and insidious. Ecko watched as Roderick slumped, staring at his hands as if he'd trashed the damn Wanderer himself, watched as Rhan tumbled down beside Amethea, Vahl with him as vast hatred and equally vast love both faded to nothing. The Kas were gone, smoke on the wind.

Comedown.

No, you're not doin' it to me, you fucker, you're so not doin' it to me...

But he could feel it, like the effects of Grey's drugs in Amal's vision.

Give up, it said, *just let it go. You'll be so much happier. There's no need to worry about anything now, no need for passion. Love and hate, elation and despair, they're all spent, all gone. Just let go...*

No I will not!

Swearing, fighting, refusing to be fucking damned, he came to his feet and walked to the edge of the hole.

It yawned for him, a mouth wide and grinning.

It beckoned.

The Monument had fallen here, The Wanderer. This was the place where all this had fucking started.

And hell, if that wasn't a goddamned message, then he didn't know what was.

Turn to 500.

Remembering how he'd once fallen from the roof of a

South Bank tower, an age and a world before, Ecko turned and took a last look at his friends. He had no words for them, no soggy goodbyes, but he wanted to hold them in his oculars like a photograph, wanted to remember this moment, all of them, always.

Rhan, Amethea, the Bard...

Triqueta.

He swallowed, blinked.

But he couldn't manage the goodbye, it was too much.

As he'd once done on London's South Bank, a world and an eternity away, he stepped over the edge.

30: CATALYST THE WANDERER

Ecko drifted through layers of consciousness.

"...a fascinating journey." The speaker was male, familiar, though Ecko couldn't place where from. His head was clouded with fug; as the voice hazed into focus, he groped for a name. "Watching your slow loss of self has been... enlightening."

Soft footsteps moved somewhere behind where Ecko lay. The voice was faintly amused, oddly paternal. "All that rage, all that passion, and in the end, you got... shall we say, 'nothing' out of it?"

Ecko couldn't think. His head and limbs felt heavy; he'd been sleeping very deeply. The last thing he remembered...

Shall we say... nothing?

The word was a shiver of unease. His mind offered images, pieces of memories; his body flickered with tension. Breathing still slow, he strove to focus, to put the images together and to remember what'd happened.

Had there been a hit?

Bloody handprints across a shattered wall?

The voice was on his other side, now, disorienting. "You failed, Mister Gabriel. It was a brave attempt, don't misunderstand.

You did manage to reach the final confrontation, and with all of the correct pieces in place – and that in itself was no mean feat. You saw it through to the end, and you gave it everything you had." His voice held a soft smile, gently patronising. "But that last confrontation proved too much for you." It was right over him, now. "The program is over, Ecko. It's time to wake up."

The program is over...

Program.

The word was like a download – a deluge of memory that blurred into a single, blazing comprehension...

Grey.

The man speaking was Doctor Slater Grey.

Program.

It's time to wake up.

He'd fallen – he remembered it now – the 'bot and the weather. They'd scraped him off the tarmac like a lump of strawberry jam. But that wasn't all – there were other memories, bright and poignant, somehow interwoven. The Wanderer, the Bard, the ruins at Tusien, Triqueta...

Gone.

And then he woke up and it was all a dream.

Stupidly, his first conscious thought was that he'd let them down.

But as the memories came stronger, faces and voices, their loss left him breathless and doubled over, a fist in the gut. His denial was reflexive – *No, it's impossible*. There was no way that they could all just be gone.

Program.

He'd lost them, failed them.

They'd never existed.

Grey's soft laugh smothered his thoughts, silenced them. A warm hand touched his face, and his eyelids flickered, he couldn't stop them. Inwardly, he cursed.

"Ah," Grey said. The touch withdrew, the feet moved again. "All that defiance, and rage, and angst, and bad language – and yet still you came to understand love." He chuckled. "How poetic."

"Fuck you." Knowing the game was up, Ecko opened his eyes. Bad language – he sounded like some fucking social skills counsellor. Ecko was fucking gonna tell this fucking asshole where he could fucking shove his fucking—

But the words died in his throat.

He stared at his surroundings in wordless bewilderment, his mind clamouring, panicked.

What the…?

He was in The Wanderer.

Or what was left of it.

He didn't understand, didn't *understand*!

This was some kinda mind game, for chrissakes – this was the same fucking *couch*. He'd woken up here, in this exact spot, when the Bard and Karine had first come to speak to him. That memory pulled at him now, like lost friendship and forgotten warmth.

For just a moment, he wanted to cry like a kid, just throw himself down and give up.

But The Wanderer itself was not the same.

The couch under him was broken, its back fractured and seats sagging. Straw stuffing spilled across stained and faded rugs. The table he'd shattered was still there, its pieces split and ageing, the wood rotten. The walls were patched with damp, their white peeling and their beams cracked. The mica windows were shot through with glittering splits, several had fallen out completely and the curtains had tumbled, forgotten and mouldering, to the floor. Dark mouths of decay ate through everything, as if the building had stood abandoned for a very, very long time.

The floor blew cold with debris.

Holy shit.

Ecko looked upwards, maybe for light, maybe for help, but the roof, too, was blotched and sagging. At one side of the room, it had fallen in completely and a hollow darkness spilled through the gap.

Horror settled over him like a shroud.

No, no, no, no, no...

His throat was tight, his eyes prickling. He blinked, breathed hard. The Wanderer's warmth, its welcome and homecoming, was something that'd once touched him to the core, something he'd missed almost as much as the Bike Lodge. How could it...?

"How long?" The question was all he could manage, but Grey understood.

He said, "There's no time here."

Ecko sat up, turned round.

Doc Grey was stood almost exactly where the Bard had once been. He'd put aside his white coat and wore faded jeans, a battered leather, a prog-rock tee so old it was more hole than fabric. With his flesh-tunnels and his long black ponytail, he looked like a direct mockery of Roderick – the old Roderick – like this whole thing was some fucking send-up of Ecko's first awakening.

Another layer of the game.

Was this what Nivrotar had meant when she'd said, *Almost to the final hand*?

Hell, maybe he *wasn't* unplugged. Maybe that was why he could still think, could *feel*, why Grey hadn't just dosed him. Maybe...

The insight brought him properly awake, adrenaline sparking, thrilled and curious. His oculars were kicked now. He needed answers, needed to understand.

He said, black teeth bared, "Whaddaya mean 'no time'?"

Hell, maybe this was the Dark Castle, and Grey was the Final

Boss, the Evil Sorcerer, the End-of-Level Mega-nasty... It did have a kinda symmetry to it.

Yeah. Whatever the hell he was, Ecko was gonna kick his fucking head clean off his fucking shoulders.

"The Count of Time is gone. Defeated at the last." Grey spread his arms, revealing vertical scars up the insides of both wrists. "Only you and I can exist on its outside." His face was calm, but his expression was oddly eager, almost whetted. "The world created for you is gone, Ecko, it died because you failed to save it. I was its first God, and its last, its forgotten God, its empty window." He gave a faint bow, gestured to the ruin around them. "This is the void."

"This is the *pub*, you asshole."

Grey shrugged and spread his hands further, inviting Ecko to see for himself.

"Dickhead." Kicking free of couch straw, Ecko stood up to look.

And as he did so, he became very aware of the darkness outside the hole in the roof – a darkness completely unlike his previous experience. This was not the starless night of the Varchinde, or living soul of dark, or the rich life and history of Mom's Underground.

This was Kazyen – true emptiness. It was an absence of all things, all passion, all feeling, all life and time.

I was its first God, and its last.

Its empty window.

There was – literally – Nothing outside the ruin of the shattered Wanderer.

The Count of Time is gone.

This is the void.

Cold crept across Ecko's skin like frost up a window. He groped for something, a key, a weapon. A magick fucking ring.

What had the Bard said?

He heard the words as if Roderick was there with him – and

now he wasn't fucking laughing at them.

At the prophecy, the memory they'd only found at the very end.

Time Nothing is more powerful, at last, than Count of Time. Then Time you bid your world farewell, your Gods, tonight, they sleep in Hell.

Oh my fucking God.

Ecko's adrenaline stopped, his breathing halted. He was too tense even to shiver – and he looked slowly down to his feet and then across the ruined rug to where the void seeped down from the broken roof.

And they were there, all of them, just as if they'd fallen down the fissure after him.

Rodcrick, lost in his own building. *The Final Guardian, defeated at the last.* Rhan and Vahl, in Selana's skin, as inseparable as they'd always been. *Then shall the mastery of light, give up...* Amethea, cured of her growth of moss – and the others were there too. Redlock as he had been, master warrior, Triqueta, younger, curled on his shoulder, her hand on his chest as if to deliberately taunt Ecko with their closeness. The stones in her skin gleamed and her eyes were open. And at the far end, Nivrotar herself, as helpless as the others, staring empty at the sagging roof.

Time when passion cannot sing, and everything held fast. Time your world farewell be kissed...

They were motionless, still as death, yet he could still see the faint misted warmth of their breathing.

"Christ." He was moving before he realised, falling to his knees beside Triqueta and looking back at Grey. *Passion cannot sing.* "What the hell did you *do*?"

"They're mine," Grey told him. He walked the length of them like some fucking sergeant, inspecting beds. "Like the first denizens of Rammouthe, so long ago, they failed to resist me, and their wills and lives are gone. Like The Wanderer

itself, they rest peaceful, contented, lost to Kazyen. *Happy.*"
He stopped to look down at Ecko, contemplative. "Now, there
only remains the question of what I'm going to do with you."

Ecko turned his head, looked at Grey out of the corner of
one eye. "You can kiss my mottled ass, is what you can do.
Wake them up, or I'm gonna pull out your lungs and *feed* them
to you."

"Why?" Grey lifted his arms, wrists out, showing the scars.
His gaze was open, eager. "They cannot live without time.
Their world is gone. No one wishes to live in despair. They're
comfortable."

Fury blazed in Ecko's heart. "They don't *want* comfort, you
fuckwit. They want life, feeling, freedom, love, hate, the good,
the bad an' the fuckin' ugly. They want—!"

"Really?" Grey's response was sharp. "Given the choice
between suffering and happiness, which would anyone prefer?"
His smile was sharp as a cut.

"They'd prefer to *live*, warts an' all!" Ecko came to his feet.
"I'm so gonna rip your head clean off—"

"And shit down my neck, yes, of course you are," Grey said,
"but before you do, consider this." He and Ecko were face
to face, yet somehow Grey was larger than he had been – the
Nothing above him framed him like an aura, made him into
some damned avatar, more than human. "You penetrated my
base, Ecko. You outwitted my staff. You eluded both Salva and
my *Takeshimi* 'bot. Yet you fell from my roof – and I found
you." His smile flickered. "I found you *first.*"

Ecko sneered, unintimidated. "What the hell does that
mean? You gonna explain the plot before you kill me?"

"I'm not going to kill you, Gabriel." Gaze brutal, Grey went
on, "Finding you on the pavement allowed me to send you
back to your boss with a little *gift*. Allowed me to introduce
your Collator to a virus. A very subtle and unique virus. I call
it," and now, his smile was beatific, "Kazyen."

"*What?*"

The inside and the outside, the reality and the program, overlapped, intertwined; his brain staggered back from the impact point. London was real, The Wanderer was real, his friends were real, Grey was real, Collator was real, all of it was fucking real. Chrissakes, he'd no idea where one stopped and the other one started...

"What the hell're you talkin' about?"

"It really isn't that hard," Grey said. "Your boss has resisted me for years. Collator is her whole organisation, mind and matter, plot and personnel. That you would undergo her Rorschach was inevitable. When she brought you home from your fall, she linked you up, and my virus became a part of your Rorschach's very earliest coding. You might say I was there from the beginning, from the world's very creation. I gave your world its nemesis." Ecko was staring at him, his oculars fixed on normal vision and his blood freezing in his veins. His friends lay at his feet, unmoving.

Inside and outside – it was like they were the *same*.

Watching Ecko's expression, Grey was unceasing, relentless. "I was there from the concept stage. I was the void into which the Goddess was born. I was the vast creature bound by the arrival of Time. And then, in my limitation and worldly exile, I dwelt upon Rammouthe, long before the Kas came. I destroyed the Ilfe, so the world would forget. I am the horror that Roderick witnessed in the water, that Ress found in the Library. I am the virus that infected Collator, infected your crafted world. As Eliza is your World Goddess, so I am Kazyen."

Oh motherfucking shit.

Kazyen.

The Final Boss.

Of *course* he fucking was. He'd been there all along. In the core code.

Forgotten.

Waiting.

Ecko had a momentary flash, a memory of the Bard in this very room saying, "...I believe you're a part of that vision. That future." He stared at Grey, could find no words, no smart-mouthed comeback. He was kicking himself.

But Grey hadn't finished.

"Of course," he said, "Eliza knew the virus was there, and she fought me. Nivrotar was her core strategy, and she orchestrated well, but not well enough." Grey loomed, right in Ecko's face. "Despite the Lord of Amos's manipulations, despite the success of the pattern she crafted, the virus has proven the stronger." He gestured at the others, fallen blank to the floor. "In short, I won." He smiled. "And so here they lie, all those little snippets of carefully crafted code, your friends, now abandoned in nothing, never to awaken or return."

I won.

Never to awaken or return.

The world created for you has died, Ecko, because you failed to save it.

Time you bid your world farewell, your Gods tonight...

Ecko's knees had folded, he was back on the floor. Triqueta still stared across Redlock's chest, empty. The Bard's Mom-crafted throat was just so much cold-steel piping.

"I am the void," Grey said, "the first God and the last, the beginning and the end. In me, all love dies, all light fades, all darkness flees. I am Grey. I am the true heart of all things."

Ecko could see it now – see it like rot in the rug. In London – his London – Grey was the crafter of passivity, of somnolence and social obedience, of the passionless drift in which the people lived their lives. In the Varchinde, that emptiness was manifest, like an elemental soul in its own right, and it had sucked all of the life from the world.

Ecko stared at the decay in the carpet, at the dust that had settled in the eyes of his friends.

His friends who had fallen because he'd failed.

"You've given this a brave effort," Grey said. "Yet believe me," he dropped to one knee to lay a hand on Ecko's shoulder, a sympathetic older brother, a priest blessing a damned man, "you could have done many things better." His gaze fell on Triqueta, and he smirked. "Your friends suffered horribly because of your distance and stubbornness. You could have saved Redlock, saved Amethea, saved the Bard his transformation." He shook his head sadly. "So, so many mistakes."

Mistakes.

You could have done better.

You could have saved Redlock, saved Amethea, saved the Bard his transformation.

...They sleep in hell.

His friends stared at the tavern's crumbling roof, their eyes full of Nothing.

Nothing surrounded them, surrounded the dead Wanderer.

There was no way out, and no way Ecko could live with what he'd done.

He saw again the scars on Grey's wrists and he understood that eventually, when it was all too much to be borne, the numbness offered was actually welcome.

He didn't feel himself topple sideways.

Didn't feel the Nothing as it settled into his soul.

But he did hear the heavy boot, the splitting, juddering impact as it struck.

And he did hear the door slamming back hard onto its hinges.

What?

Ecko blinked and stirred, trying to focus through engulfing layers of grey. There was dust in his mouth. The door teetered and swung crazily, one hinge broken. His vision was blurred, but there, in the dark of the hallway...

No. You can't be...

He swallowed, spat. His adrenaline kicked, struggled to fire, failed.

No...

It was a massive, heavy-shouldered shadow – a looming shape that didn't give a motherfucking shit for the Nothing outside the broken tavern, or for the despair that dwelled within.

Ecko tried to sit up, tried to remember fear, anger, friendship, betrayal. So many times, so many things he'd wanted to say – Christ, he couldn't recall any of them now.

Grey had turned from the window and smugness both and was staring at the doorway like a horror-movie victim.

Caught.

He whispered, "You can't be here."

But the figure was moving, black-clad and bristling with fury. Unable to stand, his muscles water, Ecko had no words, no belief. He stared.

I'll only have to tell you that I failed...

His stirring emotions evaporated, and left a dirt that felt like dread.

The figure came into the light and Ecko saw that his blond beard was long and ragged, untrimmed as if for weeks, that the hair on the back of his shaven head had grown into a comedy-thin blond fringe. His eyes were wild, pupils the size of hubcaps. But his heavy leather, the jeans, the oil stains – they were all just the same.

Lugan.

He managed the word, but couldn't say it aloud.

Lugan.

Beyond hope, beyond the end of all things, Lugan was *here*.

Stupidly, Ecko wanted to apologise. *I didn't do it, I didn't know about the virus, I swear, I didn't, I tried my hardest...* But his vision was clearing and there were so many questions and Lugan was moving too fast. The big man crossed the mouldering carpet and dragged Ecko off the floor, holding his shoulders and staring into his face like some long-lost fucking brother.

"You fucking twat," he said.

Grey had retreated to the far wall, his eyes wide. Whatever the hell game he was playing, Lugan was not a part of it.

Ecko stammered, "You're... you're not here."

Lugan released his shoulders and held up a tiny, light-emitting diode. "You little bastard, I've come all this bleedin' way!"

But Ecko's legs wouldn't hold him, and he fell back to the floor.

Grey was shouting, striving for authority and failing, "You! Eastermann! You're not supposed to be here! How did you...?"

"I'm the contingency, mate. Y'know, just in case."

Ecko stammered syllables, his heart hammering.

Grey stared at Lugan as if The Wanderer would tumble down around his ears.

But Lugan stood like some black-clad Goliath, more solid than the tavern itself. He looked along the line of the others – his eyes stopped briefly on the Bard – then he turned away.

Turned back to Grey, grinning stains and nicotine.

"You been double-crossed," he said. "But you'll stew in that shit soon enough. What matters now is finishin' this." He said to Ecko, "You didn't get all the way 'ere to go arse-over-tit at the final jump, didja?"

"Final... what?" Ecko licked cracked lips, struggled for words. The nothing was still in his head, filling him with his regrets, with failures and losses. Better to give up than live in pain. His gaze dropped to the rotted carpet, to his own now-bared feet, the colours of the mould in his skin. "I fucked this *up*, Luge." Tails of misery chased though his system. "It's over an' I lost. They," he glanced at the others, "they're all here 'cause of me. The program failed. Collator got a fucking virus. The world *died*!"

Lugan brandished the diode. "I didn't follow you 'ere to let you *quit*."

Pain twisting, Ecko said, "But why the hell should I believe you? You're just another trick, another layer, another fucking game—"

"Bloody 'ellfire, enough with the melodrama." Lugan chuckled. "I've chased you all the way from fuckin' London. From Mom's lair. From batshit Escher ruins on the wrong side of the Kartiah. Through my very own fuckin' vision quest. I followed you, you little shit, because I ain't a quitter – and neither're you."

"But I failed!" Ecko gestured at the empty eyes of Triqueta. "It was all for nothing – all the fighting, all the hate, all the anger. All that kickin' back an'... Chrissakes, Luge, I did it all *wrong*..."

Something in him was saying, *I'm sorry, I'm sorry, I'm sorry*, as if the figures on the floor could hear him.

"Quit whinin'." Lugan closed a hand at the front of his shirt. He glanced briefly at the scar Amal had given him, then glared into Ecko's black eyes. "It's all bullshit, mate, virus an' everythin' – all spin an' bollocks to make you quit. You're not 'ere."

"What?" Ecko's response was a whisper, "What the fuck're you talkin' about?"

"We're still in The Wanderer, you twat. We're under the Varchinde. This is the final level, the last confrontation. I came 'ere to tell you – you're still plugged in."

We're still in The Wanderer.

Under the Varchinde.

Ecko couldn't process the knowledge, but Lugan hadn't stopped. "Think about it, you dozy bugger. This is Grey." Lugan jerked a thumb at the doc. "We know 'oo 'e is. An' all this time, you've been fightin' against the program makin' you normal – breakin' down 'oo you are. You been tellin' Eliza you weren't gonna give in, be good, take all your tablets an' go to bed with a nice 'ot cuppa tea."

Ecko's oculars suddenly focused sharp, his understanding swelling.

What the fuck?

He pieced it together, staring demented.

Grey's the bad guy. Grey, with his social conformity, his lack of freedom and expression, his fucking pacifier drugs...

And if Grey's the bad guy...

"Then I'm s'posed to be manic," Ecko said, slowly. "I'm s'posed to be out of control. Insane. Inane." His thoughts were gathering pace now. "Oh yeah, add your own descriptions for good measure..."

It was filling him now, elation, relief, understanding. The glorious irony of it made him cackle, and then laugh aloud – a full-on belly laugh that was unlike any sound he'd ever made in his entire life.

All this time – and the joke was on him – and fuck it was *funny.*

Framing this realisation, finally and completely, felt like some huge relief – like all the tension and anger had just drained out of him, down into the carpet.

Time your world farewell be kissed, unless you find the catalyst.

The thing that makes change, without being changed itself.

Ecko felt like he could laugh forever, laugh until he cried. Lugan was right – this was his final confrontation. And he would win it by simply being who he was. Had always been.

The program ended here.

It ended with the death of Doctor Slater Grey, his Final Level Boss.

The death of Kazyen.

31: AWAKE THE PHOENIX CLINIC, LONDON

Ecko was falling.

Down between sleeping and waking, between dreaming and consciousness. Even as he felt the sensation, he jolted awake like he'd smacked into the sidewalk.

What the...?

He was startled, confused, had no clue where he was. His dreams had been so absolutely clear, but there was no remaining lassitude in which to reach for them. They were gone like they'd still been falling when he'd been jerked so rudely away.

His heart was thundering and he...

Christ. He couldn't breathe.

He panicked, gagged, heaved a crisp and antiseptic lungful. It made him cough. His mouth tasted like a bear's ass.

Jesus, what the hell'd he *done*? Meth?

There was a cold touch on one eyelid, then colours in his vision, bright in his brain. They were blinding, and he flinched, tried to blink and turn away.

"Oculocephalic response indicates consciousness." The voice was female, warm and calm. The metal touch came again, carefully lifting the other eyelid. More colours exploded – electrons, neurons, fractals. He tried to raise an arm and bat the invader aside. "Ascending reticular activating system functional, brainstem stabilising. Sensory input via thalamic pathway stable. Integrity of cerebral cortex plus ninety-seven percent and climbing. Oxygen levels good; no evidence of hypoxia. Heart rate, breathing, circulation all elevating nicely." The woman gave a slight chuckle. "Take a note: subject regained consciousness at... 5:03 a.m." She exhaled, relief or weariness. "And that, would be project complete. In the words of the prophet – I think we bloody did it."

The light withdrew, and the touch let his eyelid drop once more.

We bloody did what?

Ecko grimaced, swallowed, licked gummed lips. He wanted to tell this woman where to shove it, prophet and all, but his face was lined with ulcers where he'd chewed the insides of his cheeks, and everything was lead weights and slo-mo. Chrissakes, he felt like his whole damned body belonged to someone else. And there was this odd, ticklish shimmer in his nerve-endings, like everything'd been numb...

The sensation was a frisson, a first skittering of alarm. What the hell'd hit him? A truck? As he slowly allowed his awareness to expand, he picked up the hum of a purifier, and a soft, soothing double-thump that kept pace with his heart.

Uh-oh...

Carefully, he tried to open his eyes, but they, too, were gummed and squicky. Instead, he said, "Whmf...?"

"Shhh." The chill touch was back, this time on his shoulder. "You've been out for seventy-six hours, give or take. You're still wired to your nerve receptors, and your cortical plug is still powered. So hold still, or you'll tangle yourself in knots." The touch produced a cool cloth, wiped his face. "Okay. Can you open your eyes, now?"

Under him, the bed – chair? – moved smoothly, lifting him to a sitting position. The motion was glidingly eerie, familiar enough to creep his skin and make that audible heart rate wobble with tension. Swallowing nausea, he squeezed open his eyes, let his antidaz filter the glare.

"Oh, futhkh."

Frankly, the truck might've been the better option.

He was caught, fly-like, in clinical steel and wires and white light – trapped in its centre as if it were some vast web made for him alone. Around him, the walls were alive with a pulse of electronics.

And he was... alight, he strove to focus.

Jesus Harry, he was *alight*.

What—?

Anxiety sparked, causing a resulting surge in his surroundings. Reflexively thinking, *Fuck, fuck,* he tried to sit up, cycling ocular modes to clear his head. His digital readout said 5:05:43, 5:05:44, 5:05:45...

Time.

As his vision cleared, he saw he was covered with a sea of tiny, acupuncture-like needles, thousands of them in star-system clusters, each one ending in the minute gleam of an LED. Some of the clusters were hardlined, wires delicate and alive, others simply flickered at him, amused by his wakefulness.

His whole damn body was a pattern of lights.

Panic rose, closing his throat. Somewhere he could hear the heart-rate monitor picking up speed. He tried to move, to scrabble backwards, away from the needles and the prodding and the poking and the electronic web, right back out of the seat, but that chill hand hadn't left his shoulder. It rested harder, order rather than request.

He turned to look up at the woman.

Wondered who the hell she was.

She was slight and earnest, too young for her frown. Her

white coat was pristine, her mass of dark hair pulled neatly back. She had two steel-rimmed sockets, one under each ear – looked kinda like she'd had her restraining bolt removed.

But that wasn't the freaky thing.

Nope, the freak show was her hands, the touch on his shoulder, the gentle chill that had opened his eyes... They were graceful, perfect surgical steel; there were too many fingers and all of them with too many joints. They were fingers that ended in needles and blades and gauges and other shit he didn't even want to think about. They were arachnid, beautiful and horrifying. Christ, they were almost like something Mom would've made.

Mom...

Memories shivered in the back of his head, but he wasn't ready for them. He searched the woman's face, said, "Who're you? Esme Scissorhands?"

She smiled, stretched out her fingers. As he watched, they folded carefully down to normal sizes, each one sliding over and together with minute precision. She pulled on flesh-covered gloves. They settled into place, and the line between glove and skin faded into nothing.

Perfect.

"I'm Elizabeth," she said, flexing her new fingers. "Elizabeth Hope Shakespeare, no relation. You can call me Eliza."

Eliza.

The word was a shock of reality, a glass tumbling slowly to the clean and tiled floor.

Eliza.

Flickers and phantoms, a rush of dream-imagery. Flashes of fragments as the glass detonated. Splinters, shining in the light.

Bloody handprints across a shattered wall.

One-hand-then-two.

But he wasn't facing that shit – no way, no how, not yet.

Instead, he shoved the images aside and pulled himself further upright. He felt the tug at his brainstem, the nerve needles twitching in his skin. There was a surgical robot lurking to one side of his chair, quiescent and sinister. Behind it, a projection screen hung in the empty air. It was curved, half transparent, and it fizzed silently with a mosaic of white noise.

It revolted and compelled him – like seeing his own body opened in autopsy.

Eliza.

She handed him a steel beaker – water. "Don't worry if your memory's a little unsteady," she said. "We can help you unscramble it all, put everything back in order, that's why we're here. Do you... what's the last thing you remember?"

Falling down, down into the screaming and the dark.

Ignoring her question, he took a lukewarm sip and felt his mouth ulcers sting. The pain was good, real. It cleared his head.

"Where the hell am I?" His voice ground, metal and rust. He jerked his chin at the screen. "An' what the fuck's *that?*"

"Don't worry about that for the moment." She took the beaker back and patted his arm. "For now, you need to gather your thoughts, recover. Piecing everything back together can be a bit... strange, but we've sourced some core triggers to help you through it." She reached into a pocket of her coat, pulled something free. "Do you recognise this?"

Triggers.

Alexander David Eastermann.

Lugan's lighter.

And the memory was clear as a slap, as a glass splinter in the face – he was flicking the lid, spinning the wheel. "Outta gas." There was a man speaking to him, tall and lean, "The Wanderer finds many things... just like it found you. It's a portent, I think."

Roderick.

And now the surge rose, shattering the floodgates. The rush swamped him, bore him down. It tumbled him over and over. It robbed him of breath, pulled him under, left him gagging for bare life.

The Wanderer, the ruins of Tusien, the moss in Amethea's skin, Redlock fighting with flashing axes, monsters of stone and creatures of flame, Maugrim taunting them all. The mad old man in the corridors of Amos. Nivrotar, monochrome perfection. The stone walls of Aeona, creatures created, Amal cutting into his chest. Roderick's steel throat, Khamsin, writhing with savage power. Triqueta, glowing like opal and sunshine.

It was too much, too intense. He was shuddering with an overload of comprehension. He spread his fingers, tried to catch this image, that one. He tried to cry out but the ulcers were hurting and he'd no words to form what was—

Still, they kept coming.

Warfare before the walls of Tusien, Sical, Rhan blazing righteous. Warriors and monsters and dying children. And then dust, desolation endless, the barren and empty plain. Rural dystopia, everything dead. Those final moments as they faced Vahl across the fissure that had riven the world.

A single image, stark and jagged: The Wanderer, in ruins.

And then, rising like some deity over the tavern's broken roof, Doctor Slater Grey himself, the needle marks in his arms all puckering in invitation. He grew to huge size, his mouth widening—

No!

Grey made Ecko angry, reflexive, unavoidable. He fought the image back. But he was caught in Grey's bolt-hole, passive and obedient, he was drudging to work, empty and content; he was falling from the roof with the 'bot loosing a volley after him, hi-explosive detonations that shook the London night.

The drizzle sparkled like shrapnel.

Lugan?

The maelstrom of images passed him and was gone, burbling into the distance. He sat still, shaking, his breathing ragged, and tried to work out what the hell had just happened.

Luge?

But no, there was no Lugan. Not here.

There never had been.

In his head, the colours were gone. There was only the steel room, the steel chair, the steel lighter. Even as the memories faded, he understood that they'd been somehow false, no more than some vast and complex dream.

And as he blinked at the wires and the lights, so their cold reality sank its blade all the way home, right into his heart, grinning as it did so. All those memories, hopes, fears, lives, deaths, everything he'd seen and felt and learned and loved and hated...

Gone.

None of it... Jesus... *none* of it had ever really happened.

No.

He couldn't wrap his brain round it. It was too powerful, too recent. Too *big*. It made his brain fizz like the screen. Even as he tried to unscramble what had happened, where it all began and ended, he was trying to encompass... No, it was too much.

You can't do that... you can't've just done that... just taken it all away...

He stared at the curved screen, his own, now-blank Fourth Wall. He wanted to see something, someone, wanted to reach out for it all. Prove it had happened. That everything he'd lived through, friends and fights and foes and fuck-ups, all of it...

It was just so much Unreality TV.

His mouthful of bitterness was tangible, so strong his expression contorted.

He'd been programmed. Fucking *puppeteered*. Up on that screen like a porn star. *Daaaance.* Chrissakes, talk about a violation – boots in his brain, kicking into places that were private. Teasing him with images, people, places that hurt, that made him *feel*. Rearranging his shit, his personal shit, that was no one else's damned business. *Displaying* it. Forcing him to game, to dance at the end of a chain...

Dance, Ecko, daaaaaance—

The patterns of needles winked at him like some vast and fractal joke.

Oh, you motherfucking bitch!

Eliza's voice came faintly through a distant, tinnitus hum. Now, more of it was coming back: he was remembering *layers*. Not just the story itself, but its curses and doubts. *Eliza. Creator. World Goddess.* His clamours to be free, his determination to win through. His capitulation. His freedom, and his lack of it.

His *anger*.

Daaaaaaance, Ecko...

It made his stomach lurch. He brought up the water, puked it onto the floor. He felt unsteady enough to tumble sideways, to drown in the gleam of bile in the lights. He clung to the chair, thought of falling, of Grey, of worlds within worlds, of mirrors that reflected only mirrors. Of fractal patterns, endless. Of Lugan in The Wanderer, of Roderick in London...

Shit!

The room was spinning, now. Edges of images whispered into being, vanished again.

Too much to process. He was losing his goddamned fucking *mind*.

And hadn't she been supposed to fix it?

Hadn't that been the *point*?

He found himself laughing, rising into hysteria, and he strangled the noise to a stop.

"Ecko," Eliza said, warm and calm, as if to a child. "It's all right. Sometimes, these recollections can be... very powerful. But the shock will pass, if you give it a moment, everything will settle into its proper place. You've achieved... something phenomenal." She dropped the lighter back into her pocket. "It might help to know how it ends. Maybe give you some closure?"

Ends?

The word brought him up short, and he stared at her. *Ends?* All of those memories, everywhere he'd just been, the whole world and story that had surrounded him. He was still resonating with it, and struggling with it not being real. How could it just...?

He looked back at the screen, then back at her face. "What?"

"In fact," Eliza said, "we should take that step now. Then we can concentrate on a proper recovery."

There was a throb in his brainstem.

And the phantoms started to move.

There!

In one place, to the far right, a city. He recognised it as Roviarath, her Great Fayre rotting and ruinous. The river was empty and the wharves broken, the soil was cracked and bare. The city's people were gathering at her outskirts, stood with cart and wagon and emaciated beastie.

Roviarath was being evacuated.

Ecko stared, transfixed, biting his lower lip. There was a tiny figure on a black horse standing in his stirrups and gesturing orders. Ecko could almost hear him barking commands and rounding up the city's survivors. He watched as the people, small as toys, formed into a refugee column and headed out across the dead plain.

He'd no clue how they'd cross the intervening ground – or how many of them would survive.

Behind them, the cracks in the ground reached the lighthouse tower. It sagged sideways and fell with *Koyaanisqatsi* slowness, its great rocklight tumbling, extinguished at last.

He found a lump in his throat and he swallowed, blinking.

Ends.

There, in another place, Tusien – the great ruin black against a burning sunset. The force there was moving out, leaving its dead and its debris, and mustering to go home. Ecko saw centaurs. He saw Nivrotar, her hands full of knotted bits of cord, gesturing to the columns of warriors, all of them laden with packs. As the image moved, out through the open holes in the walls to the long staircase at the back of the ruin, he saw a slender golden figure stood alone, her gold hair blowing.

Triqueta.

Ecko found himself lifting a hand. His oculars strove to bring her closer. He realised what had happened, though he still couldn't see it clearly. There, under the great wall of the ruin, was the long barrow that was the grave of Tusien's Lord. Beside it were marks of newly dug long pits, each one headed with a cairn of broken stones. At one end stood the grave of Tan Commander Mostak, and at the other...

Before it, his axes in her hands, Triqueta stood silent and tearless. The lines in her face were somehow tempered, lean and strong, and her brassard caught the last of the light. She had a long task ahead of her, but she no longer had any fear.

And he understood, on some level, that what she had given him was the very last night of the youth she'd lost.

Triq.

He tasted her name, remembered her words...

When all this is over, is it you who fades out of existence? Or is it us? Or do we?

Another view – another grave. This one unmarked, alone amidst the death that surrounded the great fissure, and he knew before looking whose it was. Over it, Rhan was huddled on his knees, racked by sobbing, crying from heart and soul, his face contorted with the force of it. He was saying, "Thea. Little priestess. I'm sorry, I'm so sorry." *Humility is the hardest lesson of all.* The Bard stood by him, hand in his hair, and Rhan's head rested on the man's lean, black-clad hip.

But Roderick's face was turned upwards, etched in both joy and sorrow, his eyes closed at the sky. With another shock of insight, Ecko realised what the Gods had given Rhan as his final gift, his reward for his long service and his victory.

He was mortal. He would age, and he would die.

Finally, he would go home.

But the grave was changing. As the sky overhead glowed with sunrise light, so new grass was uncurling, growing where Amethea had fallen.

The Monument has my answers too, I can feel it.

She was the Soul of the Stone, the heart of the world, its new growth and recovery. Her life had cured the blight.

He blinked water, it slid down his face unheeded.

Eliza said gently, "Calm, Ecko. Watch."

And there, in the centre of the screen's curve, the rising streets of Fhaveon. People, blinking, stumbling from the Cathedral's doors and out onto the broken mosaic.

Pushing through the heaving roadways, there was a woman, tired and road-stained. She was massive in shoulder and her skin was etched with myriad elaborate scars. Ecko recognised her as the young woman from the corridor – when the mad Ress had spoken to him about Kazyen. Jayr. She seemed older, somehow, and he could take a guess at why.

She came to the great doors of the Palace and spoke to the guard. Even as she did so, the door was opened and Roderick stood there, staring at her with his face a mask of shock. As Ecko watched, she held out to him an overshirt, as filthy as she was. It seemed to be covered in some kind of writing.

Roderick took it, turned it over and over, fascinated. And then he started to laugh, to laugh as if he would cry. When the woman looked at him sideways, he apologised and then – to her surprise – he sank to one knee right there in the doorway.

"My Lord," he said. "Welcome home."

Ecko thought he was smiling, but it was too small to see.

The images on the screen were fading, now, dissolving back to white noise. He found himself almost panicking, he didn't want to lose them – he tried to think about Triqueta, about Amethea and Redlock. He tried to focus on the Bard, on The Wanderer – on the tavern created anew and *there* on the city streets of Fhaveon, warm lights in its windows. He needed it, couldn't bear to let it go.

Or is it us?

"And so we come to the resolution," Eliza said softly. "You've won, Ecko. The Lord Valiembor is returned, with her the world's memory. Fhaveon will be rebuilt, with survivors to sing Amethea's name, and Redlock's. And yours. To sing of Triqueta and her Red Rage. Of Rhan and Vahl, and their endless war. And the Bard will tell your stories, over and again, until the end of the Count of Time. Take a moment if you need one, but then we have to move on."

But...

How can he fucking sing if you turn him off?

"No." The protest was immediate, instinctive. He was still watching them, though there was little now to see. He wasn't here, in this clinical testing zone, he was there in that world, wanting it to survive and thrive and flourish. He wanted to know the rest of the story, to watch the cities rebuild, the grass regrow. He wanted to know what would happen to Triqueta without Redlock, without Amethea, without the Banned. Would she take command of the military in Fhaveon? With Jayr as her Lord and the ageing Rhan beside her? Where had Vahl gone? The Kas? He wanted to know how they'd rebuild, wanted to know if he'd missed anything, unlocked every level. He needed to be there as they recovered, needed to watch their story unfold, know what would happen next...

"You can't just flick a switch," he said softly. "They're all real, they think for themselves, they *feel.* You can't just –"

"They're code, Ecko," she told him gently. "They're nothing."

The word went through him like a shock, its symbolism knocking the breath out of him. His heart started to pound, the sound all around him, everywhere. Nothing – his ultimate bad guy, and with the flick of a finger she could condemn—

"Don't!"

Her hands were reaching for the plug in the back of his head.

"Don't fucking touch me." Sick to his belly, he was flooded with terror. Ferocious from their long hiatus, his adrenals screamed wonkily into life, making the sea of lights that covered him flicker like angry stars. "Don't you *fucking* touch me." Panicked, he wanted to take her wrist and snap it, break her to the floor and kick and kick and *kick*, but his legs were still too weak. "It's all *real*, all of it. You can't just turn them off." He barely understood what he was saying; he was pleading, panicked, words falling over themselves. "How could any *game* be that complex? Those characters, how could—?"

"You had a world made for you, Ecko," Eliza said softly. "A pattern crafted from your synapses, a fractal reality that grew with every question, that changed and shifted with every choice you made. Yes, you had characters that acted independently of your presence, that interacted with each other as well as with you." Her voice was calm, soothing as milk. "It made them three-dimensional, stopped them being the town merchant that only ever has the weapons and treasure that you sell to him. But that doesn't make them real—"

"What're you now, Philip K. Dick?" His fear was becoming anger, cleansing. His adrenals gave him energy and he could feel his limbs respond, return to life. His targetters kicked, crossing her face, her throat. "World Goddess, they called you. You *made* that world: you built it, you built yourself into it. From its earliest mythology, all the way up. You, an' Collator. An' *Grey*, my end-of-level Nasty. An' whether the characters are code or not, they believe they're real. You can't just turn them off. They'll die—"

"It's a self-adapting program, nothing more." Her voice was earnest, tense with the beginnings of irritation. "It's not real, Ecko, it's just smart enough to respond to your choices. To learn, if you like. Every decision you've made, however small, rippled out to affect the entire pattern of the program's future. You were its centre, your path undefined and free to choose whatever you wished to do. And with every choice you made, the pattern changed around you to ensure that you would still reach its end. And face your trials. And win. Without you there, it has no purpose. Does that make sense?"

"Shove it, sister." He was moving now, all pins and needles and returning circulation. He ran a hand over himself, dashing the LEDs out of his skin, then slid his feet to the floor. His knees buckled, but he stood up.

His heartbeat reverberated from the walls.

Eliza backed up a step. "Your cortical plug is still locked. You shouldn't be moving."

"You gonna stop me?" His remaining nerve-clusters sparked, ripples and galaxies. Some of the delicate hardwires were falling away, or breaking. He smashed at them again, clearing more.

His skin was stained with their light.

"If I have to." Her voice was without threat, but absolutely assured.

He bared his teeth at her. "Yeah right. So you tell me one thing," he growled, a suggestion of coming thunder. He was gonna tear this damn place to pieces, any fucking second. Anything, to keep that program alive. "You tell me *why*. If all that's not real, then why the hell go to all this trouble – just for li'l ol' me?"

"Because of your *passion*, Ecko. Your drive and savagery." She backed up, glanced quickly over his shoulder to the chair behind him. "Good, Evil, Order, Chaos, Fire, Ice, Technology, Magick. Inside, Outside. All opposites, and, at the end of the day, all the same. Whatever side of something you're on, you have to believe in what you're doing, and *roar* with that belief. Vahl was never the enemy – Roderick told you that, right at the beginning. This has been about defeating apathy, about Kazyen. Grey – *Grey* – is the enemy of all things. The enemy we face here too."

"So – what? – is this all some sneaky fucking plot to topple the bad guys? Thanks to my guinea piggin', or some unique synapse you've learned from my broken brain, you now have a program to fuck over Doctor Grey?"

That question made her smile, then she said, "I think this has gone far enough. You need that plug taken out before you can start recovery proper. Hatchetcease."

Like some damned safeword, his adrenaline was gone. His knees went and he caught himself on the side of the chair, feeling weak and hollow.

"Shit. You fucking *bitch*."

"So you've told me often enough," Eliza said, flickering another smile. "Denial is inevitable in the early stages, as is a certain amount of... emotional readjustment." She glanced again at the chair-back, a sharp glance, as if looking for something. "Just sit down, and try and breathe. If you fight this, it'll just make it harder."

So – what was she looking for? Back-up?

The thought made his adrenaline spark again, then splutter and cough like a failed engine. He was sick with nameless dread, right to his belly – like there was some monster lurking behind him.

Yeah. Take more than monsters to scare me.

He turned slowly to face it. He looked at – then past – the back of the chair.

And then he saw something else.

Behind the chair, there was a pulled curtain, heavy, white and featureless.

Before the curtain stood a silent figure in an enforcer's white suit. Her hair was cut in a strict black bob, and her eyes were covered in mirrored shades. She stood with her arms folded, and she made no move as Ecko clocked her, neither recognition nor reaction. She simply stood there, boots gleaming.

Whoever she was, she must've been there all this time. Watching. Listening.

And he'd had no idea.

"Extra security?" He rounded on Eliza. "Think I'm gonna go off the deep end? Got that much faith in your own success?"

"No need to worry." Her response was half soothing, half amused. "Ducarl's just... keeping an eye."

"On what?"

"You're not the only person in my care."

Not the only person.

The words made him stand upright, a sudden, nameless fear closing his throat. His knees shook, but he wasn't going down, no fucking way. *Not the only person.* It hadn't even occurred to him, but... were there others, in programs like his? Layers of them, like in Grey's boxes? The worlds of anywhere-but-here?

And if they were all saving fucking Narnia, why did Eliza need a criminal enforcer?

"Ecko." Eliza was speaking, urgent and soft. "We need to complete your closure." Her calm had evaporated, she sounded almost nervous. "You can't deal with the outside world with your cortical plug still powered." The smile was brief, brittle. She was jittery, fearful of something. "There are risks we don't need – ongoing depression, social maladjustment, psychotic episodes. Please, it's in your own best interests."

"You're hidin' something." His certainty was absolute. "What you got? Illegal organs? Brainwashed slaves? Human lab rats? Any combo?" He was standing straight, his energy levels rising. He was right on the edge of something – and the feeling was *good*.

"Hatchetcease." Her expression was almost panicked. "I say again, Hatchetcease." She stepped back, glanced past him to where Ducarl stood silent. "Shit!"

The safeword was a blow, a double-fist – *slam!* – in the belly. But he'd faced Maugrim, Amal, Vahl, Grey – and that which hadn't killed him was making him lace his shitkicker boots all the way to his fucking knees.

You made me like this. You deal with it.

Ironic much?

Legs firm, he took a step towards the curtain. The targetters on Ducarl's shades tracked his motion, but he didn't care, he didn't *care*. What was she gonna do anyway, spike him with a boot heel?

Eliza said, "Ecko, don't make me do this. That plug needs to come out before you leave this room. Please…"

"Please?" His adrenaline kicked again, and this time it caught, raced, sang, thrilling along his nerves, reverberating from the sensors in the room. "You put me through hell, and you say 'please'? You tease me, and taunt me, and play with me, and now you want me to play nice?" The last of his starlights glittered, his pulse beat in his ears. On the screen beside him, there were still lingering ghosts, still wistful flickers of that other world – they seemed to lean in, as if eager. "Come on, bitch, what's behind curtain number one?"

Eliza's face went white as Fhaveon stone. She said, "Ecko. Stop this. I'll put you down if I have to."

"Fuck you. For the very last goddamn time. Fuck. *You.*"

So many times, *so* many times, those words had been in his mouth and his thoughts. Now, at last, he finally had the chance to tell her exactly what he thought of her, exactly how he felt about being forced and exposed and manipulated, exactly why he'd refused to capitulate for as long he had, exactly why Roderick's sheer force of personality, his long faith and his love for his world, had affected Ecko deeply enough to make him change his mind.

But hell, she knew all that shit already.

He took another step. His adrenaline screamed at him.

He saw Eliza nod, her face a mask of regret and pain.

He saw Ducarl was moving.

His adrenaline shrilled even louder, higher than it had ever carried him – the rush was phenomenal. He wanted to cry out, laugh, cackle like some damned daemon. He wanted to tear the walls down. The world slowed round him, and he was faster than he'd thought, faster than he'd ever been.

For the first time, he was out of reach of Eliza's will and power, now answerable only to his own sense of *must*.

You can't stop me now, bitch!

The robotic doc was just close enough for him to reach.

He lunged for it, heaved the thing off the floor. In exquisite slow motion, he saw the crosshairs in Ducarl's shades track his movements, saw the pistol as she drew it from its shoulder-holster. He saw her elegantly taloned fingertip tighten on the trigger.

But he was a blur, faster than the pistol muzzle could track. The shot went off – he could almost watch the air ripple in response. He saw the screen flicker as it went through, heard the detonation as it took a chunk of plaster out of the far wall. Ducarl was swearing, her voice thick and slow; he heard her heels tick-tack on the lino. But he wasn't waiting.

With an effort that made him curse, splinters of words spat through gritted black teeth, he heaved the 'bot bodily past the enforcer, at the curtain behind her.

Watched it rip the curtain free, and tumble, tangled, onto the floor.

And his answer was there.

Right in his face.

Sleeping like some fucking giant cherub.

No cortical plug, no 'trodes, no body covered in lights.

Just a drip in his arm.

Holy motherfucking shit.

But he'd known this, all along; he'd fucking *known* it!

The sleeping figure was a man. Blond, bearded, tattooed, built like that well-known brick shithouse. His stubbled scalp was wispy with growing hair, and though his face was turned away, Ecko didn't need the shiny bald spot to tell him who it was.

Known this all along.

Lugan.

Lugan, who'd taken on Grey, who'd been there in The Wanderer. Lugan, who'd saved everything by finding Ecko just in time to kick his sorry ass...

Vision Quest.

Ecko glanced back at the fizzing screen, at the ghosts that still lurked within. He had no words, only this huge feeling of things locking into place, like everything was suddenly making sense.

He didn't understand it completely, not yet, but any minute now...

"You sent him in after me."

"No, Ecko, I didn't." Eliza's voice was alight with tension. She looked over at Ducarl, held up a hand. She seemed to be choosing her words very carefully. "I saw him but I didn't put him there. You can see for yourself – he's not wired. There's no way he could have shared your program. Lugan was spiked, hit with Lysergic acid diethylamide, not life-threatening, but enough to drop a bodyplating—"

"Bullshit," Ecko said. He was trembling. "He was in there with me."

"That's not possible." Her words were laden with fear.

Shaking now, sick with comedown, Ecko snarled at her, "He came in *after* me, you dozy bitch. Without him, I'd've failed the whole goddamn fuckin' thing!"

She spread her hands, said, "Sometimes, the subconscious mind, in times of extreme stress, conjures—"

"Fucking horseshit. Either you put him there or he... Jesus, LSD? He was *tripping*?"

And yet, his dream was the same as mine. And that means...

"Ecko." Eliza used his name like she'd grabbed his jaw and forced him to look at her. "Your program is a fiction, unique, created only for you, responsive only to you. Lugan was hallucinating after a drugs overdose."

...it means it's all connected. There's more than one way in. And that means...

His mind clamouring impossibilities, Ecko ignored her. He was heading for the curtain, the fallen robot doc.

That means it's all real.

Inside and outside, both the same. You fuckin' said it yourself.

You really did *create a world.*

The thought made him want to laugh, to cheer, to find his friends and embrace them. To tell them, "It's all right, it's all right!"

She said, "You have to let this go. Let your program run its last scenes, and let it finish."

He grinned. "I don't think so."

"Ecko, you need closure."

He gave her the finger. "Close this."

Her face tightened. She ran her hand through a mass of hair. "Please don't make me do this."

"You? Denying responsibility? Yeah right. Do your worst."

"If I have to." She nodded at Ducarl, and Ecko turned.

He saw the muzzle of the .357 come up, just like he'd once watched the whirling barrels of a minigun, seventy-six hours and a lifetime ago. He saw the crosshairs in her shades, saw them target, saw the lock, saw the pressure of the enforcer's trigger finger. He was moving, reflexive, but without the adrenaline, he'd never fucking make it...

Over his head, he saw the flatscreens change. He saw the vastness of the dead Varchinde as if he were standing on the slopes of the western Kartiah. He saw the sunrise streak the soil in pink and yellow and gold.

It was beautiful.

And down there, he could see growth – only a little – but there were tiny uncoilings of green, bright fronds of hope scattered across endless death. The sky was blue and the clouds were white.

The spring would come, after all.

Because they had won.

He didn't feel the bullet as it went through his chest. He didn't feel himself fall back, his arms flying. He didn't know that he'd hit the floor, his own blood puddling round him. He didn't feel any of it, hell, it didn't matter now. The hospital, the enforcer, the shrink, the room – the hurt – were all long gone.

He didn't see the little nerve-lights extinguishing, one after another like stars tumbling from the sky.

There was no pain, no regret.

Because there, far out across the empty plain, the flags were flying from the top of Fhaveon city, and the world would be born anew.

EPILOGUE

EPILOGUE THE BIKE LODGE, LONDON

The Bike Lodge was closed.

Metal shutters had sealed off the end of the railway arch and police barriers had sealed off the end of the road. Since the disappearance of the business's owner, the London Met had been all too pleased to remove one of the last free thorns that dug into their perfectly orderly side.

If any of them missed their custom chops, side projects that occupied garages and gleamed pointless on Sunday afternoons, then they were too smart to say so.

But Tarquinne Magdalene Gabriel was not concerned with the London Met.

Instead, she stood in the centre of the bleak and echoing space. She inhaled the smell of oil and scanned the cleaner patches on the walls where the posters had been torn away.

She tongued the diamond in her tooth, a reflexive habit when thinking.

Her ploy had succeeded.

Almost.

Everything had fallen into place – her brother had been put through the Rorschach program, and Lugan had been fool enough to touch the needle that she'd passed him. These two facts meant that Tam – Ecko – had successfully run the test gauntlet against Grey, and the program to take him down should run smoothly with what it had learned.

But Ecko had never recovered, been shot as a liability. She had no real feelings for her brother either way, but his loss was a nuisance.

She walked across the stained concrete floor, her heels clicking. The air was cold, and she wrapped her coat around her tightly with one arm as she used the other to push open the door to Lugan's office.

It, too, was empty. Even the heavy and scarred desk had gone.

Fragments of forgotten paper fluttered in the sudden breeze – but there was nothing in here of any use whatsoever.

Checking annoyance, Tarquinne turned away. As she did so, a glint of something caught her eye. And there, in the corner of the room, half-buried under the tumbleweeds of garbage and dust, she saw the gleam of chrome.

She knew what it was, and bent to pick it up.

Blew the dust from it.

Thoughtfully, she read the inscription, and then flicked the little wheel. The yellow flame was bright and immediate, warm on her face.

Tarquinne Gabriel snapped the lighter shut, and she smiled.

ABOUT THE AUTHOR

DANIE WARE is the publicist and event organiser for cult entertainment retailer Forbidden Planet. She has worked closely with a wide range of genre authors and has been immersed in the science-fiction and fantasy community for the past decade. An early adopter of blogging, social media and a familiar face at conventions, she appears on panels as an expert on genre marketing and retailing. Follow her on twitter @Danacea

WWW.DANIEWARE.COM

KOKO TAKES A HOLIDAY

BY KIERAN SHEA

Five hundred years from now, ex-corporate mercenary Koko Martstellar is swaggering through an easy early retirement as a brothel owner on The Sixty Islands, a manufactured tropical resort archipelago known for its sex and simulated violence. Surrounded by slang-drooling boywhores and synthetic komodo dragons, Koko finds the most challenging part of her day might be deciding on her next drink. That is, until her old comrade Portia Delacompte sends a squad of security personnel to murder her.

"[A] futuristic wide ride... Great fun"

Booklist (starred review)

"Richard K. Morgan's *Altered Carbon* with a dash of Tank Girl attitude"

Library Journal

"A vivid and brutal old-school (in the best sense) cyberpunk headkick"

Richard Kadrey, *New York Times* bestselling author of *The Sandman Slim* series

THE EMPRESS GAME

BY RHONDA MASON

One seat on the intergalactic Sakien Empire's supreme ruling body, the Council of Seven, remains unfilled: that of the Empress Apparent. The seat isn't won by votes or marriage. It's won in a tournament of ritualized combat, the Empress Game, and the women of the empire will stop at nothing to secure political domination for their homeworlds. Kayla Reunimon, a supreme fighter, is called by a mysterious stranger to battle it out in the arena.

With the empire wracked by a rising nanovirus plague and stretched thin by an ill-advised planet-wide occupation of Ordoch in enemy territory, everything rests on the woman who rises to the top.

"Passion, politics, and the fate of Empires hanging on the strength and courage of a single woman. You'll want to reach immediately for book two."

Tanya Huff, author of *A Confederation of Valor*

"Fast, smart, complex, and fun as hell…"

Rachel Bach, author of *Fortune's Pawn*

OBSIDIAN HEART: THE WOLVES OF LONDON

BY MARK MORRIS

Alex Locke is a reformed ex-con, forced back into London's criminal underworld for one more job. He agrees to steal a priceless artefact – a human heart carved in blackest obsidian – but when the burglary goes horribly wrong, Alex is plunged into the nightmarish world of the Wolves of London, unearthly assassins who will stop at nothing to reclaim the heart. As he races to unlock the secrets of the mysterious object, Alex must learn to wield its dark powers – or be destroyed by it.

"Crime, fantasy, time travel, horror blended seamlessly in a fascinating, fast-paced piece of dark fiction." Ain't It Cool

"A dark fantasy blending crime, horror and science fiction into something new and exciting" *Sunday Express*

"Fantastic... I couldn't put the wretched thing down." Bizarre

For more fantastic fiction from Titan Books in the areas of sci-fi, fantasy, steampunk, alternate history, mystery and crime, as well as tie-ins to hit movies, TV shows and video games:

VISIT OUR WEBSITE TITANBOOKS.COM

FOLLOW US ON TWITTER @TITANBOOKS